A SCANDALOUS ADVENTURE

LILLIAN MAREK

sourcebooks
casablanca

Published by Sourcebooks Casablanca, an imprint of Sourcebooks,
Inc.
P.O. Box 4410, Naperville, Illinois 60567-4410
(630) 961-3900
Fax: (630) 961-2168
www.sourcebooks.com

Printed and bound in Canada.
MBP 10 9 8 7 6 5 4 3 2 1

In homage to Anthony Hope, whose Prisoner of Zenda *gave me so much pleasure.*

One

Baden, October 1863

LADY SUSANNAH TREMAINE SANK INTO THE CHAIR IN the coffee room of the Grand Hotel with a sigh of pleasure mixed with relief. The pleasure was because the chairs were actual upholstered armchairs, not the spindly little things so often encountered in tea shops, and the pastries on display looked absolutely gorgeous. Every one of them was festooned with whipped cream—*schlag*.

The relief was because she had finally managed to get her traveling companions here without any disasters. That was cause for no little satisfaction. Her mother had sent her along on this trip with instructions to look out for the other two, and Susannah took her responsibilities seriously.

At first she had assumed that Lady Augusta Whyte would be the one who needed the most care. She was, after all, seventy years old, more or less. Aunt Augusta never actually mentioned her age, but Susannah had figured it out, at least approximately, from bits of information the elderly woman had let drop about things she had seen. At such a great age, Aunt Augusta might be expected to need assistance making her way onto and off of a train, or even just walking down the street.

However, it wasn't the frailty of old age that was a problem. Instead, it was Aunt Augusta's willingness to try anything once. Or twice. That café in Montmartre she had insisted on having them all visit was definitely not the sort of place a proper young lady—or a respectable old lady—should be seen. At least they had avoided any real trouble that time. Susannah had been able to get them out the side door as soon as the brawl began.

What had surprised her was that Olivia could be a problem. Olivia had been living with the Tremaines for years, ever since her brother had married Susannah's sister, so it wasn't as if Olivia and Susannah were mere acquaintances. They were almost the same age and had shared a governess and attended the same parties and gossiped over cups of cocoa. But she had never realized just how naive Olivia could be. When that artist asked her to come up to his studio and pose for him, Olivia had actually considered it. "But he needs a model and he can't afford to pay one," she had said.

Honestly!

But now they were all safe at Baden, the spa that had become wildly fashionable in recent years. Of course, it was a bit late in the year for fashion, but Susannah had been looking forward to it. Now she finally had a chance to look around the coffee room at their fellow visitors.

Hmm.

It might be just this hotel, but on the whole, the group seemed rather elderly. Or ailing. Or both. She probably should have expected that. Baden was, after all, a spa, and people came here to be cured by the waters. She just hadn't expected everyone to be an invalid. Susannah felt almost embarrassed by her own blooming health.

It looked as if the most exciting part of the visit here was going to be the pastries.

❦

Sigmaringen

Count Maximillian von Staufer, captain in the Royal Guard of Sigmaringen, grunted. Someone was pounding on the door, and that was making the pounding in his head even worse. He tried to say "Go away," but it came out as just another grunt.

Making an effort, he opened an eye. A misty gray light was sneaking around the curtains. He managed to sit up and get his feet on the floor, but then he had to pause. He rested his head in his hands with his elbows on his knees. What was wrong with him? His head was throbbing as if he had been on a three-day debauch, but he hadn't been drinking last night. The last thing he remembered was drinking coffee after dinner.

"Captain Staufer! You must come!" The pounding on the door continued.

He lifted his head enough to croak, "What is it?"

The door opened and in tumbled a young soldier—a

boy, really, disheveled and with his uniform askew. "Captain, she is gone. Princess Mila has run away."

Staufer winced at the shrill note of the boy's voice. "What do you mean, run away? Where could she go?"

"I don't know, sir. But she is not in her room, and you and the general are asleep…" The boy's voice trailed off miserably.

Staufer rubbed a hand across his face. He realized that he was still wearing his uniform, though the tunic was unbuttoned. He even had his boots on. Never in his life had he fallen into bed with his clothes on. What had happened to him? Nothing good, obviously, and it could not be overindulgence that was afflicting him. Not on coffee. He straightened up but had to close his eyes until the pain caused by the movement subsided. Stifling a groan, he asked, "What's your name, soldier?"

The boy straightened up and stood at attention. "Mueller, sir."

"Very well, Mueller. Suppose you take me to see what you are talking about," Staufer said as he buttoned up his tunic and ran a hand through his hair.

Moments later he was standing in the doorway of Princess Mila's room. Her empty room. Some garments were scattered around, but Staufer had no idea if this indicated a hasty flight or if the princess was always this messy. "Her maid?" he asked.

"She is missing too," said Mueller.

"And her guards?"

"Gone."

Staufer started to nod but remembered nodding did not help the pain in his head. The young soldier was doing his best to stand tall, but he looked terrified. "Don't worry, Mueller. This is not your fault." Staufer tried to think. "You must answer me truthfully. Who else knows about this?"

"No one, sir. I came to relieve her guard, and when I couldn't find anyone here and couldn't wake anyone in the general's quarters, I went to you."

Staufer rubbed his temples and forced himself to remain calm. From the moment they'd left Hechingen, Princess Mila had been nothing but trouble with her whining and her tantrums and her pouts. Her behavior would have disgraced a two-year-old. In an adult it was inexcusable. And now this disaster. Was the insufferable brat *trying* to cause a scandal?

"You did very well, Mueller. Now you must stay here on guard. If anyone wants to enter, tell them that the princess is indisposed and cannot be disturbed. I will go inform the general."

Mueller saluted smartly, looking both relieved and proud.

Staufer returned the salute, trying to look confident, and headed for the general's quarters. Everything was much too silent. Was everyone sound asleep? Given the way his head felt—and his stomach was also making protests—he did not think it had been an enchantment. More likely, they had all been drugged.

Blast Princess Mila. He had been sent to escort her to Nymburg, where she was to marry Prince Conrad, and he would do so if he had to put her in chains.

As soon as he got his hands on her.

Two

Baden

CAPTAIN STAUFER COULDN'T BELIEVE IT. THEY HAD been frantically searching for Princess Mila for the past three days—racing around the countryside, interrogating people along every road, river, and railway—and here she was, strolling through the formal gardens of the spa as if she hadn't a care in the world. Of all the arrogant, selfish brats, Princess Mila took the prize.

He ignored the neat gravel paths and charged across the flower beds, crushing scarlet geraniums and blue lobelia beneath his cyclopean—but beautifully polished—boots. Rage extinguished every consideration of courtesy in his breast. Coming up behind the princess, he seized her by the shoulder and spun her around.

"Begging Your Royal Highness's pardon," he began softly but couldn't keep his voice from rising to a roar. "What the devil do you think you are doing?"

Big, brown eyes looked up at him and were immediately filled with terror. The blond ringlets dangling by her ears shook as if she trembled, and the lower lip of her Cupid's bow mouth quivered. "Who...? What...?" she stammered.

He snorted in exasperation—he'd had more than enough of her dramatics—and then stumbled slightly as something landed on his back. He turned to find himself facing a young woman who was battering away at him with a parasol. What on earth did she think she was doing?

"Don't be ridiculous," he snapped. "You will break your parasol if you continue that way." Then he looked more closely at his attacker, and his glare slowly changed into a smile. She was an exceedingly pretty young woman, wielding a completely frivolous parasol—all ruffles and lace—which he caught with one hand and tossed aside.

Her eyes widened—very lovely blue eyes, he noted—and she drew in a furious breath and began to berate him. "You cad! You boor! You villain! You brute! You blackguard!"

Having been deprived of her weapon, she began to kick him. He started to laugh. Did the little wasp think she could possibly cause any damage by battering his stout boots with those dainty shoes? Well, perhaps she was not so little as all that. She came up to his shoulder, but she didn't seem to realize how futile her attack was. This was becoming more and more amusing. He was almost light-headed with relief at finding the princess, but he still had to get her back to the escort. Unfortunately, that meant he did not have time to give the little wasp the attention she deserved.

"You are going to hurt yourself if you keep this

up," he told her. To make sure she didn't, he wrapped an arm around her waist and picked her up, hoisting her onto his hip. Her head now dangled down in front of him while her legs flailed futilely behind.

He turned back to the princess, who had by now acquired some courage of her own and begun to swing her parasol at him. "Let go of Susannah, you big bully!" she demanded.

Susannah? Was that the little wasp's name? "Susannah?" He looked down at her and shook his head. "No. Susannah is not the right name for her. Too formal. Too tame. Suse. I will call her Suse. It fits her better."

"Aargh!" The little wasp gave a frustrated cry and tried to land a punch.

He laughed as it bounced off his leg.

Then the princess tried to hit his head with her parasol, but she couldn't quite reach and the blow landed harmlessly on his shoulder. He roared with laughter. They were utterly preposterous, these two.

"Unhand that lady at once, you dastard."

A new entry into the fray. This one was an elderly lady, quite elderly, and swathed in black. She carried a cane with a heavy knob. He knew it was heavy because she caught him on the knee with it, a blow that caused enough pain to make him stagger. It also knocked some awareness into him, and he paused to think for a moment.

The old lady, the young one, the princess—they were all speaking English. *English?* He had not known that the princess spoke English. It had never occurred to him that she could speak anything but her native

German. To be honest, he had not thought her sufficiently intelligent to learn another language.

Although he understood it easily enough, his
spoken English was a bit rusty. He dredged up what
he could from memory. "My apologies, gracious lady.
I wish only to…to conduct the princess back to her
party. She has somehow…become separated from
her…escort."

"Princess, my eye," said the little wasp, as he set
her on her feet again. Her hat had fallen off, and she
picked it up and plopped it on her dark curls. It was
rather dented, but he doubted she would appreciate
his commenting on that. Then she jabbed her finger
into his chest and said accusingly, "You were trying
to assault Olivia."

"Olivia?" He blinked. "Who is Olivia?"

"My dear, are you all right?" The old lady had
an arm around the princess's shoulder. The princess
herself was looking at him with terror in her eyes.

He sighed. She was going to be difficult. He
switched back to German. "Princess Mila, there is no
need to distress yourself. I will take you back to the
escort, and we will forget all about this little episode."

The princess shrank back and half whispered to the
old lady, "Do you suppose he is a madman?"

He sighed again and tried English once more.
"Gracious ladies, what stories Princess Mila has told
you, I do not know, but allow me to present myself.
I am Count Maximillian von Staufer, captain in the
Royal Guard of Sigmaringen, a member of the princess's official escort. Now, you must excuse us. The
rest of the guard awaits."

"What utter rot!" said Susannah scornfully. "You cannot seriously believe that we will let you kidnap Lady Olivia."

He tried to be patient, but he was growing frustrated. The little wasp was pretty, and at any other time he would be more than delighted to further their acquaintance. It was not every day that he encountered a woman—or anyone—who was not intimidated by his size. However, today he did not have time for explorations. Duty demanded that he get the princess back on the road to Nymburg as quickly as possible. "I assure you, *Fräulein*, this young woman is Princess Mila of Hechingen. I have for the past week been traveling with her. If she claims something else, well, I fear she has not been telling the truth."

He reached out to take hold of the princess's arm, but Susannah jumped in front of him and pushed his arm aside. Glaring up at him, she said, "And I assure you that this lady you are trying to assault is Lady Olivia de Vaux, and her brother happens to be married to my sister. Don't claim to have known her for a week. I have known her for seven years!"

"What nonsense is this?" He glared down as he loomed over her.

The old lady's cane suddenly reappeared, swinging back and forth to force them apart.

"Really, children, there is no need for you to make a public display of yourselves," she said. "Stop and think, all of you."

They all did stop. He could not say precisely what it was—her tone of voice, perhaps—but it did not occur to him to disobey. She suddenly sounded very much like his Aunt Magda. No one disobeyed Aunt Magda.

"This seems to be a case of mistaken identity," the elderly lady continued, "and I believe, Captain, that you are the one making a mistake." He opened his mouth to protest, but she raised a hand imperiously. She may have been old, but she stood firm and straight, as assured as any queen. He closed his mouth.

"Allow me to continue. I am Lady Augusta Whyte. My young companions are Lady Olivia de Vaux and Lady Susannah Tremaine. I have known them for many years. Indeed, I have known Lady Susannah all her life. Her mother is my goddaughter. They accompanied me here to Baden two weeks ago. It is quite impossible that Lady Olivia could be your princess. If you have misplaced one, as it appears from what you say that you have, I suggest that you continue your search elsewhere."

"But…but this is not possible!" He stared at her in disbelief. "Two weeks?"

Lady Augusta nodded decisively. "Two weeks. We have been staying at the Grand Hotel. If you doubt my word, feel free to make inquiries of the staff there."

With that she swept off, followed by the two young women, all of them with their noses up in the air.

Max realized that his mouth was hanging open and he snapped it shut. This was beyond belief. What sort of game did the princess think she was playing? Well, he wasn't about to let her just vanish again. He marched after them, keeping them in sight without getting too close so they would think he had believed their nonsense.

Not that it would have been easy to keep out
of sight if they had bothered to turn around. Even
without the white-plumed shako on his head, his
height—all six feet four inches of him—guaranteed
that he stood a head above the invalids tottering along
the paths of the spa gardens. He growled impatiently
as a nurse pushed her patient in a wheeled chair
through the intersection in front of him. His scowl
frightened a hobbling man back onto the bench from
which he had been attempting to rise.

Unlike many of those in the gardens, the women
moved quickly and gracefully, even the old one—
the one who called herself Lady Augusta. They
soon left the open expanse of the gardens, but the
wide streets of the town made it easy to keep them
in view. They walked past the colonnaded facade
of the Kurhaus, where the hot-spring baths were
located, but did not enter. He was grateful for that,
since he would be unable to follow them into the
women's section.

In no time at all, they arrived at the Grand Hotel, a
yellow building so festooned with white columns and
cornices and balconies that it looked like a pastry confection. As they entered, they were greeted with bows
and smiles by the uniformed concierge and porters.
So this "Lady Augusta" had not been lying when she
said she was staying there, but had there been a "Lady
Olivia" staying there as well? And for how long?

He gave them a chance to get well inside the building before he approached one of the porters. "Excuse
me, but those ladies who just entered—was that not
Baroness Lengenfeld and her daughters?"

"No, no." The fellow smiled. "They are English, those ladies."

"Really? Have they been here long? I could have sworn I saw them in Linz only a few days ago."

"Not these ladies. They have been here for more than two weeks now."

"Two weeks, you say? All three of them?"

"Indeed." The fellow began to look at him distrustfully. "Why do you ask?"

Max shook his head. "I thought... I must have been mistaken."

He turned and walked in a daze toward his own, more secluded hotel. This was impossible. Impossible. Unbelievable. Was Princess Mila—Lady Olivia, whoever she was—right? Was he going mad?

He needed to talk to the general.

Three

Lady Susannah burst into their hotel sitting room and marched furiously about, her hoops swinging wildly around her, endangering the ornaments cluttering the numerous small tables. It was most unladylike behavior. She did not care. She did not feel ladylike at the moment. Far from it. "Of all the improper, infuriating, arrogant, high-handed, overweening, pompous, insolent…" She pressed her lips tightly together.

"Have you run out of adjectives, dear?" asked Lady Augusta as she untied her bonnet and set it aside. "That was exciting, was it not? Positively exhilarating. But now, if you will excuse me, I believe I will take a short nap. Enjoyable though that little interlude was, I am not accustomed to so much excitement." She smiled cheerfully at the girls and walked to her bedroom.

"Oh dear," said Olivia. "Did we hurry back too quickly? Have we tired her out excessively? She was walking quite energetically on the way back. More energetically than usual. Unless that's why she's tired now." She sat down on the sofa of their sitting room and looked worriedly at the door Lady Augusta had just closed.

Ignoring them both, Susannah continued to pace about, pulling off the remains of her hat. Its ribbons hung down, dirty and dispirited. It looked as if that... that *creature* had stomped on it. "Look at this! It's battered out of recognition. And it was my favorite."

Olivia looked around at that. "It was? I thought you said this morning that you didn't care for it and you wished the wind would blow it away."

Susannah had the grace to look a bit embarrassed. "Well, all right. It wasn't my favorite. But that doesn't mean I want some ill-mannered behemoth to be responsible for its demise."

"He was enormous, wasn't he?" Olivia shivered delightedly. "Almost frightening, like the villain in a novel. Or the hero. You know—the dark, brooding one you can't be sure about. You were really quite brave, the way you stood up to him."

"Frightening?" Susannah raised her brows. "I wouldn't call him frightening. And he certainly wasn't brooding. He was even laughing at me. Maddening is more like it. Aggravating. Infuriating. Insufferable. I've never been treated in such a way."

"But he was so very big. And he was so angry that he certainly frightened me when he appeared out of nowhere."

Susannah wasn't listening. "Maddening," she repeated. "Insulting. Completely ill-mannered and boorish. Paying absolutely no attention to anything anyone was saying. He had one idea inside that thick skull of his, and nothing anyone said would even penetrate."

Olivia tilted her head to the side and considered. "Well, he did listen to Lady Augusta. At least, he did eventually."

"Ha. Listen to her, did he? He certainly didn't believe her. Didn't you notice that he followed us back to the hotel?" Susannah flopped down onto a chair and scowled.

"He did?" Olivia sat up in momentary alarm. "How do you know? You weren't looking behind us."

"I didn't have to. There are so many windows on the Kurhaus that they reflect everything several times over. Shop windows too."

"Does that mean he knows where to find us?"

"Well, of course he knows where to find us. Aunt Augusta told him where we are staying, remember? He was following us because he thought she was making it all up. He's obviously incapable of recognizing the truth when he hears it. As if a lady like Aunt Augusta would tell lies." Susannah sat up straighter and drummed her fingers on the arm of the chair. She ignored the fact that Aunt Augusta was capable of making up all sorts of tarradiddle if it amused her.

"Oh." Olivia sat there chewing on her lip for a long minute. "Does that mean he still thinks I'm that princess? Is he likely to try to drag me off again? I don't think I would care for that."

"I wouldn't worry about it if I were you. If he has any sense—and I'm not saying he does—but if he has any intelligence at all, he will ask about us at the hotel, and they will tell him how long we have been here.

Sooner or later he will have to accept that we are who we say we are. After all, he can't refuse to believe everyone in Baden."

Unable to sit still any longer, Susannah sprang up, shook out her skirts, and strode over to the window. Holding the heavy velvet drape to the side, she looked out at the busy street in front of the hotel. Busy, but not hurried. People walked slowly, many of them with the aid of canes. Even the horses pulling the open carriages plodded along, moving scarcely faster than the pedestrians. Every now and then a breeze would come along to swirl the leaves that had begun to fall. How depressing that the most exciting sight from her hotel window was the dance of autumn leaves.

That was the problem with a watering place like Baden. People came here to be cured, and the only reason they needed to be cured was that there was something wrong with them in the first place.

Most of them were elderly like Aunt Augusta, here because the warm spring baths would ease their aches and pains. The treatments did work, she supposed. At least Aunt Augusta was moving far more easily than she had when they arrived. And it was understandable that her mother had wanted her and Olivia to accompany Aunt Augusta. Everyone knew it would be difficult for the elderly lady to manage the trip on her own. At least that was the reason her mother had given. Susannah was beginning to have her doubts.

Though why they had to come all the way to Baden, she still didn't know. There were plenty of spas in France or Belgium, much closer to home. Was there something special about the waters here? It was possible, she supposed. But she couldn't think what it might be.

With a sigh, she let the heavy drape fall back across the window, willing herself to calm down. Soon it would be time for afternoon tea, although here people had coffee, not tea. Coffee and pastries. The pastries, she had to admit, were delectable, most of them served *mit schlag*, with whipped cream. Everything seemed to come *mit schlag*. If she was not careful, she would put on a grotesque amount of weight, since she had nothing to do all day but stroll in those boring gardens and eat pastries.

And every now and then, perhaps one of Aunt Augusta's acquaintances would appear, with a son or grandson or nephew in tow. A very proper young man, who would say all the expected things, and who would expect her to be impressed by his brilliance or his position or his cravat. A very proper, very boring young man, who would be no different from all the very proper, very boring young men to whom she had been presented in London. Or in Dorset.

She had no objection to propriety. Indeed, she valued it highly and prided herself on her own irreproachable behavior. It indicated respect for others. But was there some law that decreed that a man who behaved with propriety must be a fool and a bore? Couldn't he also have a few ideas of his own?

Olivia was still worrying, her lower lip caught between her teeth. "I suppose he isn't really likely to come here, is he? I mean, we probably won't see him again, will we?" She sounded less worried than regretful.

"No, dear, we aren't likely to see him again."

Susannah tried to keep the regret out of her own voice. At least the eruption of the enormous, though boorish, officer into their lives had meant that *something* happened today. She couldn't deny that he was something out of the ordinary. He would be out of the ordinary in any setting, not just in a spa town full of elderly invalids. For one thing, he was so big and strong—definitely strong, with those broad shoulders.

Ha. Those shoulders were probably all padding, like the ones on the guardsmen strolling around Hyde Park in London in their red tunics. She was not some silly schoolgirl to go mooning about because a handsome officer smiled at her. She knew better than that. There was probably nothing substantial to him at all.

Of course, he had picked her up and tucked her under his arm as if she weighed nothing at all, but one could hardly consider that attractive in any way. Really, it had been humiliating, not exciting. He had picked her up and warned her not to hurt herself as if she had been a child. A weak, delicate little child.

She wasn't used to feeling delicate. She might be on the short side, the smallest one in the family, but that didn't mean she hadn't always been perfectly well able to keep up with the others, whether racing across the hills of Dorset or dancing till dawn at a London ball. No one had ever treated her as if she were delicate.

She would never admit it except to herself, and she didn't like having to admit it to herself at all, but she had rather enjoyed the feeling.

She sighed. Aside from being big and strong, he was also quite handsome. Extremely handsome. Those dark curls, and those dark eyes laughing at her. Then there was the way he had laughed when she tried to drive him off—as if he thought she was being ridiculous but he enjoyed it.

She should not be thinking this way. It had all been most improper. Even if she was a bit bored—and very well, she would admit to a certain degree of boredom—there was no excuse for her to be going over the encounter and remembering every second of it, every touch.

It was high time to stop dwelling on something that was over and done with. Their little adventure had ended. It was back to pastries and whipped cream for her.

Although she did wonder about his missing princess. How on earth does somebody lose a princess? Did someone steal her? Did she run away? What might the story be there? Something interesting, she was sure. Something exciting...

Whatever it was, it was no concern of hers. She was here to watch over Olivia and Aunt Augusta, not to daydream about handsome German officers.

"We had best freshen up," she said. "It's almost time to go down for afternoon coffee." One of the high points of the day here in Baden—coffee and pastries in the coffee room, where a small orchestra played waltzes and polkas. No one danced, unfortunately, but the music was cheerful.

Olivia obediently followed her into their bedroom and started laughing when Susannah came to an abrupt halt and gasped at her reflection in the mirror.

"Why didn't you tell me? I look like—I don't know what I look like. Nothing respectable, that's for certain." Several curls had slipped out of the snood holding the heavy bun of her hair in place and were hanging in disarray. There was a smudge of dirt on her nose, and a flounce on the shoulder of her dress was torn loose. Susannah pulled the remaining pins out of her hair and attacked it vigorously with a brush, as if she could beat her wayward thoughts into submission at the same time.

Four

By the time they had washed up and changed their dresses, it was time to go down. Twisting in front of the long mirror, Susannah checked the fall of the pleats in the rear of her peach taffeta afternoon dress. It was a dress she particularly liked—very simple and ladylike, with its high neck and no decoration other than the lace appliqués at the wrists and the lace collar, but the color always cheered her up, and she liked the rustle of the taffeta. It was a pity none but aging invalids would be about to admire her in it.

She was just pinning on her hat, a small Italian straw that tilted over her forehead, when one of the hotel porters came to the door. He announced—a bit nervously, she thought—that a general wished to call upon the English ladies. Would they be willing to receive him?

Susannah looked at Olivia. Olivia looked at Susannah. They both looked at the door behind which Lady Augusta was still preparing her toilette. They looked back at each other.

Olivia looked hopeful.

Susannah shrugged. Doubtless one of Aunt Augusta's elderly acquaintances. At least the visit would be something new. "We would be delighted to receive the general," she said.

Lady Augusta joined them before their caller appeared. She was dressed in black, as she had been ever since her husband died three years ago. It was difficult to think of it as mourning garb, however, since her gowns were always in the latest style and of the richest material. This one seemed composed almost entirely of ruffles and shimmered and rustled as she moved. But Lady Augusta had never been a mournful sort of person. Her fashion choice may have been colored by the fact that black looked so dramatic with her white hair and flattered her fair complexion. Just now her dark eyes were sparkling at the prospect of visitors.

Perhaps, thought Susannah, Aunt Augusta had been feeling a bit bored too.

The general strode in, a tall, thin man with iron-gray hair cropped severely close to his head and a luxuriant mustache curling up at the ends. He carried a plumed shako under his arm and was dressed in a dark-green uniform liberally festooned with gold braid.

Susannah's eyes slipped right past the general to focus on the man behind him. A very large, handsome man, also carrying a plumed shako and dressed in a green uniform, though one with slightly less gold braid. The maddening bully from the garden. Susannah inhaled sharply. The bully was looking serious, but when their eyes met, he grinned at her and winked.

Her breath caught and, for a moment, she forgot to breathe. She had not expected ever to see him again. Admittedly she had felt some curiosity about him, but she never thought he would turn up in her sitting room. And appearing not in the least ashamed of the way he had behaved in the garden. Picking her up and tucking her under his arm like a wayward two-year-old! Holding her under his arm, his very strong arm. She could feel her face heating at the memory, while he did not seem in the least bit abashed. He just kept grinning, as if delighted to see her.

The general, meanwhile, was staring at Olivia in disbelief. "*Mein Gott,*" he whispered in German. "I did not believe it. I thought you were imagining things, Max." Then he fell silent.

His focused stare made Olivia shrink back and seize Susannah's hand. Susannah could understand her nervousness. For all her eagerness to please and be pleased, Olivia was apt to feel uncomfortable under scrutiny, and the general's scrutiny was very focused indeed. Susannah patted her friend's hand reassuringly. Protecting Olivia was a familiar occupation. Not at all like trying to keep her senses about her when a large, handsome, very *male* captain was looking at her as if he knew every uncomfortable thought that was running through her head. If only he would stop *grinning*.

For her part, Lady Augusta was staring at the general, one hand pressed to her heart. She was the one who finally broke the silence. "Otto? Otto Bergen? Is it you?"

Startled, the general turned to her and stared in

turn. His eyes widened slowly in delighted recognition. "Augusta? Augusta Lamarche? Can it really be you?"

She reached out her hand, and in two steps he was beside her, clasping that hand in his.

"By all that is wonderful—and after all these years! And looking not a day older. How came you to be here?" He shook his head in amazement.

Lady Augusta laughed softly. "Listen to you, Otto. You are as great a flatterer as ever. And a general? A very splendid one, too."

"Ach, such nonsense, these uniforms. But you—you are in black. In mourning?"

She lifted a shoulder briefly. "My husband, George Whyte. But it has been more than three years now."

He nodded understandingly and patted the hand he still held. "I know. My Elsa died almost ten years ago. Still, one does not forget."

All three of the younger ones watched uncertainly as their elders seemed to have forgotten anyone else was in the room. Finally Susannah cleared her throat. "You know the general, Aunt Augusta?"

With a start, Lady Augusta turned to the others. "Do excuse me, my dears. Indeed I do know the general. This is Otto Bergen. We met—oh, so many years ago. He was only a lieutenant then, with an embassy to London, and that was not long after the war with Napoleon had ended."

Still patting her hand, he said, "And what a beauty you were in those days. Every man in London was half in love with you, and most of them far more than half. And here you are, as beautiful as ever."

Lady Augusta laughed, her color rising. "And you are still every bit as dangerous a flirt now as you were then."

"Do you remember the time we waltzed in the garden at Apsley House?"

"Indeed I do! The waltz had barely been accepted in England, and everyone was dreadfully shocked to see me dancing under the trees with your arm around me."

"I was the envy of every man I knew."

"Aunt Augusta…" Susannah interrupted. What on earth was going on? Her acerbic Aunt Augusta had suddenly turned into a flirtatious debutante.

"Oh yes. Do forgive me. Otto, let me present Lady Susannah Tremaine and Lady Olivia de Vaux. Lady Olivia's brother, the Earl of Doncaster, is married to Lady Susannah's sister."

The general clicked his heels and bowed punctiliously. "And I believe my aide, Captain Maximillian von Staufer, has introduced himself previously."

The captain also clicked his heels and bowed, very formally to Lady Augusta and Olivia, but adding a private smile when he turned to Susannah. Really, he was behaving outrageously.

After Lady Augusta insisted that the visitors be seated, the general returned his bemused stare to Olivia. "I would not have believed it possible. I thought Staufer had been misled by some faint resemblance, the color of the hair, or some such. But it is truly remarkable."

He shook his head and smiled. "Forgive me, Lady Augusta. I am rambling. You see, I brought Staufer here partly to apologize for his behavior and partly to beg you to forget what he said. To never mention it to anyone. But now I think we must explain. The resemblance is so extraordinary." He shook his head again.

Staufer was still concentrating his gaze on Susannah, but now he reached over and took hold of her hand. "You must indeed have thought me a madman, and I fear that you were frightened."

"I was not frightened." Susannah lifted her chin. "Not frightened at all. I was angry." She tugged on her hand, unsuccessfully.

"Good. That is good."

"You enjoy making people angry?" She spoke in her frostiest tones.

"*Nein*, no, not at all. It is only that to be angry is better than to be afraid. Not so…" His voice trailed off.

"Humiliating?" she asked icily.

He smiled at that and began examining her hand, running a finger across her palm. "I do not think you are easily frightened."

"Are you setting up as a fortune-teller now? I assure you I do not wish to have my palm read." She could feel her cheeks warming and, putting more determination into the effort, succeeded in freeing her hand from his grasp.

Staufer turned to Olivia, sounding serious again. "I do indeed apologize to you as well, Lady Olivia. I know that I frightened you. In my defense, I can only say that to do so was never my intention. But the resemblance…" He raised his hand in a helpless gesture.

"You really have mislaid a princess then? Rather careless of you, I would have thought," said Susannah. She raised her brows and tried to imitate her mother's quelling look. After the way Captain Staufer had been making her blush, she hoped to discomfit him at least, but he just gave a shrug that should have been rueful but was belied by his grin.

The general seemed to take the situation far more seriously, for he nodded sadly. "I must tell you of the situation. Sigmaringen has had difficulties in recent years. Prince Conrad inherited the crown when he was still a child, and for many years the power was in the hands of his uncle, Count Herzlos, who served as regent. He…"

The general stopped abruptly, then took a breath and continued. "You will not be interested in our politics. Enough to say that there has been much unrest in Sigmaringen in recent years. Even though Prince Conrad is now fully of age, he still bows to the wishes of his uncle. But this unrest has made us appear vulnerable to our neighbors, and Prussia, you may know, is eager to take all the German states under its wing. To remain independent is becoming more and more difficult. An alliance seemed necessary, so a marriage was arranged with Princess Mila, the daughter of Prince Gottfried of Hechingen, our neighbor to the north. We, officers of the prince's Royal Guards, were sent to escort her to our capital, Nymburg."

The general stopped again.

After a glance at the old man, Staufer continued the story. "Although Prince Conrad is most attentive to duty and honor, the princess, unfortunately, is not. Also unfortunately, we were not told how unhappy the princess was about this marriage—she did not wish to marry a man she'd never met—so we had not expected her to run away. Even more unfortunately, her father, Prince Gottfried, is not a man to be… I do not know how to say it tactfully."

"It is impossible to say it tactfully. He is a man who sees insult everywhere and makes decisions in anger. Without stopping to think. Something like this—he would not only break off the alliance but might declare war. That would make both our countries more vulnerable to Prussia," said the general.

"Dear me, he sounds like a most foolish and unpleasant fellow," said Lady Augusta, frowning. "I assure you we will not say anything that might create difficulties for you."

"It all sounds very unfortunate," said Susannah. "However, I can understand why your princess might have been reluctant to accept a marriage arranged by a man like her father. She seems to be nothing but a pawn in all this."

"She is no more a pawn than Prince Conrad is." Bergen lifted his hands in a pacific gesture. "A ruler— any member of the royal family—has a duty to do what is best for his country. A princess just as much as a prince. And this princess is in many ways very foolish indeed. Unlike her father, Conrad is a man of much honor and kindness, and he is most concerned to do what is right."

"Then I cannot approve of the princess's behavior," said Olivia. "If she truly did not wish to marry your prince, she should have told her father so. She should not go around creating difficulties for other people. That is simply selfish." She stopped suddenly and blushed, as if embarrassed to have spoken so forcefully.

Susannah smiled at her. It was so like Olivia, this

outburst. Having suffered so much from the thought-
less selfishness of her own parents, Olivia was not
tolerant of selfishness in herself or in others. Susannah
was not a particularly selfish person herself—at least
she didn't think she was—but she didn't have Olivia's
willingness to sacrifice herself for others.

She noticed that Captain Staufer was smiling at
Olivia too, a gentle, kindly sort of smile. Far more
respectful and admiring than the impudent looks he
had been directing at her. With a sniff and a toss of her
head, she looked away from him.

Lady Augusta apparently decided that this was a
social occasion and rang for coffee and cakes. She
began to make smiling chitchat with the general,
giving Olivia a chance to recover her composure. The
general responded, but almost without thought.

Five

STAUFER DID NOT KNOW WHAT HAD GOTTEN INTO THE general, but he seemed to have withdrawn into his own thoughts and was listening with only half his attention. Lady Augusta chatted away at him, and Bergen responded with smiles and nods, but his glances kept sliding over to Lady Olivia. She, in turn, grew more flustered every time the general looked at her.

Max did not mind, since this left him free to concentrate on Lady Susannah. She was every bit as attractive as he had first thought—even with her hair pinned back severely, her posture stiffly perfect, and her dress buttoned up to her chin. Did she think that buttoned-up dress disguised her curves? It just made them more tantalizing, especially since that peach hue was deliciously close to the color of her skin.

She was being a most proper lady. Oh, so very proper. She had poured coffee for everyone and seen to it that they all had pastries. At the moment, she was using her fork to take tiny little bites of her slice of raspberry pastry and then sipping delicately from her

cup of coffee. Not a crumb fell on her pretty dress, and
whenever a speck of whipped cream escaped to land
on her upper lip, she promptly blotted it off with her
napkin. He kept hoping she would lick it off instead.
He would be glad to do so himself.

She was so very prim and proper that he could
barely keep from laughing out loud. Did she think she
was fooling him? He had seen her fly into action when
her little friend seemed to be threatened. She was not
so prim and proper then. Her wariness was that of a
warrior, prepared to go into battle when necessary, not
that of a shy little miss.

What amused him most was the way she tried to
avoid meeting his eye. Did she think he would eat her
up? It was a temptation. And then she kept glancing
over at Lady Augusta and Lady Olivia, as if to make
sure all was well. Or to make sure they were behaving?
*No need to worry about them, pretty Suse. What can happen
to them here?*

So he let the silence between them stretch out.
When it seemed to be growing uncomfortable for her,
she asked, "What made you think the princess might
be in Baden, Captain Staufer? Is this not rather far
from Sigmaringen?"

"So very formal, Suse. Surely you can call me Max.
After all, you did attack me with your parasol. That
makes us friends, doesn't it?" He spoke in German,
partly to see if she understood, and partly because he did
not speak English well and disliked sounding foolish.

A delightful shade of rosy red crept up her cheek.
She definitely understood, and replied in excellent
German. "That would be most improper, Captain."

"Proper, improper—we must be beyond that, no? After all, you did kick me. And I picked you up and held you on my hip. Does that mean nothing?" He put his hand over his heart and looked soulful.

"Really!" Her mouth pursed up. She was either annoyed or trying not to laugh. "If you were a gentleman, you would forget that ever happened."

"But was it not more interesting than the usual stroll through the gardens?"

She did laugh then. "You are dreadful, Captain. Even if it was, I should not admit it."

"How does it happen that you speak such excellent German?" He was curious.

The question seemed to startle her, as if she had not even realized that they were no longer speaking English. For that matter, she noticed, the others had all drifted into German as well. "Our governess—Olivia and I had a German governess. She was from Vienna, and while she was with us, she would speak only German. If we wished to converse, we had to learn."

"An obviously effective method."

Susannah smiled.

"And did she call you Suse?"

"Most certainly not, Captain Staufer." She made an effort to look affronted, but he did not find it successful. "She called me Lady Susannah, just as she should."

"You should call me Max," he persisted. "My name is Max."

She ignored that. "You did not answer my earlier question about the princess."

He gave a plaintive sigh. "I do not want to talk about the princess. She is a very stupid and tiresome creature. I would much rather talk about you. Why do you keep looking over at your friends? Are you their guardian?"

The question seemed to startle her, and she gave a little laugh. "Why…I suppose I am, in a way."

It was as he had thought. She was a companion to the old woman, though obviously not a servant. Probably a poor relation if it was her task to watch over the others. "There is no need to worry about them. I promise you no harm will come to them at my hands—or at the general's hands either." He offered a reassuring smile and held out his cup. "Might I trouble you for some more coffee?"

She blushed again and took the cup to refill for him, adding cream and sugar just as he had requested the first time. It delighted him that she remembered. When she handed it back to him, their fingers brushed and he sucked in a sharp breath. There had been something, a spark between them—he would have sworn it was powerful enough to set the table aflame. Whatever it was, it wiped the smile from his face and left him so shaken that his coffee splashed into the saucer.

❦

Susannah pulled back abruptly. What was that? Surely the mere touch of a man's hand could not have such an effect. This was ridiculous. It was like touching that voltaic pile her brothers had made one summer. Except that it hadn't been that kind of shock. She did not know what to think.

Mercifully, the general sat up, looked around, and

waved the remaining waiter from the room. He stood and walked over to the door, pulling it open quickly and checking to see if anyone was nearby before he returned to his seat.

"Otto…" Lady Augusta began reprovingly, but she stopped when he shook his head.

"You all showed some sympathy with my country's plight," he said.

Olivia and Lady Augusta nodded. Susannah simply looked at him blankly. His country's plight? Oh yes. The missing princess. The diplomatic worries. The possibility of war. She had forgotten all about that. She focused her eyes on the general, trying to concentrate on his problems and forget the presence—the very disturbing presence—of his aide.

"I assure you we will say nothing of this." Lady Augusta smiled and patted the general's hand. "If there is any other way we could be of assistance, you need only ask."

"There is." But having said that, the general fell silent again. The silence drew out uncomfortably.

"If you don't tell us what it is, we cannot know if it is something we could do," Susannah said, trying to be helpful. To her annoyance, that remark prompted a choked laugh from Staufer. She thought she had sounded quite reasonable and didn't see what was funny about it.

The general smiled slightly. "It will sound mad. It is mad. But I think it can be done. It is just possible that it can be done." He looked at Olivia. "You, my dear lady, are the image of Princess Mila. No one in Sigmaringen could tell the two of you apart. No one anywhere could. I would swear that her own father would be unable to tell you apart."

"Yes, we understand that," said Lady Augusta. "That accounts for Captain Staufer's confusion."

"Yes, but don't you see? If she comes with us to Nymburg as the princess, no one will know that she is not. That will give us time to find the real princess and avoid any problems with Hechingen."

There was a brief silence while they all looked at him dumbfounded.

"That's preposterous," said Susannah, putting down her cup with a clatter. "Absolutely insane."

"Oh, I couldn't possibly," said Olivia at the same time.

General Bergen ignored Susannah, but took Olivia's hand in his. "Ah, but you could. It would not be difficult. You are a lady, and you have been to court in your own country, have you not?" At her hesitant nod, he beamed and continued. "It is not just the way you look, but the way you behave, the way you speak. You have the manner. No one would question it."

"This is ridiculous," said Susannah, putting an arm around Olivia to pull her away from the general. "How can you possibly make such a lunatic proposal? One simply doesn't do things like that. It does not matter that Olivia resembles your missing princess. She can't possibly lend herself to such an idiotic scheme."

The general concentrated on Olivia, still holding her hand. "It will not be for long. A few days only. Just to give us a chance to find the princess and bring her back to her duty. No one will ever know."

"But I wouldn't know what to do, what to say." Olivia sounded hesitant, but not nearly hesitant enough. A chill made its way down Susannah's spine. Olivia couldn't possibly be considering this, could she? Not really. This was insane.

"I don't know, Otto," Aunt Augusta said slowly.

Good heavens, not Aunt Augusta too. Susannah closed her eyes and took a deep breath. "Yes, you do know, Aunt Augusta. You know perfectly well that this is utterly impossible. Think of your position. Think of Olivia's position. We're not a troupe of strolling players, for goodness' sake!"

"Of course not," said the general. "If you were actors, we could never manage it. But Lady Olivia here, she knows how to behave, how to hold herself, how to speak. Listen to her. Her German is perfect. She is as much a princess as the real one, isn't she, Max?"

And Max—Captain Staufer—that traitor, was beginning to smile as if he actually thought this was a reasonable proposal. He looked at Susannah. "She is, you know. In fact, she seems more like a princess than the real one does. Much more gracious. Much better behaved."

"What does a princess have to do, actually?" asked Olivia. Her eyes were starting to sparkle dangerously.

"Stop it!" Susannah wanted to shake her.

"Don't be such a cabbage, Susannah," said Aunt Augusta. "Think how exciting it would be. What an adventure!"

"Exciting? Think what a disaster it would be. It's probably high treason or something. They would chop off our heads as soon as we were exposed."

The blasted captain was grinning now. Did he take nothing seriously? He said, "Do you know, now that

I think about it, it might work. The princess would not be expected to know much. Everyone knows she is not an intelligent woman. Quite ignorant, in fact. And it could win us the time we need."

"It would not be for long." The general turned to Lady Augusta, obviously having realized that she would be the easiest to convince. "A few days at most. It will not take us more time than that to locate her and bring her back. It is not as if she is someone who will know how to hide. As soon as we discover the road she has taken, we will be able to find her. And in the meantime, you could prevent a disaster for my poor country."

"Honestly. Have none of you any sense?" Susannah stood up and glared at the two officers. "This could not possibly succeed." There were a hundred reasons why it would fail. Now all she had to do was think of one. Of course! She smiled triumphantly. "For example, the princess must have attendants who will know she has gone and who will know at once that Olivia is not the princess."

"Yes, of course," said Olivia, looking regretful. "Her maids, her ladies-in-waiting would know right away. It's almost impossible to fool servants."

Max shook his head, still smiling. "No, they would not know, not the servants who remain. Only her maid and her bodyguards knew her well, and they vanished with her. Suse, you and Lady Augusta can be the princess's attendants, her ladies-in-waiting. You will travel to Nymburg and be in the castle with her. You will be with her all the time."

"Stop calling me Suse!" When she turned back, she could see Olivia and Aunt Augusta looking hopefully at each other. Surely they could not be seriously considering this lunacy. Olivia was always throwing herself into things before she thought them through, and Aunt Augusta—Great God in Heaven! Aunt Augusta was thinking it would be fun. Susannah knew she had to inject some common sense into this discussion. "How long has your princess been gone?" she demanded.

"Three days," Max—Captain Staufer—said.

"And if you haven't found her yet, what makes you think you will find her in another few days? Or weeks or months? What if you don't find her before the wedding? Surely you don't expect Olivia to marry your prince, do you?"

The general shook his head. "We have men, trusted men, searching all the ways out of the country, but we have not yet heard from them all. It will not take long. A few days will surely be enough."

Lady Augusta cocked her head. "How have you explained the delay so far?"

"We sent a wire ahead to say that the princess has a slight indisposition and is staying at a *schloss*, a manor house, on my estate until she recovers," said Staufer.

"Lady Olivia, you cannot know how much it would mean to us if you would undertake to do this." The general took her hand again. "You would save not only the prince, but the people of Sigmaringen."

Olivia looked at Susannah, eagerness in her eyes. "It does seem that they really need our help."

Susannah wanted to shake her. "You do not have to help everyone who asks you! This could be an utter disaster."

"No, no, don't think that way. Instead, think how exciting it would be." Lady Augusta turned to Olivia, beaming with delight. "Imagine having a chance to be a real princess. You can't possibly refuse."

"Imagine me being a princess." Olivia giggled. "Wouldn't those nasty cats in London have a fit!"

Susannah wanted to scream, but Max took her hands in his—in his big, strong hands—and suddenly her knees felt weak. He grinned at her. "Ah, Suse, don't turn timid on me. You know you could do it. Think what an adventure we will have. And you need not worry. I will not let anything happen to you."

She could feel herself wavering, and then she pulled away. Once he was no longer holding her hands, sanity returned. "*I* will not let anything happen to me. You are mad, all of you. Completely mad. You"—she pointed at the count and the general— "out of here. Get out right now! I am going to talk some sense into these two ladies."

The general was still pleading and the captain was still smiling as she pushed them out and slammed the door on them.

"Really, Susannah, don't you think you were being rather rude?" Aunt Augusta pursed her lips and frowned.

"Rude? When they are proposing to involve you and Olivia in some harebrained scheme? Words fail me!"

They did not fail her, of course. She spent the next several hours explaining to Lady Olivia and Lady Augusta why they could not possibly allow themselves to be dragged into General Bergen's lunatic scheme.

"But they need help," Olivia pleaded.

"The fact that they need help does not mean that we have to give it to them. Nor does it mean that this plan of the general's has any chance of success."

"Honestly, Susannah, I don't understand how your parents ever produced such a cowardly little mouse." Lady Augusta sniffed.

"Cowardly? A mouse?" Susannah was outraged. "Just because I am the only one with at least a smidgen of common sense?"

"Yes, cowardly. If you aren't careful, you will turn into a shriveled old maid who's afraid of life, never daring to step outside her own front door." Aunt Augusta glared at her. "Where's your sense of adventure?"

Susannah was so furious she could not speak, but just stood there with her mouth opening and closing.

"And besides," said Olivia, totally ignoring all of Susannah's objections, "I would have a chance to be a princess for a few days. You know how everyone always looks down on me because of my mother, and because no one believes that my father really was my father."

"That's not true," Susannah protested, but she knew that it was. She just hadn't realized that Olivia was so aware of it.

"Just for a few days, everyone would be looking up to me instead." Olivia's eyes were shining at the very thought of it all.

The next day they were en route to Sigmaringen.

Six

ANNE, LADY PENWORTH, WALKED INTO HER HUSBAND'S office waving a piece of paper. "Phillip, I have just received the oddest letter from Susannah."

The Marquess of Penworth looked up from the pile of papers on his desk and smiled at his wife. "An odd letter from Susannah? I didn't know our daughter knew how to write odd letters."

"That's what makes it so odd." Lady Penworth settled herself in the comfortable chair by the fireside that her husband kept for her in his office. "She says that they are going to Nymburg. I've never even heard of Nymburg. Where on earth is it?"

Penworth called his attention back from admiring the picture his wife made in her green dress with that lacy confection on her head. "Hmm? Nymburg?" He frowned for a moment. "Ah, yes. It's the capital of one of those little German states in the south, near Switzerland. But I thought they were settled in Baden for the time being. What do they want to go to Nymburg for?"

"I'm not sure. She doesn't say. Is it far from Baden?" Lady Penworth was staring at the letter.

"No, I don't think so." Lord Penworth got up and went over the enormous globe in the corner of the room and turned it slowly until he found what he was looking for. "Ah, there it is, in Sigmaringen, which is just south of Hechingen, and the two of them are tucked in between Baden and Württemberg. A pair of those tiny little states that are likely to be gobbled up soon by either Prussia or Austria." He shrugged. "I don't know of anything interesting about either one of them. I should have thought Baden would be more pleasant for them."

"I would have thought so too, but she definitely says they are off to Nymburg. The truly odd thing is that she says we shouldn't bother to write to them there because she doesn't know precisely where they are staying, but it will be for only a few days. She'll tell us all about it later."

"She doesn't know where they will be staying? You're sure the letter is from Susannah?" He laughed and put up a hand to ward off his wife's glare. "It just doesn't sound like our Susannah. Before they set foot out of the house, she had every stop on their itinerary planned down to the minute."

"I know," Lady Penworth said. "That's why I found it so disconcerting. It doesn't sound like Susannah at all."

Lord Penworth began to frown. "You don't suppose she's allowed herself to be dragged into some mad scheme of Augusta's, do you? Or of Olivia's?"

His wife was frowning too. "I wouldn't have

thought that possible. I was relying on Susannah to keep them in check. Perhaps I was asking too much of her. She has always been so sensible and mature that I tend to forget how young she is."

"I'm sure that if there is any serious problem, she will let us know." He gave the globe a worried turn.

"Yes." Lady Penworth drew the word out as she stared at the letter. "I'm sure she will. But it is odd."

Seven

No trains ran from Baden to Wald, the town—village, really—closest to Staufer's schloss, so they went by carriage. Even the sturdy coach could not disguise the fact that the roads they traveled were little more than unpaved country lanes. If this had been Princess Mila's introduction to her new home, Susannah could understand why she had fled.

They all rode in the coach, a nondescript black one, to preserve their anonymity. That meant they were a bit crowded—more than a bit. Their crumpled skirts might never recover. The ladies were crushed together in the forward-facing seat with Olivia sandwiched in the middle, making it even less likely that she might be seen along the route. Facing them, Captain Staufer took up more than his fair share of the space here as he did everywhere.

To Susannah's annoyance, he took up more than his fair share of her thoughts as well. How could she ignore him when he was right there in front of her with that smile on his face? That smug smile, as if he knew…

Blast!

As if he knew that he was the real reason she had agreed to this idiocy. The chance to learn more about him had proved irresistible.

She could not have him think that she was a coward, that all she cared about was propriety, that all those things Aunt Augusta had said were true. He didn't know what Aunt Augusta had said, of course, but he would probably have thought the same things if Susannah had adamantly refused to allow this…this whatever it was…to go forth.

Having common sense is not cowardice. And behaving properly is not prudishness. It's simple courtesy. Good manners make people comfortable. They…

Why wouldn't the blasted man stop smiling at her in that infuriating, knowing way!

Susannah turned her head determinedly to look out the window at the trees. That was all there seemed to be—trees. Endless forests of dark evergreens, with occasional bursts of color from the yellow and orange leaves of birch and beech trees. Were there no people in this land? No towns or even villages? Nothing but forest?

And dust. The horses kicked up a cloud of dust as they trotted along, and it crept into the coach despite the closed windows. Her nose was filled with dust and the smell of dust.

The coach hit a bump that sent her up in the air, and then it lurched to the side. She would have landed on the floor had Captain Staufer not caught her. He held her suspended, a look of concern on his face, while she tried to remember how to breathe. When she could manage a smile, he placed her gently back on the seat.

In her corner, Lady Augusta was not smiling. "I do not wish to be insulting, but the roads in Sigmaringen leave something to be desired."

"My apologies to you all," said the general, frowning but not looking at all apologetic. "I thought it best to avoid the main roads. Here in the forest, we are unlikely to be observed, and if we are, it will be only by woodcutters and huntsmen."

Lady Augusta did not look appeased, but Lady Olivia smiled cheerfully. "Well, that makes it even more of an adventure, doesn't it?"

The prospect of an adventure appealed to Susannah less and less. Baden may have been dull, with its rigidly formal gardens and broad paths for invalids in wheelchairs, but it had become familiar. Safe. Now they were traveling into the unknown, and she was worried. Worse, she was cold—so cold that she shivered.

"It will not be much longer, perhaps an hour, until we reach the schloss." Captain Staufer seemed to be addressing all of them, though he was looking only at Susannah. "There you will be able to recover in comfort."

❧

Suse, Lady Susannah, had been right, Max acknowledged to himself. This was a foolish scheme. Yes, they might be able to pull it off, especially if they could find the princess within the next few days, as the general had said. Find her and put her back in place with a minimum of temper tantrums.

It might well be more sensible to tell Prince Conrad that the princess had run off. It would doubtless make a scandal if the news got out, but they might be able to keep it quiet. Her father could hardly complain when his daughter was the one creating the problem.

Sensible, but was Conrad ready to deal with such a problem? He was still, in many ways, so very young and inexperienced. Above all, it was Max's duty to protect Conrad, and that often meant taking care of problems that would be too much for the young prince to handle.

Besides, even if telling Conrad might be sensible, it would not be nearly as much fun. They would be playing a huge joke on everyone, and they could do it. Max was sure of it.

There had been a chance that Susannah would convince her friends to refuse, but she did have a sense of adventure. He had suspected it from the start. A woman who flew to protect her friend armed with nothing more than a frivolous parasol was hardly a prim and proper mouse.

This way he would have a chance to further his acquaintance with her. At the very least, they would have a few days at his schloss while they all prepared for the masquerade.

To allow her to disappear from his life after such a brief encounter would have been a pity.

❧

Susannah knew that a schloss could be anything from a

castle down to a cottage with dreams of glory. Captain Staufer's home was one of the middling sort—three stories high but very plain, with unornamented walls of white stucco and a red roof. It was approached via a bridge over a small lake that bordered one side of the building and looked as if it might once have been part of a moat.

The coach drew up not at the main entrance but at a small side door, and the ladies were whisked silently up a back staircase to the rooms in which, Staufer explained, the princess had been "recuperating."

To Susannah's delight, a lively fire was burning in the sitting room. She pulled off her gloves and held her hands out to the warmth. A small sigh of pleasure escaped her.

"It is chilly here," Staufer acknowledged. "The schloss is fairly high up in the mountains."

"Do you keep fires burning all the time in empty rooms? It seems a bit extravagant."

He laughed. "Hardly. But it is important to keep up the pretense that the princess is here, keeping to her rooms. And it seemed unlikely that she would wish to sit in the cold, so the fires have been kept up, and light meals have been brought for her."

"How...thorough of you." Susannah was not sure she liked it that he was so adept at—well—lying, to call it by its rightful name.

The smile twisted, and he averted his eyes. "That is one of the less pleasant lessons one learns at court—how to create a false image. And that the image is what people will believe."

There did not seem to be anything one could say to

that, so Susannah did not try. Olivia and Aunt Augusta had discovered the wardrobe that the princess had abandoned and were exchanging squeals of delight.

"What…?" Susannah started to speak but decided that this was not a conversation Max needed to hear. She turned to him with a formal smile. "If you would excuse us, Captain?"

He blinked but bowed with equal formality. "Of course. We will see you at dinner."

As soon as the door closed behind him, she turned on Olivia and Augusta. "What do you think you're doing? You can't raid the princess's wardrobe! That's no different from stealing."

Olivia looked mortified, at least briefly, but Aunt Augusta said, "Nonsense. If she had wanted her clothes, she would have taken them with her."

"All that means is that she couldn't carry them all with her," Susannah said.

"Besides," Aunt Augusta continued as if Susannah had not spoken, "if Olivia is to portray the princess, she must look the part. How better to do that than in the princess's clothes?"

"They won't fit." Susannah tried to close the door of the wardrobe.

"We won't know that until Olivia tries them on." Augusta pulled the wardrobe open again and took out a green taffeta trimmed with yellow. "Hmm. Scheele's green. I don't care for this color." Tossing it aside, she took out a beige silk trimmed with purple grosgrain. "This is better. The neckline is low enough for evening, and the full sleeves will be needed. The rooms here seem to be chilly despite the fires."

Olivia held it up. "The length seems about right."

"And the color is good on you. Try it on, and we'll see how it fits." Augusta smiled happily.

"This just is not right," Susannah protested, but she knew she had lost the battle.

A few hours later, they went down to dinner, the "princess" having recovered sufficiently to make an appearance. Olivia wore the beige silk, which was a trifle tight across the bosom but needed only a few stitches to take in the waist.

Susannah's misgivings about the dress paled beside her fear that at any moment someone was going to say, "But that's not the princess!"

No one did.

To Susannah's amazement, the servants—even the ones from Hechingen—accepted Olivia as the princess with no comment, not the slightest look of surprise or doubt. They accepted as well the sudden appearance of two new attendants. Apparently Captain Staufer had mentioned that the ladies-in-waiting had just arrived from Vienna, and everyone accepted this with no question. Susannah realized that she had been expecting some sort of denunciation and could not decide if she was relieved or not when none was forthcoming.

Standing at the window, she looked out at the lake—yes, she now knew it had once been part of a moat. When the need for that sort of protection became less urgent, Staufer told her, his grandfather had turned part of it into a lake and filled in the rest for a garden.

Still, moat or no moat, the schloss was a modest building inside as well as out. The furnishings were comfortable enough, though edging past worn on their way to shabby. The captain might be Count von Staufer, but the title did not seem attached to any great wealth. He probably spent most of his time in the capital, either at court or in the barracks. She had met enough young officers like that in London. Some of them had titles too. And all of them neglected any estates they might possess.

This house was pleasant and could be made attractive easily enough, but it did not have the air of one in which the owner lived. That made it seem even more likely that the court was his real home.

"Are you pleased with the success of the masquerade so far?"

Susannah jumped slightly at the sound of his voice and looked up to see that Staufer was standing right behind her. "I don't know," she said slowly.

"You have not yet decided if this is a good idea or a foolish one?"

"I'm quite sure it's a foolish one, and I do not know why you lend it your support." She knew she sounded irritated, but she did not care.

"Don't you?" His smile caressed her. She could almost feel it glide across her cheek, and it was all she could do to turn her face away.

"Stop flirting. That is hardly an adequate explanation."

Staufer stepped back with a look of regret. "No, you are right. I wish that my only motive was to find a chance to flirt with you, but the prince and I... We are cousins, you know." He nodded at her look of surprise. "Not close. My father used to say our family is close enough to be loyal, and distant enough to be safe. But when I was a boy, I was one of those sent to be educated with Conrad, to provide him with some companionship. And then when the riots happened in '48, my parents were killed along with his. It gave us a bond."

"Yes, of course." She wanted to reach out to him but stifled the impulse. "But even so, I don't understand why you don't tell him that the princess has run away."

His mouth lifted in a half smile. "I am the older, you see, by three years. My father always told me that I must watch out for Conrad, protect him. That was the duty, the most important duty, that he laid on me. And I fear Conrad is not yet ready to deal with a crisis." A shadow crossed his face. "Or is he? It is hard to know. Sometimes I think that perhaps I—all of us—protect him too much. He is a bit timid, yes, and unsure of himself. He remains more willing to let others set the course than to take charge himself. Still, he must learn to make decisions, and I sometimes fear he will never learn if we keep him in ignorance."

Susannah opened her mouth to agree that too much protection was not good for a ruler, but decided it was pointless. Advice from a stranger, especially a stranger who had never even seen the prince, was unlikely to be welcome. So she simply nodded.

"Besides," he said, grinning once more, "it will be fun."

Eight

WHILE THE GENERAL INSTRUCTED OLIVIA IN THE protocol of Hechingen and those bits of history that even Princess Mila would be expected to know, Susannah hovered over them. This, Max decided, would not do. She was making her friend nervous, and the general's temper was beginning to fray.

"You are not needed here," he said. "Come for a walk with me. The fresh mountain air will blow your worries away."

Susannah allowed herself to be led, but continued to look distressed, even when they reached the lake. Max tucked her hand under his arm and began the walk along the path circling the water. She seemed to be sufficiently agitated to run the entire circuit, so he made his pace deliberate to slow her down.

"It is not a race, you know," he told her.

"Isn't it?" She stopped completely and stared across the lake at the road they had come on, the road that would lead them away tomorrow. "We may all be racing headlong toward disaster. Olivia will never master all that history."

"No? She did not seem to be having any difficulty that I could see."

"She always hated lessons."

He could see the uncertainty on Susannah's face. "Perhaps this time she is having lessons that she wants to master."

"She doesn't seem to realize the danger she faces— the danger we all face. And you are the same. You treat this all as a joke. How can you?"

"Why not? Will it change anything if I put on a long face and say *tsk-tsk* all the time?"

She stopped and glared at him. "Is that what you think I am doing?"

Max didn't say anything, but he answered her glare with a smile. She was adorable, but she took things much too seriously. He answered her with a question. "Do you think smiling will make things more dangerous?"

"You don't understand." Susannah turned away and waved a hand at the schloss. "Olivia and Aunt Augusta, they're my responsibility. I'm expected to keep them safe and out of trouble."

"That is a great deal of responsibility for such a young lady." He tried to sound serious, but he wanted to laugh. No matter what she thought, he doubted anyone expected a pretty girl like her to be responsible for anything more than choosing a bonnet.

She looked annoyed. "Well, I'm a very responsible person. Everyone in my family says so. And those two need looking after."

That he could believe, but Susannah needed to be looked after as well. How could their families have sent these ladies off on a trip without a man to take care of them? Max shook his head. She was fortunate that he was here to see to her protection. "Well, you do not need to worry. I will make sure that none of you come to harm."

She looked even more annoyed at that. Did she think he was unable to take care of three women? He smiled to reassure her. "Come, let us forget all these worries. Let us pretend you have just come for an ordinary visit and we are out enjoying the sunshine. It is a pleasant day, is it not? Warm for this time of year."

She looked at him as if he had suddenly lost his mind.

His smile turned into a grin. "Is that not what a proper Englishman would do? Talk about the weather?"

Her annoyance dissolved into reluctant laughter. "Yes," she said when she recovered, "very proper indeed. All right then, let's pretend we are not engaged in a lunatic enterprise and just stroll about admiring the scenery."

Max tucked her hand under his arm again, and this time Susannah relaxed and walked comfortably beside him. It had been a while since he had walked for pleasure with a pretty girl. He had almost forgotten how enjoyable it could be. If she was laying her worries aside for the moment, so was he. Neither of them spoke for a while, but the silence was companionable.

She broke it eventually. "Your mountains are very impressive and dramatic. They surround us, and I keep wondering if they are protecting us or imprisoning us." She interrupted herself with a smile.

"You mustn't mind me. It's only that I've never seen mountains before."

"Never seen them?" He was startled, but then he thought about it. "Of course. That sounds strange to me because I have seen these mountains every day of my life. But in England there are not high mountains, only hills. Am I right?"

She nodded. "And where I live, even the cliffs leading down to the sea are not all that high."

"You live near the sea? Then we are even. You have never seen mountains, and I have never seen the sea."

"Really?" Susannah stopped and stared at him. "You've never been to the ocean?"

She was looking at him with wide-opened eyes, eyes of such a deep blue. Darker than the sky. Was the ocean that color? "Consider where we are, Suse. In the middle of mountains in the middle of Europe. There is no seashore in my country."

"Yes, but you are a man. You can travel any time you want to." There was a note of envy in her voice.

Max shook his head, wishing that were true. "No, I have too many responsibilities."

"Yes, I know," she sighed. "To the prince."

He shrugged. "Not just to the prince. I have aunts and uncles and sisters and cousins. You would not believe how many cousins I have." He rolled his eyes in mock horror. "And somehow I am responsible for all of them."

He had made her laugh again. "Well, I do not have any cousins," she said, "except very distant ones, but I have brothers and sisters, and when they marry, they bring a great many relations into the family, with a great many responsibilities. I think we are not very different after all."

They continued on their way. Perhaps she was right. They were not very different. He liked that thought.

Nine

THE PRINCESS'S PRIVATE TRAIN TRAVELED THROUGH the pine forests covering the lower slopes of the mountains surrounding the country. Endless forests, it seemed to Susannah, with only an occasional village and an occasional vista of snowcapped mountains.

Yesterday at the schloss had been both confusing and reassuring. The general drilled "the princess" in the minutiae of court etiquette and had her memorize facts about people she could be expected to know. For the first time in her life, Olivia was being a brilliant scholar, absorbing all the information like a sponge.

At times, it seemed as if Olivia was forgetting that she wasn't really a princess. What on earth were they going to do with her when she had to go back to being plain Lady Olivia, daughter of the scandalous Lady Doncaster?

Yesterday when Susannah confessed her worries to Max—she had given up trying to think of him more formally—he had teased her out of them, but they had returned this morning. She went to him again, and his laughter comforted her once more.

"After all," he said, "what is the worst that can happen? We will be exposed; the prince will be angry with me and with General Bergen; and you and your friends will be scolded and sent back to Baden. Is that so very dreadful?"

"It will be dreadfully humiliating," Susannah said. "And I'm not at all convinced that is the worst that can happen."

Max took her hands in his—those big, warm hands that made her feel both fragile and protected—and said, "You are not to worry, Suse. I will take care of you. I promise that I will not let any harm come to you, or to your friends."

She almost believed him.

Almost.

It was not that she did not trust him because—for reasons she did not quite understand—she did. It would only be for a few days, and a part of her was looking forward to the adventure. But what if he was wrong? She could not rid herself of the fear that some unknown danger was lurking out there in the dark forest.

Gradually the landscape changed. The forest thinned, and the train tracks ran alongside the river. Sharp hills on the other side kept the train close to the bank, but on the other side of the river, a wide plain was covered with the stubble of this year's harvest. Distant slopes were home to grazing cattle and sheep.

One of the servants came in with a question for Max. At least she thought it was a question. Both the servant and Max spoke a language that was unknown to her. When the servant had left, she could not keep from asking, "Why do you have foreign servants?"

He looked startled. "But I do not."

She frowned. "But you speak to them in a foreign language."

His face cleared and he smiled. "No, not a foreign language. The people here mostly speak the Schwäbisch dialect."

Olivia's head spun around and she looked appalled. "But I didn't understand anything you said to him. That was Schwäbisch? I don't know how to speak Schwäbisch! How will I manage? I won't understand anything people say."

The general smiled and patted her hand. "There is nothing to worry about. Only the peasants speak Schwäbisch. The nobility and anyone you are likely to encounter will speak proper German, *Hochdeutsch*."

"Only proper German? They do not speak the local dialect?" asked Lady Augusta. She did not sound as if she approved.

Staufer nodded. "I fear that is too often the case."

"But that's preposterous," said Susannah. "How can you work with people if you can't understand them?"

The general looked surprised at the question. "One has agents, stewards. And the upper servants always speak proper German."

"But you speak Schwäbisch," she said, looking at Staufer.

He smiled. "I like to work with people I can trust. How can you trust a man if you cannot even speak to him?"

The general shook his head. "Radical notions. Staufer here would be a revolutionary himself if he were not so closely tied to the prince."

"The prince himself speaks Schwäbisch well enough," said Staufer mildly, "and would speak it more often if he were not always tucked away in his castle."

The general opened his mouth as if to argue but then glanced around at the women and settled back in his seat with an irritated grunt.

Olivia had been listening in growing distress. "This will not do," she said firmly. "If I am to pretend to be the princess, I cannot make things more difficult for her and for the prince by insulting the people. There will be people at the station, along the way, in the town... At the very least, I must learn a few phrases so that I can speak to them."

The general seemed about to protest, but Lady Augusta overrode him. "The princess is quite right." When the others looked startled, she continued, "If we are going to succeed in this masquerade, you had better start thinking of her as Princess Mila. And that means that when she asks you to teach her some phrases in Schwäbisch, you obey."

Olivia sat up a bit straighter and smiled, as if the idea of being obeyed had a decided appeal.

⤝⤞

Nymburg

Dressed in the formal uniform of the Supreme Commander of the Armies of Sigmaringen—white tunic, dark-green trousers with a gold stripe down the sides, high black boots, and a saber at his side—Prince Conrad paced back and forth across the carpet in his private sitting room. He was generally considered a handsome man, not much above average height, but slim and graceful in his movements. His light-brown curls were brushed severely into place, and a small mustache graced his upper lip.

His pacing did not lead him to step off the carpet, because once on the marble floor, his steps would have been audible to the guards at the door. The prince was nervous, but he did not want everyone in the castle to know it.

He wished he could have kept awareness of his state of mind from his uncle, but Count Ludwig Herzlos had come into the sitting room an hour ago and showed no sign of leaving. He would have liked to tell the count to leave but couldn't bring himself to do so. When his parents were killed in the rioting in 1848, Conrad had inherited the Grand Duchy but Herzlos had been named regent. That regency had ended four years earlier, on Conrad's twenty-first birthday, but the habit of obedience was too ingrained to be shaken off easily.

The portly, gray-haired Herzlos was punctilious in his deference to Conrad. He would never sit in the presence of the prince until invited to do so, and even then he would not sit unless Conrad was also sitting. Indeed, he insisted on the observance of ceremony at all times. On the rare occasions when an exasperated Conrad suggested any relaxation of the rigid protocol, the count declared that informality would be the death of monarchy. It was ceremony that kept the ruler above the ruled, he insisted.

Protocol did not, however, keep Herzlos from

walking in on Conrad any time he chose. Privacy, it seemed, was of a part with informality, something indulged in only by the bourgeoisie. There were days when Conrad dreamed of being someone, anyone, other than the Prince of Sigmaringen.

"Enough of this, Your Highness. There is no need for you to worry yourself over a few days' delay. The message from General Bergen said 'a mild indisposition.' She probably ate too much fruit. I'm sure there is no need to be concerned."

Conrad came to a halt and looked at the count. The prince's mild gray eyes showed a trace of annoyance. "There is no need for you to be concerned, perhaps. You are not about to be married to a woman you have never even seen, no less met and spoken with."

"Bah." Herzlos gave a dismissive shrug. "You worry about nothing. I never met my wife before our marriage either, and we have a perfectly good marriage. My father chose her for her family and for her connections, just as Princess Mila has been chosen for you. What more is needed?"

Conrad doubted he could make Herzlos understand. The Countess Herzlos appeared at court on ceremonial occasions, a thin, timid creature who rarely spoke. Conrad wondered if she had always been like that, or if she had simply been unable to stand up to her forceful husband.

Herzlos patted the prince on the shoulder. "You must not distress yourself. Those older than you, and more experienced, will arrange things as they should be arranged. That is why a prince has advisers. Just trust me."

The prince wanted to say that he was tired of having advisers arrange his life for him, that he wanted to make his own decisions for a change. But Count Herzlos stood there so smugly assured that somehow Conrad couldn't manage to open his mouth.

Doors were being flung open, and someone was being announced. Conrad could hear each announcement coming closer, but could not make out who it was. He wasn't expecting anyone, and, to judge by the scowl on his face, neither was Herzlos. Soon enough his sitting room doors were opened, a liveried footman holding each one at a precise ninety-degree angle, and today's herald announced, "Baron Hugo Herzlos. Baroness Helga Herzlos." As if Conrad might be unable to recognize them.

His cousins, the terrible twins, marched in, looking much as they always did. They were a good-looking pair, tall and imposing in stature. No one could deny that. Yet somehow they never managed to be attractive.

Hugo held himself stiffly, with a vague air of defiance, as if uncertain of his welcome. Helga was more assured, wrapped in smiling perfection that seemed somehow inauthentic, as if it imperfectly covered a festering discontent with life in general, and her own circumstances in particular.

They stopped the precise ten feet away demanded by protocol.

Protocol must always be observed. Throughout their childhood, that dictum had been drummed into them all by the count.

Conrad always felt vaguely guilty in their presence.

He ought to like them. They were his cousins, close to him in age, and Hugo had shared lessons with him and Max. But there was always a distance.

He had not realized it at the time, but he now saw that the distance had been created by the count, who never let his children forget that it was Conrad who was the heir to the throne and they were only his subjects. The count had tried to impress that on Max as well, but Max had ignored him. Perhaps that was why Max was Conrad's friend in a way that Hugo was not.

Hugo bowed and said, "Your Highness."

Helga curtsied and said, "Your Highness."

Conrad gave them a smile as false as their own and inclined his head briefly.

The count, however, scowled. "What brings you here, Hugo? I did not know his highness had invited you."

Hugo flinched, but only slightly. The dismissive tone had doubtless been expected.

It was Helga who replied, looking coldly on her father. "Since Hugo was part of the delegation that arranged the alliance with Hechingen, we thought it only considerate to be on hand to greet the princess when she arrives. She might be glad to see a familiar face."

Considerate? Helga? Conrad thought it unlikely.

She turned to Conrad and continued, "The poor girl must find it all rather overwhelming, going off to a strange country to marry a stranger. I do feel for her." She smiled faintly.

That smile chilled Conrad, and he shivered just as he did every time he recalled the suggestion—he did

not know where it had come from—that he marry
Helga. Fortunately the count had poured scorn on
the idea. Conrad had no idea what Princess Mila was
like, but she would have to be better than Helga,
who quite simply terrified him.

"Very considerate of you, I'm sure," said Conrad,
his irritation at the intrusion growing. "However, I fear
you will all have quite a wait. The princess's train is not
due in Nymburg until two, and the procession through
the town should take at least another half hour."

Hugo looked taken aback. "Not until two? But the
schedule I arranged had her arriving at noon."

"Oh, didn't anyone tell you?" Conrad smiled.
"General Bergen and I arranged a different schedule,
providing her with a more scenic route than the one you
had planned." He took a surely reprehensible pleasure in
seeing Hugo try to conceal his annoyance, and that little
exercise of power encouraged him to try another. "Now
there are some matters that require my attention. You
may all feel free to wait in the anteroom."

Herzlos nodded stiffly. He was frowning, but he
would never protest his dismissal in the presence of his
children. In front of others, he always pretended that
Conrad was prince in fact as well as name. Helga was
about to object—her mouth was open—but Hugo
tugged on her arm. They all left, and the doors closed
behind them.

Conrad felt rather proud of himself. His nervousness about the princess remained—the delay in her
arrival had done nothing to calm him—but at least he
had arranged some privacy for himself.

Ten

THE TRAIN PULLED INTO THE STATION AT NYMBURG
at two in the afternoon precisely. The general checked
his pocket watch with a smile of satisfaction. He and
Staufer were the first to descend from the car, followed by Susannah and Lady Augusta.

The railway station was not what Susannah had
expected. Unlike the stations of London, this was not
an enclosed building. Even though Nymburg was the
capital of the country, the station would have been
more appropriate in a country village. There was
only a single platform, open to the sky, and a small
station house. The building was cheerfully painted in
green and red, and even this late in the season sported
window boxes full of flowers like those on village
houses they had seen. All told, the station house was
attractive, but far from impressive.

Although sunny, the day was chilly. So was the
crowd on hand to welcome the princess. It was a
crowd of respectable size, Susannah supposed, but
people seemed far from enthusiastic. Their stolid
behavior could, perhaps, be accounted for by the

presence of numerous soldiers at the front of the crowd. They wore dark-green uniforms like Max and the general, so she supposed they were members of the Royal Guard.

In front of the crowd were two nervous men carrying top hats and wearing broad sashes across their chests. One of them had his hand on the shoulder of a little girl with an enormous bouquet of flowers.

Susannah's doubts about this masquerade continued, but she offered a smile before she took her place beside Max, facing the general and Lady Augusta, to create a pathway for the "princess."

Then Olivia appeared at the door of the carriage. She stood there for a moment, hesitantly, then smiled shyly at the crowd.

The air of tension seemed to dissipate slightly, and the murmurs that ran through the crowd seemed friendly.

Susannah tried to make out the words. "What are they saying?" she whispered to Max.

"Pretty," he whispered back. "They think she is pretty."

Well, Olivia certainly was that. She looked almost magical in her cream-colored velvet traveling dress with her blond ringlets falling over her shoulder. The green of her collar and of the plume curling down from her hat matched the guards' uniforms almost precisely. Aunt Augusta had determined on that touch.

After a push, the little girl came forward and held out the bouquet. "For you." The words were barely audible.

Bending down to the child, Olivia took the

flowers. "I thank you," she said, "*Dangschee*," speaking to the child almost as softly in her best effort at the local pronunciation.

The two welcoming gentlemen, the only ones close enough to hear the exchange, looked at each other in surprise. Then one of them tucked the paper he had been holding into his pocket and stepped forward.

"Welcome to Nymburg, Princess Mila," he said, and waited uncertainly.

Olivia came forward and smiled at him and at the crowd. She spoke a bit haltingly in her best Schwäbisch, thanking him—"*Dangschee*"—for the welcome and proclaiming her delight—"*I frai mi*"—at being here. The words were clear enough and loud enough to be heard by the crowd.

After a stunned moment, people burst into a cheer, grinning and turning to each other in delight. Olivia ducked her head and blushed prettily, which produced even more cheers.

"She was right," said Susannah. "It is important to speak Schwäbisch."

"I never doubted it," said Max.

The general harrumphed and signaled to the troops to clear a path to the carriage for the princess. But when they arrived, there was a slight disturbance— not from the crowd but from the general. He had been handed a message that brought a frown to his face, and his mood did not improve when they reached the carriage.

"This is the wrong carriage," he said in a furious undertone. "I ordered the state coach. Who is responsible for this?"

A frightened underling saluted and replied, "Baron Hugo Herzlos ordered it. He said the open carriage would make it easier for the people to see the princess."

The carriage looked perfectly acceptable to Susannah. It was a wildly ornate landau, white with gold trim and a coat of arms—presumably that of Sigmaringen—on the door, and was drawn by four white horses. The weather was cold enough that the ride would probably be chilly, but other than that, Susannah did not know what the general's objection was. Nonetheless, he and Max were exchanging worried glances.

The general tugged at his mustache briefly, then decided, "It will have to do. It cannot be changed now. Come ahead."

The ladies were seated in the carriage with fur rugs tucked over their laps, Susannah and Lady Augusta riding backward and Olivia in the middle of her seat, the cynosure of all eyes. She looked nervous, but managed a smile, and they set off.

Once they were out of the station area and riding down a broad avenue, Susannah had an opportunity to see something of the city and the castle on the hilltop high above it. The avenue had the breadth that Susannah had seen in Paris and other cities that had been shaken by all those revolutions and riots in the wild year of 1848. Wide avenues let in the light and gave cities an air of elegance. They also made it difficult for people to erect barricades to impede the passage of troops.

The buildings lining the way were as new as this

thoroughfare. They were tall edifices, many of them as much as six stories high, built of stone with large windows that would provide plenty of light for the inhabitants. On the ground floor were shops offering a wide variety of goods. Nymburg looked prosperous and remarkably clean—far cleaner than London. Occasionally, however, the cross streets offered a glimpse of an older, shabbier, less pristine city. That was rather more like London.

High above them, separated from the town by a swath of forest, loomed the walls of the castle. Those grim fortifications contrasted badly with the cheerful banners flying from the buildings in the town.

News that the princess had spoken in Schwäbisch spread through the crowds with amazing speed. One could almost see the tide of the news moving along as smiles appeared on faces that had, moments before, been almost hostile. Shouts of welcome in Schwäbisch were directed at the princess, and she responded with smiles and waves. Such a simple gesture made such a difference. Olivia was a perfect princess.

Susannah turned to share her delight in Olivia's performance with Max, riding beside the carriage, but he was not looking at her or at Olivia. He was scanning the crowd, looking at rooftops, staring at anyone who was moving through the crowd. On the other side, the general was doing the same. They both looked intent and serious. Deadly serious.

As if they thought there was some danger threatening.

Eleven

THE FANFARE ANNOUNCING THE APPROACH OF THE
princess startled Conrad out of his reverie. He had
been imagining what it would be like if he gave an
order and Count Herzlos actually took it seriously,
rather than dismissing it as idle speculation. What
would it be like to actually rule Sigmaringen?

But the trumpet blare called him back to reality. He
stood up, straightened his tunic, adjusted his sword,
and set out for the Rudolf Room, where the princess
was to be received.

Conrad was not to be allowed to receive her on
his own, of course. Count Herzlos awaited him in the
anteroom, and the twins were there as well. Ready to
walk beside him, as always, but kept a few feet behind
by the presence of the count.

"Well, the great day has arrived, has it not, Cousin?"

Conrad swung around and gave Hugo his best icy
glare. It was enough to make Hugo pull back the hand
that had been about to clap Conrad on the shoulder.
That, plus his father's growl, forced Hugo to grind
out, "Your Highness, that is."

Helga was less easily cowed. She gave her irritating trill of a laugh and said, "It is to be hoped that all is well."

"Why shouldn't it be?" Count Herzlos scowled at her.

The baroness gave a careless shrug. "It is only that the escort for the princess was left in the hands of General Bergen."

"Bah. A simple task like that should be no problem, even for a simple soldier like Bergen." The count harrumphed and kept his eyes ahead of him.

That was enough to irritate Conrad. "General Bergen has ever been a loyal and devoted champion of my house. I will not have him insulted."

"No one would dream of insulting the old general," said Hugo. "It is just that he is so, well, *old*. One always worries if he will be up to a task."

"Indeed." Helga laughed again. "I wouldn't be in the least surprised if he misplaced the princess and brought a milkmaid instead."

"Your disrespect is unbecoming," said Count Herzlos stiffly. "No more of this."

Helga stopped speaking, but she did not bother to suppress the little smile tugging at the corners of her mouth.

They neared the Rudolf Room, an enormous chamber almost one hundred and fifty feet long. The plan was for Conrad to stand before his throne at one end of the room while the princess entered from the far end and walked the entire length of the chamber to present herself to him.

That, he decided, was ridiculous. When they came to the doors, he kept going.

Hugo had started to turn in and stopped in confusion. "Cous—Highness, where are you going?"

The count also tugged at his sleeve. "The plan, Sire, was to…"

"I have changed the plan," Conrad said, cutting him off. "I will greet the princess at the castle entrance." He continued on his way, walking too quickly for the others to do anything more than follow, and ignored the disgruntled mutters behind him.

At his approach, the guards promptly opened the huge castle doors and stood at attention while he passed through to stand in the sunlight at the top of the stairs. In the courtyard below, a company of the Royal Guard snapped to attention, and he could see the heads of innumerable servants peeking out of windows and around pillars to catch a glimpse of the princess.

"An excellent idea, Highness," said Hugo. "This way, the people will soon know all the details about the princess's arrival."

"Yes," said Helga. "I only hope it hasn't been too much for the poor old general."

Conrad ignored them.

Another fanfare sounded, and the wrought iron gates leading to the courtyard swung open. General Bergen and Captain Staufer rode in on their white steeds.

"The general does not appear to be suffering any ill effects from the journey," said the count.

His daughter smiled.

Conrad continued to ignore them. He stood as immobile as the guards in the courtyard.

Next came the princess's carriage, pulling to a halt at the foot of the steps, while the troop of Royal Guards on horseback formed a line behind. The general and the captain dismounted and came to stand at the door of the carriage. Two ladies descended, one old and one young. The princess's ladies-in-waiting, presumably. They stepped to the sides to allow the princess room to alight. The general held out his hand to assist her.

And there she was.

Conrad drew in a sharp breath. Her portrait had lied. It had shown only a conventionally pretty girl. And this woman before him? He did not think he had ever seen a more beautiful creature. Golden ringlets framed a heart-shaped face. Huge brown eyes looked up and locked with his. A smile trembled on the lips of a beautifully bowed mouth. She stood proudly erect, with a tiny waist beneath a glorious bosom.

Behind him, Helga also drew in a hissed breath and Hugo uttered an abrupt expletive, but Conrad barely heard them. His entire being was focused on his future bride.

                              ✒

The attention of the bridal party was on the prince and his companions.

As they neared the foot of the stairs, the general murmured to Olivia, "The old man is Count Herzlos, the First Counselor. The young man is his son, Baron Hugo Herzlos. He was part of the delegation to Hechingen, so you have met him. The woman is his sister. You do not know her."

Olivia gave a tiny nod and stepped forward, holding the general's arm.

Susannah, who had heard every word, kept her

attention on those surrounding the prince. She had not missed the horrified shock on the faces of the baron and baroness when Olivia stepped from the carriage. They were aghast at the sight of the princess. They covered it up quickly and now wore masks of frozen courtesy, but Susannah had seen.

So, apparently, had Max. When she glanced to her side, he was staring at them with a scowl on his face. Scowls were hardly appropriate for the occasion. He had wanted this masquerade. The least he could do was play his part properly. She smiled and jabbed her elbow into his side. An elbow, but only because she did not have a knife. He jumped and looked at her. She smiled more broadly, baring her teeth and wishing they were fangs. He recovered himself and smiled as well. It was no more convincing a smile than hers, but it would do. He was not a fool.

"You have been lying to us," she said, whispering through her smile. "There is more going on, more danger threatening, than we were told."

There was no more time to speak, for they had reached the prince. Olivia began to curtsy to him, but Conrad caught her hands to raise her up. "No, my princess. You need never bow to me."

He introduced her to the count, who clicked his heels and bowed.

"Count Herzlos," she said. "I have heard much of you. You are greatly admired all across Europe."

The count flushed with pleasure. "And I believe you have met my son, Baron Hugo Herzlos?"

Hugo also clicked his heels and bowed.

Olivia looked at him, slightly puzzled, and then her

face cleared. "Oh yes, you were one of the delegation that came to my father's court to arrange this marriage. I do remember you."

The look of annoyance on Hugo's face at this snub was undeniable, but Olivia had already turned away to look coolly at Helga. The baroness tried, but she was finding it difficult to stand up to Olivia's clear gaze.

Sounding dismissive, the count said, "My daughter, Baroness Helga Herzlos."

The baroness sent a quick glare at her father and then sank into a curtsy.

It was not quite deep enough. Olivia looked at her with raised brows and turned back to the prince.

They all proceeded into the castle, Olivia on Conrad's arm, Lady Augusta on the general's arm, and Susannah on the captain's arm, with the Herzlos clan trailing behind. The general turned back and said softly to Susannah, "That was clever of her, to flatter Herzlos. One cannot offer too much cream to that old fool."

Max glared, but the general simply smiled and shrugged before moving on with the procession.

"We have to talk," Susannah muttered to Max, keeping her smiling gaze on the couples ahead of her.

Something was bothering him. He was so tense that she could almost feel his frown in the muscles of his arm. She did not, however, think that the scowl was for her. He was silent for a minute or two, but then muttered, "Yes. I must find out what is going on. Stay together, you and your friends. Do not allow yourselves to be separated. I will come to the princess's rooms as quickly as I can."

She had to be satisfied with that, mysterious and worrying though it was, because Olivia soon pleaded weariness after the journey, and the welcome broke up.

The chamberlain hurried over from a corner of the room, where he had been in conference with the baron. He was a portly fellow with a supercilious expression beneath his powdered wig, dressed in a particularly showy version of the green and gold castle livery. In his arms he cradled an elaborately carved and painted baton, presumably his badge of office. He bowed to the princess and, at a word from the prince, turned to lead the ladies to their rooms.

As Susannah was about to follow, Max caught her arm. "Remember," he said, "stay with the princess. Do not allow yourselves to be separated."

She nodded, feeling more and more worried. The captain had not struck her as a man given to foolish alarms. A foolish disregard of danger was a more likely fault. As they left, she noticed the baron watching them carefully. The baroness must have slipped away earlier, for she was not to be seen.

Twelve

SUSANNAH KNEW THAT SHE HAD BEEN MAD TO AGREE to this adventure. She was supposed to be the sensible, responsible one. Olivia always agreed to be helpful. It scarcely mattered what was suggested. Olivia would agree to any mad scheme if she thought it would please others. And a scheme like this? Pretending to be a princess? How could anyone expect her to resist?

As for Aunt Augusta… When Mama had told her to watch out for Aunt Augusta, Susannah had originally thought it was because of the old woman's health. She'd thought she was supposed to make sure Aunt Augusta didn't overtax her strength, not make sure she didn't go off on some harebrained, madcap adventure. She hadn't realized that white hair did not mean common sense. If anything, it seemed to mean the reverse.

No. Susannah gave herself a mental scold. There was no point in trying to shift the responsibility. The blame for this adventure did not belong to them. It was her own fault. She could have prevented it if she had really wanted to. Instead, she had allowed herself to be swayed by the prospect of furthering her acquaintance with a handsome, laughing officer. She had no business giving in to this attraction, a purely physical attraction, no matter how strong. That admiration had been added to the attraction—admiration for the way he could combine his own sense of responsibility with a sense of humor—did not absolve her. She had her own duties. The failure was hers.

Her spirits found no encouragement on the long walk to their chambers. They passed through a huge, vaulted chamber that belonged to the Middle Ages, with a stone floor and painted medallions of strange beasts on the walls. The sort of beasts that lived in nightmares. The medallions themselves were outlined in red, the color of blood. The groins of the vault rested on pillars topped by grotesque figures with hideously distorted faces. Whether they were threatening her or merely mocking, she did not know.

When they finally left that room of Gothic horrors, they entered a more modern corridor that was only marginally more cheerful. The high ceiling was covered with elaborate white plasterwork that could be considered pleasant, even elegant, but the walls were lined with paintings of battle scenes, huge paintings with larger than life-sized figures. The battles had doubtless been victories for Sigmaringen since they were commemorated in the castle, but the scenes were full of the dead and dying. Occasional groupings of chairs, presumably for those who enjoyed contemplating bloodshed, were covered in brocade in the same shade of red that had decorated the Gothic medallions.

The windows of the corridor opened onto an

inner courtyard paved with flat, gray stones. No color enlivened the courtyard, but an excessively large fountain in the middle sent up fierce jets of water for the entertainment of those who chanced to look out.

Eventually they reached a broad staircase decorated with statues of ancient and imposing deities, all in chilly white marble. This led them to still another corridor, bright with more plasterwork surrounding tall windows overlooking still another courtyard.

The steady tapping of Lady Augusta's cane marked their progress. Susannah walked beside her, worried that the pace set by the chamberlain might be too rapid for the old woman, but Lady Augusta showed no signs of weariness. Instead, she looked about her with lively interest.

Finally the chamberlain stopped before a pair of gilded doors, which were promptly pulled open by the footmen who waited in the hall.

"Your chambers, Highness," said the chamberlain.

Olivia entered, with Susannah and Lady Augusta behind her, to find two strange women awaiting them. They were a sour-faced pair, but dressed far too finely to be servants. Olivia turned a questioning look on the chamberlain.

"May I present Madame Kroeger and Madame Glantz."

The two women curtsied.

"They will serve as your ladies-in-waiting," the chamberlain continued. "They will occupy the rooms on either side of yours so that they will be available whenever you need them, and we have also provided a maid for you."

Olivia's eyes widened. "And my own ladies?"

"Rooms will be found for them elsewhere in the castle."

"No," said Susannah flatly. She was going to panic any moment now, but she fought to keep calm.

The chamberlain, who seemed astounded by this rebellion, glared at her. She flushed slightly at the realization that she was probably not the one who should be objecting. She needed to remember that it was Olivia who took precedence now. She was not even certain that the chamberlain did not outrank her in this palace.

Before he could speak, Olivia raised a hand to silence him. "No," she said, not even sparing him a glance. "That will not do. I prefer to have my own ladies beside me. You may find rooms elsewhere for these women. I have no need of them." She indicated the sour-faced ones with a dismissive wave of her hand.

Both women stared at her in outrage, perhaps at being referred to as *women*.

The chamberlain recovered and smiled condescendingly. "You do not understand, Highness. Baroness Herzlos chose these ladies for you herself. They have been provided to help you learn our customs."

Olivia turned a look of affronted astonishment on the chamberlain, a look of regal assurance. The silence stretched out uncomfortably before she spoke. "It is clearly you who do not understand. When I express a preference, those who serve me know enough to consider it an order. Those who do not understand that do not remain in my service."

The chamberlain blanched. That threat was clear enough. "Of course, Highness."

Without even looking at them, Lady Augusta waved a hand at the waiting ladies, who stood there in silent fury. "You may leave."

Noses in the air, the ladies did so. One of them hissed to Lady Augusta, "The baroness will hear of this."

"That presumptuous upstart? She will indeed," replied Lady Augusta, feeling no need to keep her own voice down.

The chamberlain, obviously torn between his desire to serve those currently in power and his concern for his future, stood there as if his feet could not decide on the correct direction in which to carry him.

"You too," said Lady Augusta, waving a hand in the direction of the door.

He fled behind the two women.

No sooner had the door closed behind the shocked trio than Olivia collapsed into a chair with a gasp. "I can't believe I did that."

"You were magnificent!" Susannah collapsed with laughter, her relief bordering on hysteria. "I didn't know you had it in you to be so, so arrogant!"

"Neither did I," said Olivia. "The thought of being left in here with those two horrors gave me strength. I pretended I was Cleopatra. Remember that scene where she dismisses her servants? The way she held her head?"

"Well, I must say you played your part with aplomb. I was quite convinced that you were born to rule." Lady Augusta smiled approvingly as she set aside her bonnet and removed her gloves. "And I am pleased to see that you have been given appropriate quarters."

Susannah looked around. It really was a regal setting, a cavernous and extravagant room. The walls were crimson with gilded trim. Gold brocade covered the chairs and hung at the windows. A gilt chandelier hung from the ceiling, and the paintings on the walls were set in elaborate gilded frames.

Regal, but not precisely inviting. The paintings were dark, but not dark enough to obscure the subject matter—some of the less cheerful Biblical scenes. On one wall, Abraham raised his knife, prepared to sacrifice Isaac, and on the opposite wall Roman soldiers enthusiastically engaged in the Slaughter of the Innocents. Still, the tiled stove radiated welcome warmth.

"This is exciting, is it not?" Lady Augusta settled herself in one of the chairs, "However, I did not care for that baron and his sister. They looked at us with positive dislike. In addition, they were far too presumptuous. The idea of the baroness taking it upon herself to decide who the princess's attendants should be!"

"I was terrified when that man said they were to be my attendants," said Olivia. "I couldn't imagine what I would do if you weren't with me and I had to be with strangers. And they looked so grim. Positively witch-like."

While they talked, Susannah recovered herself and wandered around the room, examining the windows, which looked onto the gardens, and the doors. One led to what must be the princess's bedroom, an almost equally large room, this one with bedding, draperies, and upholstery in the green and gold that were the

Sigmaringen colors. Another door led from the sitting room to a smaller, more modest bedroom for an attendant, and a second modest chamber was entered from the princess's bedroom.

It was an arrangement that could be kept reasonably secure. Hardly the sort of thing she normally thought about, but Max's obvious concern on the way from the station had made her doubly nervous.

"Well, it appears that we can be on either side of you," she told Olivia. "That is good. And there are keys in the doors to the corridor, so I assume we can lock them."

"Lock them?" Olivia straightened up in alarm. "Why would the doors need to be locked?"

"I don't know, but Captain Staufer said that we should stay together until he comes to explain. I don't want to alarm you, but I think that when we were at the station, the general received a message that upset him."

"Heavens! I knew that something was going on here." Lady Augusta shook her head, but looked more thrilled than distressed. "This is turning out to be even more exciting that I had expected."

Susannah looked at the old woman with fond exasperation. It was no wonder that her mother had offered to let Susannah and Olivia accompany Lady Augusta on this trip. It was less an offer than an order, she realized. They had been sent to rein the elderly woman in—or try to do so. So far, Susannah had been markedly unsuccessful in that endeavor, and "exciting" did not begin to describe this adventure.

Footmen appeared with the trunks, followed by

maids to unpack them and more footmen bringing pots of coffee and trays of pastries. The three women remained in the sitting room, sipping and nibbling and occasionally giving orders about the unpacking until they were finally alone. Then there was nothing left to do but wait for Max.

Thirteen

Max wanted to smash something. Preferably Hugo Herzlos's face. That, however, did not seem to be a possibility at the moment.

He had spent a nightmarish hour with the prince and the Herzlos clan, while Conrad burbled happily about the princess's beauty ("So much lovelier than her portrait"); the count grumbled about the reports that the princess had spoken in Schwäbisch ("It will just encourage the reformers"); and Helga had returned to make her usual not-quite-offensive comments ("Somehow I expected a princess to be more regal"). Hugo had soon disappeared, however, and Max was increasingly worried about what he might be doing.

When Max finally escaped the royal chambers and managed to confer with the general, his mood plummeted further. The situation was far worse than he had feared. This masquerade had put Lady Susannah—all the women—in real danger, and it was his fault. They were in danger because he had thought the masquerade would be fun.

Fun! He must have been mad.

Not entirely mad. Part of his motive had been purely selfish. He had wanted the opportunity to further his acquaintance with Lady Susannah. That part he could not regret. She was extraordinary. Such beauty! Not the fragile prettiness of Lady Olivia of the golden curls. No, underneath that prim-and-proper pose of hers, Susannah had the wild beauty of a warrior queen and the spirit to match, only waiting to be set free.

And she was no fool. She had seen that there would be problems facing them and had not hesitated to warn them. He was the one who had been a fool, promising her that there would be no danger, that he would be able to protect her.

He berated himself for failing to recognize the seriousness of the situation. How could he have been so stupid? He should have seen at once that the princess's disappearance had to be more than the childish tantrum of a spoiled brat. He did not care about himself, but until now, he had never put a woman in danger, and that was tormenting him.

Susannah was in danger because of his rashness. The others too, of course, he reminded himself. Now the only thing to do was to get them out of here—not just out of the castle, but out of the country.

And then he would never see Lady Susannah again. That would be just as well for her, since he was unlikely to get out of this with his head still attached to his neck. An exaggeration, but the best he could hope for was utter disgrace. Losing a princess and attempting to palm off a pretender was hardly the sort of behavior to be approved by a ruler. Conrad was no tyrant, but there were limits to what a prince could accept, even from a boyhood playmate. But still… *Damnation!* He did not want to lose Susannah. Not when he was just getting to know her.

The princess's suite was in the south wing of the inner courtyard, almost as far as it could be from the royal chambers without being obviously insulting. Max saw Helga's jealous hand in this, but it was just as well. The isolation would make it easier to spirit the women away.

When he finally reached the corridor, two footmen were standing outside the door to the suite, but none were at any other doors. Good. That meant the rest of the corridor was unoccupied. His own men of the Royal Guard stood watch, two at either end of the corridor. That should keep out any intruders, so the women were safe enough for the moment.

When he reached the gilded door, he stopped the footman who was about to open it. "Wait. Do not open the door yet. Knock first and wait for a response. No one is to enter these rooms unless the princess or her ladies give permission. Is that understood?"

The flicker of surprise in the footman's eyes was followed by a nod. That would have to suffice. Even if these men had been put here by Hugo, they were unlikely to disobey a direct order. And he didn't want the women to be surprised by unwanted visitors.

Max rapped sharply on the door.

Lady Susannah opened it so quickly that she must have been waiting right there. She started to speak but noticed the footmen and stepped back. Good. She had enough sense not to trust the castle servants. He entered and closed the door firmly behind him.

She had not stepped back very far. Not because she wished to be close to him, but because there was no room. They were in a tiny antechamber, which had barely enough room for two people. She was looking up with a mixture of irritation and worry, probably because it had taken him so long to get here.

He breathed in the scent of her. Something floral. Roses? But not just roses. Not just sweetness. There was something else. Thorns? Did thorns have a scent? If they did, then that was the scent of Lady Susannah—roses and thorns.

Through the doorway, he saw Lady Olivia and Lady Augusta sitting up, blinking their eyes as if they had been dozing in their chairs. He put an arm around Susannah's shoulders—the closest he dared come to an embrace—and led her over to join them before he sat down himself.

He leaned forward, his elbows on his knees and his hands clasped before him. "I am sorry. Problems have arisen. Things are not quite as we had thought." He tried to think of a way to phrase it without frightening them. He couldn't. "We—the general and I—think we should be able to smuggle you out of the castle tonight."

That made all three women straighten up in surprise.

"But why?" asked Olivia. "I thought I did quite well. Was I not convincing after all?"

"You were indeed convincing," he assured her. "No one doubts that you are the princess. But—" He paused. "I must tell you everything. When we first approached you, we thought Princess Mila had run off in a fit of pique while we were all asleep—so sound asleep we suspected she had drugged us. Her servants—her maid and the members of her immediate guard—had vanished with her, and some of her things as well. We assumed we would find her quickly.

"But today at the station, there was a message for the general. One of the princess's guards has been found dead. The body had been dragged from the road and hastily buried under leaves in the forest." He paused again. "That has changed everything."

Lady Olivia gasped and looked distressed. Lady Augusta straightened up, her eyes full of interest.

Susannah frowned in concentration. "That suggests the princess did not leave voluntarily after all. Unless...unless there was a disagreement among her guards? Might he have been trying to keep her from leaving?"

"I wish I could believe that," Max said. "Unfortunately, the road where he was found leads only to the neighboring estate, which is owned by Hugo Herzlos. She would have had no reason to go there."

"An unpleasant fellow, that Herzlos. I did not care for him." Lady Augusta spoke firmly, and then she frowned and added, "Nor did I care for the rest of his family. His sister is presumptuous far beyond anything her title or her person might support. And his father is a relic from an earlier century. Do you think they have kidnapped the princess?"

Max blinked, taken aback. He had been trying to lead up to that gently so that he would not frighten the women, but Lady Augusta was asking as if it were nothing more than an item of gossip.

"You needn't try to soften it for us, you know." Susannah sounded impatient. "We could see that there was something wrong before we even reached the castle. You and the general were obviously worried. And Horrible Hugo looked positively astounded to see the princess step out of the carriage. We could hardly fail to notice, so naturally we assume that he is involved in whatever has gone wrong. But I don't see why he wanted to carry off the princess. Don't tell me he fell madly in love with her and wants to marry her himself."

Max laughed shortly. "In love? Not Hugo. But that he might want to marry the princess?" He considered. "That is a possibility. Yes, that is possible. But for that to happen, or at least for it to be of any use to him, Conrad would have to be removed."

"He cannot mean to harm the prince!" Lady Olivia looked distressed at the idea.

"No, not personally, at any rate. But if Prince Gottfried decides that the princess's disappearance is an insult to Hechingen and threatens to punish Sigmaringen, there might be riots as there were in '48, when Conrad's parents were killed by the mob. Then Hugo could step in to save the situation, rescue the princess, marry her, and claim the throne."

"The blackguard!" Lady Augusta sniffed her disapproval.

"Would that work?" asked Susannah. A reasonable question.

"Possibly." Max sighed. "Probably."

"And his father and sister? Are they involved in this plot of his as well?"

Susannah did ask sensible questions. Max could not keep from smiling at her before he answered. "Helga, yes. The twins are very close, and she has always been part of his plotting, even when they were children. His father, no. The count may be a stubborn old fool, but he would never do anything dishonorable. For Hugo's plot to succeed, his father would have to be…removed from the picture."

The three women looked at each other, holding some sort of silent conference. Max broke in to say, "Hugo is confused at the moment. He cannot understand how the princess can be here. Did she escape? Did he kidnap the wrong woman? Until he can speak with his confederates, he cannot act because he does not know what to do. That gives us at least a day or two. We will have you out of the castle and out of the country before he knows for certain that you are imposters."

They all stared at him. Then they turned away to look at one another, then back at him.

Susannah tilted her head to one side, considering. "It would perhaps be sensible for us to leave," she said slowly, "but do you want us to leave?"

That was not a question he wanted her to ask, and certainly not one he wanted to answer. He said, "It is not a question of what I want, but of what is needed for your safety."

They looked at one another again. Susannah looked uncertain, and Lady Olivia was frowning and chewing on her lip, but Lady Augusta sat there stiff and erect and shook her head.

"No," she said firmly.

"No?" Max didn't know what to say. He had expected them to be frightened, distressed, worried, perhaps even a bit hysterical. He did not expect a flat refusal—and certainly not from a fragile old lady.

"We gave our word," that fragile old lady explained with a tolerant smile for him. "We do not go back on our word."

"How difficult will your situation be if we disappear? Yours and the general's?" Susannah asked. "It will be apparent that you tried to pass off an imposter. Will you be safe?"

"And the prince," said Lady Olivia. "What will happen to him? Will he be safe?"

"You see," said Lady Augusta, "we cannot consider only our own safety. When we agreed to this adventure, a certain train of events was set in motion, so to speak. We cannot very well disembark and leave others to suffer in the crash."

This was preposterous. Lady Augusta clearly had no notion of the risks involved. Max could not permit them to remain. It was his fault that they were now in danger, and it was his responsibility to get them to safety.

"No," he said, rising to his feet. "Your offer to help is beyond anything the general and I could have expected, but we cannot allow you to put yourselves in jeopardy."

Lady Augusta smiled kindly at him, and he felt himself flushing. It was the way his Aunt Magda smiled at him when he said something foolish. "My dear boy," she said in dulcet tones, "I am sure you mean well, but it really is not up to you to decide what we may or may not do."

"If we simply vanish, it will put the prince in danger, will it not?" asked Lady Olivia, looking at him solemnly with those huge brown eyes. "And he does not even know that there is danger."

Why on earth was she so worried about Conrad? It was all very well and good for a woman to have a tender heart, but…Conrad was the prince. It was not for women to rescue the prince. He turned to Lady Susannah. "Lady Susannah, Suse, you saw at the very start that this was a foolish endeavor. Now you cannot let these other ladies persist in an escapade that has turned seriously dangerous. Make them see sense."

She looked at him for a long minute, but finally shook her head. "I admit that I thought it was foolish at the beginning, but that was because I did not think it would be possible to make people believe that Olivia is the princess. Obviously I was wrong about that. And I also admit that I thought it improper for us to get entangled in your country's situation. We could, and perhaps should, have refused to involve ourselves.

"However, things have changed. Whether properly or not, we are entangled in this situation, and what we do, or fail to do, will affect others than ourselves. You cannot expect us to turn aside just because we have encountered a few difficulties."

Then she smiled at him, as if she expected him to understand.

She looked reasonable. She sounded perfectly reasonable. How could she sound reasonable when she was uttering such idiotic nonsense?

"A few difficulties?" Max exploded. "Are you out of your mind, woman? You could all get killed and it would be my fault."

"You must keep your voice down, dear boy," said Lady Augusta. "The footmen at the door are not deaf, and I have no idea if they can be trusted."

He sat down abruptly and closed his mouth. He was losing his self-control as well as his mind, and he'd had to be warned about the most elementary precautions by a white-haired old lady covered in silk ruffles.

"That's better," said Susannah. "Now, Lady Augusta is right. It would be dishonorable of us to abandon this cause when we are in part responsible for the current situation."

"You are not responsible!" He wanted to shake her. "*I* am responsible. The general is responsible. But not you ladies."

"Actually," said Lady Augusta, "the people responsible are the ones who kidnapped the princess. That would be your friend Hugo, it appears."

Max made a strangled noise.

Lady Augusta ignored him and continued, tapping her chin thoughtfully. "Or one might say that the fault lies with whoever made the decisions that led to the unrest in the country, which in turn made an alliance with Hechingen so necessary. That, I gather, would be Hugo's father, Count Herzlos."

"Or Prince Conrad," put in Lady Olivia regretfully, "for failing to take charge of the country himself."

"At this point it no longer matters who is to blame," said Susannah. "But if we run away, we leave the field to Horrible Hugo and Helga the Hag. It may sound petty, but I cannot bear the thought of letting them win."

"Neither can I," said Olivia. "Imagine her setting herself up to give orders to the princess. I know I'm not, really, but she didn't know that."

"Stop that!" Max was outraged. "You cannot turn this into a joke by giving them silly names. These people are dangerous. You must not forget that at least one man has already been killed."

"True enough," said Susannah, "but silly names remind us that they are not infallible. If they were, we would not be here and they would not be so confused. And I refuse to let them drive me away as if I were some timid little mouse."

"Bravo!" said Lady Augusta, beaming a smile at Susannah. "I knew you had it in you. No child of your parents could be a coward."

"You don't understand." Max rubbed the back of his neck as he shook his head. "During the riots in '48, when Prince Conrad's parents were killed… If Conrad had died as well, Count Herzlos would be the prince now and Hugo would be his heir."

"Ah," said Susannah. "Hugo looks at Conrad and thinks, 'There but for the grace of God go I.'"

Max glared at her. "It is not funny. And then there is Helga." He paused.

"Can women rule here?" asked Olivia. "Could she be the princess?"

"She thought at one point that she might be. There was talk of a marriage between her and Conrad." A corner of Max's mouth twitched up. "I'm not sure where the talk started."

"So there is personal animosity here as well as ambition." Lady Augusta frowned. "A dangerous combination, but one I have encountered before. We need only keep our wits about us."

Olivia was frowning. "It does all seem a bit unfair."

"Unfair?" Susannah looked confused.

"Yes. I mean, the way their father kept ignoring them or dismissing them as unimportant, when the baroness would probably have made a very good princess. She's so beautiful and regal. I'm sure she looks more like a princess than I do." Olivia lifted an apologetic shoulder.

Max snorted. "She would have eaten Conrad alive."

Susannah swung around on him in annoyance. "That is a criticism of Conrad, not of Helga. Or do you think a woman must never have any ambition?"

"No, of course not," Max said quickly, though he was inclined to think so. But he didn't want to argue with Susannah about that.

Olivia was continuing on her own line of thought. "In fact, the count seemed to deliberately humiliate both his children. That isn't right. You can hardly blame them for resenting it. I feel rather sorry for them."

That won Susannah's attention. "Olivia, stop that right now. They do not deserve your sympathy. Your own parents were far worse—the best that can be said of them is that they generally neglected you—but you don't go around kidnapping people or getting them killed."

"Well, of course not." Olivia looked horrified at the suggestion.

"Quite right," said Lady Augusta. "You can feel sorry for them after we have stopped them."

And that was that as far as the ladies were concerned. Struggle as he might, argue as he could, Max could not budge them from their purpose. It was a battle he could not win. He had expected Susannah to see that it would be far more sensible for them to leave immediately. Although he admired her courage, the thought of her in danger tied knots in his gut.

There was nothing he could do except try to see to their protection. He would bring some of his own people to the castle to serve them and to stand guard at the door. They agreed to keep together and to be cautious about allowing anyone into their rooms. A promise to be on their guard was the most he could get from them.

There was to be a grand ball in four days' time to celebrate the princess's arrival, and three weeks after that, the betrothal would be solemnized in the cathedral. Prince Gottfried was expected to be present for that occasion, and they could hardly expect their masquerade to fool the princess's father. That gave them twenty days in which to find the princess, get her into her proper place in the palace, and somehow explain all of this to the prince.

The ladies seemed convinced it could be done. *Ha.* The more Max thought about it, the more impossible it seemed.

But that plan would keep Susannah here.

She should not be here. It was insanity to keep her here where she would be in danger. How could he be so selfish? He should insist that she leave.

But how could he let her go?

Susannah escorted him to the door. Before he left, he seized her by the shoulders and pulled her to him, holding her in a fierce embrace. "Ah, Suse, if you come to any harm in this, I will never forgive you."

Fourteen

If she had been asked, Susannah would have been hard pressed to say just what she had expected after the dramatic events of the previous day. However, she was reasonably certain that a lengthy, interminable tour of the Nymburg castle would not have been high on the list.

She trailed listlessly behind the others. Aunt Augusta would probably tell her to stop behaving like a ninny, but Aunt Augusta was too busy flirting with the general to notice Susannah's behavior. Olivia would normally have asked what was wrong and fussed over her, but Olivia was hanging on Prince Conrad's arm, too engrossed in whatever he was saying to notice anything else. As for what her mother would say—Susannah did not want to think about that. Fortunately, her mother was back in England, busy spoiling her grandchildren, and had no idea what her youngest daughter was doing.

Susannah was not feeling neglected and ignored. Well, perhaps a bit. But not neglected by Olivia and Aunt Augusta. She was delighted that they were able to enjoy themselves under the circumstances. Really.

What bothered her was that after the tumult of the revelations last night, after that parting embrace, Maximillian von Staufer had simply vanished. *Poof.* He was nowhere to be seen. He had left no word of explanation. No letter, no message. Nothing.

Had she completely mistaken his feelings? Perhaps the embrace had just been a kindly gesture, designed to encourage her. That seemed unlikely since he had been trying to *dis*courage her. She did not think she had misunderstood, but it was possible that she had.

And how to explain her own reaction? It was not as if she had never been held by a man before. She was almost twenty-two years old, after all, and she had been out in society for ages. London was hardly a nunnery, and she had her share of curiosity. But never before had she experienced an embrace that dissolved her bones and set off fireworks inside her. Last night, however, when Max had held her in his arms, she'd felt as if she had finally come home, as if she was at last where she belonged.

This was nonsense. She had to stop thinking this way. She should not start thinking that it meant anything special to him or to her.

She should not think there was anything more than attraction in her feelings for Max. Not really. Just because he was so big and strong and handsome and dashing and laughed as if he would defy the world. Just because he made *her* laugh too. Just because his arms around her made her feel safe and protected. She gave herself a shake and straightened her back. This was infatuation, nothing more. And his determination to protect her? Lady Susannah Tremaine did not need to be protected. Her parents had raised their children to be independent and self-reliant.

She stiffened her back and tried to feel self-reliant. It would be easier if that melting warmth deep inside her would go away.

Given the heated direction her thoughts were taking, it was obvious that she had been reading too many novels of late. Tonight she would have to take up something dry and boring. Thucydides, perhaps. Greek history always put her to sleep.

Meanwhile, she needed to pay some attention to her surroundings. The prince may have thought he was showing his bride-to-be her new home—and from the soft glances that Olivia was resting on him, she was playing her part as the princess a bit too well—but Susannah wanted to study the geography of the castle. They had determined to stay and play their parts until Max and the general found out what had happened to the princess and where she was now. However, it would be wise to find an escape route or two, just in case.

Insisting on carrying on with this masquerade when Max wanted them to leave was not, perhaps, the most sensible thing she had ever done. She did not intend to examine her motives too closely. Even so, she was not so foolish that she did not realize there was danger in this enterprise. "Secure your line of retreat" was a piece of advice that she intended to follow.

As they ascended still another staircase—more marble and more statuary—to turn down still another corridor—more tapestries and more windows over-looking a courtyard—she was learning this could be more difficult than she had expected. Over the past five centuries, princes had been altering the castle and adding what seemed to be an endless array of halls.

The tour had taken them through the medieval great hall with its cavernous fireplace, stone floor, and vaulted ceiling. That was where the first ruler, a Hohenstaufen count, had held court. Then they had traversed a Renaissance throne room with its coffered ceiling and checkerboard floor. That was the work of the first prince, Rudolf. Now they had reached the seventeenth century and were admiring the intricately carved paneling with its acanthus leaves and grotesque animals. Above the fireplace was a huge carving of the royal coat of arms. The lions rampant on either side were as large as the real beasts would be. The fourth Prince Rudolf had presided here.

What she had yet to see was a way out that did not require marching through the public corridors, all of which were lined with footmen awaiting the orders of the residents of this complex. There must be discreet passages for the servants who kept the rooms gleaming, but the doorways for those were too well disguised in the paneling for a mere visitor like herself to find.

Eventually she realized that the basic design of the castle was not all that complicated. When they had arrived, they had gone through the iron gates of the castle walls into the first courtyard. The medieval wings surrounding it housed the offices of the castle staff in small, dim rooms with slits for windows. The only part of the medieval castle still in use by the court was the great hall.

The Renaissance rooms, serving various official

functions, surrounded the second courtyard, culminating in an enormous ballroom dividing the second courtyard from the third.

Around the third courtyard were the private rooms, in what was almost a separate palace built in the eighteenth century. Their suite of rooms was in the south wing, while Prince Conrad resided in the north wing. Susannah asked and was told, reluctantly, that the Herzlos clan was also housed in the south wing, but on the lower floor.

She wasn't sure if a lower floor meant higher or lower status, but at this point she didn't really care. They had been walking so long on these marble floors that her feet were beginning to hurt.

Finally, Olivia noticed that Lady Augusta was leaning rather heavily on the general's arm and whispered something to the prince. He promptly invited them all into his private quarters.

These proved to be much cozier rooms, filled with comfortable chairs and with the draperies open to let in the sunshine. Even the paintings on the walls were cozy—genre scenes with rosy-cheeked children. Not particularly good ones, either. The sentimental sort, full of apples and woolly lambs. If Conrad was the one who had chosen them, his taste in art did not seem to be terribly sophisticated. Or he truly was childish.

Almost immediately a servant brought in coffee and cakes. This appeared to be the inevitable form taken by Sigmaringen hospitality. Susannah did not mind. The cakes, which came in an enormous variety, were delectable. There were sweet buns filled with fruit, sponges with cream filling, bundt cakes rich with almonds and raisins, and so many varieties of biscuits that she never saw the same one twice. Just breathing in the rich, sugary odor was going to make her fat.

Between the pleasure of being off her feet and the delight in sampling a new biscuit—this one chocolate with a filling of raspberry jam—it took Susannah a bit of time to realize that Olivia and the prince seemed to have forgotten that there were other people in the room. They were too busy looking at each other like a pair of mooncalves.

That could not be a good idea.

Susannah was not concerned about the prince. He was doubtless a nice enough fellow, but he could take care of himself. Her concern was for Olivia, who had a tender heart. Too tender. As if by caring for others, she could make up for the care she had never received from her parents.

Olivia must not fall in love with the prince. The pretense was one thing, but the reality would be an absolute disaster. Nothing good could come of it.

Susannah turned to Lady Augusta, only to discover that lady and the general equally engrossed in each other. Susannah raised her eyes to the heavens, or at least to the ceiling. What was happening here? This would be fine if they were safe in London, where they could all flirt safely to their hearts' content, but they were in Nymburg. Had they forgotten why they were here? Had they forgotten the danger of their situation? Had they lost all sense?

Was she the only sane one here?

She coughed. No one noticed.

She coughed more loudly. They still did not notice.

This was ridiculous.

She reached over and balanced Prince Conrad's coffee cup on the edge of the table. Then she sat back and stuck out a foot to jiggle the table.

Success.

The coffee cup fell to the floor with a satisfying crash, splattering the prince's trousers with a mixture of coffee and whipped cream. He jumped up. Everyone else jumped up. Olivia began dabbing at the mess with a napkin. Aunt Augusta fluttered and the general hovered. Conrad assured everyone that it was nothing.

Susannah rang the bell for a servant, who promptly appeared, assessed the situation, and began to clean up the mess. At least the royal servants had some sense.

"I don't know how that happened," said Conrad apologetically, apparently forgetting that princes are not supposed to apologize for anything.

Susannah waved a dismissive hand. "One never knows what will happen while one is distracted." She glared at Aunt Augusta, but that lady, whose age should have given her some notion of propriety, simply looked confused.

While one servant was carrying out the remaining dishes and pastries, another entered with a message for the prince. Looking delighted by the distraction, Conrad announced that Captain Staufer requested an audience.

Well, it was about time he put in an appearance. Susannah did not know what the appropriate demeanor was for a woman who had been passionately embraced and then ignored, so she decided on chilly indifference.

She tightened her lips and tried to appear unin-
terested, but she could not keep from immediately
turning to look at him.

Max entered with a broad smile, saluted the
prince, who seemed delighted to see him, and
greeted the rest of the company. Their meeting
should have been easy enough. A cool smile from
her would have been appropriate.

Unfortunately, he was accompanied by a pair of
huge dogs and one small one, along with a short,
wiry man. The wrinkles on his face claimed he was
an old man, but the vigor of his step and the twinkle
in his eye denied it.

The small dog, which looked vaguely like a red
dust mop, was on a leash. The other two, with heavy
cream-colored coats and dark masks, stood calmly
beside the count, observing the company with intelligent eyes. She had never seen dogs quite so large—
their heads were well above her waist. They made the
carved lions she had seen earlier seem positively puny.

Prince Conrad was regarding the dogs with approval.
"A magnificent pair." He turned to the others. "They
are similar to the Leonbergers, but Captain Staufer
breeds these himself. They are the finest guard dogs I
have ever encountered."

"With Your Highness's permission, I would like to
offer one to Princess Mila and one to Lady Susannah,
and the small dachshund to Lady Augusta." Max
turned to Susannah and winked.

Olivia looked nervous. "They are very impressive
dogs, Captain Staufer, but…but they are very large."

"Don't worry about that." Max smiled in

encouragement. "I also brought Josef, their trainer. He will remain until the dogs understand whom they protect and until you feel comfortable with them." The old man grinned at them cheerfully.

Aunt Augusta looked at the small red mop. "Am I to understand that I am too old to need protection?"

"Not at all, my lady. Little Hans here is a ferocious guardian for all he looks like an innocent toy. He will bark furiously at any intruder, and though he may not be able to knock down an enemy, he will most certainly attack his ankles."

"That is indeed true," said the general with a smile. "They are very loyal, these dogs, and prompt to send out an alarm."

While Lady Augusta, with the general's help, bent down to make the acquaintance of her small protector, Susannah stepped a bit closer to one of the large ones. She looked into a pair of dark eyes that looked calmly back at her.

"This is Lev. His brother here is Lezo."

Max was watching her as he made the introduction so she nodded calmly and put out a hand. Lev sniffed it politely, and she was emboldened to scratch behind his ears. He seemed to enjoy that and tilted his head toward her. She ran her fingers through the thick coat and found it surprisingly soft. When she looked up, she found herself ridiculously pleased to see the gleam of approval in Max's eyes, but she concealed that pleasure by looking away immediately.

"You are annoyed at me?" he asked. "Ah, you thought I had deserted you."

She looked up to deny it, but the words died

unspoken. His eyes were not laughing now. They looked tender, almost caressing.

"I will never desert you, never leave you in danger. So long as it is in my power, I will protect you. That much I can promise." He took her hand.

Her throat felt dry, and she licked her lips. "I do not ask for any promises."

"No, you do not." His mouth quirked in a slight, sad smile. "And I cannot make all the promises I would like. Not right now. But I will do all I can to keep you safe." He lifted her hand and pressed a kiss on her palm.

It was just as well that Lev was so big. It was only the fact that she could lean on the dog that kept her from collapsing in a puddle as that kiss sped from her hand to pierce her heart and spread fire through her. It was an outrageous thing for him to do, here in a room full of people. Once she had begun to breathe again, she glanced quickly around to see if anyone had noticed.

No. The prince was introducing Olivia to Lezo. She reached out timidly to the dog, who stood there phlegmatically. Aunt Augusta was sitting stiffly erect, but her expression as she fondled the small dog on her lap was unexpectedly indulgent. As usual, they were not paying attention to Susannah.

Perhaps Max had not noticed her reaction either, for he continued to speak in an undertone. "You are all safe at the moment because Hugo does not know what is happening. Is this the princess? Is this an imposter? He does not dare to say anything or do anything until he knows, and it is difficult for him to find out. He sent a messenger last night, but the messenger ran into some of General Bergen's troops." Max smiled. "There are troops on all the roads leading from the castle. We should be safe for a few days more."

"And the princess?" Susannah darted a glance at Olivia. "The real princess, I mean. Are you any closer to finding her?"

Max lifted a shoulder. "We can only hope. At least we will no longer waste our time searching the routes leading out of the country. Now I have asked my people to find out what they can from the servants on Hugo's estate. They may know something and be willing to speak of it, at least to other servants." He grinned. "Hugo thinks all peasants, especially those who speak Schwäbisch, are fools. This does not endear him to those who work on his estate."

Susannah nodded, trying to look attentive. Of course Max needed to concentrate on thwarting Hugo and finding the princess. That was his duty, and she would not want him to fail in it. Her own thoughts, however, kept returning to the kiss he had pressed on her palm. The warmth of it did not seem to fade.

Fifteen

TOO RESTLESS TO SLEEP, MAX TOOK HIMSELF DOWN TO the palace gardens just as the dawn was breaking. He filled his lungs with the cold, crisp air drifting down with the mist from the neighboring mountains. Already he could smell the approach of winter.

He hated it here in the palace. Always and everywhere there were plots and counterplots, backbiting and jostling for position. General Bergen was always jealous of Count Herzlos's influence over the prince, the count was jealous of the general's control of the army, Hugo and Helga were jealous of everyone, and the courtiers were in constant turmoil, trying to decide which one to support today and which one would be on top tomorrow.

Prince Conrad seemed to ignore it all—or perhaps he simply accepted it as the usual way of things. Did he not see his own responsibility in this? If he did not take control of his principality, if he continued to leave the reins of power dangling, there would always be someone trying to pick up those reins himself. Someone like Hugo.

Max rolled his shoulders, trying to ease the tension in his muscles. How he longed to be back in his own castle at Ostrov, among his own family, his own people, where there was none of this insanity. Would he ever be able to return there to stay, or would he be trapped here forever, protecting a prince who could not seem to protect himself?

A movement in the mist caught his eye and immediately he was on guard, every muscle tense, his hand at his sword. Then the movement resolved itself into Lady Susannah, accompanied by Lev, and suddenly his spirits lightened.

Dressed simply, with a large shawl wrapped around her against the morning chill and with her dark hair just pulled back with a ribbon, she looked absurdly young. He felt a rush of tenderness, more than tenderness, at the sight of her. She was reaching out to touch a flower, caressing its petals.

His footsteps on the gravel path must have startled her, because she swung around, alarmed, until she recognized him. He was glad to see that Lev had also gone on guard.

"You are an early riser," he said.

She nodded, turning back to the flower, fingering its light-pink petals. "I like the peace of early morning. The silence when there is no one around."

"Should I leave?" He didn't want to, but he could understand the yearning for solitude.

She looked up quickly, flushing slightly. "Please don't. I didn't mean you. You aren't…" Her color deepened, until it almost matched the flower she was caressing.

"I am not someone you are responsible for?"

"Yes," she said, sounding almost guilty. "It's not that I don't love them, you understand."

"I know precisely what you mean. We sometimes feel the need to snatch a moment just for ourselves."

They stood there in companionable silence, not quite touching.

"Is that a rose?" He bent his head toward the bush in front of her. "Is it not late in the year for roses?"

"Yes. This one is called Autumn Damask. It has a lovely fragrance. Can you smell it?"

Indeed he could. It was the scent of Susannah, richly fragrant but with something sharp. He couldn't tell her that, so he simply nodded.

"I love this rose for its history as well as its scent. It's descended from the cuttings that crusaders brought back from Damascus, and they say it may be the rose that the ancients called the Four Seasons Rose of Paestum. It humbles me to think that this fragile flower has survived for hundreds, even thousands of years."

"A reminder that our worries are not nearly so important as they seem?"

"Something like that." She smiled at him and then turned back to touch the flower. "My mother has this rose growing in her garden, and now my sisters, the married ones, have planted cuttings of it in their own gardens."

"And you will one day do the same?"

"I hope so. That way, we will always have a piece of home binding us together."

"A lovely thought." He reached down to touch

the velvety petals and brushed her fingers at the same time. "Lovely."

She stilled for a moment as their fingers touched before she drew back with a sigh. "But roses are for another time. At the moment, we have responsibilities. I have to protect Lady Olivia, and you have to protect Prince Conrad."

"Yes, we both have responsibilities, but…" He picked up her hand and placed it against his, palm to palm, their fingers entwined. "But I think that those responsibilities have become entwined. Do you agree?"

She stared at their hands, and the moment stretched out before she gave a tiny nod. "That worries me," she whispered.

≈

"Olivia…" Susannah began, but she didn't quite know how to continue. She didn't like to talk about her own feelings, so she hesitated to probe other people's. But she did need to talk to Olivia, and now, while Aunt Augusta was taking a nap, was an ideal time.

Olivia was happily draping a shawl in various ways around herself and examining the effect in the mirror. "The princess does have lovely things, doesn't she?"

"Yes, but don't you think it might be better for you to wear your own things?"

Olivia thought for a moment, still looking in the mirror, and then shook her head. "No, because when I'm wearing my things, I feel like Olivia de Vaux, and when I wear her things, I feel like a princess."

"Yes, dear, but you *are* Olivia de Vaux. You

aren't Princess Mila. Isn't it a little dangerous to get the two confused?"

Suddenly serious, Olivia turned and sat down facing Susannah. "You have no idea how wonderful it feels to be someone—anyone—other than Olivia de Vaux. When I stayed with your family, I tried to pretend I was one of the Tremaines, but I know I'm not. Not really, no matter how much you treat me like one of you. Any time I go out, any time I'm at a party or a ball, any time I'm even in a shop, I know that people look at me and think, 'Oh, there's that de Vaux girl. She's the daughter of that dreadful Lady Doncaster. One of the Degraded de Vaux.' And they wonder if I'll be a whore like my mother."

"Oh no, darling Olivia, no one could possibly think that way about you." Susannah jumped up to put her arms around her friend. "Not possibly!"

Olivia leaned into the hug, not quite crying. "They do, you know. Some of them like to whisper just loud enough for me to be able to hear them."

"Who?" Susannah demanded. She pulled back and straightened up, preparing to do battle as soon as they returned to London.

"It was Mary Penobscot and her set this season."

"That rat-faced scarecrow? How dare she! That nasty little piece of work is jealous of everyone. You're so sweet and pretty that she knows you make her look like the viper she is."

Olivia managed a slight laugh. "Well, she was slithering around so much that your mother decided to send me on this trip with you and Lady Augusta."

"She never said anything to me." Susannah sat down with a frown.

"Well, of course not." Olivia did laugh now. "You would have charged into the ballroom and started pulling Mary around by the nose."

"Humph. Well, it's long enough to serve as a leash."

They sat there for a few minutes while Susannah considered the ways she could make Mary Penobscot's life a misery as soon as they got home. Then she remembered where they were right now.

And what their immediate problems were.

"Olivia," she began again, "about Prince Conrad…"

"Isn't he wonderful?" Olivia smiled dreamily. "He isn't just handsome. He's kind and considerate and not at all domineering or arrogant. Not at all what I thought a prince would be like. He's…he's *sweet*."

"Yes, dear, he's very sweet, but you have to remember that he *is* the prince. He's supposed to marry Princess Mila. And you aren't really Princess Mila. It's just a masquerade."

"I know that. It's just that I feel a bit sorry for him."

"Sorry for him? But he's a prince. People don't feel sorry for princes!" Susannah was getting a bit exasperated.

"Yes, I know that, but he seems so lonely. As if he doesn't really have anyone to talk to. And from what Captain Staufer said about the princess, I don't think she's going to be much of a companion for him."

"That is the prince's problem, not yours. Don't try to make him happy. Be a bit stiff and standoffish. Because we are going to vanish from his life as soon as Max finds the real princess."

Olivia's head came up. "Max?"

Susannah could feel herself blushing. "Yes, well, he asked me to call him Max, and it seemed sensible."

"Sensible," repeated Olivia. The corners of her mouth tugged up.

"We do have to work together, remember."

Olivia didn't say anything, but her smile broadened.

"The problem is the prince." Susannah was determined to change the subject.

Olivia sighed. "All right. The prince. You know, I really think we should tell him what is going on. This doesn't seem fair."

"I know," said Susannah. "I know. But that isn't our decision to make."

&c&

"What did you need to see me about so urgently? It's getting too cold for conferences in the garden." The general stamped his feet and shivered.

Max ignored the complaint. He thought the shivers were more playacting than anything else. The general didn't want to have to talk to him, so it was best to state his position baldly. "I think we should tell the prince what is going on."

The general snorted dismissively. "That would be a disaster. Telling Conrad would be no different from telling Count Herzlos, and we know that would mean ruin for all of us."

"I am not suggesting we tell Count Herzlos, but Conrad is the prince. He has a right to know."

"He is a boy, Max, not a prince."

"He is only three years younger than I am."

"Years don't matter. You are a man, but he is still the little boy who obeys Herzlos's every command. He never thinks for himself. We cannot let him find out." The general waved his hand dismissively and turned to return to the castle.

Max stepped quickly to block the general's path. "That is because no one tells him anything. He is told only the decisions, never what he needs to know in order to make the decisions himself."

"And that is how it will be as long as Count Herzlos rules the prince. Don't you see? Hugo is actually playing into our hands."

"Hugo is?" Max frowned. "By creating this disaster?"

"Yes." The general smiled. "We can foil his plot. We will find the princess and expose Hugo. When the son's treason is uncovered, the father will be forced out. Even if he is not branded a traitor himself, he will be too shamed to be of any influence. Conrad will have to turn to us."

"To us?" Max was horrified. "What do you mean, to us?"

"To the army, of course." The general looked at him impatiently. "It is the army that can keep Sigmaringen free and independent. There is no need for alliances with Hechingen or any place else."

Max exploded. "That is not your decision to make! It is the prince who decides whether or not Sigmaringen shall enter into an alliance."

The general backed up a bit and made a placating gesture. "Of course it is the prince's decision. And once he is free of Count Herzlos's baneful influence, he will see who his true friends are."

Max closed his eyes in despair. "You are just using this as one more step in your endless battle with Herzlos. Think, General, of the damage you can cause. We must let the prince know what is going on."

"No, *you* think, Max. Think it through. If Herzlos finds out, his son will find out, and what happens then? There are two possibilities. First, Hugo will decide his plot cannot succeed. To save himself, he will make the princess disappear. Then he can deny everything and we are the ones who have plotted to foist an imposter on the prince."

Max shook his head. Conrad was not a fool. He would see through that…wouldn't he?

The general continued. "The other possibility is that if his plans are far enough advanced, Hugo will set his little revolution in motion. Even if we manage to defeat him in the end—and there is no guarantee of that—all our lives will be at risk, the prince's most of all. You think those women are in danger now? Just think of the danger they will face in that situation."

This could not be right. But…but the general might be right. Could Max insist on a course of action that would put Susannah in even more danger? "You don't know," he said. "You don't know that Conrad would tell Herzlos. Not if we warned him that Hugo is involved."

"But he might."

"It is the prince's right to know," Max insisted stubbornly. "You cannot keep this from him—not the princess's disappearance, not Hugo's plotting."

"And you cannot put Sigmaringen at risk by placing such a burden on a boy who is not yet ready to bear the burdens of rule. Those who serve the prince have a duty to protect him, and sometimes that protection means we must conceal situations from him that he is not prepared to handle."

"And the ladies who are engaged in this masquerade? What of them? This is not their country. Their loyalties are not involved. How can you expect them to endanger themselves for your purposes?"

With a flourish, the general dismissed that concern. "You can handle them. Lady Olivia thinks this is a game and looks no further than that. Lady Susannah— well, she could be a problem, but you can manage her. She may not be a fool but she is clearly enamored of you. You have enough experience with women. You can use her emotions to bend her to your will."

"You dare to speak of her in such a way? You dare to suggest...?" Max could not speak, but his hand flew to the hilt of his sword.

The general's eyes widened, but he straightened and stared at Max. "Captain Staufer, you are a soldier, and you are under my command. I order you to keep silent."

Max stood at attention and stared back for a long minute before he spoke. "Three days. I will give you three days. If we have not found the princess by then, I will tell the prince everything. And if any harm comes to those ladies..." He saluted stiffly, spun around, and marched away.

Sixteen

Bradenham Abbey

ONCE THEIR CARRIAGE HAD PULLED TO A STOP, LADY Penworth flung the door open and leaped down the moment the footman lowered the steps. The butler barely managed to open the door of the Abbey in time to let her in.

"Where are they?" she demanded, barely pausing.

"The blue drawing room," the butler called after her as she raced down the corridor, not bothering to remove her cloak or hat. Lord Penworth hurried along in her wake.

She burst into the drawing room, where her oldest daughter—Elinor, Lady Doncaster—was sitting beside her husband, Harry. Lady Penworth halted so abruptly that her husband almost crashed into her.

The Doncasters looked up in surprise. Harry jumped to his feet. Elinor, who was extremely pregnant, tried to rise but everyone waved her back into her seat.

Arms akimbo, Lady Penworth looked at her

daughter, her anxiety giving way to irritation. "You look perfectly well," she said accusingly.

"I am." Elinor blinked. "Except for looking like a whale and being unable to find a comfortable position for sleeping, I'm fine. Why wouldn't I be?"

Her mother sat down in the nearest chair and pulled off her gloves, finger by finger, with great concentration. She laid them on the table beside her. Next she undid the fastening at the neck of her dark-blue woolen cape and pushed it off her shoulders onto the back of the chair. She then folded her hands in her lap and looked at her daughter.

"When one receives a telegram from one's daughter—one's daughter who is barely weeks from giving birth—and that telegram says, 'Come at once,' it is not unreasonable for one to assume that something dire has happened."

Harry's jaw dropped and he looked at his wife. "*That's* what you said in the telegram?"

Elinor looked defensive. "Well, telegrams are supposed to be brief, aren't they?"

"Not so brief that they strike terror into the hearts of the recipients," he said, starting to smile.

Lord Penworth handed his hat, gloves, and coat to the servant who had followed them in. "Well, now that we are here with hearts beating normally again, perhaps you could tell us *why* we are here."

"I'm sorry. I truly am. It never occurred to me that you would think…" Elinor broke off. "Now that I hear it, it does sound rather drastic, doesn't it? But the thing is, I don't know if it's something dire or not." She looked at her husband.

"We've had a letter from Olivia, you see," he said.

"Ah." Lady Penworth nodded. "And what does your sister say?"

"Not a great deal. She says they are off to Sigmaringen for a few days to have an adventure." Harry looked worried. "But that's all she says about it."

"You know how enthusiastic Olivia gets," said Elinor. "It could be anything from a trip to buy a new bonnet to an expedition to climb an unclimbable Alp. But I don't like the sound of that. We were hoping you had heard from Susannah and could tell us what it's all about."

"Oh dear." Lady Penworth and her husband exchanged worried glances. "We did have a letter from Susannah, a rather odd letter. All she said was that they were going to Sigmaringen, and she didn't know where they would be staying so we couldn't write to them."

"That doesn't sound like Susannah." Elinor looked worried as well.

"The situation doesn't improve," said Lord Penworth, removing a paper from his pocket. "I had a letter from Augusta. It didn't arrive until today because she sent it to Penworth Castle rather than to London."

Lady Penworth turned a look of astonishment on him.

"I didn't tell you about it because by the time I saw it, you were already distressed about Elinor's telegram."

His wife closed her eyes and took a deep breath. "Very well. What does she say?"

"That they are going to Sigmaringen, which we already knew. However, she adds that they are going to be staying in the royal palace, but we should not write to them there because they will be incognito."

"What?" Lady Penworth leaped to her feet in outrage.

Harry and Elinor echoed her.

Lady Penworth began to pace back and forth across the room. "I'll wager Augusta sent that letter to Dorset on purpose. She knew we were in London. She just didn't want us interfering before they had their little adventure."

"She wouldn't do such a thing, would she?" Harry looked shocked.

Lord Penworth looked not in the least surprised. "Yes, of course she would. That's why we sent Susannah with her."

"Now that was not at all fair," said Elinor. "You shouldn't expect Susannah to rein in Aunt Augusta. You can't do it yourself." She stopped and a slow smile appeared on her face. "On the other hand, Susannah might have decided that she'd like a bit of adventure herself. It's high time she broke out of that prim-and-proper mold."

Her parents looked at Elinor in surprise. Then Lady Penworth, unaccustomed to uncertainty, said, "You may be right. About her wanting to break out, I mean. I'm quite certain you are right that we were unfair in expecting her to shepherd Augusta, who is old enough to be her grandmother. That still leaves us with a problem. Susannah is all alone in a strange country with no one to watch out for her. She certainly can't rely on either Augusta or Olivia for help."

"If they were going to be in Sigmaringen for only a few days, they should have left by now. It's been a week since we got the first letter." Lord Penworth was frowning. "We should have heard from them."

"Something has gone wrong," said Harry. "Olivia is my sister. I should go…"

He looked at his wife. His very pregnant wife who had a sudden flash of panic in her eyes before she resumed her look of calm interest.

"No, Harry. You cannot possibly leave Elinor at this point," said Lady Penworth. "Phillip and I will go." She began putting her gloves back on. "After all, we were the ones who sent the girls off on this trip."

Lord Penworth nodded. "We can set out tomorrow."

Seventeen

It was just as well that Mama had taken them to Paris in preparation for this trip, Susannah thought. Her own gown didn't matter so much—well, of course it did. One's gown *always* mattered, and she loved the blue and lavender brocade of hers. The color made her eyes look more violet than blue, and the rich fabric was enhanced by the simplicity of the cut. It was perfect for a lady-in-waiting—rich but not gaudy.

However, what mattered for this ball was Olivia's gown, and tonight she was wearing one of her own, not one of the princess's. It was of pale-gold satin, almost the exact shade of Olivia's hair, with lace-trimmed scallops over an underskirt of soft green. The same green trimmed the wide bertha collar that skimmed over the top of her shoulders, baring just the right amount of space for the filigree necklace of gold and peridots.

The sight made Susannah sigh with pleasure. It also made her nervous. Was Olivia having doubts? Did the fact that she was wearing her own gown mean that she wanted to stop being the princess? A grand ball in honor of the princess did not seem the best time for such indecision.

Olivia did not look as pleased with her appearance as she should. She held herself very still as the maid adjusted the ribbons in her hair and twisted a ringlet into the proper position, but she did not seem to be taking any interest in the process.

Lady Augusta sighed impatiently. "Really, Your Highness. Anyone would think you had never attended a ball before." She waved a hand to dismiss the maid and waited for the door to close before she began to speak softly. "Surely you are not worried about your ability to play this role. The prince, the court—everyone has accepted you. And the prince seems quite entranced by you."

Olivia's lower lip stuck out the way it did when she was about to be stubborn. That was enough to worry Susannah. There were times when Olivia was impervious to reason. She took Olivia's hand. "What is the matter? Is it the danger? Are you afraid? If that is it, I will tell Max and he will have us out of here tonight. You know he will."

"No, no, it's not that at all." Olivia wrapped her arms around herself and looked angry. "It just isn't right. The prince has been so kind, so trusting. We should not be playing this dreadful trick on him. Think how humiliated he will feel when he discovers it. We should tell him what is going on. We really should."

That prompted a snort from Lady Augusta. "Stuff and nonsense. Just what do you think will happen if we tell him what has happened, or what we *think* has happened, since we do not really know? I'll tell you

what he will do. Like a child, he will run to Count
Herzlos and ask what to do—because that is apparently
what he has always done. It seems to be accepted here
that Conrad is the prince, but Count Herzlos is the
ruler. And then? Why, then Herzlos will confront his
son, who will realize that his only recourse is to stage
his revolution immediately and kill the prince, the
count, and all of us. Is that what you want?"

Susannah felt slightly ill. What Aunt Augusta said
sounded frighteningly possible. On some level she had
known all that. She just hadn't thought of it in quite
such brutal terms.

Olivia grew pale and looked about to burst into
tears. "I feel so sorry for him."

"Stop that," commanded Lady Augusta. "You are
not to pity the prince. It seems to me that the problems in this country have been caused by his weakness.
If he had taken up the reins of government himself and
not just sat there in his pretty uniform, he would not
have been vulnerable."

"He's not weak," insisted Olivia. "He's kind. All of
you seem to think that's some sort of weakness, but
it isn't."

Lady Augusta held up a hand. "Whether he is kind
or weak is not the issue at the moment. Do you want
to put Captain Staufer and General Bergen at risk, to
say nothing of Susannah and me?"

"Oh no!" protested Olivia.

"Then stiffen your spine. Now that we have put
this masquerade in motion, we have no choice but to
follow it through. Hold up your head and remember
that you are a princess."

Lady Augusta flung open the door, and Olivia did as she was told. It was the princess who walked into the corridor to lead the procession to the ballroom. Susannah took a deep, steadying breath and followed.

Sometimes Lady Augusta could be quite frightening, Susannah thought. That thought was followed by another one. Would Lady Augusta be quite as vehement about preserving the secret if General Bergen were not involved?

Eighteen

THEY HAD SEEN THE BALLROOM ON THEIR TOUR OF THE castle, but that had been in the daytime. Susannah had thought the white and gold space cold and cavernous. Intimidating. Certainly not at all appealing. Now, however, it was magical. Three enormous gilt-and-crystal chandeliers, each with three tiers of candles, hung in a row down the center of the room. A dozen smaller ones marched down either side, brilliantly illuminating the festivities. Flowers, banks of flowers, perfumed the air as in an eternal summer. The sweet strains of a few violins floated over the chatter of those awaiting the start of the ball.

For a moment, Susannah forgot all about the masquerade, the danger, Olivia's fears, and Aunt Augusta's warning. The splendor of the scene drove all those worries away. She had wandered into an enchanted world.

She had never been to a ball at Buckingham Palace—such frivolity had died with Prince Albert—but she could not imagine that the Queen had ever presided over an event so lightheartedly joyful. It was not just the magnificence of the room and the glamour of the guests. Yes, the women wore beautiful gowns and dripped with jewels. Yes, many of the men wore splendiferous uniforms and glittered with decorations so that they were even more colorful than the women. But Susannah suspected that the real source of joy on this occasion was the prince.

He had greeted his princess with a look of delight that cast a glow over the room. When he held her by his side as he welcomed people to the ball, a faint sigh of pleasure rose from the onlookers. The court was as delighted with the princess as the prince was, and as the crowds greeting her arrival had been.

Susannah felt a twinge of something. Guilt? Not really. Concern, perhaps. It was not quite the earlier worries returning. This worry was something new.

Olivia was such a perfect princess that she was going to create problems for Princess Mila when she reappeared. But from what Max and the general had said, Mila was a foolish and self-centered girl, so perhaps Susannah's concern should be for the prince. It was the reverse of all the fairy tales. His charming princess would turn into a toad.

She shook off the regret. Mila was the princess he was supposed to get in the first place, and all they were doing was preserving his realm for him. He would have to be grateful for that when he eventually found out what had been happening. But she doubted that would happen. He would have to be inhuman to be anything other than furious at the deception. To be offered happiness and then have it snatched from you? She knew how she would feel, and it would not be grateful.

Enough.

She could do nothing about the prince and his troubles, present or future. For tonight she was going to set all her fears and worries aside, seize the moment, and enjoy it. The problems would still be there in the morning, but for once in her life, she was going to ignore her responsibilities.

This night was going to be for her.

Never again would she dance in a royal ballroom. It was quite possible that never again would she dance with Captain Maximillian von Staufer.

She stepped forward to take her place beside Max in the opening polonaise, and her breath stopped when she looked up at him. He was magnificent. He was tall and strong and incredibly handsome. He was a knight in shining armor, no matter that instead of armor he wore a white uniform festooned with gold braid. Instead of a shield, a green velvet cape lined with gold satin hung over one shoulder.

The warmth in his eyes when he looked at her fanned an unaccustomed flame inside her. His hand enveloped hers, and even through their gloves, she could feel the heat crackling, welding them together.

They moved through the gliding steps of the procession, bowing and twirling as the dance demanded, but she felt separate from all the others. It was as if she and Max were the only ones there. The orchestra slipped into the first waltz of the ball, and she was spinning to the music with only his strong arm around her to keep her from flying off into space.

Susannah had heard this music before. It was one of the Strauss waltzes that had been played when they were in Vienna. It had been lovely then. Now it was perfect. *Dum-de-dah, dum-de-dah*—rising and swirling, inscribing itself in her heart. Never would she lose this melody. This music was hers for all eternity.

She looked up into Max's eyes, his dark, dark eyes, and could not look away. One was expected to talk to one's partner while dancing—she knew that—but she could not think of anything to say. Her heart was overflowing, but with feelings she could not put into words. His eyes told her it was the same for him. They spun and whirled and floated on a cloud of music, alone in the universe.

Eventually the music came to an end, and slowly she grew aware of the quiet. Max had whirled her out of the ballroom and onto the balcony. The chill of the evening meant that they were utterly private here, but with his arms around her, she did not feel the cold.

"Suse." He breathed out her name almost as a prayer. "Ah, Suse, there is so much I want to say, so much I want to promise, but I cannot. Not yet. Do you understand?"

She nodded. She could not speak, not now, but she did understand. Duty was something everyone in her family understood. Duty always came first.

But duty was not the only thing in the world.

She moved her hand from his shoulder to pull his head down to her. Then the voices from the ballroom penetrated her consciousness—voices that seemed to be coming nearer.

Regretfully, she stepped back, and after a moment, Max's arm loosened to let her go. He led her sedately back into the ballroom.

"Staufer." The sharp voice made her jump, and she turned to see another officer, tall—though not so tall as Max, of course—and fair, with a thin, blond mustache. He was smiling, but only with his mouth. His gray eyes were cold and swept over her in a quick assessment before turning back to Max. "Will you introduce me?" he asked. His tone made it more demand than request.

Max looked at him with equal coldness, then turned to Susannah with warning in his look and in his voice. "Lady Susannah, may I present Lieutenant Dieter Angriffer, a friend of Baron Herzlos. Angriffer, Lady Susannah Tremaine, companion to Princess Mila."

The lieutenant clicked his heels and bowed.

Susannah did not need Max's warning. This was the end of her plan for an idyllic evening at the ball. The romantic fantasies that had filled her mind on the balcony faded, leaving her feeling resentful at their loss. The resentment focused on Lieutenant Angriffer.

Although he was good-looking enough with his blond hair and chiseled features, there was something distinctly reptilian about him. The coldness of his pale eyes, perhaps, and the way they stared at her without blinking. However, she did not consider it politic to refuse his request for the next dance. That would be rude, and though there might be need for rudeness in the future—she was fairly certain that he was an enemy—that time was not yet.

The waltz began conventionally enough. They kept the proper distance apart, and he held her and danced correctly, without flourishes. The difference between this waltz and the one she had just shared with Max was indescribable.

The silence between them was a trifle awkward, but Susannah felt no need to break it. Angriffer was the one who had requested—demanded—this dance. And she still resented his intrusion.

Finally he gave a short bark of laughter. "You are not a fool, I see. You know to keep silent."

That hardly needed a response, so Susannah remained silent. She kept her face averted, ignoring him, though she could feel his eyes boring into her.

He gave that barking laugh again. "Very good." He sounded approving. "Where did Staufer find you? Are you whores? Actresses?"

She did look at him then, startled.

He looked back, studying her. "No, probably not actresses. When actresses portray ladies, they cannot avoid excess. Too much pride, too much condescension. You do it as if it is all natural. Minor gentry, perhaps? Impoverished gentlewomen?"

She found her tongue and spoke coldly. "I cannot imagine what you are talking about."

"No need to play insulted with me." His smile looked smug. "You see, I know where Princess Mila is."

Susannah looked pointedly at the end of the room, where Olivia was standing beside the prince.

"An excellent imitation, I admit, but not the real thing." Angriffer spun her into a twirl, beginning to enjoy the dance. "I was introduced earlier, and this one is much pleasanter than the real one. Princess Mila keeps whining and fussing. I was finding her quite irritating and came to ask Hugo what he wants me to do with her."

She couldn't keep from stiffening, and he smiled at her reaction.

"Yes," he continued, "all is known, at least in some quarters. I can stand up and say, 'Your Highness, these women are imposters.' And then where will you be? On your way to the gallows?"

After a moment, during which Susannah thought frantically, she smiled slowly. "Oh, I don't think so, Lieutenant."

"No?"

"No. Because, after all, what are you going to say? That this princess is an imposter, and I know because I have kidnapped the real one? Then you would be the one on the way to the gallows."

He regarded her with amusement. "Definitely not a fool, not if you see the problem so quickly. You interest me."

"And you also have another problem. How can you be certain that your prisoner is the real princess? Perhaps you have kidnapped an imposter."

"Another possibility, which leaves us at a stalemate. Whatever shall we do?" He seemed both amused and pleased, as if enjoying this exchange.

"Well, you could always return the princess."

He laughed out loud at that suggestion. "Somehow, I do not think that the baroness and her brother would think much of that idea."

Susannah found his phrasing interesting. "The baroness is the one who would object? Not the baron?"

"You are quick indeed." He looked at her with

admiration. "Yes, the baroness is the one who plans, and her brother follows her lead."

"But why is she so ambitious for her brother? Can it possibly make that much difference to her life? She is already the daughter of the country's first minister."

"It is never wise to offend that lady. Her father should never have dismissed the suggestion that Conrad marry her with such disdain. Not that Conrad showed any enthusiasm for the prospect. And then when she turned her attention to the possibility of becoming Countess von Staufer, Max didn't even notice her advances to him." Angriffer shook his head in mock reproof. "Helga does have her pride."

"She is doing this out of wounded vanity? That is preposterous." Susannah's common sense was outraged.

A touch of sympathy entered Angriffer's look. "A word of warning. It has not escaped her that Max is a bit taken with you. If she offers you a glass of wine, I recommend that you decline."

As the music drew to a close, he whirled her to a halt just beside the prince and Olivia. Hugo and Helga were also standing there and acknowledged them with a nod. Angriffer stepped to Helga's side, and she placed a possessive hand on his arm while sending a look of cold calculation at Susannah. Her face smoothed out as she returned her attention to Olivia, who was standing up bravely but looked hunted.

The prince did not seem to notice this, though how he could be so oblivious Susannah did not know. Perhaps he was so accustomed to the Herzlos pair that he no longer noticed their vitriol.

"How curious that both your attendants should be

English ladies," said the baroness. "One would have expected you to bring your own compatriots with you. To keep you from being homesick."

Olivia smiled sweetly. "That had occurred to me, but I decided against it. After all, this will be my home, and I do not need ties to another country. Lady Augusta and Lady Susannah are old friends from my travels and, as such, provide enough connection to my old life without distracting me from my new loyalty to Sigmaringen."

"Bravo," said Conrad. "The perfect answer from my bride-to-be."

That comment, combined with Olivia's condescending smile, froze the baroness's smile into a grimace.

Ordinarily, Susannah would wager on her friend in this contest. Olivia looked so sweet that people frequently underestimated her, though she only defended herself when she was actually attacked. At the moment, however, Olivia was handicapped by her ignorance. She did not know that their masquerade had been exposed—at least to the villains of the piece.

Helga did not just suspect. She now knew that Olivia was an imposter and was trying to unmask her. All Olivia knew was that Helga was being poisonous, and she probably thought Helga was no different from all poisonous ladies she had encountered in London. Nor was Lady Augusta any help. She was off on the floor, waltzing with the general. Again.

In preparation for her next foray, the baroness narrowed her eyes and prepared to strike. "You know, Princess, I find myself puzzled by your accent. It seems a bit strange to me."

The prince stepped in. "Really? It sounds charming to me." He smiled at Olivia and lifted her hand to kiss it.

Helga seemed about to burst, so Susannah said, "To tell the truth, Baroness, your accent seemed a bit strange to me. A trifle countrified, perhaps. But then, I don't imagine you have spent much time at the court in Vienna, have you?"

"In Vienna?" The baroness spun around to look at Susannah. "What has Vienna to do with anything?"

"Nothing at all," said Susannah, patting Helga's arm sympathetically. "I am sure there has never been any need for you to visit Emperor Franz Josef's court there. Just because Sisi—the Empress Elisabeth—made such a pet of Princess Mila, you should not feel slighted. After all, very few are invited to join the empress at Bad Kissingen."

Susannah heard a snort of laughter from Angriffer. She also heard a hiss from Helga, whose claw tightened on Angriffer's arm. Hugo was saying nothing, just standing there looking rather as if he had indigestion. He was not the leader in this plot, Susannah realized. But whether the real leader was Helga or Angriffer, she was not sure.

Mercifully, the music began again, and the prince excused himself to whirl Olivia into another waltz. Susannah reached a hand out to Max, who had been glaring at Angriffer. "I believe this is our dance," she said, and stepped out without waiting for his reply.

He joined her, still looking thunderous, and swept her into the dance. "I do not like the way Angriffer

looked at you. He has a bad reputation where women
are concerned. What did he say while you were
dancing?"

Susannah sighed. She hoped Max was not going
to be difficult. "He knows that Olivia is not the real
princess because he has the real princess himself."

Max stumbled slightly and corrected his rhythm
before he spoke. "How do you know?"

"I know because he told me. I see no reason to
doubt his word."

"But…" Max frowned. "But why did he not
denounce Lady Olivia as an imposter?"

"He said he might, but I pointed out that he could
not. What would he do, confess that he kidnapped
the princess?"

"Ah." Max tightened his grasp on her but then
vanished into his own thoughts.

∽

The waltz continued, and Max did not miss a step, but
Susannah could have been a mop in his arms for all the
notice he gave her. At last his thoughts returned to the
ballroom. He glanced around and steered them through
one of the windows onto a balcony once more.

"Yes, I see," he said. "It is a stalemate. He cannot
denounce Lady Olivia as an imposter without admitting that he kidnapped Princess Mila. Hugo must
also know now that she is an imposter. He was not
certain, but Angriffer will have assured him that the
princess did not escape. That is why Helga was playing
her little games. But what is that nonsense you were
spouting about Empress Elisabeth?"

"It wasn't nonsense. One of Olivia's cousins is with the embassy in Vienna, so she and I visited there before we took Lady Augusta to Baden. And the empress was quite taken with Olivia."

"Ah," said Max again. "I had not realized... I am not familiar with the nobility of England. Lady Olivia's family is important?"

"Her father was the Earl of Doncaster. Her brother holds the title now. Lady Augusta's brother is the Earl of Greystone." Susannah sounded surprised that Max did not know, but why would he?

"And these are all important men, are they not? Men who will not be happy that I have put their daughters and sisters in danger?" When she nodded, he grinned. "Then I shall have to see to it that I keep you safe while we outwit Angriffer and Hugo. A pretty problem, is it not?"

His smile faded. "It is not that easy, though. I must warn you, Dieter Angriffer is dangerous. He is more intelligent than Hugo and more vicious. He especially dislikes me." His mouth twisted at his memories. "When we were cadets, I always seemed to come out ahead of him. Some of it he could blame on favoritism—I was a count; he was the son of a trades-man. But I was the better swordsman, the better rider. That he could not forgive."

"How ridiculously childish." Susannah sounded impatient.

"Unfortunately, calling it 'childish' does not make it go away. It makes me all the more concerned for you." Max took her hands. "It does not take a blind man to see that you matter to me, and Dieter is not blind. He may try to strike at me through you. You must be very careful."

"Of course I will be careful. We are all being careful."

He pulled her into his arms and held her tightly. "Ah, Suse, I want so desperately to protect you. What if I cannot?"

The strains of another Strauss waltz came through the window, mocking their earlier pleasure in the evening. Susannah shivered. Max wrapped his arms around her to keep her from the cold, just to keep her warm, but he could not resist doing more. His mouth descended slowly to cover hers.

The embrace seemed to surprise her. She stiffened at first, but then, as his lips moved over hers, she yielded. Her body melted against his, her lips softened and parted for him, and her arms crept up to cling to his shoulders. Ah, yes. Yes. His arms pulled her even closer.

She felt so perfect in his arms, so right. He lost all sense of time, all sense of his surroundings.

The kiss was more than he had thought it possible for a kiss to be, more than he had ever dreamed. It was full of sweetness, full of hope, full of promise. It was everything he had ever wanted.

It was breaking his heart.

Nineteen

Susannah lay in her bed, staring at the canopy over her. There was a slight stain on the silk lining in one corner. Trying to think of ways the stain could have gotten there served to distract her thoughts for a while, but could not occupy her for long. She kept reliving the kiss that had turned her topsy-turvy, the kiss that had shaken the very core of her being.

It was not as if she had never been kissed before. Other men had begged or stolen a kiss from her, but those kisses had been, it must be confessed, boring. She hadn't minded them, precisely, but they were not experiences she longed to repeat. However, last night's kiss, Max's kiss, had no sooner ended than she had longed for another. No, not for another, but for something else, something more. This was the feeling her sisters had told her about. They couldn't describe it, but had told her she would recognize it when it happened.

When she had imagined it, she dreamed that magical kiss would happen in a moonlit garden. Well, a moonlit balcony would do. But she had thought that

then they would go to her parents, and everyone
would be smiling and happy. Instead, she was surrounded by danger and uncertainty. If there was a
protocol for this situation, she did not know it.

Beside her bed, Lev snuffled in some doggie dream.
Lucky Lev. He knew he was supposed to protect her,
and that was all he needed to know. She knew the
commands, both the hand signals and the words, to
direct him.

What she didn't know was when she should use
those commands.

She flopped over on her side and stared at the
window. She had shocked the maid by insisting on
not only having the bed curtains drawn back, but
having the window drapes pulled back as well. The
maid was convinced Susannah would catch her death
of cold, but she had always disliked being closed in.
Mama said she had even fought against swaddling
clothes when she was an infant.

She might just as well be swaddled at the moment.
The moonlight shining on the walnut paneling of
the room might give aesthetic pleasure but did nothing to illuminate the problems swirling through her
mind. And the kiss was not the only thing disturbing
her sleep.

It was all well and good to say that they were
at a stalemate with Hugo, that neither he nor his
agents could betray them. But how could they
break that stalemate without bringing disaster down
on themselves?

She flopped onto her back and sighed. Then she
noticed a change in the near-silence. Lev was no

longer snuffling in his dreams. He had raised his head—she could see the top of it above the level of the mattress—and was growling softly.

Susannah sat up and looked at the section of the wall that Lev had focused on. Bizarre though it seemed, the wall was moving. A piece of the paneling was swinging out. Slowly. Very slowly.

Lev stood up. She put a hand on the dog's head to keep him still while she thought furiously. There was no time. She had to act quickly.

Keeping as quiet as she could, she pushed aside the covers and swung her legs over the side of the bed. The moonlight made it easy for her to see where she was going, but it would make things easy for the intruder as well. Behind the door that was appearing in the paneling would be the safest place to be, she decided. Snatching up a heavy candlestick, she moved into place as quickly as she dared. Mercifully, the thick carpet allowed Lev to move silently as well, and they were in place before a figure emerged from the opening.

Hunched over, the intruder moved cautiously, as intent on silence as she had been, and paused to look at the bed. Since his back was toward her, this would be her best opportunity. She swung the candlestick with all her might at his head. It connected with a satisfying *thunk*. Unfortunately, the thunk was insufficient. The man staggered but did not fall.

Susannah did not know what to do now. That blow had been as hard as she could strike. In the books she had read, a blow with a heavy candlestick was always enough to lay the villain out.

As the intruder began to turn, Lev leaped. That proved to be far more effective than her blow had been. The intruder gave a cry of terror as he crashed to the floor under a hundred and fifty pounds of dog. Growling dog, with teeth bared.

Susannah leaned back for a moment to allow her knees time to stop shaking. She felt quite proud that she was still standing, but her satisfaction immediately vanished to be replaced by uncertainty. Very well. She and Lev had captured the intruder. That was good. Definitely good.

What was she supposed to do now?

A creak as the door in the paneling swung a bit reminded her that it was still open. That couldn't be good. Where one intruder had entered, others might follow. She started to push it closed but realized that she had no way to secure it. There didn't seem to be any sort of latch or even knob on this side.

She peered into the opening, but all she could see were stairs leading into blackness. Should she go see where the passage led? That would be beyond stupid. What would she do if she found someone else in there?

Also, the prospect of going down a dark staircase terrified her.

She looked at the intruder, who seemed even more frightened that she was. His eyes were white with fear as he lay there, staring up at Lev. The dog stared back, his mouth open, allowing drool to drip onto the intruder's face. The intruder was too frightened to even wipe it off at the moment, but how long would that last?

What if he called for help and another enemy came up that staircase?

What if she called for help and another enemy came instead of an ally?

She could hit the man with the candlestick again, but her blow hadn't been all that effective the first time. Also, it was one thing to hit an unknown intruder. It was another to hit a man who was lying terrified under a dog.

But she couldn't just do nothing. Lev couldn't stand over the man forever. Sooner or later the man might try to move, and she had no idea what she ought to do in that case.

She needed help.

Yes, she definitely needed help.

Help appeared.

A sleepy Olivia stumbled into the room, yawning and stretching. By her side was Lezo, looking far more alert, with the hair on his neck bristling.

"Is something wrong?" Olivia asked, still yawning. Then she noticed Lev and his captive. Suddenly she was wide awake. "Oh."

"Yes," said Susannah. She gestured at the section of paneling standing ajar. "It seems we didn't secure all the doors to these rooms."

They heard a door slam somewhere down below, and Olivia walked over to peer through the opening into the darkness. "This must be a servants' staircase. I wondered how they managed, since I never saw any servants wandering around the castle. This sort of arrangement keeps them out of sight."

"Oli… Mila, this is no time for a disquisition on household management."

"It was just that I had wondered. But I don't suppose this fellow came to dust the furniture." Olivia turned to the man on the floor. His color was returning, but he remained motionless, staring at the dog standing over him. He gave a slight moan when Lezo came over to peer down at him too, but did not speak.

Susannah forced herself to take a deep breath. "We need help," she said and handed the candlestick to Olivia. "If anyone else comes up, you can hit him with this and set Lezo on him. I'm going to send for Max."

Josef and Emil, another of Staufer's men, were on guard in the hall and jumped to attention when she appeared.

"What is wrong, my lady?" asked Josef, instantly concerned. "Has something happened to my dogs?"

"The dogs are fine. They are guarding an intruder." She ignored the old man's gasp and turned to Emil. "You must find Captain Staufer and bring him here at once."

"The count? Here, my lady? In the middle of the night?" Emil, a fresh-faced young man, looked scandalized at the impropriety.

"Yes, here, and right away," she said impatiently. "Josef, you must come with me. I don't know what to do with the intruder, and I don't want to make poor Lev stand guard over him all night."

Josef grinned. "My Lev will have no trouble with that, but if it makes you happy..." He trotted into Susannah's room and, after a glare from her, Emil hurried off in search of Staufer.

❧

Max burst into the room barefoot, wearing only trousers and shirt, his saber in one hand and its scabbard in the other, and skidded to an abrupt halt. There on the floor, tied up in a neat package, lay what he assumed was the intruder. Josef was putting the final touches on the bonds, which looked like drapery cords, while Susannah stood over them, observing.

He dropped the saber and seized her by the shoulders to spin her around. No blood, no wounds. He crushed her to him and buried his face in her hair until he calmed down enough to speak.

"You are uninjured?" He forced the words out.

"I am fine." Her voice was muffled, and he realized he was pressing her face against his chest. She did not seem to mind. Her hands were clutching his shirt, keeping him close.

He seized her shoulders again to hold her away from him and shake her in a mixture of fear and anger and a maelstrom of other emotions he didn't recognize. "This is why I told you to leave! You could have been murdered in your sleep, you fool woman. And I could not have prevented it!"

She did not even look frightened, the idiot. She smiled at him and put a hand to his cheek as if to soothe him. "But you did prevent it." She sounded as if she were talking to a child, and he wanted to shake her again. "You did," she insisted. "You set Lev to watch over me. He warned me and knocked the intruder down."

Max could not think. All he could do was pull her close once more and wrap himself around her. He wanted to hold her and protect her forever.

As his turmoil subsided, he began to notice things. First, that Susannah seemed perfectly content to rest her head against him, as if she belonged there in his arms. Where he wanted her. Then, he remembered that they were not alone in the room. Josef was standing nearby, his eyes averted and his boot keeping the prisoner's face to the wall. A pair of dogs—Lev and Lezo—stood on guard. And Lady Olivia was there as well, watching Max and Susannah with considerable interest. She was holding a tall candlestick, resting it on her shoulder like a club, and had a shawl wrapped around her over her nightdress.

Nightdress.

Susannah was wearing nothing but her nightdress. It was not cold in the room. Someone had built up the fire, but still, there was nothing but thin lawn between her body and his hands. He should not be holding her this way. It was improper. He had no right.

He did not think he could let her go. Not when her hands were pressed against his back, only the fine linen of his shirt…

"What, may I ask, is going on here?"

The icy tones of Lady Augusta, coupled with the furious barks of little Hans, dispelled the fog that had been descending on Max's mind, and he and Lady Susannah sprang apart. At least they put a few inches between their bodies. His fingers slid slowly down her arms before leaving her entirely, and his eyes did not leave hers at all.

Then the general appeared, not barefoot, but with his tunic hanging open. His words echoed Lady Augusta's. "What is going on here?"

What was the general doing here? The question popped into Max's head, and he pushed it aside to be considered later.

Little Hans continued to yap at everyone, ignored by Lev and Lezo as well as the humans, but no one spoke. "Susannah captured an intruder," said Olivia brightly when the silence started getting awkward.

Everyone, including the dogs, turned to look at the creature trussed up on the floor. The handkerchief stuffed in his mouth made him look rather like a fish, especially when he heaved about impotently.

Lady Augusta sniffed. "Not very impressive, is he?"

Josef coughed. "Perhaps not, my lady, but he carried an impressive knife. This was tucked into his boot." He held out a dagger with a blade close to a foot long.

Lady Olivia gasped and Susannah's eyes widened, but Lady Augusta just raised her brows. "Not a visitor on a friendly errand, I gather."

"He also had this." Josef held out a bottle wrapped in a cloth.

The general stepped forward to take it and cautiously removed the cork. He brought it near his face, grimaced, and quickly replaced the cork. He set it down among the trinkets on a table. "Chloroform and ether. A powerful mixture. Was he coming to kill or to capture? Or perhaps both?"

"I checked the staircase, my lord. It is one of the old servants' passages, but the door to the kitchens and workrooms is barred from this side. The door at the bottom leads out to the gardens. Someone had been waiting there with horses—I could see the prints—but they fled before I got there." Josef flicked a glance at the women and lowered his voice. "He is wearing…"

Max nodded, hoping to avoid frightening the

women further. However, Susannah immediately demanded, "What about what he's wearing? It doesn't seem to be a livery. What does it tell you?"

Josef looked apologetic, but Max's mouth twitched up in a half smile. Of course she was paying attention.

"Not livery precisely, but Hugo likes to have all his people wear his colors, black and red." Max had picked up his saber and used the tip of it to lift a corner of the captive's short black jacket with red lapels. "This is the way he dresses his foresters."

"Do you suppose he came here to kill us?" Susannah sounded calm enough, but he could see that her fists were clenched.

The captive shook his head wildly in denial.

"To kill only one?" Max asked, sounding equally calm.

The captive shook his head wildly again.

"To carry off the princess," said Max.

The captive looked relieved and nodded.

"But," Max continued, putting the point of his saber at the man's throat, "prepared to kill if anyone interfered. Is that it?"

The captive froze and stared at the blade, glittering in the light from the fire.

Max looked down at him, unsmiling, and neither of them moved. Finally he lifted the blade and thrust it into the scabbard. The three women stood around him, watching with more interest than fear. What did it take to frighten them, he wondered. He hoped he never found out.

The general started to speak, then glanced at Lady Augusta and changed his mind. He turned to Max.

"We will need to question him elsewhere. Staufer, have you more men available?"

At least Bergen had that much concern for the women. Max nodded and asked Josef, "Where are the others?"

"Bedded down in the stable loft," the old man said. "They didn't want to leave the horses unattended."

Max nodded. "Good. Can you get this one there by yourself? I'll meet you there shortly."

Josef waved a sort of salute and dragged the prisoner to the staircase behind the paneling.

They could hear the thumps as he bounced down the steps. Olivia winced, but Lady Augusta was examining the dagger. "I do not find myself troubled with much sympathy for the fellow," she said.

Susannah, meanwhile, picked up the bottle of chloroform and ether and tucked it into a drawer. One never knew when such an item might prove useful.

Twenty

London

LADY PENWORTH LOOKED UP FROM SUPERVISING THE packing and regarded the itinerary with horror. "We have to change trains *how* many times?"

"Six in all," said her husband. "And I believe we will need to stay overnight at least twice, in Metz and in Stuttgart."

"That is preposterous. It will take us three days to get there? When Lady Woodhouse's son went to join the embassy in Berlin, he was there the next day." She scowled at the offending pile of papers. "And we need all those documents?"

Lord Penworth regarded his wife sympathetically. "I know you are worried about Susannah, but I'm afraid Nymburg is not the most accessible city on the Continent. All those little German states mean there are numerous borders to cross, and each one has its own rail system that doesn't always coordinate its schedules with others."

"They are all utterly ridiculous," she snapped. "It

almost makes me sympathize with Herr Bismarck's ambitions to unify the whole thing."

In an effort to be soothing, her husband said, "It's still faster than when we went to Rome and had to make almost the entire journey by carriage."

"But that was ten years ago, and I was ten years younger!"

She closed her eyes and rubbed her temples. "Tell me why Augusta decided she had to go to Baden rather than Vichy, for example. No, never mind. It's fashionable now, and she wanted a bit of excitement. But a spa should not be dangerous or even exciting. If she has led the girls into danger…"

Lady Penworth stopped and stiffened her shoulders. "Enough of that." Turning to the maid who was continuing to pack, she said, "Put together a small valise for me to take on the train—the trains, that is. Lord Penworth and I will be traveling as quickly as possible. You will have to follow with the trunks."

Twenty-one

"YOUR HIGHNESS...SIRE...I DO NOT THINK... ARE YOU sure this is a good idea?" Olivia felt even more flustered than she sounded. She watched the prince stride back and forth in his study, a pleased look on his face.

The problem was that it had been her idea in the first place. It had seemed like a clever notion when she was waltzing with the prince and, it must be admitted, after she had drunk several glasses of champagne. Just how many she could not recall.

Now she was afraid that the plan was not just foolish but dangerous. Unfortunately, she had no idea how to stop him. She was not good at stopping people. People always stopped her when she got carried away, but the prince hadn't done that. He had listened to her.

Where was Susannah? She would know what to do. Olivia looked at the door, but no one magically appeared. She looked back at Conrad. "Have you discussed this with anyone?"

He frowned. "With my uncle, Count Herzlos, you mean? Certainly not. He would attempt to forbid it, even though he is no longer the regent. He would talk of nothing but the danger."

"Are you certain he would be wrong?" Olivia had begun to think of Sigmaringen as a very dangerous place indeed. Villains literally coming out of the woodwork did not inspire a feeling of security.

The prince shook his head dismissively. "My uncle sees danger everywhere. Fifteen years ago, when my parents were killed by the revolutionaries and there were riots everywhere—yes, there was danger then. But now? There have been no reports of unrest."

"No reports, perhaps." Olivia pounced on that. "But there might be dangers you do not know of." There were indeed dangers he did not know of. Should she tell him? But that would put Captain Staufer and the general in a dreadful position. Perhaps it would even put the real princess in more danger. She had no idea what to do.

"That is precisely the point—I do not know. You were the one who said that a prince ought to know what his people think, what they want, what they need."

"But I only meant that perhaps you should hear from their representatives." Why on earth had he paid attention to what she said? No one paid attention to what she said. She often didn't pay attention to it herself.

With a sigh and a sad smile, he took her hands. "Ah, Mila, no one tells the truth to the prince. You must have learned that at your father's court."

Olivia had a moment of confusion. She did wish the prince would stop calling her Mila. Everyone else called her Princess or Highness, which made it much easier to remember that this was a masquerade, that she was just playing a part. Calling her Mila made it all seem too personal. And why did he have to talk about people not telling him the truth? "But, Sire…"

"Conrad. You must call me Conrad. No one else does, not since I was a child. It is as if I no longer have a name. I am not a person, I am only a title. But at least when we are in private, my princess will be able to call me by my name. You have no idea how I long to have someone call me Conrad once more." He took her hands and pulled her toward him.

Much too personal. But he smiled so sweetly that she was sorely tempted. She started to return his smile and let herself be drawn closer, but then she remembered herself and pulled back. "There must be people you can ask, people you trust." *Not people like me. You must not trust me.*

He shook his head. "My advisors are all my uncle's men. They tell me what he thinks I should hear. But if I am to do my duty by my people, I must know them. So I thought about what you said, and then I remembered Haroun Al-Rashid."

"What is that?"

"Not what. Who. Haroun Al-Rashid."

She sighed. "*Who* is that?"

"Do you not know the story? He was an ancient prince off in the East somewhere. He used to disguise himself and wander around the city to hear what his people were saying."

"You are going to wander around Nymburg in disguise because of a *story*? *A fairy tale*?" Olivia could not believe her ears. He was a prince, for goodness' sake. How could he be such a noddy? Yes, he needed to know what his people were thinking, but a prince could not go around in masquerade. A twinge of guilt pierced her. That was precisely what she was doing. But she wasn't a princess. She was just trying to help one.

He smiled again, that sweet smile. Why did he have to be so sweet? "You are very good, you know, and you are right to remind me. It is my duty that should concern me. And I cannot do my duty if I do not know my people." Growing serious, he reached out and touched her cheek, sliding his fingers gently across. "You are good for me, my princess."

Olivia turned away, a flush of embarrassment flooding her face. "You must not speak to me so," she said.

"Why not? Shall I call you my bride?" He smiled again. "You will be so soon enough…"

❧

The door to the study opened and Max led Lady Susannah in, both of them looking a bit distracted. Olivia turned to them, half alarmed and half questioning, but Max shook his head a fraction. The intruder had not provided any helpful information. At least not yet. They still had no idea where the princess was being held.

"Ah, there you are Staufer. Good," Conrad said. "I want you and Lady Susannah to accompany us."

"Of course, Sire," said Max automatically. Then he paused. "Er, accompany you where?"

"This was really Princess Mila's suggestion." The

prince took Olivia's hand and smiled at her. "I wasn't sure how to go about it, but then I thought of a way."

Max and Lady Susannah stood there, waiting for an explanation, while Olivia looked down at the hand clasping hers.

"We are going to go for a walk through the marketplace down in the town."

Max waited, but Conrad was smiling as if that was all the explanation anyone could need. It wasn't. "Do you wish to go in procession, Sire?"

"No, no. We will go in disguise."

"In disguise?" Max was confused. What on earth was the prince thinking?

"Yes, in disguise. We shall look like ordinary peasants." Conrad sounded perfectly assured.

"But…but why?"

"Princess Mila has pointed out to me that I do not really know what my people think because all I ever hear are reports from officials who are more concerned with their own positions than anything else. Today is a market day. There will be people from the countryside as well as the town, and I can hear for myself what they have to say."

The prince was breaking out of the cocoon Count Herzlos had wrapped around him. This was what Max had been hoping for. It had been bound to happen sooner or later, but now? Now, when danger was all around, when they had no idea where Hugo might strike next? Why did Conrad have to choose this moment to assert himself? He looked down at Lady Susannah, who seemed equally appalled.

She sent a quick glare in Olivia's direction, the likely

origin of this notion, but Olivia shook her head help-lessly. With a sigh, Lady Susannah turned politely to the prince. "But Your Highness, how can you possibly disguise yourself? Surely people will recognize you."

"No, they will not." He looked delighted with himself as he picked up a green hooded cloak of boiled wool, like the ones half the population of Sigmaringen wore. "No one will recognize any of us. We will wear these cloaks, and people will think we are just some of the peasants come to town for the weekly market."

The others looked at him, then at each other. There were so many problems with this that Max did not know where to start. He threw a helpless glance at Lady Susannah. She gave him a tiny nod before she spoke to the prince. "Boots. Look at your boots. No one would believe a peasant has boots like that."

Conrad looked at his boots. Their black leather, polished to a mirror shine, covered him from toe to knee. Not a scar, not a scuff, not a fingerprint marred their gleaming surface. He frowned slightly. "Perhaps I should wear my hunting boots."

"Sire," said Max gently, "you do not own anything that a peasant might wear. Not a shoe, not a shirt, not a glove."

"And you do not stand or walk or sound like a peasant," put in Lady Susannah.

Conrad drew himself up, offended. "I can speak Schwäbisch," he said, switching to that dialect. "Tell them, Staufer."

"Yes, but you speak the Schwäbisch of an educated man, not the Schwäbisch of a peasant," replied Staufer in the same dialect.

Conrad scowled and paced over to the window to stare down into the courtyard. The wind played with the spray from the central fountain, blowing it first one way and then another. Servants and officials hurrying on one errand or another gave it a wide berth. One fellow, a clerk by the look of him, was caught unaware and cuffed a boy who was foolish enough to laugh.

The prince turned, smiling again. "There is no need for us to be peasants. People from the castle frequently go down to the town. And the market will be full of townspeople as well. We will wear the capes and mingle."

"But Sire," Max protested, "people know you. They know what you look like."

"People see me standing on a balcony or riding in the state carriage. No one would ever expect to see me on foot in the marketplace, so they will not recognize me. At worst, they will say that I look like the prince."

Max wanted to protest, but he couldn't deny that the prince was right. People saw what they expected to see, and no one would expect to see Prince Conrad walking around the city in ordinary clothes.

Perhaps that would be enough to keep him safe.

Twenty-two

ALL THEIR ARGUMENTS PROVED FUTILE. LADY SUSANNAH tried to send an appeal to Lady Augusta, but she had disappeared again, off for a carriage ride with the general. So the four of them found themselves riding down the road from the castle in an ancient barouche driven by Josef. He had found the dusty vehicle in a distant corner of the royal carriage house, and a pair of nondescript horses to pull it. The hood over the rear seats sufficed to hide both the prince and Lady Olivia.

Once down in the town, Josef stood, stiff with disapproval, at the door of the inn's stable where the prince and Staufer were divesting themselves of uniform tunics while Susannah and Olivia replaced their hats with bonnets, the old-fashioned kind with deep, concealing brims. All four stepped out into the sunshine of the inn courtyard wrapped in green cloaks.

The prince looked around happily and clapped a broad-brimmed hat on his head. One side was pinned up rakishly with a feathered brooch. He had the air of a schoolboy on holiday.

Josef, his eyes darting about the courtyard, muttered

to Staufer, "No one seems to have taken any notice."
The captain nodded an unsmiling acknowledgment.

"I think we should speak only proper German,"
said Conrad. "If people think we do not understand
them, they will speak more freely to each other."
With a gallant gesture, he held an arm out for Olivia.

Max grimaced and took hold of Susannah to follow.

They strolled among the stalls and carts to not much
effect. There was an awkward moment when Conrad
sought to present a bunch of violets to Olivia and realized that he had no coin to pay for them. Fortunately
Max, not being a prince, was accustomed to carrying
money and tossed a few groschen to the flower girl.
He also bought some violets for Susannah to hold
under her nose. Market day was full of odors, and they
were about to pass a butcher's stall.

After an hour or so, they paused at a shop where a
pretty girl was standing at the window, directing her
sister in arranging the display of laces. "Well?" asked
Max softly.

Conrad grimaced, but spoke equally softly. "There
is not much to hear, is there? People seem to worry
more about how bad the winter will be than they do
about the prince."

"That is probably as it should be. People have their
own lives to worry about."

A young boy dashed up and called into the shop,
"Black Star soldiers are coming!"

An older man hurried out. "Have they been drinking?" When the boy nodded, he shooed the girl into the
shop. "Anna, Josie, into the back, quickly." He looked
at the party from the castle and spoke in hesitating

German. "Good sirs, the ladies might perhaps want to join my daughters inside?"

"Because soldiers are coming?" Conrad looked startled.

"*Drunken* soldiers," said the shopkeeper, watching the square nervously.

Max swore under his breath and started to usher Susannah and Olivia into the shop.

Before they could move, a trio of officers—a lieutenant and two cornets, all wearing red tunics with black stars on the shoulders—swaggered into the square just as a young woman stepped out of a shop. She was looking over her shoulder, laughing and saying something to the young man following her, and stepped right in front of the lieutenant leading the group.

"Well, well, well, what have we here?" The lieutenant swung an arm around her to pull her against him. "What a pretty little piece it is. Ah, we shall have a pleasant time of it today after all, won't we, cornets?"

The girl gave a shriek of fright and tried to push free. The young man behind her rushed forward and tried to pull the lieutenant away from her, but the lieutenant shook him off with sneer. When the young man threw himself at the lieutenant once more, shouting in Schwäbisch, one of the cornets held him back and tried to hush him.

"You are insolent," snapped the lieutenant. Turning to the remaining cornet, he pushed the girl to him. "Hold on to her while I teach this clod a lesson."

The young cornet took her arm but looked worried. "Lieutenant Gruber, this is not right. She is not a whore."

"She's a peasant. They are all whores. This fellow can have her back when I am finished, and should be grateful for what I'll teach her."

The cornet who had pulled the young man away was having difficulty holding him and did not look happy with the situation either. The young man was struggling and shouting almost incoherently. The cornet glanced around. No one was interfering, but the faces watching from doorways looked far from friendly. "Lieutenant, we are attracting too much attention. Let's just go on to the tavern."

"No," Gruber snapped. "He laid hands on an officer. He needs to be taught a lesson. Now let him go."

Gruber took up the stance of a boxer and got in several hard blows when the young man flew at him, sending him sprawling on the ground. The lieutenant laughed as his opponent looked up warily from the ground. "Had enough, peasant?"

But the young man did not seem ready to surrender. He rose to his feet cautiously, keeping his eyes on Gruber. The lieutenant relaxed too soon. The young man tackled him, landing them both on the ground with Gruber on the bottom, and he set in to pummel the lieutenant.

By the time the cornets pulled the young man off, Gruber had a bloody nose, a loose tooth, and was shaking with fury. While the cornets waited nervously, he stood up and brushed himself off, too angry to speak at first.

Finally he burst out, "You have attacked an officer of the Sigmaringen army. You will hang for this."

"Lieutenant," one of his friends protested, but Gruber turned on him.

"Did he not strike me?"

"Yes, but the girl…"

They looked around, but the girl had disappeared.

"Bring him to the prison." Gruber marched off, and the others followed, perhaps unhappy but unwilling to disobey.

❧

The girl had not gone far. Looking for help, she ran straight to Max, by far the largest man around, and began babbling a plea for assistance. At least that was what Susannah thought she was saying—she couldn't entirely understand the dialect. That had been sensible of her. Susannah couldn't suppress a small smile of pride. Any girl in her right mind would run to Max for help, immediately recognizing that he would give it.

Max made reassuring noises, patted the girl on the back, and handed her to Susannah. He then tossed back his cloak and, with a grin on his face, started to head toward Lieutenant Gruber.

"No." The prince held up a hand.

"No?" Max stumbled and turned to look at the prince. "*No?*" he repeated in outrage.

"You can't mean that, Sire," protested Susannah.

Even Olivia made a protesting sound.

But the prince frowned them into silence.

When Gruber began to lead his party to the prison, the prince nodded to himself and told Max to follow him, leaving the women behind.

Susannah snatched hold of Max's sleeve. "What's

going on? He can't mean to let Lieutenant Gruber take that poor young man to prison."

"I don't know." Max looked furious. "But do not worry. All will be well. I will make it so." He pressed her hand. "You will take care of the girl?"

"Of course."

"Yes. That's my Suse." He smiled and bent down to give her a quick, fierce kiss before he hurried after the prince.

She believed him—he would make it well—though she was appalled by Conrad's behavior. *This* was the prince they had all been trying to protect? This coward? He could at least have allowed Max to take care of the beastly Gruber and not just run away. Now she was left here in the shop with the peasant girl sobbing on her shoulder and Olivia looking stricken. What was she supposed to do? She took a deep breath and let it out slowly. She would have to do what she always did—keep the others safe and make sure they did not do anything too foolish.

Twenty-three

MAX FOLLOWED THE PRINCE IN A FURY. CONRAD was almost running in his haste to get back to the stable. Was he that eager to escape from trouble? The royal tunic was neatly fastened and smoothly in place by the time Conrad stepped out into the road.

What was Conrad doing? Max had expected him to duck out of sight into the carriage. The road was the one leading to the prison. Hurriedly buttoning his own tunic, Max followed and stood just behind the prince. They were blocking the way as Gruber turned the corner with his own unhappy party following.

The prince examined the newcomers with raised brows, then turned to his companion. "What is this, Staufer? Has one of my officers been brawling in the streets, do you suppose?"

"It certainly appears that way, Sire." Max did not know what was going on, but he had no trouble scowling fiercely at Gruber. "Disgraceful."

"Your Highness!" Gruber stumbled to a halt and stood openmouthed before he pulled himself together enough to stand at attention and salute. "Not a brawl, Your Highness. This peasant attacked me."

The prince stared at the lieutenant, who fidgeted nervously.

"Identify yourself, Officer," Max said softly.

The lieutenant flushed and stood still more stiffly. "Lieutenant Augustus Gruber, Black Star Regiment, sir!"

Max nodded absently and looked at the prisoner. "This fellow attacked you? Well, he must have taken you by surprise. You certainly seem to have come off the worse in the encounter."

Gruber's embarrassed flush turned to one of anger. "I am taking him to the prison."

The prince looked at him and waited.

"He must be punished. Hanged," said Gruber, sounding defensive. When he saw no approval on the faces before him, he continued, "Or flogged perhaps. Villains like this cannot be permitted to attack officers."

Max cocked his head and looked at the captive, who sagged in the grip of Gruber's companions but nonetheless stared at Gruber with eyes filled with furious resentment. "Not a very large fellow, is he? Smaller than you, at any rate. Why do you suppose he did such a thing?"

"Who knows why these peasants do anything?" said Gruber. "They are all animals and must be punished like the beasts they are to teach them how to behave."

The prince looked at Gruber long and hard. "Yes, there are lessons here that must be taught. However, lessons taught in the dark of the prison are meaningless. There must be no punishment without a trial,

and everything must be done in the light of day."
He looked around and spotted a shopkeeper peering
around his door. "You there. Go fetch the mayor. He
must set up a tribunal in the marketplace. We shall
hold a trial there, where all may see and hear, and I
will preside myself."

Max looked at the prince. Suddenly the prince's
behavior was making sense. He had not been running
away. He had planned this! Conrad caught Max's eye,
and his mouth lifted with the hint of a smile.

Susannah peered out the shop window. News of what
was happening quickly spread through the town, but
no one seemed to know how to react. She didn't
know herself. At least the prince had not really run
away, pretending nothing had happened. That was
good, she supposed, though she couldn't see why he
hadn't just let Max handle the situation. He could
have done so easily.

The nervousness in the square was almost palpable.
She could not help but share in it.

The mayor had done his best. The stalls and wagons
had been pulled out of sight, and the cobblestones of
the square had been swept clean. A small dais covered
with green fabric was set up at one end of the market
square. On it stood a carved armchair draped with a
brighter cloth. A clerk, all gray and dusty, and armed
with paper, quills, and ink, sat at a table off to one side.
Beside him stood Lieutenant Gruber, and across from
them on the other side of the dais the young peasant
stood between two constables.

No one looked happy.

The mayor paced back and forth. His mustache drooped over his downturned mouth, and he looked around with worried eyes, as if he feared his efforts were more likely to win him a trip to the dungeons than to gain the prince's approval.

The prisoner was the picture of dejection, slumped between two guards who looked no happier than he did.

"Why do they look so fearful?" Susannah asked the shopkeeper. "Are they so afraid of the prince?"

"Of the prince?" He sounded startled. "No, not of the prince, but of the soldiers."

"But it was the soldiers who were in the wrong—or at least the lieutenant. Not that young man."

The shopkeeper looked at her pityingly. "The soldiers of the Black Star Regiment do as they like. No one can stop them." He waved at the people in the square. "They all know it—the prisoner, the constables. Everyone."

Susannah looked out. Max was going to see to it that everyone was proven wrong. *She* knew it.

She looked with distaste at Gruber, who maintained a certain swagger as he stood on his side of the dais. But every now and then she could see a shadow cross his face. Perhaps it was beginning to occur to him that this trial might not underline the power of the Black Star Regiment. He glanced over to the side where his erstwhile companions were trying to fade into the woodwork. He needed them to support his version of the encounter. Would they?

Most of the square was filled with townspeople and peasants who seemed more curious than anything else. Small children darted in and out around adult legs as small children always do when a crowd is gathered. The stone buildings around the square, three and four stories high, had people watching from all the windows.

Susannah had never seen anything quite like this crowd. There was none of the eager anticipation that usually greeted a spectacle. It wasn't fear either. No, it was resignation, she realized. People had gathered as if their attendance was required, not because they expected to find any pleasure in the coming scene.

Even the peasant girl had stopped sobbing and was simply leaning against the wall, utterly resigned to whatever fate awaited her.

Susannah felt as if she were the only one looking forward to the coming scene. That was because she knew that Max could be relied on. He would see to it that justice was done.

⤜⤏

From the shadow of the arcade where he had been standing with the prince, Max looked at the setting in the square with approval. There would be a good audience for this little drama they were staging. The crowd was subdued now, but that would change.

"Is everything ready?" Conrad sounded tense, but that was understandable.

"Ready, Sire." Max stepped out into the sunlight and then swung to the side, making way for Conrad's entrance. The mayor was there, gripping his hat in both hands and bent over in a nervous half-bow, as he waited to lead the prince to the dais.

Conrad stepped up onto the green carpet and the crowd cheered. It was not an enthusiastic cheer, to be sure, but neither was it ironic. After all, one was supposed to cheer a prince, and this one was at least providing a new bit of entertainment.

Then the prince spoke first in formal German and then in Schwäbisch. "This is not, as you can see, an ordinary trial. Our only goal is to arrive at the truth. So that everyone, particularly the accused, can understand what is happening, the proceedings will be conducted in Schwäbisch."

A moment of stunned silence ensued. A wild light of hope flared briefly in the prisoner's eyes, and a true cheer went up from the crowd. When it subsided, Lieutenant Gruber, who had been trying to catch the prince's attention, said in an undertone, "But Your Highness, I do not understand Schwäbisch very well. And I do not speak it, of course."

"No? How odd that you should not speak the language of the country in whose army you serve," said the prince, his words loud and clear for all to hear. "In that case, we must provide a translator for you. Mayor, can you take on the task?"

When the mayor choked out his agreement, bowing and twisting his hat in his hands some more, Conrad turned to Gruber with a smile. "Don't worry. My German is good enough to make certain that your words are translated correctly."

Max smiled to himself. Conrad was playing his chosen part beautifully.

With a graceful flourish, the prince seated himself on the improvised throne. The sun struck his blond hair, burnishing it into a golden crown. He waved a hand to signal Gruber to begin.

The lieutenant licked his lips and swallowed nervously. Max smiled at him, but this was a smile that made Gruber jerk even more nervously. Then he managed to pull himself together. Standing at attention, he told his story stiffly, pausing when the prince raised a hand to let the mayor stammer out a translation for all to hear. The constant pauses seemed to throw the lieutenant off, but his story was simple enough. He had been walking peacefully with his companions when he was assaulted for no reason by this peasant.

"No reason at all?" asked the prince with a glance at the peasant, who seemed to be simmering with fury.

Recovering at least some of his assurance, Gruber sneered. "He shouted something I could not under-stand in that gibberish the peasants speak. Some treason, no doubt."

"There must have been witnesses to this encounter." The prince looked around in inquiry.

"My companions will corroborate what I have told you," said Gruber quickly. He glared at the two cornets until they came forward.

Max watched them approach the dais. They were very young, not yet out of their teens, and seemed frightened, though whether of the prince or of Gruber was uncertain. Perhaps of both.

"And do you indeed corroborate Lieutenant Gruber's account?" Conrad looked at them sternly.

They looked at each other nervously.

"It all happened very quickly," said one.

"And I really couldn't understand what the peasant was saying," added the other.

The prince sat silent, waiting to see if they had anything to add. Gruber glared at them, and they looked uncomfortable, but said nothing more.

"Very well," said the prince, turning to the peasant, "let us hear your story. Your name?"

The young peasant did not present a prepossessing figure. Dressed in trousers and jacket a bare step above rags, he was short, not above five and a half feet tall, but broad shouldered. His face was also broad, and hair of a muddy brown hung in unkempt fashion across his brow. Nonetheless, he stood as straight as the lieutenant, proudly defiant. "I am Franz Bauer, Your Highness. The officer lies. I did not attack him. He attacked my wife. I only tried to protect her."

"How dare you call me a liar, you dog!" Gruber snatched up a riding crop and advanced on Bauer. He came to a halt when the prince held up his hand but demanded, "What wife? I see no woman here with you."

"Is this man's wife present?" asked the prince.

Max looked over to the shop where the young woman huddled in the shop doorway beside Susannah. At his nod, she walked hesitantly across the square and fell into an awkward curtsy in front of the dais. "Your Highness," she gasped in a trembling voice. Unable to say any more, she stood there, twisting her hands in her apron.

The prince smiled kindly at her. "Don't be afraid, my dear. We only need you to tell us what happened."

She stared up at him, still twisting her apron. "It

wasn't our fault. Really it wasn't. I know I bumped into the officer because I wasn't watching where I was going, but then he wouldn't let me go. Franz was only trying to help me. Truly."

"Lies!" spat out Gruber. "Your Highness, she lies. You cannot take the word of a peasant against an officer."

The prince looked around calmly. "The square was crowded today. Were there no other witnesses?"

People looked about them nervously, and some wriggled uncomfortably. There were a few whispers. Finally a woman burst out of the crowd. She was perhaps fifty years of age, round of face and body, dressed respectably though far from richly. She looked around at the crowd, hands on her hips, and said, "If none of you fine fellows can find your tongue to speak the truth, I'll have to do it myself."

She stepped up to the dais and bobbed a curtsy. "Marta Schwartz I am, Your Highness. The lass and her man are telling the truth. That officer grabbed hold of her and wouldn't let her go until her man came to protect her. And that's the truth as anyone here will tell you." She looked aggressively around.

The prince looked out at the crowd. "And is that the truth?"

A man shuffled forward. "Aye, it is. I saw it all."

"And so did I," said another, a bit more boldly.

"I saw it as well. Marta told you the truth."

In moments, it seemed that the entire crowd was prepared to bear witness.

The prince held up his hand for silence, and the shouts subsided. He turned to the two cornets. "And you two, what have you to say?"

They looked like guilty schoolboys as they exchanged glances.

"There was a girl," admitted one. "We didn't know the fellow was her husband."

"We only did what Lieutenant Gruber told us," said the other, looking up at the prince with sad eyes.

"But they are all peasants," burst out Gruber, gesturing at the crowd. He was answered with threatening murmurs from that very crowd. While he might have been unable to understand the words, the tone was unmistakable.

"Enough," said the prince, rising to stand at the front of the dais.

His tone commanded obedience, and he received it. In the attentive silence that followed, he said, "The army exists to protect the citizens of Sigmaringen, not to abuse them. You three have disgraced the uniform you wear and betrayed the oath of loyalty you swore, loyalty to me and to Sigmaringen." Looking down at the cornets, he said, "You two are young, young enough, I hope, to learn from this experience. You will report to your barracks and remain there until your punishment is decided."

The white-faced boys—for they were little more than boys—saluted and stepped back.

Then the prince turned to Gruber, who looked far more angry than penitent. "As for you, Lieutenant, I can conceive of no excuse for your behavior. As of this moment, you are cashiered from the army. Before you are taken to prison to await trial, Captain Staufer will strip you of the insignia of your rank."

"No," roared Gruber, stepping toward the dais

in a rage. "No, you cannot..." He halted as the constables who had originally guarded the young peasant seized his arms. A wild look around showed no sympathy anywhere.

"Do not make things any worse for yourself," the prince said softly.

Gruber stood, stiff and furious, as his epaulets were ripped off and his sword was broken over Max's knee. He muttered, so that only Max could hear, "You will pay for this. You will all pay."

Max grinned.

The crowd watched in awed silence until the constables led Gruber out of sight.

"My people," said the prince, standing on the dais, "justice is what you all deserve, and justice you will have. I will not tolerate officers or officials who abuse the people they should serve. I vow to stamp out such violations of trust wherever I find them. This I promise you."

This time, the cheers were heartfelt and lasted for many long minutes. Max caught Susannah's eye, and they smiled in shared delight. The prince had come into his own.

Twenty-four

NEWS OF WHAT HAD TRANSPIRED IN THE CITY REACHED the castle more quickly than the prince did. His progress was impeded by cheering crowds all along the way, and the presence of Princess Mila beside him was cause for even more cheering. The horses had been unhitched and replaced by half a dozen young men who insisted on being given the honor of pulling the prince's carriage.

It would be difficult to say which delighted the prince more, the admiration of his people or the admiration of the lady seated beside him, for Olivia was indeed looking at him with something verging on adoration.

Sharing the carriage with them, Max and Susannah smiled too. She suspected her own smile was as tinged with worry as his was. He kept watching the people surrounding them, craning his neck to check for danger points ahead. An ambush could not have been planned, he whispered to her under the cheers of the crowd, since no one knew ahead of time that the prince intended this escapade. Still, an opportunist might take advantage of the absence of guards.

The prince's safety might have been Max's main concern, but it was not Susannah's. Her worries were focused on Lady Olivia, who showed all the signs of having fallen in love with the prince. Susannah's earlier fears had been confirmed. This was a disaster. Nothing good could come of it. At the very least, Olivia would come out of this with a broken heart.

That the prince looked equally besotted might also be a problem. He was not precisely a confident man—at least he had never seemed confident before. Would he feel humiliated when he found out that he had fallen in love with the wrong woman? Would he strike out at Olivia?

This was a horrendous mess!

Max took her hand in his just then and held it tightly while he smiled down at her. "Ach, Suse, there are complications we never considered, aren't there?"

She could only smile in acknowledgment.

"I know I should never have involved you in this, but…" He shook his head.

"No. It was not your decision. It was mine. I will not let you blame yourself."

He lifted her hand and held it to his cheek. "I should regret it, but I cannot. That is nothing to be proud of, I know, but it makes me so happy to have you by my side."

They might be facing disaster. They *were* facing disaster. It did not matter to her any longer. What was important was that they were facing it together. She knew that whatever happened, she would always cherish this adventure.

❦

They rolled through the gates into the courtyard, still pulled by half a dozen young men, still accompanied by what looked to be half the population of Nymburg. Leading Olivia by the hand, the prince stopped at the top of the steps to turn and wave once more to the crowd. The resulting cheers followed him into the castle.

Staufer looked quickly around. A detachment of his own men, members of the Royal Guard, stood at attention around the courtyard. He would be willing to swear that they stood more proudly than usual, just a hair away from bursting into cheers themselves. The master sergeant standing close to the castle door could not quite keep the smile from twitching at his lips.

Staufer wanted to smile himself. It struck him that whatever else this escapade had accomplished, it had made Hugo's task that much more difficult. It was one thing to usurp the throne of a prince whose rule was oppressive and who was himself disliked. It was something else entirely to overthrow a popular prince, and Conrad had just made himself very popular indeed.

Angriffer apparently shared that thought. He was standing just inside the door, watching the prince lead his princess down the hall, and turned to Staufer. "A very clever move, Max. Your idea?"

Staufer raised his brows. "You are surprised? How foolish of you, Dieter. You, and perhaps your friends, may have seriously underestimated the prince. He has no difficulty recognizing injustice when he sees it, nor in taking steps to combat it."

"Injustice?" Angriffer laughed. "A prince worried about injustice? What an outré thought. No, I suspect it was all done to impress his pretty little pseudo-princess. Nonetheless, you have posed an interesting problem for Hugo. Or more likely for Helga. I wonder how long it will take her to determine a countermove. Amusing, is it not?"

∽

Floating along on the cloud of euphoria created by the cheering crowds, Conrad started to lead Olivia toward the private wing, but he was interrupted by a cough from one of his secretaries. He paused. "Yes?"

"Excuse me, Sire, but Count Herzlos begs for a word with you. He is waiting in his office."

Conrad automatically began to drop Olivia's hand and turn toward the prime minister's office, but he felt her hand tighten and stopped. Slowly he smiled and said to the secretary. "Tell the count he may come see me in my study in half an hour's time." Turning to Olivia, he said, "Will you accompany me, my princess?"

"I would be honored, Sire."

The secretary stood immobile, feeling rather as if the earth had shifted on its axis. Then he too smiled and started off to the office where Count Herzlos and his son and daughter were waiting. There was a spring in his step. He looked forward to delivering this message.

∽

The trek from the castle entrance to the prince's private wing was every bit as long as the trek to the princess's apartments, though today they turned right instead of left. Still, it wasn't the distance that bothered Susannah. It was almost as if, when those massive doors at the entrance thudded to a close, the real world had been shut out.

She was probably being ridiculously fanciful, but Susannah could not help feeling that something was inherently unreal about the castle, or at least about its inhabitants. They were all pretending, all of them. It was one enormous masquerade. The only one who did not seem bothered by this was the prince. He had not looked in the least bit worried when he reached the castle. In fact, he had been looking rather smug.

Max, on the other hand, was looking very worried indeed. As she walked beside him with her hand on his arm, she could almost feel the waves of distress coming from him.

"Are you not pleased to see the prince taking charge?" she asked, keeping her voice low.

One side of Staufer's mouth lifted in a half-smile, half-grimace. "A few weeks ago, I would have been delighted. Once this…this…*confusion* is over, and he is safe on his throne, I will be delighted. But at the moment, no. It is hard enough to predict what Hugo will do, and now Conrad has added to the uncertainty."

"But it must be good that he has made himself popular."

"For the moment, yes, but how long will this last? If we do not find the princess quickly, if the country is plunged into war, how popular do you think Conrad will be then? For that matter, what if there is another incident like this in Nymburg or elsewhere in the country, and the prince does nothing about it?

Because there will be other incidents, and the prince will not even know about them."

"You are being exceedingly gloomy."

"Am I? Yes, I suppose I am." Max huffed a small laugh. "It is this waiting. I fear I am not a patient man."

"Has the intruder told your men nothing?"

He shook his head. "I have the impression that he fears Hugo more than he fears me and my men. But the general has sent one of his intelligence officers. Perhaps he will be more successful." He sighed. "Or perhaps our prisoner really has no idea where the princess is being held."

Susannah would have liked to say something encouraging, but she couldn't think of anything. The waiting was undeniably frustrating, but Max's mood was no more depressing than the castle itself.

They trudged down long marble corridors lined with marble statues of statesmen in classical poses standing between gloomy portraits of dead princes. It was a heavy weight, this constant reminder of the past. Susannah could not help feeling that it was not really necessary. Surely a prince had the authority to do something to lighten the atmosphere in his castle. But she supposed that he had to really be the one in charge, and Conrad wasn't. Not yet.

The prince's mood was still euphoric when they reached his private study, a room mercifully free of gilding. Three tall windows set in arched bays looked out on a garden where a venerable beech tree was displaying its bronze autumn foliage. The walls were painted a soft green, and deeply cushioned chairs covered in darker green were set in groupings around the room where tables held oil lamps, books, and periodicals. In the corner, a tall stove covered with painted tiles in cream and yellow kept the room pleasantly warm.

The far end of the room was dominated by a large desk with inlaid panels of walnut burl. The only thing that broke the broad expanse of the leather surface was an elaborate inkstand of brass and crystal.

Conrad had seated himself behind the desk. Leaning back in the high, leather-covered chair, he said. "Do you remember my father sitting at this desk, Max?"

"Indeed I do." A slow smile appeared on Max's face. "I remember being called in with you when we had been caught out in some fault. It seemed a very long walk from the door to the front of the desk. My knees would be trembling by the time I arrived before him."

"Mine too. I swear I always found him more intimidating here than in the throne room. But I think he would have approved of our prank today, no?"

"Indeed." Max's smile faded to seriousness. "I believe he would have been very proud of you today."

Olivia and Susannah must have looked confused, because Conrad turned to them. "Did you not know? Staufer and I were playmates when we were children. We were close enough in age, and he was of high enough birth for my father to allow it."

The prince turned his eyes to Max, suddenly serious. "Perhaps that is why he is the one man I trust."

As Max stood motionless, a dozen emotions could be seen flashing across his countenance. Guilt, concern, loyalty, determination, even love—all were there. He bowed to the prince, his hand on his heart. "I will never betray you. I swear it. What I have done, anything I have done, has been to protect you and your throne." Then he turned to the two women. "I must tell him everything. Do you see that?"

"Yes, of course," said Susannah. She now understood more of the conflict that had been raging in him. Loyalty to a prince is one thing, but when loyalty to a friend is added to the mix... No wonder he had been so torn.

Olivia had eyes only for the prince, eyes in which tears were welling up. "Yes, I know. I have known for an age that he must be told. Your Highness, I have felt so guilty..."

The sound of approaching confusion interrupted before any explanations could begin. The prince frowned and held up his hand for silence. "Whatever it is, there is no time for it at the moment. I must first deal with the Herzlos clan. You will wait."

With a wave of his hand, he directed them to seats in front of the windows, where they sat in shadow.

The approaching clamor softened into a mutter of voices—angry voices—and the door opened to give entrance to a footman. "Count Herzlos, Baron Herzlos, Baroness Herzlos, and Lieutenant Angriffer beg an audience with you, Your Highness."

"Ah yes," said the prince, as if he had just remembered the appointment. "Send them in."

Twenty-five

THEY DID NOT PRECISELY MARCH IN. COUNT HERZLOS, at the head of the party, moved at a stately pace that accentuated the distance from the door to the prince. Hugo, fuming, stumbled over his feet every few steps in an effort to keep himself behind his father. Helga, on the arm of Angriffer, floated behind them. The determined smile on her mouth was not quite good enough to counteract the effect of the angry color on her cheekbones.

In contrast, Angriffer looked not only calm but faintly amused. He caught Susannah's eye and winked at her, prompting a low growl from Staufer. Helga also noticed and tightened her grip on Angriffer's arm while darting a glare at Susannah.

Count Herzlos paid no attention to this byplay. He was stiffly proper as he came to a halt before the prince, clicked his heels, and bowed. Hugo managed to do the same, but with far less grace. While his father looked icy, he was seething with ill-concealed rage.

"How could you—" burst out of Hugo's mouth before his father held up a hand to silence him.

Conrad looked coldly at the son for a moment before granting the father a courteous smile. "Good afternoon, Count. You wished to see me. It was something urgent?"

"My apologies, Sire," said the count, his face impassive, "but my son shares my distress at your recent actions."

"Distress? At my actions? Dear me, have I failed to recognize someone whom I passed in the hall? Greeted someone I should have ignored?" The prince's voice was pleasant, though there was an edge to it.

Susannah, sitting between Max and Olivia, watched with nervous interest as Count Herzlos stiffened even more. She would not have thought such a feat possible, but he managed it.

"You must know, Sire, that your safety, the safety of your realm, rests upon the loyalty of the army. To undermine the authority of your officers is an act of folly, dangerous folly."

"Really, Uncle, I assure you that I have done nothing that would undermine the lawful authority of my officers."

None of the three observers made a sound, but their eyes brightened at the emphasis on the word "lawful."

Hugo could no longer be restrained. Stepping forward, he slammed a fist down on the desk. "You humiliated one of my officers in front of the entire town. You disgraced him, and I will not stand for it."

The prince did not move for a long moment, then looked down at Hugo's fist resting on the desk before raising his eyes to look directly at Hugo. "You forget yourself, Baron." His voice was soft, but cold enough to drop the temperature in the room by several degrees.

There was a hissed intake of breath—Susannah thought it came from Helga, but she could not be sure. In the silence that followed, she held herself very still, as did Olivia and Max. This was the prince's scene, and they had no desire to draw the attention from him. From the corner of her eye, Susannah could see Angriffer. He had detached himself from Helga and was standing in a relaxed pose with a glint of wicked amusement in his eyes.

The count pulled Hugo back. "I beg you to excuse my son, Sire. He is naturally distressed, since it was an officer of his regiment who was humiliated. News of this has already spread throughout the town and throughout his regiment. Through all the regiments. This will have a serious effect upon discipline, upon morale."

"And you think I caused this disruption?" The prince responded so calmly that Count Herzlos hesitated, momentarily uncertain.

Hugo, however, showed no hesitation at all, and jerked his arm free of his father's grasp. "Who else?" he demanded. "You took the word of a peasant over the word of an officer. You must have been mad to do such a thing."

"It was not a single peasant, you know." Conrad smiled pleasantly. "There were a dozen witnesses to say that Lieutenant Gruber was lying. To say nothing of the two cornets."

Hugo slashed a hand through the air in dismissal. "The cornets are young. They were probably frightened. And everyone knows that peasants, townspeople will tell any lies they think they can get away with."

Helga put a hand on her brother's shoulder as if to calm him, but Susannah could see that she squeezed tightly enough for her knuckles to turn white. It served to silence him. "Really," she drawled, "you must look at this sensibly, Your Highness. One can hardly take the word of peasants over the word of an officer."

Conrad tilted his head consideringly. "So you think everyone was lying. Only the lieutenant was telling the truth. Is that it?"

"Precisely." Helga smiled condescendingly, as if at a child who has recited his lesson correctly.

"Of course," snapped Hugo. "Anything else is impossible. These people all hate the army. Everyone knows that."

Helga shut her eyes briefly and gave a gasp of annoyance as she tightened her grip on her brother again.

"Hate the army? Now why would they hate the army, which exists for their protection?" The prince turned to Staufer. "Captain, do your men complain that people hate them?"

Staufer spoke from the shadows. "No, Sire, I have never heard such complaints from my men. Perhaps it is only the baron's Black Star Regiment that has such problems. Perhaps it is the way they behave that causes the problems."

"What you suggest is impossible," Hugo said, dismissing the suggestion with a sneer. "My officers are gentlemen."

"No, not impossible." Conrad leaned back in his chair and smiled. "Tell him, Captain Staufer."

Staufer slowly unfolded himself from the chair where he had been sitting quietly. He stepped over to stand beside the prince's desk and faced the Herzlos clan. "I was in the marketplace myself today when this incident occurred and saw the whole thing. Lieutenant Gruber attempted to assault a young woman, and when her husband came to her defense, he threatened to have the husband hanged for his impertinence."

With a look of disgust, he turned to Hugo. "Your drunken lieutenant lied through his teeth."

Hugo's anger abated not at all. "I don't believe it!"

Staufer smiled then. "Are you calling me a liar?" he asked softly, pulling off a glove and fingering it gently.

Susannah stood up before things could get further out of hand. Standing tall, with her head high, she faced the Herzlos family. "I too was in the marketplace and saw it all. It happened as Captain Staufer said."

"I saw it all as well, and I say the same." Olivia rose and put her arm through Susannah's.

Helga hissed in an angry breath, and her lips could be seen to form the silent word "imposters." A dozen angry impulses flashed across Hugo's face, each one uglier than the last.

Conrad stood as well. "And I was also in the marketplace and saw it all. I think, Cousin, that you need to point out to your regiment that their duty is to Sigmaringen, not to themselves. And perhaps you might remind them that an officer is expected to be a gentleman, and a gentleman does not tell lies to escape the consequences of his own misdeeds."

Prince and cousin stared at each other in silence. It was as if the prince's steady but unsmiling look slowly drained away Hugo's bravado, and the count seemed to deflate in concert with his son. Helga simmered impotently, but for some reason she seemed to be directing her fury at Susannah, who could not understand why. It was uncomfortable.

Finally the prince said, "You may leave us."

Twenty-six

CONRAD WATCHED THE DOOR CLOSE BEHIND THE Herzlos party before he turned to Staufer. "Well?"

The three of them stood before the prince, a cloud of guilt hanging over them.

Staufer shook his head and forced himself to meet the prince's eyes. "It is my fault. I was wrong. I should have trusted you. I should have had faith in you. I failed in my duty. I failed you."

"Failed me?" Conrad looked understandably confused.

Susannah wasn't going to let Max take it all upon himself to clear up that confusion, not when it had all been General Bergen's idea in the first place. "It wasn't Max's fault. I should never have agreed…" she began, but was interrupted by Olivia, who stepped forward and knelt.

"No, Your Highness, the greatest betrayal is mine. I know you will never be able to forgive me." Olivia lifted eyes glistening with unshed tears. "I am not a real princess."

"What nonsense is this?" Conrad frowned. "Of course you are. You must not kneel before me." He went to lift her to her feet, but she turned her face away and wrapped her arms about herself.

"She only wanted to help," said Susannah, reaching down to lift Olivia up. "That's all any of us wanted to do."

"I beg you, Sire, let me speak." Staufer tried to step in front of the women.

Protocol was blown to the wind as all three supplicants tried to speak at once.

It was the prince who finally brought about order with a single sharp word. Faced with his stiff frown, the others were shamed into silence. When the prince finally gave him a nod, Staufer began to provide the explanation.

There was dignity in his recital. Staufer spoke in the unemotional tones of a soldier reporting to his commanding officer. He told of the princess's disappearance, their belief that she had run away, the hope that using Lady Olivia as a substitute would give them enough time to find Princess Mila and avoid a scandal.

"I'll not believe it!" Anger and shock fought for dominance on the prince's face. "It is impossible. There are people who have met the princess. An impostor could never…" He turned to look at Olivia. "Impossible."

After staring at her for a long minute, he turned back to Max. "A few days. You said you needed a few days to find the princess. But it has been almost two weeks."

"We were mistaken." Staufer's mouth was white at the edges. "It was far worse than we had thought." Still in that flat, military report tone, he recounted the discovery of the dead guard, the revelation of the kid-napping, the involvement of Hugo and Helga Herzlos, the midnight intruder.

Fury flared in the prince's eyes as he stepped toward the captain. "There was danger, real danger? You knew this and still you allowed the princess…" Conrad caught himself. "…these ladies to continue with this masquerade?"

The pain in Max's eyes was unbearable. Susannah stepped forward. "It was our decision, Sire. Max—Captain Staufer—wanted us to leave, but we felt an obligation to continue."

Conrad turned his anger on her. "An obligation? An obligation to make a fool of me?"

Max flinched but Susannah continued in a steady voice. "We were afraid that if we fled, you and your country might be in greater danger."

"So I am such a weakling that I must be protected by women," Conrad said bleakly. "I could not be trusted to deal with a crisis. What did you fear? That I would collapse like a frightened child? That I would go running to my uncle?" His mouth twisted in a bitter smile. "Yes, that would have been General Bergen's great fear. Those two old men—their hatred of each other rules their every action. But you, Max, I thought you at least were my friend. Had you no faith in me? Why did you…?"

He turned to look at Olivia, who was by now sob-bing into Susannah's shoulder. "Was it all lies, then? Yes. All lies. Get out of my sight, all of you."

❧

Staufer accompanied them back to their quarters, but he might as well have been somewhere else. Anywhere else. They walked through the endless marble corridors—those blasted endless corridors—as if they had some purpose, but their only purpose was to hide their distress.

Max's face showed such pain that Susannah wanted to weep. Why was he taking all the responsibility on himself? She also wanted to shake him. She wanted to say, "Dammit, it wasn't your fault! This was the general's idea, not yours. You wanted to end it. You wanted to tell the prince the truth, but we wouldn't let you!"

It had never been his idea, and if at the beginning he had thought of it as a lark, a joke—well, so had they all. No one expected it to turn so serious. And when it had turned serious, when they discovered that the princess had not just run off by herself in a fit of temper, Max was the one who wanted to end it. He had seen the danger, but they had forced him to go on with it, and he couldn't end it without betraying all of them.

Instead, they had betrayed him. *She* had betrayed him. And the others—Aunt Augusta hadn't wanted to give up the excitement; Olivia hadn't wanted to lose the chance to help the prince; the general... Susannah had no idea what the general wanted, unless it was to thwart Count Herzlos and his family. But what they all wanted would not have mattered if she had not insisted on staying. She knew that. Max would have overridden the other protests. Hers was the only one that had stopped him.

Were it not for her, he would have done the honorable thing. To protect them, he would have sent them all to safety. Then he would have told the prince everything, doubtless taking all the blame on himself. He had put aside his best judgment because she insisted on staying, and though she had not admitted it, she had insisted for the purely selfish reason that she wanted to stay with him. She hadn't thought about what would be best for him, only about what she wanted for herself. She was an arrogant, selfish fool.

When they finally reached the princess's suite, Olivia ran into her bedchamber, probably to weep in private. That was something else for Susannah to feel guilty about. She had seen that Olivia was falling in love with the prince. She should have done something to stop it. There must have been something she could have done.

She spun around and faced the wall, her hands pressed to her mouth. What was she to do? She was supposed to be the sensible one, the one who would take care of the others and see to it that they did not get into trouble. Instead, she had thought only of herself and ignored her responsibilities. Well, what she had to do now was deal with the consequences of her failure.

It was all too humiliating.

She took a deep breath and turned back to face Max, who was staring at the floor, his jaw clenched.

"Forgive me," she said, as he raised his eyes to look at her. "I should have listened to you when you wanted us to leave."

He shook his head. "No, you must forgive me. It

is all my fault. I should have trusted him. I decided, when I had no right to decide. I was too sure I could protect him, protect you. In my pride, I thought I could do it all, and I failed. I have dishonored myself." He reached out and touched her cheek, just a feather of a touch. "The truth is that I wanted to keep you near. I did not want you to disappear from my life."

"I wanted to stay near you too," she whispered.

They began stumbling over each other's words, reaching out their hands first in supplication and then to offer comfort. Before they knew it, they were clinging to each other in desperate longing. He rained kisses on her face, on her hair, and crushed her to him. She clung to him, sobs punctuating the kisses she pressed on him.

Finally, Max lifted his head and slowly stepped back from her, his arms resting on her shoulders as if he could not bear to stop touching her. "I must go. You understand, do you not? In my arrogance I have failed my prince. Honor demands that I redeem myself."

Susannah nodded but did not speak.

"To do that, I must find the princess. I should never have left the search to others. I should not have…" He stopped with a short laugh. "Useless now to say what I should not have done. All I can do is try to repair the damage."

She nodded again. Painful though it was, she understood. Apologies were meaningless now. Action was needed to bring things around. "Where will you go?"

He lifted a shoulder. "I must start where she disappeared. Someone may have seen something. There may be witnesses, some hint. I was careless at first, thinking she had just run off, and later…" He smiled wryly and lifted a hand to touch her cheek. "Later I left things to the general, and now I am not even certain that he wanted to find her. I should not have done so, but…"

"No matter. When you find her, you will return." She spoke with absolute conviction.

"You will wait?"

"Here, if the prince permits. Otherwise…"

"I will come to you. Whatever happens, wherever you are, I will come to you."

"And I will be waiting."

When the door had closed behind him, Susannah stood, frozen, until Lev padded to her side and pushed his head under her hand. She ran her fingers through the thick fur as he looked up at her face. "You saw all that, didn't you? And you understand."

The dog nudged her toward the bedroom, and she obediently allowed herself to be herded to the bed. "Yes," she told him, "I would like to lie down." She did so, and Lev remained beside her, standing guard.

She smiled when she realized that the dog was watching the wall where the door to the staircase had opened only a few days before. "Clever Lev," she murmured. "You remember where the danger came from. If only I knew where the danger lies now. If only I could help Max now."

She sat up abruptly and focused on the panel that disguised the door to the staircase. Her eyes narrowed. It had been night, and it had been dark. Josef had checked it, but only by candlelight, and he was looking for other intruders. The next day, when they looked more carefully, they were only interested in finding the mechanism to open the door. Once they had done that, they had simply wedged it shut.

However, they had not bothered to examine the passage itself. Not carefully. The intruder could have dropped something. There could be some clue in there, something that could help them.

She walked over to the panel, removed the wedge, and pressed the board that released the latch. The door swung open silently. The silence gave her pause. There had been no noise the other night either when the intruder came in. Only well-oiled hinges move so silently. Had they been specially oiled in preparation for the attempt to kidnap Olivia? Or was this a regularly used way of moving around the castle? Or perhaps of spying on guests who were given these chambers?

Returning to the sitting room, she lit one of the oil lamps, adjusted the wick, and carried it back to the staircase. It provided some light in the stairwell—more than a candle, at least—and she descended carefully. A thud behind her almost made her drop the lamp, but her heart resumed its normal rhythm when she saw that it was only Lev, following behind her. "You should have told me you were coming," she scolded. "If I had dropped the lamp on this wooden staircase, I might have burned down the entire palace. I don't think that would have pleased the prince one bit."

Lev just looked at her. The dog's calm was reassuring. She took a deep breath and continued the descent. Unfortunately, there seemed to be nothing on the staircase but dust. Plenty of dust. She held up her skirts with her free hand in an effort to keep from getting them filthy. Then she reached a landing and she saw that although the staircase continued down, there was an opening to the side. It was so dark that she would not have noticed it had there not been footprints in the dust to show the way.

As she moved slowly through the narrow passage, she could hear voices. She stopped to listen, but could not make out the words. The voices were up ahead. She almost turned and ran back. What excuse could she possibly give for being here?

She rallied her courage. If the voices belonged to servants, she would not need to give any excuse. And if they belonged to any of the villains? Well, she doubted they had any more business being in this passage than she did, and she had Lev to protect her.

So she continued cautiously down the passage and soon realized that the voices were coming not from the passage but from one of the rooms. Of course. The passage had been built for servants, so naturally it would open into more than one room. As she drew closer, she could recognize Helga's shrill accents and Hugo's rumble. At the door, she pressed her ear to the crack.

Hugo was railing about the prince's sudden popularity with the populace. "…Showing off for that insipid little blonde. We must do something about it."

"It won't last." Helga sounded amused but definite. "Our dear papa will have him do something stupid, and his bubble of popularity will burst. You really must learn to keep your head, Hugo."

"But suppose Staufer persuades him to do something else?"

"No need to worry about that." A third voice, with a bark of laughter. Dieter Angriffer? It sounded like the sneering tones of that reptile. "Our friend Maximillian von Staufer will no longer be a problem. I've taken care of him."

"You have?" Hugo sounded hopeful, but Susannah felt a stab of panic and clenched her fingers in Lev's coat.

"I've had a message sent to him, telling him that the princess is in your hunting lodge at Krassau."

"What?" Helga screeched, no longer amused. "But that's where she is!"

"Indeed, my love," Angriffer drawled. "Considerate of me, is it not? When my men ambush him, they will not need to carry him so far. He is such an ox."

"But why…" Hugo was sputtering.

Angriffer sighed. "Be sensible. The original plan, in which you rescue the princess after her father invades—or threatens to invade—Sigmaringen may no longer be possible. The appearance of this imposter has thrown all in disarray. Even Mila is not stupid enough to believe that she has been held for weeks in your hunting lodge without your knowledge. We may have to eliminate her just to save our necks. If that becomes necessary, I would prefer to have Staufer available to take the blame as her assassin."

Susannah came dangerously close to dropping the lamp. It was only the need to keep it steady and upright that gave her time to tamp down her fury. The sensible part of her knew that she could not physically tear Angriffer to pieces, that she was too weak, but the sensible part of her was fading fast. Every muscle in her body was tensed, ready to leap.

"But you can't just keep a dead body sitting around until you need it!" Hugo sounded ready to explode in panic.

"Calm yourself, Hugo." Helga seemed to have recovered her control. "Let us hear what Dieter has to propose."

Angriffer sighed again. "Really, Hugo, you talk as if I'm as much of a fool as you—your father. I'm not going to kill him yet. I'll just keep him in the cellar until he's needed. And, at the same time, that will keep him out of the way while your father helps the prince make a fool of himself."

"Yes…" Helga drew out the word. "That could work. And these imposters will be destroyed with him. Yes."

Twenty-seven

Susannah forced herself to back away slowly, pulling Lev with her. Helga's voice followed as Susannah turned around and ran back to the staircase, no longer caring if her footsteps made any noise in the passage.

She raced up the staircase and through her room, and burst out into the corridor. Two of Max's men were still on guard there. She grabbed the nearest one, a slim fellow, scarcely more than a boy, with flaming red hair. "Do you know where Captain Staufer is?" she demanded.

He shook his head, wide-eyed. "No, Lady."

"Find him," she said. "Find him at once and bring him here. And you!" She turned to the other man, who was staring at her as well. "You go find Josef. Now!"

Then she flung back into her room and tried to think. What should she do? What if Max had already left?

She would have to go after him. There was no other choice.

In the wardrobe she had her sister's exploring outfit, the one with the divided skirt that Elinor had worn in Italy. Elinor had told her to take it along, "just in case you have an adventure too." Susannah had thought it ridiculous—she wasn't the sort to have adventures, and she was hardly going to be exploring anything at a spa with Aunt Augusta. Now, however, she blessed her sister for the thought. And her brother Ned for the pocketknife he had given her. Just as a precaution, he had said. She would take that along, and also the bottle of whatever it was that the intruder had left behind. She took it out of the drawer and checked that the cork was tight.

She intended to be prepared for whatever was to come.

In a trice, she was out of her dress and out of her corset. By the time she finished dressing, Josef was knocking at the door.

She swung open the door. "Is Captain Staufer still here?"

"No, Lady, he rode off. There was a message for him…"

She interrupted with an impatient gesture. "It was a false message. He is on his way to Krassau, but it's a trap. Angriffer's men are waiting to ambush him. Take me to the stables. We must catch him."

She was prepared to drag Josef down the hall, but there was no need. He did not hesitate to believe her, thank goodness. Instead, he immediately headed off, barking an order to the guard who came running toward them, the guard she had sent in search of Max.

They hurried along and turned down a staircase she had not seen before—wood, not marble, but not as steep or grimy as the servants' stairs had been. In no time they were in the stables and three horses were being saddled. The gray mare, she assumed, was for her. The young guard was arming himself with a bow and arrows. She stumbled when she saw that. A bow and arrows? This was the nineteenth century, not the Middle Ages! She looked at Josef in surprise.

"Emil knows the forest near Krassau," he said with a grunt. "He will make sure we do not lose the route."

Well, that was useful, she supposed. At least Josef was armed with a rifle. She looked again. Two rifles. She had been afraid he would not take her seriously. She did not know if she should be grateful that he had listened to her—or worried that he did not seem to consider this an unexpected development.

They were out a gate at the rear of the castle before Susannah realized that Lev was accompanying them. Josef turned at her exclamation of distress but grinned. "Have no fear. If he cannot keep up with us, he will still be able to follow, and he may be of use."

Remembering how Lev had terrified the intruder in her room, Susannah did not doubt the dog's usefulness. Besides, the large, white shape trotting beside her was comforting.

As they plunged into the forest, she had need of comfort. These were not the shady woods of England with gentle paths kept clear for ladies' rambles. This was the setting of an ancient folk tale, the sort of place that was inhabited by witches and trolls. Though it was still afternoon, the dense trees cut off the light so that it seemed almost like night. What would it be like when the sun had set? The darkness would then be impenetrable.

They proceeded slowly, often riding single file because the path was so narrow. Actually, it hardly deserved to be called a path. Often it seemed to be little more than an opening between trees. Emil peered ahead as if he were uncertain himself. They moved at little more than a walk. She could have gone faster on foot.

Frustrated, she longed to gallop so she might reach Max before he rode into the ambush, but she could see that would be madness in terrain like this. Reckless speed would only endanger the horses. She tried to tell herself that Max would have had to go slowly too, but she only half believed herself.

She was finding it difficult to believe anything about her present situation.

What was she doing here? How had Lady Susannah Tremaine, a very proper English lady—all the dowagers approved of her and introduced her to their grandsons, their very boring grandsons—come to be here? What was she doing riding through some foreign forest in an effort to rescue a Sigmaringen officer?

She did not do this sort of thing. She was cautious, careful—not the sort of person who went dashing off into forests. She did not recognize herself.

All she knew was that she had to help Max. She had to save him. If she could not do that, nothing else in her entire life was of any importance.

They had been traveling for nearly two hours—two endless hours—when Emil pulled to a halt. Another wider trail crossed the one they were following. He looked down, frowning.

She pulled up next to Josef. "Are you sure he knows the way?"

Without taking his eyes from Emil, Josef nodded. "Yes. He has been taking us on an old way that is shorter. Rough, but it cut many miles off our trip. He is looking now to see if any have been here before us."

Emil made a satisfied noise and looked up. "The count passed on the main path, not long ago. We will follow him now."

"No worry," Josef assured her with a proud smile. "Emil knows. He is my grandson."

Susannah followed obediently, praying that Emil did indeed know what he was talking about. She was none too certain of that herself, but at this point, what choice did she have? At least they were moving more quickly now. The path was wider and, without trees pressing in on all sides, it was brighter too. She trotted behind the two men with Lev at her side, thinking that they really should go faster. Max might not be far ahead of them, but he still was ahead of them and riding into an ambush.

Emil pulled up suddenly and raised a hand. Josef stopped as well, so perforce she had to halt too. She started to ask why, but Emil said, "Do you hear?"

She looked at him in annoyance. "I don't hear anything."

"No birds, no animals moving about." He nodded, frowning. "We must hurry."

The two men kicked their horses into a gallop, and Susannah followed. Moments later, they heard a shot, followed by shouts.

Too late, too late. Fear was a hard rock in her stomach.

The noise ahead continued. That must mean that he was alive, mustn't it? A cry of pain, but a high-pitched voice. Not Max. *Good*, she thought viciously.

Josef shouted something, and Lev went charging ahead, a huge, spectral creature moving silently.

The dog was just ahead of them when they burst into a clearing, where two men were bent over a third. Without a sound, Lev leaped on the closer one. The man's cry was cut off abruptly when he thudded into the ground.

When the second man saw them, he pulled out a wicked-looking knife, but an arrow struck his chest. He stared at it as if amazed before he fell to the ground.

It was all over very quickly. While Emil and Josef collected the attackers, Susannah flew to Max. He was collapsed on the ground, his head and his jacket bloody. She felt his head around the bleeding wound very gently, but there seemed to be no broken bone. With trembling fingers she pulled his jacket apart and off his shoulder. No wound, there was no wound. It was not his blood.

But he was unconscious. From the blow on his head? The cut had not seemed that serious. He groaned slightly when she lifted him, and there was a smell. She sniffed. It was familiar.

Then she saw the bottle, spilling its drug into the ground. Of course. It was the smell of that stuff her intruder had carried, the stuff she was carrying herself in the bottle in her pocket. If she had needed evidence that all these events were connected, she had it now.

She sat back on her heels. That's right. They used

that *stuff* on Max because they hadn't planned to kill him. They had intended to capture him. She shook her head to clear it. The smell was making her dizzy too. Well, their plan had been disrupted. Right now, she needed to take care of Max.

She pulled him away from the spill as best she could, fearing that it could be dangerous for him to keep breathing the stuff in. It was making her light-headed just being near it. She knelt beside him, laying his head in her lap, and gently brushed the hair from his face. With a sigh, he turned his cheek into her hand, almost as if he knew she was there.

Josef appeared at her side and stared down at Max, a puzzled frown on his face.

"I don't think he is wounded," she said. "I think they used that drug on him." She inclined her head to indicate the bottle.

He nodded, still frowning. "There were four of them. My lord laid out two of them." He shook his head. "Only four. I would have thought…"

Emil appeared beside them, leading a horse. "The count's horse," he said, gesturing at a cut across the forelegs.

"Ah," said Josef. "That explains it. But stupid, if they wanted him alive. He could have broken his neck."

Susannah had no idea what they were talking about, and her confusion obviously showed in her face, because Josef gave her an understanding look.

"They put a cord across the path to trip his horse. It's an old trick to bring down a rider, who is always thrown. But it's dangerous."

"No way to know how badly the rider will be hurt," said Emil, scowling in the direction of the captured men.

"But it explains why there were only four of them," said Josef. "I would not send so few to take down Count von Staufer." He sounded affronted, as if odds of four to one were an insult.

She nodded, looking down at the unconscious count. "I do not think he will awaken quickly."

"No," agreed Josef. "What should we do?"

That was not a question she had expected. Why was Josef asking her? When she looked up, she saw that Emil was also looking at her for instruction. Were they mad? They could not possibly expect her to know what to do now. But they obviously expected precisely that. Turning back to stare at Max's unconscious form, she chewed her lip as she thought furiously.

"We cannot wait here for him to recover consciousness. There is no way to know how long that will take." She spoke slowly and was relieved to see the two men nodding agreement. "And then there are the attackers. Are they dead?"

"Only the one Emil shot." Josef sounded regretful. "The others still live. Should we…?"

Good heavens! She was accustomed to giving orders to servants, but she was not going to give an order like *that*. "No, but…" She had an idea. "Are they going to be expected somewhere?"

Josef shrugged. "I will go and ask." He strolled over to the spot where Lev kept guard over the men.

She could not make out what was being said. The voices were indistinguishable mutters. Then there was a growl, followed by a shriek—of fear, not pain, she thought.

Emil smiled. "They will tell Josef. No worry."

She looked down at Max, cradled in her lap. No, she was not worried. Lev was welcome to nip off as many pieces of them as necessary to persuade them to tell what they knew. They deserved it.

It did not take long. Josef came back with a contemptuous look on his face. "They have no loyalty, no courage, these pigs. All my Lev needs to do is bare his teeth and they begin to babble."

"But what did they say?" She did not really care whether or not they were cowards. She only wanted to know what their plans had been.

"They were to keep the count prisoner in a gamekeeper's hut until they received word to take him to Krassau. Beyond that, they say they know nothing."

Susannah nodded. "Good. Then if they are not left here, no one will know they did not succeed. Can you hide them so they cannot escape and will not be found?"

Emil smiled. It was a confident smile, though not a particularly nice one. "Oh yes. I can do that. Is easy."

She had a momentary qualm, suspecting that she would rather not know what Emil was planning. Then she remembered what had been planned for Max, and her qualms vanished. "And we need a safe place for Captain Staufer. It may take a while for him to awaken."

At that, Josef and Emil conferred, but she could not follow the discussion. They seemed to come to some desirable conclusion, because they were both smiling when they turned back to her.

"We are not far from the count's lands. I know a small hunter's camp near here. The count will be safe there," Josef said.

That seemed likely to be a good refuge. "But how can we get him there?" she asked. "He cannot sit on a horse by himself, and none of us is strong enough to hold him."

"The cart," said Emil.

"They would not have been able to carry him either," said Josef with a satisfied smile, "so they brought a cart. It will do as well for a rescue as for a capture."

Really, she thought, Josef had a very strange sense of humor. However, a cart would be necessary, so she nodded.

In short order, all was arranged. Josef drove the cart with Susannah supporting Max in the back. Lev stretched out beside Max, helping to keep him warm. Their horses, including Max's wounded one, were tied behind. Emil took care of the other horses, riding his own and leading the others with their burdens of bound villains.

Some misgivings prodded at Susannah as she watched Emil and his prisoners ride off. "Where will he take them?"

Josef smiled slightly, a smile that made her glad he was on her side. "No need to worry. He will manage."

Just how he would manage was what worried her, but she pushed that worry to the side while she concentrated on Max. He was so pale. She tried to tell herself it was nothing more than a deep sleep that held him in thrall, but he was so pale and so cold.

She wrapped her thick green cloak around him and pulled one of the blankets that cushioned them over him. It was a horse blanket, and smelled like one, but it would provide some warmth as the day chilled with the setting sun.

She held Max cradled in her arms to cushion him as the cart bumped along another narrow trail, jolted by ruts and roots and stones. Her fear was tinged with anger, and her jaw clenched. Had the Herzlos twins been within reach, she would cheerfully have dismembered them—and that loathsome Angriffer as well. She would not allow them to harm Max. Not now. Not ever.

It was dark by the time Josef pulled the cart to a halt beside a low timber building. Telling her to wait, he went inside to light a lamp. With the door open, they could at least see what they were doing. Together they pulled Max to the edge of the cart so that Josef could carry him by the shoulders while Susannah took his legs.

"Not a man to take lightly, eh?" Josef grinned at her.

She glared at him instead of answering. How could he be so cheerful?

The building seemed to consist of a large room that served as both kitchen and sitting room with several smaller rooms opening off it. A huge fireplace, a simple wooden table and chairs, and a few comfortable chairs served as the furnishings for the main room. They carried Max into one of the smaller rooms, which was almost filled by a large bed but also had a fireplace. While Josef started a fire, Susannah found a stream outside and filled a bucket with water. She set it beside the fire to warm, then they managed to pull off Max's boots and remove his jacket and shirt.

When Josef went off to take care of the horses and cart, Susannah took a basin of warm water and began to wash the blood and grime from Max. None of the cuts and scrapes seemed serious, and he did not seem to have any broken bones. At least, she hoped he did not. She had no idea how to tell if any of his ribs were cracked. He would suffer enough from the bruises tomorrow. When she had finished, she pulled up the thick quilt to cover him.

An arm snaked out to pull her down beside him.

"Suse," he murmured.

She tried to get up, but his arm held her fast, and she did not want to hurt him. He was injured, and she was trying to care for him, but that hardly meant she could lie in bed with him. It would be utterly scandalous. Unthinkable. She couldn't possibly...

After a moment's consideration, she stopped struggling. They were hiding in a hunters' shelter in the middle of a forest. Who would even know? And it was important to keep invalids warm. Everyone knew that. She tugged the quilt up to cover her as well, rested her arm across his chest, and closed her eyes. She was too tired to do anything else. How could this be wrong? It felt so right.

Twenty-eight

Stuttgart

IT WOULD BE DIFFICULT TO SAY WHICH ONE LOOKED
more exhausted, Lord Penworth or his wife. They sat
in matching horsehair armchairs in the lounge of the
Royal Hotel in Stuttgart. Lady Penworth had taken
one look around the gloomy, over-furnished room that
was apparently the best the hotel had to offer and had
retreated downstairs to recuperate from that day's travel.
The lounge was also gloomy, but at least it did not make
her feel as if the walls were falling in on her.

Leaning her head back, eyes closed, she said, "I had
not realized how difficult travel can be when people are
not tumbling all over themselves to be helpful. When
there are constant delays, so many frustrations."

Lord Penworth glanced about, but the only other
traveler in the lounge was a hearty burgher being presented
with a stein of beer by a young waiter. They were too far
away to overhear, even assuming they understood English.
"I'm sorry, my love. It's just that since we don't know
what is happening in Sigmaringen, what the situation is,

why on earth they are incognito—it seemed wiser to travel anonymously. At least, without mentioning the title."

"I do realize that, and you are quite right, my dear. It is just that it seems strange to be plain Mrs. Tremaine after all these years. And it is doubtless good for me to be reminded what life is like for the rest of the world. Under other circumstances, I would be enjoying the adventure." She shifted slightly in her chair and winced. "Perhaps I should rather say, twenty years ago I would have enjoyed the adventure."

Her husband looked at her with a smile. "I'm sure that twenty years from now, when someone offers you an adventure, you will be off in a minute."

"And you will be with me!" She returned his smile, but then it faded. "It's not the discomfort. It's the worry."

He nodded. "Elinor and Harry know where we are. They will send a telegram if they hear anything."

"And since there has been no telegram, they haven't heard anything." She completed the thought with a sigh. "Are we likely to reach Nymburg tomorrow?"

He shook his head. "Probably not. We can take a train as far as Tübingen, but then we will have to hire a carriage for the rest of the trip."

"Damnation!" she burst out. "Does that benighted country not even have a railway?"

"It does, but unfortunately there is only one train a week, and that will run four days from now. It will have to be a carriage."

"Augusta must have been out of her mind to take the girls to such a preposterous, backwards, uncivilized place. I am going to drag them all home the instant I lay my hands on them."

Twenty-nine

Max awoke in the pale light of dawn. His head ached, his shoulder ached, his back ached. Everything ached, and his stomach felt uncertain, but at the same time he was comfortably warm and...and something else. He could smell roses. No, he could smell roses and thorns. He managed to force his eyes to open.

Yes. Roses and thorns. Susannah was lying beside him, her head on his chest, his arm around her. He smiled contentedly and closed his eyes again.

His eyes snapped open.

Susannah was lying beside him?

He looked around in the dim light. Where the devil were they? Rude wooden walls, plain curtains on a small window, a cabin of some sort. It looked vaguely familiar. He had been here before, though he couldn't think when.

But Susannah? What could she be doing in a place like this? He had left her safe in the castle. No matter how angry the prince was, he would never have simply thrown the women out. Not Conrad. That was unthinkable.

What had happened? He remembered setting out for Krassau, but this was not Krassau. He knew Krassau. It might be rough and crude, but it had walls of stone, not wood.

And wherever he was, Susannah should not be here. She should be safe in the castle where he had left her.

She should be safe. Not here, wherever "here" was.

Grimly, he eased himself out of the bed without waking her and got to his feet. He almost fell back when a large, white beast rose beside him and waited. Lev. The dog was still protecting her. Max gave a sigh of relief and nodded his approval. That, at least, was as it should be.

The dog returned to his position, guarding the bed and its sleeper. Leaning a hand against the rough wall—he was feeling a bit shaky—Max made his way out of the room.

He found himself in a larger room of what looked like a hunters' camp. Rough, but comfortable, with antlers decorating the walls. A man wrapped in quilts was sleeping across the door. Josef? Max leaned over, holding on to the wall to keep his balance, and gave the man a shake. Yes, it was Josef, who growled before finally opening his eyes.

Once he looked up, Josef was immediately awake. "Count! You are all right then?"

"As you see." Max was somewhat comforted to see his servant here, but not comforted enough to relax. He was far too confused and worried for that. "What the devil is going on here? Where are we? And what is Lady Susannah doing here?"

Josef smiled. "Ah, she is a fine lady, that one. A warrior. It was she who saved you."

"Saved me? From what?" Max demanded.

And so Josef told him the whole tale—Angriffer's plot, Lady Susannah's spying on the Herzlos twins, the ambush and the rescue. Max had to sit down when he realized that Lady Susannah—his Suse—had been risking her neck. This was impossible. It could not be allowed.

"How could you let her endanger herself like that?" he demanded furiously. "She was supposed to be safe in the castle. How could you let her go with you?"

"Ach, you should have seen her. A Valkyrie she was. How could we stop her?" The old man shrugged. "And why would we try?"

"Because she should be kept safe, that's why!"

Max shook his head in confusion. She had raced off to protect *him*? No, it was for him to protect her! What madness was this? Everything was topsy-turvy.

How could Josef have allowed her to run into such danger? There had been an ambush; there had been weapons, gunshots. Did she think she could wave off bullets with her parasol? She had not been injured, true, but she could have been. It was a miracle that she had not been killed! He was ready to kill her himself.

And then he had awakened with her beside him...

"You let her sleep in my bed?" he roared at Josef.

The old man shrugged again. "You were cold, and we needed to keep you warm. I did not think it would matter."

She had been here all night with him? She had slept in his bed? She was willing to ruin herself, all to protect him? He shook his head in silent amazement. Was there ever such a madwoman? His woman. He was ready to kill her. Or to burst with pride. One or the other.

But just as she had protected him, it was now time for him to protect her. He had to keep her safe. He had to think.

It was not even a question of her reputation. She had been gone from the castle overnight. That was probably known by now. But no one except Josef would know what had actually happened, and there was no doubt of Josef's loyalty. That could be managed.

The real danger came from the Herzlos twins. There was no knowing how much disruption their plotting might cause, how much turmoil they could create. Things seemed to be approaching a crisis. They were taking more risks now if they were willing to try to capture him. That meant they no longer felt as if they were in control.

Yes, it would have been Dieter Angriffer who ordered the attack on him. Dieter would also take steps to ensure that his own head stayed on his shoulders. In many ways, Dieter had always been a daredevil, but he would not deliberately sacrifice himself. He would rather sacrifice others.

Max sat there trying to analyze the risks, the possible dangers. He needed to think clearly. Too much depended on him. He needed to think. But a bubble of joy kept rising to take over his thoughts: *She threw herself into danger to rescue me! She is mine!*

He had to concentrate.

Things had become more dangerous now. Even if

an open conflict with Hechingen and Prince Gottfried
could be avoided, it would be easy enough for Dieter
and the twins to start riots in Nymburg. If that happened, there was no way of controlling the outcome.
His own parents had died simply because they were in
the castle when the rioters broke in all those years ago.
What security would there be for a woman—a lady, to
be sure, but one who was without the protection of a
powerful family? One who was nothing more than the
companion of an elderly lady?

Susannah needed his protection, the protection of
his family.

She would be out of harm's way on his estates. It
was the only place he could be certain of her safety.
There, his men—all his people—would guard her.

Especially once she had the protection of his name.
Once she was Countess von Staufer.

That was it. Until she was his wife, he could not be
certain of protecting her. They had to be married right
away. No one would touch his wife.

"I don't know this place," he said abruptly. "Where
are we?"

"On your lands. This is one of the hunters' camps.
Your grandfather had them built."

Josef had moved over to the fireplace and was
calmly kneeling there to lay a fire.

A fire—that was good. It would be more comfortable for Susannah when she woke. "We'll need some
food," Max said absently. "She'll be hungry."

Still kneeling, Josef turned to look at Max. "We
didn't stop to pack a lunch when we went chasing
after you. I could try to catch a hare."

Max flushed. Of course they didn't have food. He wasn't thinking properly. But… "How far from Ostrov are we?"

Josef shrugged. "Not far. Perhaps an hour's ride. Maybe two."

"Good. You will ride to tell my aunt to prepare for a wedding today. And tell Father Milan." He rubbed a hand across his forehead. "A wedding in the village church. It must be there so all will see." He thought some more. "Lady Susannah will doubtless need some things for the wedding. Tell my aunt to be prepared."

The old man sat back on his heels and looked at Max. Then he smiled slowly. "She will be a worthy countess."

Max smiled too, the first time he had smiled since his confession to the prince. "I know." Suddenly he felt lighter, almost happy.

Josef paused in the doorway. "Emil should be here soon. He will tell you what he has done with the prisoners." It was almost a question.

"We will wait for him. I would not want him to worry," Max replied, answering the unasked question.

He heard a step behind him and turned. Susannah was standing there, one hand on the bedroom door. Her face was still flushed from sleep, but there were rings of strain under her eyes. She was wearing some bizarre costume that was all wrinkled and twisted, streaked with mud and dark blotches that were probably blood. His blood. Her hair was a tangled mess.

She was beautiful.

His bride-to-be. Happiness blossomed and filled him. She began to smile at him, but then her eyes filled with concern. "Should you be out of bed? Are you recovered?"

Such foolish questions did not require an answer. In two strides he was at her side and she was in his arms. His mouth claimed hers, and he drank deeply of her sweetness. After a moment's hesitation, she responded with all he sought and more, her softness yielding to his touch.

The sound of horses outside called him back to himself, and he lifted his head to listen. That Susannah was none too steady as he relinquished his hold gave him a rush of satisfied pride. Still, there was no time for that. Not yet. He pushed her behind him when he hurried to the window. It was one of his men, almost ghostly in the lingering morning mists, leading a string of horses.

Susannah recovered from his kisses more quickly than he would have liked, because she was right behind him, peering around his shoulder. "Oh, there's Emil," she said. "Has he been gone all night? What has happened?"

Ah yes. Josef had told him that his grandson was disposing of the attackers. Max opened the door and stepped out to be greeted by a flood of words as a grinning Emil proudly described his activities.

Max could not suppress an answering grin. It seems that his attackers were now tethered in various places in the forest: one in a cave, one in a thorny thicket, and one on a rock in the middle of a stream. They would all be able to untie themselves eventually, but that would be just the beginning of their woes. Emil had left them stark naked. It would be some time

before they found their way out of the forest—and
even longer before they would be able to convince
anyone that they were not escaped madmen.

"What is it? What has he done with them?"
Susannah had followed and was tugging at Max's sleeve.
She could not follow the Schwäbisch dialect easily yet.
"He hasn't killed them, has he?"

"No, no. They are a bit uncomfortable, but
unharmed." He had no intention of enlightening her
any further than that.

"What's this?" She had gone over to a couple of sacks
tied onto one of the horses.

He was curious as well, and went over to inspect them.

Emil explained, with a satisfied look. Since the attackers had all worn the Herzlos colors, he thought it might
be useful to bring their boots and clothes along. One
never knew when a disguise might be useful.

Max nodded appreciatively. Emil was a clever lad.
"You have done well, and I have another task for you.
I will write a letter, and after you have had some sleep,
you will take it to the prince."

The lad went off to take care of the horses, beaming
with pride.

"That really was very clever of him, bringing back
their clothes." She looked after Emil with a smile.

Her approval relieved Max, though he could not
think why he had worried that she might be overly
scrupulous. She had never shown herself to be anything less than practical. Good. She would see the
sense, the necessity of their immediate marriage.

But perhaps he ought not to mention it just yet.

Of course he should. What was he thinking? She

had just spent the night with him. No matter that it was all innocence, if only because he had been unconscious throughout. The first words out of his mouth should have been a proposal. Emil could have waited.

"Suse…" He reached out and tucked one of the dangling locks of hair behind her ear. She was so very dear to him, this woman who had come racing to his rescue. The love in his heart drove the words from his mind. "Suse," he said again.

She smiled.

There must be words he was supposed to say. He tried again. "I love you."

Her smile illumined her face. "And I love you," she said.

The joy in him burst out in laughter, and he pulled her into his arms and swung her around in a circle until she laughed as well.

He slowed the spin to a halt but kept his arms around her. "We will marry," he said.

She still laughed. "Is that a proposal?"

"Oh yes." He pulled her close and buried his face in her tangle of hair. "Yes."

She lifted her face to look at him. "Then my answer is yes."

Now she was his to kiss, now and always.

When he lifted his head again, his breathing was rough. "We must go to Ostrov now."

Thirty

SUSANNAH WAS HUNGRY AND TIRED AND SORE. THEY
had left the hunters' camp shortly after Emil's arrival
and before they had anything to eat. That was because
there hadn't been anything to eat except for a few sour
apples hanging from a tree by the door. And water, of
course. Plenty of fresh, cold water from the pump in
the yard.

Just the memory of washing in that icy water made
her shiver.

Now they were riding through endless forest—they
had been riding for almost an hour through the blasted
forest—and she was so far beyond uncomfortable that
she had no idea how to describe it. She was not accustomed to riding astride, not since she had been a child
racing across the moors near her home at Penworth
Castle. She was a young lady now, and she rode the
way a young lady should, decorously sidesaddle. At
least she usually did.

Yesterday she had ridden astride without a thought
of the discomfort because fear for Max had driven every
other concern out of her head. Today, he apparently

assumed that this was her normal way of riding and was setting the pace with no concern for her.

What's more, they were riding in silence. This was his land, he had said, but they did not want to attract attention, just in case. Just in case of what, he had not explained, and she had no energy to spare for demanding explanations. She had trouble enough just staying in the saddle.

She could not understand how he managed. It was not as if he had escaped yesterday's adventures unscathed. Aside from being drugged, which should have left him groggy, he had to be suffering from all those bruises. The black eye he was sporting made him look like a pirate, especially with the unshaven stubble covering his face.

Instead, she was the one suffering. A small moan escaped her as he increased the pace to a trot and her horse followed.

Apparently he noticed the sound, because he turned and asked, "Is something wrong?"

She gritted her teeth before replying. "No, what could be wrong?"

He beamed a smile at her. "We are almost there. The horses know and are eager for their own stable."

In that case, the horses knew a lot more than she did.

Where were they going?

"To my home," he had said.

Did he say anything more about it?

No.

Did he say why they were going there, rather than back to the castle?

No.

Where was Josef?

"He went ahead to get everything prepared," he had said.

What things?

He smiled and said nothing.

She was filthy, she was hungry, she was tired and sore. The blasted green cloak was all that was keeping her warm, and she had no idea where she was or where she was going. Max hadn't said a word about the fact that she had rescued him. Well, Josef and Emil had rescued him, but they couldn't have done it if she hadn't told them he was in danger.

He had said he loved her, and he said they were going to be married. She could not fault that. But then after just a single kiss he had practically shoved her back on this horse without a word of explanation except that they were going to Ostrov.

It took every shred of pride she possessed to keep from bursting into tears.

They came to the end of the forest, and at last they entered sunshine in a valley looking up at a hill.

"There it is!" Max sounded almost smug, as if the sunshine had been his accomplishment.

She realized that he was pointing at something off in the distance, so she looked. Then her jaw dropped. She made some sort of strangled noise.

He seemed pleased by her reaction. "My home. Ostrov."

"No, it isn't." Her voice returned, but as a cracked squeal of protest. "I saw your house. We went there when we left Baden."

That had been a pleasant, if neglected, residence.

This was… She didn't know how to say what this was. It was the entire top of a mountain, that's what it was. She could see at least two separate encircling walls with towers and more towers within the walls.

It was the size of a small city.

Off in the distance were fields, some with the stubble of this year's harvest, others with herds of cattle. A church steeple and a few roofs indicated a village or town not too far off at the base of the mountain, and a small river appeared and disappeared as it wove through fields and forests.

Above all this, Ostrov floated, a city in itself, looking as arrogant and assured as a lion, too powerful to worry about any possible challenges.

She was impressed.

She was terrified.

"When we left Baden?" He looked momentarily confused, then his face cleared. "Ach, no, that was not my home. That was only a small hunting lodge on one of my estates. Ostrov is the family seat."

"The family seat," she repeated.

Max was a count, Count von Staufer. She had known this, but she had not thought of his position as anything so, so *regal*. After all, her own father was a marquess, but their home, Penworth Castle, was modest compared with this. She didn't know any house in England that took its role as a castle so seriously. This wasn't the home of a gentleman or the estate of a nobleman. This was the seat of a ruler.

After a quick swallow, Susannah forced up the corners of her mouth into what she hoped was a smile. "Goodness, it's large."

"Large?" He looked at it with a slight frown, as if he had never noticed its size before. "I suppose it is."

"You suppose it is? Of course it is! For goodness' sake, it must be bigger than the prince's castle in Nymburg." This was not the time for false modesty.

"Perhaps. But we do not have a throne room." He grinned. "Do not worry. You will soon grow used to it."

"I will?" What did he mean? How did anyone grow used to a palace?

"Assuredly." Max sent her what was obviously intended to be a reassuring smile, rather like a pat on the head. "Come. They are expecting us." He kicked his horse into a trot and headed down the hill.

She bounced after him, calling, "Wait. What do you mean? Who is expecting us?"

He slowed until she was riding beside him again. The smile was still on his face. "Truly, there is no need to worry. It is only my family. I sent Josef ahead to tell them that we were coming."

"Your family. I am about to meet your family." Susannah thought she kept her voice admirably cool. At least she didn't shriek.

"Not all of them, of course." He grinned. "My parents are dead, I have no brothers, and my sisters have married and moved away, but I have a great many cousins and uncles and aunts. I think only my Aunt Magda is in residence—she makes her home here most of the time—and probably a few cousins."

She pulled up her horse. It took him a moment to realize that she was no longer riding beside him. He turned back, the grin fading to a look of concern.

"Count von Staufer," she said.

The look of concern deepened at her formal address.

"Count von Staufer," she repeated. "Look at me."

He looked, but in a puzzled way as if he had no idea what the problem was.

"I am a mess, a filthy, bedraggled mess!" Her voice was definitely approaching shriek level now, and she tried to lower it. "I am in no condition to meet your family."

He laughed. "You look far better than I do."

That was possibly true but only because she didn't have a black eye.

"Do not worry," he continued happily. "Aunt Magda will have arranged things. We will both be able to clean up and change before…"

"Before what?" Susannah asked suspiciously.

"Before the others arrive." He shrugged and waved at Ostrov once more. "Look. It is not far. We can be there within the hour."

Thirty-one

SUSANNAH BOUNCED ALONG BESIDE MAX—THERE didn't seem to be any alternative—but she had not failed to notice that he hadn't looked her in the eye when he replied to her question.

They rode up a grassy path. It was quite steep, but through the trees she could see glimpses of a paved road that wound more gradually up the mountainside, presumably for carriages. A stone bridge, wide enough for the largest carriage to cross in comfort—and for both of them to cross side-by-side in equal comfort—brought them across a sort of chasm to the gate in the first wall. Whether the chasm was natural or man-made, she could not tell, but both the bridge and the wall were of carefully dressed stone and well maintained. A stout defense.

At the gate, which stood wide open, an elderly man in a uniform of sorts stood at attention with a broad smile on his face. Max sent a smile and wave in his direction, which made the man smile even more broadly. Several faces could be seen at the windows of the gatehouse, but Susannah had no chance to observe more than that.

It was perhaps a quarter of a mile to the next wall, and she could see a dozen cottages, each with its own garden, in the space with an orchard beyond. All the inhabitants seemed to be standing in their doorway or hanging out the windows, calling welcomes and smiling at Max. A small boy ran alongside the road, blowing a cacophonous tattoo on a tin trumpet.

It was a bit unnerving.

Max continued smiling and waving as they rode on the paved road to the second gate. It struck Susannah that he had grown more and more cheerful as they neared this place. It might be an intimidating pile, but it was also his home.

The moment they passed through the gate, the intimidation increased tenfold. The Gothic buildings of some sort of golden stone bristled with spires and turrets of slate. Beyond the courtyard immediately in front of them, she could see further spires and turrets, all rising higher and higher.

But buildings, no matter how impressive, she could deal with. The problem was the people.

There was no possibility that she could sneak into Ostrov unnoticed. Max had lied. Well, he had misled her. It was one thing to say that they were expected. She had thought he meant that there would be hot baths and food when they arrived. It was outrageous to find herself faced with a formal reception committee. What had he been thinking?

She closed her eyes. Why was she asking herself such an idiotic question? He was a man. He had not been thinking. It would never have occurred to him to think that she would object to being introduced looking like a…like a… Oh, she couldn't even think what she looked like. It was fine for him. They all knew him, and besides, he looked damnably attractive despite his dirt and bruises.

She, on the other hand… It didn't bear thinking of.

Servants lined up to bow and curtsy, and by the time she and Max had dismounted, three young men were surrounding them and clapping Max on the shoulder. All Susannah could do was try to hide behind him, feeling disgracefully grubby. This was not the way she presented herself to strangers. Not usually. But her life had left its usual path the day she first encountered Max von Staufer.

"Max, my boy. This is wonderful news." An elderly lady stood at the top of the stairs, leaning on an ornate walking stick. She was dressed in a beautiful mauve gown trimmed with lace. A cap of the same lace topped her white hair, and she was draped in pearls and diamonds. She could not be dressed more elaborately if she were awaiting a visit from the prince.

What was going on here?

Susannah did not have an opportunity to ask Max, because he had pulled her beside him and was propelling her toward the elderly lady with his arm about her shoulders.

"Suse, this is my aunt, Countess Magda von Staufer. Aunt Magda, may I present my betrothed, Lady Susannah Tremaine."

She smiled weakly. This was not precisely how she had expected her first introduction as a future bride to go. All right, she might expect to meet some members of his family before the formal betrothal ball that would be held at Penworth Castle, or perhaps in their London house…

Her attention returned to Max, who continued to speak to his aunt as if she—his *betrothed*—wasn't even there. "Is everything prepared for the wedding?"

Wedding? What wedding?

"As much as could be done on such short notice has been done." There was a touch of acid in Aunt Magda's voice. "Really, Max, you should have given us a chance to prepare properly. This haste—it is not seemly."

"It is necessary. I will explain later." He turned the power of his smile on his aunt, and her irritation seemed to melt away.

Susannah's irritation, or rather her distress, was growing stronger every second. It was rapidly turning into utter panic. She stood as tall as she could, and in the grande dame tones she had learned from her mother, she demanded, "What wedding? What will you explain later? Just precisely what are you talking about?"

Then, to her eternal humiliation, she burst into tears.

"Suse?"

Max's confused question was overridden by his aunt's exclamation. "Max, what is happening here? Are you telling me that you have failed to explain yourself to this poor girl? You are impossible!"

Susannah's feet were swept out from under her; Max carried her up some steps; and a minute later she was deposited on something wonderfully soft. Her sore muscles moaned with pleasure. She heard Countess Magda order a protesting Max from the room, and the next thing Susannah knew, she was sitting up on the sofa, sobbing on the countess's shoulder.

"He never said anything…not where we were going…or why…and I don't know what's happening…"

Countess Magda held an arm around Susannah and patted her gently. "Yes, I know my nephew. He means well, but he can behave like an arrogant ass, always assuming that he is the one who knows best. He is so accustomed to being in charge that he neglects to explain himself."

"He doesn't ask me, he doesn't even tell me…"

"Ach, that is so like him. It is because he has had to make all the decisions for so long now, since his parents died, since he was just a boy. He forgets that sometimes others must be consulted."

Susannah managed to slow her sobs to a sniffle. "He didn't say anything…and I didn't know there would be people. He introduced me to his family, and I look like a bedraggled frump!"

"Yes, men can be very stupid at times."

"And what does he mean about a wedding? Who is getting married?" Her sobs were subsiding into hiccups.

Aunt Magda pulled back and looked horrified. "You mean he didn't even ask you…?"

The door to the parlor was flung open, and Max strode in. "Aunt Magda, I am sorry, but I must speak with Suse."

"You certainly must. You should have done a great deal more speaking a great deal earlier, young man."

"Not now, Aunt Magda. You can scold me later." He sat down beside Susannah, drawing her away from his aunt and into his own arms. "Oh my love, my darling Suse, I never meant to upset you."

Aunt Magda sniffed. "You have a great deal of apologizing to do, Max. I suggest you get on with it. The poor child is worn out and bruised with you dragging her about." She stood up, but before she left, she looked back and smiled approvingly at them both.

The smile did not help. Susannah started sobbing again, and Max was trying desperately to stop the tears.

"You must stop this crying, *Geliebte*, beloved. It was important that we get here quickly. You must have realized…"

She sniffed, gulped down a few gasps, and pushed away from him. "Realized what, you foolish man? What was I supposed to realize when you didn't tell me anything?"

"But…but I thought you knew. We were too close to Hugo's lands. We had to travel quickly and quietly. I needed to get you here, where you would be safe."

"And there was some reason why you could not say so?" Anger had dried her tears. "And what is this nonsense about a wedding?"

"Nonsense?" Max pulled back himself in confusion. "I do not understand. You said you would marry me."

"Yes, but…but today?" The tears were threatening to return. "People don't get married just like that. There are things to do, preparations, and…and I should be married at *my* home." The sobs began again. "I can't be married without my family. I want my mother!"

"No, no, don't cry, my love. Don't cry!" He wrapped his arms around her and held her close, murmuring gentle endearments as he dropped kisses on her hair, on her cheeks. "I never want to make you cry. Please, you must understand."

The tears subsided again, and the sobs degenerated into sniffles as Susannah leaned against him. "What must I understand?"

Some of his tension eased. "I have to know that you are safe. Once we are married, you will have the protection of my name and title, but even more, you will have the protection of my family."

"Yes, but why can we not wait? My parents will not object. We could be married at Penworth."

"Suse." He sighed. "Think, Suse. We cannot wait. After last night, there would be scandal."

She sucked in an irritated gasp. "That is nonsense. We weren't even alone. But even if it were true, we could at least wait for Olivia and Aunt Augusta. They could be here—"

He interrupted her. "Hugo and Dieter will soon discover that the trap they set for me has failed. Before that happens, I must find the princess. Try to rescue her."

"Try?" Susannah's voice felt very small.

"No, I will rescue her." He smiled and rubbed a knuckle across Susannah's cheek to wipe away the tears. "But something could happen, something could go wrong. I must know that even if something happens to me, you will be safe."

She stared at him in sudden realization and nodded slowly. Yes, she did see, though not precisely what he intended her to see.

He thought there was even more danger coming. She knew it was real—she had heard that dreadful

Angriffer talking about killing Max and the princess as casually as one might discuss a move on a chessboard. They were evil, these people, with no conscience, only greedy ambition. That was why Max had brought her to this castle, this fortress. She had thought he seemed happy to reach here because it was his home, but she realized now it was relief he felt, because this place was safe. He had brought her to the one place where he believed she would be out of danger.

That might be his reason for urging an immediate marriage. It was not hers, of course, but now that she realized the situation, she saw that she had a motive of her own that was just as compelling.

The danger—and she no longer doubted that it was imminent—meant that there might not be another chance for them to marry. There was no way of knowing how much danger would be facing him— facing *them*—when they went to rescue the princess. No matter how big and strong he was, no matter how brave he was, there was risk. He could be killed. Since his life was going to be in danger, this might be the only chance she had to marry him.

Whatever was to come, she would be his wife. On that she was determined. She had known when she set out with Josef and Emil to save him. She had known then that she was committed to him, bound as completely as any marriage ceremony could bind her.

But if he thought she was going to let him go charging off and get himself killed while she stayed safe here in his castle, he had a great deal to learn. Yes, he would rescue the princess, but he was not going alone. She was going to be right there to keep *him* safe. Marriage would give her the indisputable right to do so.

After that, after the physical danger was past, they could face the problem he did not yet know about— her parents. They would not be pleased to find that she had married a man they did not know, a man she had known for only a few weeks.

They would not be pleased to find that she had been married without any of her own family present.

They would not be pleased to find that her marriage meant she would be living in a foreign land.

She did not want to think about her mother's reaction when she learned that a third daughter was being married in another country, and not from her own home.

Her parents were not going to be pleased.

❧

At least she did not have to be married in her sister's grubby exploring outfit. Aunt Magda—it was hard to think of her as anything but Aunt Magda after sobbing on her shoulder—Aunt Magda had not only provided her with a huge tub of steaming, scented water and a maid to brush all the tangles and dirt from her hair. She had also produced a wedding gown.

It had been the wedding gown of Max's mother. It was a bit old fashioned, with its pointed waist and the elaborate embroidery down the front of the skirt and around the hem. But once the enormous puffy sleeves and the odd little cape were removed, it was quite lovely. The heavy cream satin had not stiffened or discolored with age in the slightest. When Susannah first tried the dress on, it had fit almost perfectly.

"Ah good, very good." Aunt Magda smiled approvingly. "We wore our skirts a bit shorter in those days, but Elisabeth was very tall. The length is just right for you."

Susannah was not sure she liked being dismissed as short, but when she saw herself in the cheval glass, she saw a princess from a fairy tale. Her hair had been curled into ringlets, and the lace veil was held in place on her head with a crown of pale-yellow roses— yellow roses symbolizing joy. Where they had gotten the roses at this time of year, she did not know. But they were perfect.

She blinked back tears and turned to Aunt Magda. "My mother would love this dress. And my sisters too."

The older woman smiled with understanding. "As soon as all this"—she waved a hand dismissively— "this foolishness about that princess is settled, Max will take you to your family. Do not fear."

And then it was time.

The fairy tale continued as she and Aunt Magda rode to the church in a carriage pulled by four white horses. With them was an old man who looked to be at least a hundred years old, a mere memory of a man, a fragile creature dressed in the embroidered silks of a century ago. He said nothing, though he smiled constantly. Aunt Magda said he was her uncle, Baron Arnost, and would walk Susannah down the aisle. Susannah couldn't help worrying that he might be too frail to make it, but apparently he had accompanied all four of Max's sisters down the aisle at their weddings. He had become a symbol of good fortune.

When they arrived at the church, a pretty yellow building with an odd, bulbous roof atop the bell tower, Susannah helped Baron Arnost to descend from the carriage. After teetering for a few moments, he found his footing. With a beaming smile, he offered her his arm.

Which of them was supporting the other was unclear. Susannah's head was spinning with the oddness of it all. Nothing seemed quite real, neither the four white horses, nor the lace veil on her head, nor the little gnome walking beside her.

But then she stepped into the church and saw Max standing at the altar, tall and strong and solid. He was real, and nothing else mattered.

Thirty-two

MAX FLOATED ON A CLOUD OF EUPHORIA. WHATEVER might happen in the future, at this moment everything was right. Susannah, his *wife*, was on his arm, smiling and charming the villagers as they came up to offer their good wishes. Never did she put a foot wrong. She knew, somehow, precisely what should be said to everyone who spoke to her.

How did she know? She managed to make sense of even the strangest bits of Schwäbisch dialect and laughed at her own efforts to reply, enchanting everyone. And when the fiddlers began a lively polka, she looked at him with a question in her eyes. He knew the answer that had to be given and swung her, laughing, into the dance while his people cheered.

They loved her already. Josef had doubtless told them of the way she had flown to Max's rescue, and if he knew Josef, the tale had lost nothing in the telling. Except the part about where she had slept last night, of course. Josef would never mention that. But her courage? Her daring? Those the old man would have praised to the skies.

He needed to have no fear. Today in this celebration she had wordlessly told his people that she would shelter and protect them as well, and they had sworn to protect her. She had become one of them. She had in no way sacrificed her dignity or denied her station, yet she had bound herself to them. Where had she learned that? Learn it she had, however.

More than he had known, he had found his perfect countess.

In a few hours—less than that, for the sun was vanishing behind the mountains—she would truly be his.

❧

Aunt Magda and Mama had much in common, thought Susannah. They both set the world around them into order with seemingly effortless efficiency. Ordered it, that is, in the way that they thought proper. They would have been astonished had anyone suggested a different organization.

It was not that Susannah was complaining. To arrange a wedding and a wedding banquet on mere hours' notice was a Herculean task. She doubted any royal household or any army quartermaster corps could have accomplished it. In fact, she was quite sure those bureaucracies could never have managed. They lacked the imagination.

Even here in the bridal chamber the results of Aunt Magda's care could be seen. Six gardenias floating in a shallow bowl lent their fragrance to the air. Yellow roses, gardenias—the castle greenhouses must be extensive. A fire blazed in the fireplace—less efficient than a tile stove, perhaps, but more romantic.

Susannah stood before it, burying her bare toes in the fur hearth rug, and a shiver trembled through her.

It wasn't that she was cold. She was covered neck to toe in a nightgown of fine white cotton, trimmed with lace and delicate white embroidery. That would not have kept her warm, but over it she wore a robe of soft blue wool and had a cashmere shawl draped over her shoulders.

No, it wasn't the cold that made her shiver. It was the uncertainty. She didn't know what she was supposed to do. Should she stand here by the fire? Should she get in the bed? It was an enormous bed. Well, Max was so big that he doubtless needed an enormous bed. She had a momentary vision of him sprawled out on top of it. Just the thought flashing through her mind was enough to make her blush furiously.

She blinked to clear away the vision and studied the bed. There were several feather beds piled up on it, and quilts—white, with complicated stitching—on top. If she lay down on it, would she disappear, swallowed up by the feathers?

Perhaps she should stay right where she was.

She knew what to expect. Sort of. It was just as well that her sisters, Elinor and Emily, had decided that there was no point in her waiting for Mama's talk the night before the wedding. They had assured her that it was really marvelous, the most wonderful thing she could imagine.

She hadn't been entirely convinced. It all sounded awkward and uncomfortable, not at all delightful and exciting.

Except…

Except that whenever Max held her, even when she thought about being in his arms or just stood next to him, there was this unfamiliar heat flooding deep inside her, and she felt this yearning.

A small noise, a mere click, made her jump. Max was there. He had just come through the door from his dressing room and had a quizzical look on his face. She could feel herself blushing furiously. Could he possibly know what she had been thinking about?

He came over to her and took her hands in his. She smiled at the way her hands vanished in his big ones. His big, strong hands that made her feel cherished. She looked a little higher, not quite ready to meet his eyes. He was wearing a blue satin robe with velvet lapels. It looked very dashing. She started to say so, but the words froze on her lips.

He wasn't wearing anything else.

She was looking straight ahead, and in the vee between the lapels of his robe, she could see the dark curling hair on his chest. It wasn't as if she had never seen a man's chest before. She had seen his yesterday. But it hadn't seemed the same. Yesterday she had been washing the blood and dirt off him. With all the worry about how badly he might be hurt, she hadn't been able to appreciate it properly. This was different. She lifted up a hand to touch the curls.

"It's soft and sort of bouncy," she said.

"Does that please you?" His voice sounded odd, as if he were being strangled.

She did look up at him now and smiled. "Yes. Yes, it does."

The kiss that followed was sweet and tender, at least at the start. Then it grew warmer and warmer.

When Max broke off the kiss, Susannah couldn't restrain a little whimper of protest. He rubbed his cheek against her hair. "Ah, Suse, I don't want to hurt you."

She rubbed her cheek against his chest. She did like the way those curls felt. "Elinor and Emily—my sisters—said it doesn't hurt, not really. Well, Emily said it hurt a little the first time, but she thought that was because she hadn't been expecting it."

"Your sisters told you...?"

She could feel a rumble of laughter in his chest. It was reassuring, somehow, so she nodded. "And they wouldn't lie to me."

"Well, in that case, do you think we could...?" He lifted his head and indicated the bed.

Her nod was all that was required. He picked her up and carried her over to the bed, the shawl and robe getting lost somewhere on the way. When he sat her down on the edge, she discovered she had been right. She sank into a sea of feather beds and couldn't help but giggle.

He laughed as well. "I see Aunt Magda is determined that we shall be cushioned against any pebbles or peas, at least for this night." He touched a finger to the lace at the neck of Susannah's nightgown. "Pretty."

"That's from Aunt Magda too."

"In that case, perhaps we should remove it. We would not want to damage Aunt Magda's nightgown."

She shifted to allow him to lift the nightgown over her head. Then she lay back amid the billows of the feather beds and watched as he tossed aside his robe. He was magnificent. She must have actually said the word aloud, because now he blushed.

He joined her, sinking down with her into the cushioning feathers. They began with laughter and kisses and caresses. He touched her breasts and she gasped in surprise. She knew gentlemen seemed to find breasts fascinating, but she didn't know they were a source of pleasure for her too. Especially the nipples. Then he touched her in other places, even more surprising, and she gasped and cried out until a conflagration consumed her completely.

Some time later, she was lying on his chest, his wonderfully broad chest, tangling her fingers in those soft curls of hair.

"You cry out in English, you know." His word caused a tremor in his chest. A pleasant tremor.

"Do I? Do you mind? You cry out in German. I think." She was not really certain.

"Why would I mind? What we do, what we say, it is all ours. Only ours."

His laughter was silent, but she could feel it deep inside him and she smiled. As she fell asleep there, with his arm around her to keep her safe, she thought she would have to tell her sisters that they had been wrong.

It was far more wonderful than they had said.

Thirty-three

Nymburg

PRINCE CONRAD STRODE DOWN THE HALL. GUARDS sprang to attention, but he ignored them all. They looked sideways at each other, nervous. They had never seen the prince up this early in the morning. Nor had they ever seen him with such a stern expression on his face.

He marched down the marble corridors alone, with no trail of courtiers, servants, or minions waiting to do his bidding. His boots, and his alone, created an echo as he left the royal apartments and advanced on the apartments that had been allotted to the princess and her ladies. As he bore down on the door, one of the guards hastened to swing it open before him.

A wry smile lifted one corner of Conrad's mouth. Even the guards sent by Captain Staufer recognized that a prince did not wait to be announced. He stood in the center of the sitting room, waiting, while the door closed behind him.

Was she asleep, whatever her name was? The thought

that she might have slept the night away peacefully while he had tossed and turned and paced the room—it was not to be borne. He had not had a moment's peace since her confession, and she was lying abed?

No, she wasn't asleep. Someone was moving around in the bedroom. Feeling no need to be courteous, he flung that door open and marched in.

There she was, as beautiful as ever, with those huge brown eyes and those golden curls. At least she looked pale and drawn, as if she had slept no better than he had. Good, he thought savagely. He wanted her to suffer too.

Her belongings were strewn about the room, and she had been piling them into the open trunk. He frowned. A servant should be doing that. Why had she not called for one? Did she think she could simply slip away from a palace without attracting any notice? She could not be so foolish as that.

She stared at him wide-eyed, looking more like a frightened rabbit than a princess. Was that what she really was? A rabbit that had been caught up in someone else's scheme? But whose scheme? Staufer's? General Bergen's? Hugo's?

She dropped into a deep curtsy, ever graceful. "Your Highness," she said in that soft voice that he had found so charming. That he still found charming.

He shook his head to dispel the charm. She was false, entirely false. A creature of someone's imagination—his own, at least in part. He would not allow himself to be charmed by a lie.

"Why?" The word burst from him like a sob. "Why did you do it?"

She shrank back, looking down, and shook her head just a little. Her voice shook as well. "I only wanted to help. We didn't mean any harm. None of us. We were only trying to help."

"Help? By making a fool of me? By…by *seducing* me?" He spun away, unable to look at her.

"No, please…" She began to sob. "I know you're angry, but…but the general said it could mean war… and it would only be for a day or so…and…and…and I wasn't supposed to fall in love with you!" Heaving sobs made more words impossible.

Those last words…he couldn't deal with them. Not now. But her earlier statement… "War? There is no war. What are you talking about?"

She was taking great gulping breaths in an effort to stop crying. She did not cry attractively, he noted. Her face was all splotchy and the noises she was making were not pretty. He should have been disgusted by the sight, but somehow he wanted to comfort her. She cried like a small child. "Here," he said gruffly, handing her a handkerchief.

With a silent nod, she took it, blew her nose rather loudly, and blotted her eyes. "Thank you," she whispered, still not looking at him.

He kept his face impassive, his voice cold, as he asked, "Now, what is this nonsense about war?"

"Princess Mila ran away while the general and Captain Staufer were escorting her. He said—the general, that is—he said that her father, Prince Gottfried, might use her disappearance as an excuse to invade Sigmaringen."

Conrad snorted dismissively, but then paused.

Gottfried was always casting covetous eyes in the direction of Sigmaringen. The marriage was supposed to create an alliance, but still… Then his anger returned. "Even if that was not a completely ridiculous idea, why keep it from me? Is not the prince the one to be told of threats to his realm?"

"I don't know." Her voice was still a whisper, a fearful whisper. "There was a message when we arrived in Nymburg—they were worried. I think that is when they found out that the princess hadn't simply run away, and they weren't sure who had taken her." She looked up at him uncertainly.

"Bergen and Herzlos!" He spit out the names. "Those two old men, forever mistrusting each other." He ran a hand through his hair. "They will not tell me what I need to know for fear that the other will find out too. Is there no one I can trust?"

"Captain Staufer wanted to end it. He wanted us to leave." She reached out to touch his arm. Her hand fluttered there, but then fluttered back. "I wanted to stay. I thought you might be in danger—but you might be safe if we stayed until they found the real princess."

"Even you thought I needed to be protected? Does no one think I can be a prince?" He gritted his teeth against the pain of that thought.

"Oh no! That is not what I thought at all! I just wanted…I just wanted to stay a little longer. To pretend I was the princess you might someday love."

He gave a bitter laugh. "Oh, you did that well enough, my princess." Turning his head to look at her, he said, "I don't even know your real name. Who are you?"

"Lady Olivia de Vaux, Sire." She dropped an automatic curtsy.

"Olivia." He was trying to hold on to his anger, but a small smile tugged at his mouth. "A pretty name, that."

For a moment they stood there, teetering on the edge of something neither one quite understood. Each one took a slight step toward the other. Her hand rose in an uncertain gesture. Offering? Pleading?

A moment later they were in each other's arms. She was hiding her face against his chest and was sobbing again. He rested his cheek on her head and rubbed her back gently. Through the soft wool of her dress he could feel the stiff corset. It seemed wrong that her garments should be stiff when she was so soft herself. He murmured words, sounds with no meaning, but full of meaning. Words of comfort. He knew now. This was what he must do—comfort her, protect her. This was his true purpose.

Her sobs slowed, and he put a hand under her chin to ease her face up. "There now. You will bruise your face on all this silly braid. I can see the imprint of it on your cheek already." He dropped a light kiss on the mark. "Now there will be no more tears, and you will tell me about yourself."

With his arm around her, he led her into the sitting room and seated her beside him on the sofa. "Now then, Lady Olivia de Vaux, you are English? How is it that you speak German so well?"

She lifted a shoulder dismissively. "My nurse when I was a small child was German, so I spoke German before I spoke English. And then Susannah and I had a German governess."

He frowned, confused. "She is your sister, Lady Susannah? You do not look alike."

"No, no." She smiled slightly. "Her sister married my brother, Harry—he is the Earl of Doncaster—and her mother, Lady Penworth, took me in hand, so to speak. I stayed with them, and Susannah and I shared a governess."

A flash of hope sprang up in him. "Your brother is an English nobleman, then? And your parents, they are dead?"

"No. My mother is living." Her lips tightened into a thin line.

He ignored the expression on her face and continued his own train of thought. "You are of the English nobility, all of you. Lady Susannah and Lady Augusta as well?"

"Oh yes. Lady Susannah's father is the Marquess of Penworth. He is very important. And Lady Augusta's brother was the Earl of Greystone."

"But this is excellent!" He cupped her face in his hands and turned her toward him. "Do you not see? An English noblewoman, the daughter of an earl— that is someone I could marry. It is not what was expected, but it would not be a mésalliance."

But instead of responding to his feeling of joy, Olivia looked at him in despair and shook her head.

"You do not wish to marry me," he said flatly.

The sound she made was half laugh, half sob. "There is nothing on this earth I could wish for more. But I could not let you marry me." She raised a hand to silence him while she turned away to collect herself. "I told you my mother is not dead. She is living, I am told, in Naples these days, but her notoriety is still remembered in England. Officially, my father was the Earl of Doncaster. He acknowledged us all, at least. Unofficially, no one knows who my father was, not even my mother." Olivia smiled bitterly. "She could not even be faithful to her lovers."

Conrad stood up and marched stiffly over to the window. He wanted to smash something. Anything. He slammed his hand against the glass. It shuddered, but did not break. Outside, the wind ripped the last leaves from the trees.

Can I have nothing?

Turning back to her, he demanded, "Do you love me?"

"Yes, oh yes. You must know that I do."

In two strides he was beside her again and pulling her up into his arms. His kiss was fierce, devouring. She responded with equal hunger and yearning.

When it was again time for words, he spoke hoarsely. "I will not give you up. I will find a way. You must trust me."

"I do."

He kissed her again, but this time their embrace was interrupted by a shriek.

Lady Augusta burst into the room, still in her bedclothes though it was almost noon, waving a sheet of paper. "What is this? What is this?" She halted abruptly and stared at the couple, still locked in an embrace. "Oh no, my dear, oh no. This is not wise. Really, it is not. And you, Sire, you should not be here at all." Then she looked down wildly at the paper again. "And this!"

Stepping away from Conrad, Olivia led the old woman to a chair and took the paper from her hand. She returned to Conrad's side so they could both read it.

"No, O—princess!" Lady Augusta started up in protest. "He must not… You must not…" She pressed her hands to her mouth.

"Hmm?" Olivia looked back at her and smiled. "It's all right. The masquerade is over. We have told the prince everything."

"Oh dear." The old woman sat back down, chewing her lip. "You should not have done that. You know what the general said. He was quite insistent that you should not tell the prince anything. He will not be happy."

"*Gott im Himmel!*" Conrad stared at the paper in horror. "That fool!"

"What is it?" Olivia snatched the sheet to read it herself.

"Max went off on his own to hunt for the princess, with no one to help him, and your friend discovered that he was heading into a trap. So she went after him!"

"Susannah went after him?" Olivia looked up wildly. "Susannah?"

Lady Augusta rocked in her seat and moaned. "How could she do such a thing? Whatever will I tell her parents? She really should not have done it."

"But where did they go?" Olivia tried to get a look at the letter.

"She doesn't say! She can manage to say that she went down the servants' staircase to eavesdrop, but she doesn't have the sense to say where this trap was. Damnation!" He crushed the letter in his fist.

"But Otto told Max to just wait," Lady Augusta said, still moaning in distress. "Why didn't they do as he said?"

Conrad glared at her. "Otto said! Otto said! General Bergen has said a great deal too much. If he is wise, he will have nothing more to say." He reached out a hand to Olivia. "Come. We will see if we can find some hint at least of where they have gone."

Late that afternoon, the prince was pacing back and forth in his private study. He had dismissed servants and secretaries, all of whom fled with relief. They were accustomed to dealing with a prince whose most characteristic temper was a kind of shy courtesy. They did not know how to react to this sudden onslaught of demanding irascibility.

General Bergen and Lady Augusta sat in a pair of chairs off to the side. They had chosen hard, uncomfortable chairs, the ones usually reserved for unwelcome visitors, as if they sought penance. The general seemed to have shrunk since his earlier private encounter with the prince. Although his bearing was still stiffly military, his lips were pressed tightly together and he no longer seemed to dominate the room. As for Lady Augusta, she kept uncharacteristically silent, though her eyes darted from the prince to Lady Olivia and back again.

Although Olivia shared the prince's worries, she was less concerned about Susannah and Max than she was about Conrad himself. She was cocooned in the comforting cushions of the plush chair in which he had placed her, but her face showed nothing but worry.

It was the prince who dominated the room. Even the desk with its broad expanse seemed to have shrunk to an accessory. When his pacing brought him in front of the window, the late-afternoon sun seemed to seek him out to bathe him in light.

He did not notice. He stared out the window as the shadows lengthened across the courtyard garden.

A servant entered almost soundlessly, but the faint click of the door latch was enough to make them all swing about to face the intruder, who gulped nervously before he managed to speak. "Baron Herzlos and the baroness left early this morning, in some haste their servants say. They left no message about their destination, but they were seen on the road that leads to the baron's hunting lodge at Krassau."

The general raised his head and demanded, "And Count Herzlos? Where is he?"

The servant looked at the general and blinked nervously. "I believe he is still in his office." Turning back to the prince, he continued, "The count did not know that his son had left the castle. Do you wish…"

The prince made a dismissive sound and waved the servant away. He waited until they were alone once more before he turned on the general. "Have you not done enough harm with your stupid feuding? Never an honest discussion. Oh no. Instead, you are forever undermining each other so that neither of you can ever be trusted to give me an honest answer."

The general's mustache quivered, but he did not speak.

The door opened once more, and the nervous servant crept back in, holding a tray before him like an offering. "Excuse me, Sire, but a messenger brought this from Captain Staufer."

Conrad almost leaped at the servant and snatched the letter from the tray. "A messenger? Send him in. I may have questions."

Ripping open the letter, he scanned it quickly and gave a shout of laughter. He handed the first page to Olivia and said, "While we have been driving ourselves half mad with worry, Max and Lady Susannah have gotten themselves married."

"What?" Olivia read the letter quickly and handed it back to him. "Goodness gracious. How? Where? I never would have expected Susannah to do such a thing."

Lady Augusta started to rise and then fell back in her chair, clasping her hands to her breast. "Oh dear, oh dear, oh dear. They will never forgive me. How can I ever explain to Anne and Phillip? How could I let such a thing happen?"

Conrad looked at Olivia in confusion.

"Lady Susannah's parents," she said.

"Ah. But will not be pleased by the match? Max is, after all, a count."

"And her parents are the Marquess and Marchioness of Penworth," snapped Lady Augusta, twisting a handkerchief in her hands. "I should have been watching over her. They trusted me."

The general reached over to pat her hand but thought better of it and shrank back into his own seat.

"But what is the problem?" Conrad asked Olivia, still looking confused.

"I don't think they will have any objection to Max. Not really." Olivia sounded doubtful. "It's the suddenness of it all. And it's so far from her home."

Conrad continued to look confused but returned to the letter. His expression immediately turned to satisfaction. "Yes! He knows where she is. Krassau—Hugo's hunting lodge. No wonder the twins are fleeing there." He turned to the final page and gave a shout. "Yes! At last!"

They all turned to him.

A smile of delight spread across his face. "Max proposes to rescue the princess tomorrow. It is as well that he is sharing his plan because he does not know that Hugo and Helga will be there. He will stop at a farmhouse we both know—we have stopped there when we were out hunting—and will wait there until three if I care to join him. If!" He threw his head back exultantly. "At last!"

Olivia laid a hand gently on his arm. His expression softened as he looked down at her. "This is what I have been waiting for. You understand, do you not? It is not only that he has left it to me to decide whether I shall join him or not. I must join him, for he does not know what he will be facing. He does not know that Hugo will be there—and doubtless accompanied by Angriffer."

Conrad began to pace about the room, thinking. "General, you are about to be of use. I will need a troop of your men to accompany me, and you may come as well if you choose. Have them ready to leave by six tomorrow morning. That will get us there in good time."

"As you wish, Sire." The general stood and saluted formally, but his fierce mustache did not quite cover his hopeful smile.

Thirty-four

Ostrov

THE SUN HAD NOT YET RISEN, BUT IT WAS NO LONGER night. The chill gray light that precedes the dawn had crept into the room. Max could see well enough to dress himself, and he did so silently so that he would not awaken his bride.

His bride. His.

In the dim light, her hair was a dark shadow on the pillow and he could make out only a faint suggestion of her face. Not that he needed light to know what she looked like. Her face in all its many moods was always with him. Longing for her stabbed through him. His great regret was that he had never had a chance to watch her while she slept.

Perhaps he would. If all went well, they would have a lifetime together. There would be a thousand mornings when he could watch her while she slept and awaken her with a kiss. She would turn to him, all soft and rosy with sleep. They would have a lifetime of love and joy.

And if all did not go well—at least she would be safe. His family, his people would protect his wife against all danger. No matter what Hugo might intend, Susannah would be safe. That was what was important. She must be kept safe.

He leaned over and brushed a kiss on her hair. *Sleep well, my love.*

Stepping carefully, he left the bedchamber.

❧

As soon as the door clicked softly shut, her eyes opened and she sat up in the bed. Foolish man. Did he really think she would not notice his departure? The moment he moved away from her, she had felt the loss of warmth from his body. A week ago—a day ago—she would not have known what a sharp pang that loss could cause. But there was no time for such thoughts.

In the dressing room, her clothes from the day before—Elinor's exploring outfit—lay ready for her. Good. The maid had followed her instructions and brushed it all clean. Well, reasonably clean. Grateful once again that she needed no assistance to don these clothes, Susannah dressed quickly, pulled on her boots, and headed for the stables.

She kept out of sight and waited while they rode out. Max had Josef and two other men with him. Not exactly an army. He could not be planning any kind of frontal assault on Krassau. He must be intending to somehow sneak in and then sneak the princess out.

That meant she could be of help to him.

Max did not even realize how intimidating he could look. Not to her, of course, but to other people.

If he appeared suddenly before the princess and demanded that she go with him and obey his orders, she was quite likely to get hysterical. It was all very well and good to think that she would recognize him since he had been part of her escort in the first place, but she hadn't wanted to be escorted to Nymburg. She hadn't wanted to marry the prince. She needed to be assured that she wasn't just trading one imprisonment for another.

If he was accompanied by a woman who could speak to the princess calmly and reassuringly—namely, herself—it would all go far more smoothly. At least Susannah could help convince her that the prison of duty would be pleasanter than the prison Hugo had contrived. It would also keep her alive.

Susannah waited until they were safely out of sight before she moved toward the stables, then had to stifle a shriek when something brushed her leg. Lev looked up at her as if to ask why she had stopped. While her heart gradually slowed to its normal rhythm, she leaned on the dog.

"Well, Lev, it's probably just as well that you're here. You'll be able to help me if I get lost in the woods." She rubbed him behind his ears, and he rested his huge head against her. "But first I need a horse."

The dog trotted behind her into the stables. The grooms were apparently still asleep. A few horses turned and looked at her with sleepy indifference. It was fortunate, she decided, that her father had insisted that all his children be able to care for their own horses. That included saddling them. So she located the gray mare she had ridden before and set to work.

She would have used one of the sidesaddles in the tack room, but she wasn't sure the mare was accustomed to one. At least she and the mare were accustomed to each other by now.

In very little time, she and Lev were following Max and his men. It wasn't even difficult, she realized. Four men on a forest path created enough disturbance to make their passage clear.

It took about half an hour before she was close enough to hear them up ahead of her, and she kept back for another half hour before she heard Max say sharply, "Listen!" The horses up ahead stopped then. Since neither she nor Lev was attempting to be particularly silent, Susannah was surprised at the length of time it took Max to realize that he was being followed. He really hadn't been expecting it. There was something sweet and innocent about that. Any of her brothers would have been on their guard before they even left the house.

She stopped too, but then decided she might as well travel with them at this point, so she nudged the mare onward.

Max was in the middle of the path with Josef and the others behind him. He looked utterly dumbfounded when she rode into sight, so she smiled cheerfully.

"Suse." It sounded like a sigh. "What do you think you are doing?"

"I'm going with you, of course. I assume you are on your way to retrieve the missing princess."

"No." He lifted his riding crop to point in the direction from which she had come. "You are going back to the castle. Now."

"Don't be foolish. You need to take me along."

"Oh? Should Hugo's men decide to resist, you will be of great assistance, I am sure."

"You needn't sound sarcastic. Of course I won't interfere if there is any actual fighting." She tried to look shocked at the very thought. "But the princess is likely to be frightened—and just as frightened of you as of Hugo. You probably don't realize how intimidating you look. I'll be much better able to reassure her that we have come to help her, not put her in even more danger."

Max exploded. "For God's sake, woman, I married you to keep you safe, not to let you run into danger!"

He was going to be difficult. That was obvious. She tried to look upset. "I hope that wasn't the only reason you married me."

"No, of course not." He ran a hand through his hair and rubbed his neck. "You know that wasn't…"

She caught herself up. No, this was all wrong. This should not be like trying to wheedle her brothers into letting her do something. She must begin as she meant to go on. Max was her husband, and there would be no games, no trickery between them. She was not going to pretend that he had hurt her feelings, but she had to make him understand. She had to make him understand by giving him the truth. "No, I do know that's not why you married me, any more than I married you to keep myself safe. So you must know that I will not be tucked safely behind the castle walls. Not when you are going into danger. There is no safety for me without you. There is no life."

He froze in place, his hand still on the back of his neck. When he finally did move, it was to pull his horse up next to her. He did not touch her, but his look enveloped her as tightly as any embrace. "My love, you must be sensible."

"I am being sensible." Her words were half whispered so that only he could hear. "You must understand. You are my life. I cannot lose you. And so I cannot let you go off into danger without me. Not when there is a chance I could help you. Would you let me go off into danger alone?"

"Of course not!"

She pulled back enough to look up at him. "Then how can you expect me to stand by when you are in danger?"

"My love…" He groaned in protest.

She held firm. "Together, or not at all. That is how it must be, now and always."

The argument continued, more pleading than argument. How could he act, knowing she might be in danger? How could she stay behind, knowing he might be in danger?

Josef coughed to get their attention. "We need to be going."

"But Suse…"

The old man shrugged. "She is the countess. She has the right to go with you. And if you do frighten the princess, she will be able to calm her down."

"And I promise I'll keep out of the way if there's any fighting," she said.

"Ah, Suse." He took her by the shoulders and gave her a little shake. "I would have someone take you back and lock you in your room, but you would just climb out the window."

She offered a half smile. "True."

"So you must promise me that you will obey orders, just as my men will. I cannot be worrying about you all the time."

"I promise. I will not do anything to cause problems."

The five of them rode on through the forest in near-silence. The morning mist hovered in the hollows, and the damp earth muffled the hoofbeats. Lev trotted beside her, his white coat making him appear almost like a piece of mist himself. No one else seemed surprised by the dog's decision to join them, so she kept silent as well.

After another hour, keeping silent required a major effort. Under some circumstances she might have enjoyed the ride. Once the mist had burned off, the air was crisp but not really cold, bits of colorful foliage still hung on a few of the trees, and they were surrounded by the fragrance of the pine trees. Unfortunately, Susannah was still sore from all the riding yesterday and the day before, to say nothing of other activity.

Eventually—to her relief—they stopped beside a small stream to rest the horses and themselves. She sat down on a log. It was no softer than the saddle, but at least it did not move. Breakfast appeared from Josef's saddlebags—bread, a hard yellow cheese, and garlicky sausages that he cut into chunks with his hunting knife. To wash it down, there was icy water from the stream. Like the others, she ate with her fingers and drank from a shared tin cup.

It was a meal unlike any she had ever eaten, but somehow one of the finest. Max sat beside her, close enough for her to feel the warmth of him. It was enough to make her feel safe. He always made her feel safe.

"Do you see them smile?" He smiled too. "They are yours now."

She blinked in confusion.

"My men," he said, tipping his head toward Josef and the two other men—they had been introduced to her as Hans and Gustav—who had ridden out with them. "You sit here and eat with them, and do not scorn their food. You ride with them and do not complain. They would have protected you in any case because you are my wife. But now, now they will follow you because you have won their respect."

"Because I ate a sausage?" She choked down a surprised laugh. "They are easily won over."

He continued to smile at her, and there was pride in that smile. "Not easily. Josef will have told them that you rode with them to my rescue, that you never flinched on the journey, that you never complained. And now they see for themselves that you are prepared to ride with them, to face hardship, to do what must be done. My warrior countess."

"Goodness. All that from a sausage?" She flushed, embarrassed by the thought. She was about to protest that she was really a very conventional person, a proper English lady, but then a smile began to spread. Was she a warrior? Was that who she really was? A warrior countess. She liked that image of herself. It was certainly better than Susannah, the dutiful daughter, who always knew the proper thing to do and never caused anyone a moment's worry. That Susannah who had somehow become very boring.

She held her chin up a little higher. But a warrior countess did not mean she had no questions. She felt a bit foolish that she had to ask, but she could not see how she could be expected to know, so she asked, "What are we going to do? Is there a plan?"

Max grinned at her. "Is that why you insisted on coming along? You thought me such a fool that I would go running into danger with no plan?"

To her annoyance, a blush was heating her face. "You know I didn't think anything of the sort. But *I* don't know what the plan is. And if I don't know, I could be more of a hindrance than a help."

"Ah, don't worry, Suse. I will not let any harm come to you."

She sent him an exasperated look. "You are enjoying yourself, aren't you? You know perfectly well that I'm not worrying about myself."

"Yes, and yes." He was still grinning. "It is a pleasure to tease my wife. No, no, do not distress yourself." He raised his hands in surrender. "I will tell you all."

With a glance at his men, he said, "First we go to the farm of Hans's uncle. It is on my lands, but not too far from Hugo's hunting lodge. Only a few miles. There we may be joined by another."

"Another?" She could swear Max looked a bit shamefaced.

"I could not deny him the chance. He was right. We—I—must stop trying to protect him and allow him to rule."

"Him? Do you mean the prince?" Her voice rose almost to a shriek.

"Hush." He glanced over at the men, but they did not appear to have heard. "I do not know. It is his choice. I told him I would be at the farm until three."

She gnawed on her lip briefly. "Do you need his help?"

He looked down at her in surprise. "I? No. It is he who needs to act. Not for me, but for himself."

The farm was at the edge of the forest. The house itself was on a hill near the trees, a whitewashed building two stories high. A wooden balcony with a fancifully carved railing looked out from the upper floor. Nearby stood a barn and other buildings. Stubble in the rolling fields beyond showed that the harvest was over, though close to the house rows of vegetables were still flourishing. Farther off, cows stood about in a field. No other houses were visible, but a broad road at the bottom of the hill meant that it was not too isolated. It looked very peaceful, with smoke drifting lazily from the chimney.

It was not, however, quiet.

Aside from usual farm noises—chickens in the farmyard, ducks and geese by the pond, pigs somewhere out of sight but not out of smell, and the steady *chunks* of wood-chopping—a pair of dogs came running up, barking furiously. Large dogs, looking much like Lev, with loud barks. Threatening barks. Very loud threatening barks.

Susannah had been riding next to Max, so when he pulled up, she did too. Had she been alone, she would have turned her horse and galloped off in the opposite direction, but no one else seemed disturbed by the canine threats. Lev took up a stance in front of her and uttered a low growl that seemed to keep the others at a distance.

One of their young companions—Hans—continued past them, ignoring the dogs. Or being welcomed by them, since their barking changed in tone as soon as they recognized him. They let him through but remained on guard, keeping the rest of the party at bay while he disappeared into the barn. A few minutes later, he reappeared, accompanied by a sturdy man of middle years, struggling into a jacket as he hurried along.

"May I present my uncle, Johann Tischler," said Hans.

"Excellency," said the man, bowing to Max, "and Excellency"—bowing to Susannah—"welcome to my home. How may I serve you?" He looked up at Max nervously.

"We will be meeting some friends here, but until they arrive, we would like to wait out of sight. And if our horses could rest in your barn?"

"Of course, of course..." Tischler almost tripped over his feet in his eagerness. Susannah offered what she thought was a friendly smile, but he seemed to be knocked sideways by it. It was startling. She snuck a glance at Max, but he did not seem to consider this anything out of the ordinary.

Nothing seemed to strike him as out of the ordinary. He led her into the farmhouse kitchen as if he were leading her into the reception hall at the castle, ducking his head to avoid banging it on the door frame as if that were the way he always entered rooms. But he stopped, looking around with a pleased air.

A smile broke across his face. "Ah, it is just as I remember it. The most welcoming kitchen I have ever seen. You brought us here once before, Hans, when we were hunting." He turned to the woman nervously twisting her hands in her apron. "Frau Tischler, you had been baking, and served us some of the finest bread I have ever tasted."

The woman's eyes widened and she gasped as her hands flew to her cheeks. "Count von Staufer, you *remembered*?"

"But of course. We were all tired and hungry, and you welcomed us in and shared your meal with us. How could I not remember?" He brought Susannah forward. "And now I present to you my countess."

A flurry of greetings ensued. Lev followed Susannah into the kitchen, though the other dogs remained outside. However, a dog in her kitchen did not appear to distress Frau Tischler, who provided him with a bowl of water and a large bone.

Soon they were all seated around the large table that filled the center of the room, a table that had been scrubbed so clean it was almost white. In fact, when Susannah looked around, she thought this was the cleanest kitchen she had ever been in. The floor had been scrubbed as clean as the table; the whitewashed walls were indeed white; and the windows sparkled behind the deep sills on which herbs flourished in pots. A large pot of something that smelled deliciously savory simmered on the rear of the iron stove.

Pitchers of beer were placed before them, and for Susannah, a thick cup—almost a bowl—of milky coffee with lumps of sugar for sweetening it. Then came platters of bread and cheese, and a dish of bright yellow butter. When Susannah tried to give smiling thanks to their hostess, she discovered that the Tischlers had retreated to the shadows at the end of the kitchen and were keeping nervous watch over everything and everyone.

This was confusing. Not the coffee, or the bread and cheese. What confused Susannah was the awe with which the Tischlers seemed to view their guests. At one time or another, she had visited every tenant on her family's estate at Penworth. Sometimes she had been alone, sometimes with one or both of her parents. And while the tenants had been respectful, they had also been friendly. There had been none of this awe. This was almost medieval.

She froze with the cup of coffee almost to her lips. That was precisely what it was. Medieval. Feudal.

She carefully put the cup down, trying to keep her hands from trembling, and looked back over the past few weeks in Sigmaringen. How had she not seen it before? It was not simply that Baron Hugo was plotting against the prince. She had heard enough political talk in England to know that people were always jockeying for power, trying to engineer their opponents' falls. She knew they were not always overscrupulous about their methods, and she knew that the Irish Fenians were perfectly willing to use violence.

But this was different.

The Black Star Regiment was part of the Sigmaringen army, at least in theory, but in actuality, it was Hugo's private army. Max didn't have an army in that sense, but when he spoke of his men, when he said they would protect her, he did not mean they would protect her from social gossip and sniping. He meant they would physically defend her against attack, and he obviously considered that a real possibility.

The walls around Ostrov were not a fanciful decoration, like the Gothic walls and towers at Eglinton Castle or Strawberry Hill back in England. Ostrov's walls, like its hilltop setting, were intended to hold off an army.

Now that she had married Max, this was the world she would live in. How had this happened? She—cautious, always proper, unquestionably ladylike Susannah Tremaine—had barely hesitated before she had thrown herself headlong into adventure. Could she do this? Could she accustom herself to this alien world?

Panic began to rise in her throat, and she turned to look at Max. He must have felt her glance because he immediately turned to look at her and smiled, a wide, glorious smile that banished fear. Yes, at Max's side she could do whatever was needed.

As it turned out, they did not have a long wait. Less than an hour after they had arrived, a second party came down the road and turned in to the farmhouse. Although the man at the head of it wore ordinary hunting clothes, complete with a brush in his hat, he was followed by a small troop of soldiers wearing the uniform of the Royal Guard. They rode, unsmiling, in precise formation.

The Tischlers looked ready to faint.

Susannah stood beside Max in front of the house, waiting. There was so little expression on his face that she could not tell if Max was pleased that the prince had come or not.

The prince also looked impassive as he trotted up and pulled his horse to a halt only steps away from them. Then his face broke into a grin. "Well, Max, we go hunting together once more, eh?"

She could feel Max relax beside her, and he too grinned. "As you will, Sire."

Conrad swung down from his horse and came over to clasp Max on the shoulder. "It will be like old times when we were boys, will it not?" The grin faded. "Ah, my friend, I have missed you."

"Sire, I…" Max's voice broke. "I have been a fool. Can you forgive me?"

Conrad shook his head dismissively. "My fault as well. I should not have allowed myself to be ruled by others so long. But there is something I am not certain I should forgive." He smiled again, and shook a mock-chiding finger before he turned to Susannah. "Well, Countess, what have you done?"

She dropped into a deep curtsy, as gracefully as she could wearing such outlandish clothing. "Your Highness."

The prince held out a hand to raise her up. "Your friends are very angry with you—and with you as well, Count von Staufer. That you and Lady Susannah should wed surprised no one, of course, but that you should fail to invite us to the wedding… Severe penance will be required. At least two weeks of balls and parties will be needed before you can be forgiven."

He turned back to Max. "But first we must take care

of this little problem of ours, eh? Let us go inside, and you can tell me what you have planned."

Susannah followed them in, feeling bemused. Was this the same prince who had been so stiff, almost shy, when she first met him? Now he was not simply relaxed. He was jovial and, somehow, regal.

Things kept changing—people kept changing. She had always known who she was, where she belonged, what she should do. But ever since they had left Baden, she felt as if she could not be certain of anything.

Back in the kitchen, there was no longer a place for her at the table. Herr Tischler was invited to join Max and the prince, while she sat by the stove where Frau Tischler was trying to pretend she was busy stirring the soup. In actuality, both of them were listening carefully to the men's discussion.

Herr Tischler proved invaluable to the plotters. Although their village was on Max's land, it was the closest one to Krassau. Hugo's men had no desire to travel further than necessary to find a tavern—or to get home from one—so they had been frequent visitors of late. They had not been popular visitors, however. The innkeeper did not dare refuse to serve them—one does not refuse service to men bearing arms—but after the first few days, the barmaids had been replaced by the burly blacksmith and his sons.

Villagers had also been commandeered from time to time to work at Krassau. As a result, not only could Tischler provide a general plan of the hunting lodge, but he also knew the schedule of the guards. Two of them were drinking at the tavern now, and in about two hours, they would return to Krassau to relieve the guards on duty at the rear entrance. That was the entrance close to the cellars, the most likely place for prisoners to be held.

Next came a debate over the best way to gain entrance. Should they force the door while two of the guards were away? Should they follow the returning guards and force their way in when the door opened for them?

"How much do they drink?" asked Josef. "Enough so it would not be unusual if they need help getting back?"

Tischler shrugged. "Maybe, from time to time."

"Ach," muttered his wife, "they stagger so much they can barely stay on the road."

Max glanced over, having caught the mutter, and smiled. "Then it would be a kindness if a couple of strangers helped them to their door, no?"

The prince smiled as well. "And if a few more strangers enter with them, there may be very little difficulty at that end."

"Especially if important visitors appear at the front door, keeping everyone occupied." Max and the prince smiled at each other.

To Susannah's eyes, they bore a marked resemblance to her brothers when they were home from school and about to embark on an adventure that would certainly be forbidden if their parents heard about it. Shaking her head, she fished the bottle out of her pocket, walked over, and put it on the table in front of Max.

"What is this?" He frowned at it.

"This is what the intruder carried when he came

into my room. It is the same thing that they used when they attacked you, and you were unconscious for hours. With this you should be able to incapacitate the guards with a minimum of bloodshed," she said, thinking that might also mean a minimum of danger.

The prince widened his eyes in surprise. "Ah, Max, your new wife is a formidable woman."

Max fingered the bottle and looked at her with a smile. "And a formidable partner."

Thirty-five

WHATEVER IT WAS IN THE BOTTLE PUT THE GUARDS out very neatly, and they were tossed into the back of a wagon to be hauled back to Krassau. The wagon was something of a compromise. A vehicle would be needed to transport the princess if she was unable—or unwilling—to ride, but there were no coaches or carriages in the village. Something was also needed to transport the guards, and while they could have been draped over the back of a donkey, something with wheels was easier. This wagon was the cleanest one to be found, and it had not been used recently to transport anything particularly odiferous. No more odiferous than the guards, that is.

Princess Mila would probably throw one of her fits about the inadequacy of the arrangements, but Max did not really care. She would have to deal with reality at some point. The pampered and petulant princess had nothing in common with Susannah—his wife, his countess—who rode beside him through the darkening forest.

Soon enough they came to a fork in the road and

the party paused. Max beckoned Susannah to ride on with him the short distance to the edge of the forest. Ahead of them, the hillside had been cleared of trees for a hundred yards. Beyond that, Krassau loomed, dark and threatening.

Built of dark, almost black stone, it stood on a low hill. The entrance, through a round tower, was guarded by four armed soldiers. On the lower levels, the windows were mere slits in the thick walls. Not until the third story were there windows large enough to let in sunlight.

"Good heavens!" Susannah gasped. "How gloomy it is."

Max grinned. "Not very welcoming, is it? Hugo calls it a hunting lodge, but in reality it is an old fortress. Once upon a time, there were lords of Krassau, more robbers than lords, who preyed upon this area. That may have been what recommended the building to Hugo. It certainly couldn't have been the beauty of the place, because it has none."

Susannah was frowning at the castle. "I don't see how we're going to get in. They'll see us coming as soon as we leave the woods."

"That's why we aren't going in the front door. We'll leave that for the prince. The guards may belong to Hugo's regiment, but I doubt they know his plans. They'll not dare deny entrance to the prince. We'll be going through the rear entrance, the one provided for peasants and prisoners." He led her back to the fork, and they all followed a narrow track through the woods that came out farther down the hill.

It was almost dark when they faced the door at the

rear of the castle. It was wide enough for wagonloads of necessities, and though battered by the years, it still looked sturdy enough to withstand a siege. Max had no intention of testing it. Not if they could persuade someone to let them in. They left their horses tied in the trees, and Hans drove the wagon while the others walked beside it, virtually invisible in the dim light.

Max had been tempted to leave Susannah back in the trees, but the thought of leaving her alone in the night, even for a short time, filled him with dread. And that would have been if she had been willing to wait. So he had her walking behind him, with Josef behind her.

The hundred yards across the barren hillside stretched out forever. They all moved as silently as possible, but the jangle of the horses' harnesses seemed as loud as cathedral bells. When they finally reached the door, Max pulled Susannah to the side behind him, flattened himself against wall, and drew his saber. On the other side, Josef and Gustav did the same. Hans waited until they were all in position. Then, at Max's nod, he went to hammer on the door.

But his knock never came. He stood, his fist raised for a moment, and then stepped back in confusion. "Count, the door is open!" He kept his voice down but the tone was urgent.

The others cautiously stepped forward. It was perfectly true. The door stood slightly ajar. Max pushed it wider with the tip of his sword. The hinges creaked, reverberating in the silence. Signaling the others to wait, he stepped inside.

The dirt on the floor crunched under his boots, but there was no other sound. It was almost impossible to see anything in the gloom, but there was a lantern on the floor. He gave it a shake. There still seemed to be some oil in it. It was the work of a moment to light it, but it illuminated only an empty room.

Proceeding cautiously he came to a room with a table bearing the remains of a meal—some crusts of bread and a bit of sauerkraut on a platter, as well as a pitcher that, from the smell of it, had held beer. One of the mugs was overturned, as were the two stools. Several cloaks and hats hung from pegs on the wall, and a few boxes of ammunition sat on a shelf.

Of the guards there was no sign.

Josef appeared almost silently at his side. "What the devil is going on here?" the old man muttered.

Max wished he knew. He moved across to the door in the far wall and used his sword tip to push it open. He could hear a faint rumbling noise. A staircase led down, turning sharply. He followed it until the lantern illuminated a pair of cells. The rumbling noise came from four men lying on the floor, their loud snoring interrupted from time to time by grunts. They had no boots, though each had an ankle cuff chained to the wall, and they wore the uniforms of the Black Star Regiment.

"Well, now we know where the guards are," said Josef, "but where are the prisoners?"

"And who were the prisoners?" added Max, shining the lantern into the corners. It was unpleasantly damp down here, and it stank of filth. "I can't believe Hugo would keep the princess down here. Even if he had no respect for her rank, she is too valuable to him." He shook his head, frowning.

Back upstairs, Max waved the others in and had his men take the unconscious guards from the cart to join their colleagues in the cells. Leaving Josef to guard the door, he proceeded cautiously up the stairs to the main level of the castle. Susannah followed close behind.

They stopped at the top, where an ill-fitting door allowed voices through. Max recognized one of them immediately—Dieter, an angry Dieter, shouting loud enough to be heard.

"What do you mean, they aren't here? They should have been here with Staufer hours ago."

A mumbled response in an apologetic tone—a servant, no doubt—was cut short by a blow.

"Dieter!" That sharp tone belonged to Helga. Max was momentarily surprised to hear her address Dieter so informally, but he forced himself to concentrate on her words. "…the princess?"

"Sleeping, Baroness."

"At this hour?" Helga's annoyance was showing.

"Her maid said she was not feeling well and did not wish to be disturbed." The servant sounded frightened. Hardly surprising, if he served Dieter.

"She'll be disturbed soon enough." Dieter laughed unpleasantly. "Get out of here."

That dismissal must have been for the servant. Footsteps faded and a door closed. Was Helga still there? Yes.

"What can have happened to your men?" Her voice. She sounded uncertain. Max took some pleasure in that. It was high time her assurance was shaken. She should be the one worrying for a change.

"Either Staufer was killed in the ambush and they

were afraid to tell me, or he escaped and they were afraid to tell me. Either way, my little plan to blame the princess's death on him has been ruined." Dieter laughed again. "Pity. I would have enjoyed destroying Staufer's reputation along with his life."

A sudden onslaught of rage choked Max. He did not realize that he had stepped forward until he felt Susannah's hand holding him back. Even so, he had to breathe deeply several times before he could nod to her and ease back.

"But what are we going to do now? What if everyone accepts that imposter? That…that *creature*!" Helga was starting to sound more panicked than merely worried.

"Yes, her appearance did put a crimp in your brother's plans, didn't it? Now here we are with the real princess tucked up in the tower and no way to reveal her without admitting that we kidnapped her in the first place. A pretty puzzle."

"You find this all amusing? Well, it will be your neck as well if we don't find a way out of this. Don't think you'll be able to escape."

"I assure you, I have never thought that you would fail to throw me to the wolves if you were caught. I would naturally do the same. What, did you think I had joined in your little plot because I was besotted with you?"

There was the sound of a slap, a sucked-in breath, and then another slap, followed by a cry from Helga. Footsteps stumbling, then hurrying, and a slammed door. Then more footsteps, unhurried, and a door closing with a creak.

Silence.

Max waited, but the silence continued. Finally he nodded to Susannah and slowly inched the door open. He stepped out, sword in hand, and found himself in the Great Hall, a cavernous room with stone walls, barely illuminated by a dozen torchères bearing fat candles and an iron chandelier hanging from the beamed ceiling some thirty feet above them. Long windows on one wall must have allowed plenty of sunlight into the hall during the day, but now they were only stark, black oblongs, unsoftened by any draperies.

An oak table in the center of the room might have had some function in the past, but at present it held nothing but an empty decanter and an empty glass. A fireplace large enough to roast an ox was cold and empty. A stone staircase along the wall rose up to the balcony that circled the hall, presumably providing entrance to various chambers. It was there that the princess was most likely to be found.

Motioning Susannah to wait, Max began to climb the stairs as quietly as he could, but boots on stone steps did not allow silence. Any noise he made was drowned out, however, by a commotion at the front of the building. Before he could get very far, one of the rear doors was flung open and Dieter appeared. He halted abruptly on seeing Max.

A dozen expressions flashed across his face—surprise, anger, confusion—before he settled on unholy pleasure and drew his saber. "How kind of you to drop by, Max. It seems my plans may work out after all."

Max dropped down off the stairs and landed in a

swordsman's crouch. His own pleasure welled up in him. This is what he had been longing for—an open battle. He threw his head back and laughed. "You sent four men after me, and they did not succeed. Do you really think you are my match?"

"Yes!" snarled Dieter, and he drove at Max.

A flurry of thrusts and slashes were beaten back with no trouble, and the two separated and began to circle to room, each watching for an opening.

∽⌘∾

Susannah watched from the door in horror. They were smiling. Both of them were smiling, as if they were enjoying this. Were they out of their minds? Another flurry and clash of swords. She closed her eyes. Silence again. She opened her eyes. They were circling again.

They were out of their minds, both of them.

The door burst open, and they both jumped farther apart, thank heaven! In came Hugo, with Helga right behind him. They were in a state, wild-eyed and almost hysterical.

"The prince!" gasped Hugo. "He's here!"

"So?" drawled Dieter, not taking his eyes off Max. "If they all die here, your troubles are over."

"He's not alone, you fool," cried Helga. "He has a troop with him, and General Bergen as well."

"Ah. Then it seems we may have lost. Pity." Still keeping his distance from Max, Dieter took a quick glance around the room.

The door opened again, and this time the prince strolled in, still pulling off his gloves. "Dear me,

Cousin Hugo, have you been allowing your minions to play with swords? You know Angriffer has never been a match for Captain Staufer."

Angriffer ignored the prince, but Hugo slammed the door and barred it, throwing his back against it to face the room.

The prince gave him a pitying look. "You've lost, Hugo."

"That doesn't mean you win." Hugo drew his sword. "I can at least make sure you die too."

Conrad tossed aside his gloves and drew his sword as well. "This is foolishness. You have never been able to match me when we duel."

"No?" Hugo sneered. "But perhaps I just thought it politic to let my cousin the prince win."

In a moment the room was filled with the sound of sabers clashing and sliding and an occasional shout from one of the swordsmen. They had all stopped laughing and watched each other with deadly intent.

Susannah had no idea what to do. What she wanted to do was tell them all to stop acting like idiots. When her brothers and their friends started fighting, she had been able to stop them by dumping cold water on them, but they hadn't been using swords, at least not real ones. They had also been small boys at the time. Cold water would be unlikely to work this time, even if she had any.

She didn't even dare try to distract them. Perhaps if she opened the door, the troops the prince had brought would be able to separate them safely. She started to edge her way around the hall when she noticed Helga. The baroness was also edging her way along, but she was trying to get to Max and Dieter. And she had a knife. It was unlikely that she was planning to use it on Dieter.

Susannah quickly reversed course. The swordsmen were all moving so quickly, attacking, retreating, leaping from side to side, that Helga was having difficulty positioning herself behind Max. Her concentration on them gave Susannah a chance. One of the torchères was close to Helga. Susannah reached it just as Helga was raising her knife, and she sent it crashing down on the baroness. The weight of it knocked Helga to the side, and the candles went rolling about.

The clatter, combined with Helga's screech, momentarily distracted Max. With a shout of victory, Dieter charged, only to step on one of the candles and go flying himself, losing both his footing and his sword.

On the other side of the room, Hugo let out a screech as well when Conrad's blade pierced his shoulder, and he fell to his knees.

Max recovered more quickly than Dieter and kicked his opponent's sword to the side. Dieter rose slowly to his feet and backed away, with a glare for Helga.

"Dieter!" she cried out. "I was only trying to help."

"As usual, my sweet, your interference has done more harm than good."

"No!" She leaped up suddenly and ran for the stairs to the balcony.

This distraction gave Dieter a chance. He made for the rear door, only to run right into the waiting arms of Josef and the rest of Max's men.

Susannah opted to follow Helga. She could not see

any reason to allow the baroness to escape. When she reached the balcony, one of the doors was standing open and she could hear laughter, hysterical laughter.

The baroness came out slowly, still laughing, and waving a sheet of paper. "You've lost as well," she finally managed to say. "We've all lost. She's gone." She looked down at the confused faces below and shouted, "She's run away! Your precious princess has run away. She's made fools of us all."

Thirty-six

IN THE FIRST FLUSH OF VICTORY MAX AND CONRAD
had embraced and pounded each other on the back in
manly and brotherly exuberance. Max had embraced
Susannah with a somewhat different but even more
enthusiastic exuberance.

Then reality intruded. There were things that had
to be settled, decisions that had to be made.

A physician was called to deal with Hugo's wound.
It was not dangerous, but Hugo was nonetheless a
problem. They were, after all, in Hugo's castle surrounded by Hugo's presumably loyal servants and
members of his regiment. Those soldiers may not
have been aware that Hugo was intending to usurp
the throne, but that meant they had no idea why the
prince and Captain Staufer were here, in effect usurp-
ing that baron's castle.

Nor were they pleased to find themselves surrounded by the Royal Guard. The rivalry between
the two regiments had grown notorious over the
years, and they bristled at being given orders by
General Bergen.

It wasn't until Prince Conrad appeared and reminded them that their oath of loyalty had been to Sigmaringen, not to Baron Herzlos, that they settled into a kind of sullen acceptance.

A bandaged Hugo and a snarling Dieter were taken down to the cells to join the guards already chained there. The previous residents had been members of the princess's escort who had taken exception to her confinement. The guards didn't know how they had come to escape. All they knew was that their beer had tasted a bit odd—but not too unusual to drink.

Conrad and Max thought that Helga could not be confined with her brother in the dungeon. Susannah did not see why not, but she knew that men had these odd fits of what they considered chivalry. At any rate, Helga was locked in the room that had earlier held Princess Mila. She did not seem particularly pleased about this and tried to claim feminine weakness that had enabled her brother to lead her astray. Susannah intervened and made clear that Helga could quietly accept the princess's former quarters or she could share her brother's cell.

Eventually, the prisoners had all been provided for, the hunting lodge had been secured, sleeping quarters had been arranged, since it was much too late for a return to Nymburg, and everyone had been fed. But once all that had been taken care of, the euphoria of victory faded.

Prince Conrad sat at the head of the table with Max and Susannah on his right and General Bergen on his left. The dishes had been cleared away, and once the wineglasses had been refilled, the servants were dismissed. The candles on the table flickered in the drafts that seemed to be everywhere in Krassau, but still provided reasonable light.

They now had to face their final problem—Princess Mila. She was gone—that much the brief, jeering note for her captors had made plain. But where?

She had also left a letter to be delivered to her father. That would, presumably, contain more information. But it was addressed to her father, Prince Gottfried. Conrad, Max, and General Bergen were all agreed. They could not read a letter that was addressed to someone else. So there it sat, on the table within reach of each man but untouched.

Susannah now understood her mother's exasperation when her father was describing various diplomatic or parliamentary maneuverings. Men clearly had no common sense. They were perfectly willing to try to kill each other with swords or any other weapon that came to hand, but they boggled at reading a letter addressed to someone else.

"This is ridiculous. Suppose that letter contains information about some danger she is running into? Or some danger she is creating for others? You could be putting people at risk with your silly scruples." She took the penknife out of her pocket, warmed the blade in the candle flame, and slipped it under the seal on the letter.

The men gasped or choked or growled but made no move to stop her as she unfolded the missive.

Then she leaned back in her chair and began to read—silently. It was a lengthy letter. She smiled understandingly a few times and nodded more often. Once she emitted a sympathetic sigh.

When she turned to the third page, Max exploded. "Damnation! What does she say?"

She considered asking if their scruples extended only to reading the letter themselves but not to hearing someone else read it, but she decided she had teased enough. "Well, much of the letter is devoted to telling her father what she thinks of him in less than devoted terms. I'm afraid, Your Highness, that she was not enthusiastic about marrying you."

She couldn't resist. She stopped talking and returned to reading.

"Suse!" Max looked ready to throttle her.

"Countess!" The prince stretched out his arm to point his finger at her. "I would hesitate to put you in the dungeons, but you could be required to share Helga's room."

She smiled and put the letter back on the table. "I'm sorry. You can read it yourselves. Princess Mila, it seems, is in love with a Lieutenant Bauer. It sounds as if he was in charge of her escort?" She raised her brows in inquiry.

The prince and the general looked blank but Max nodded. "Yes, I think that was the fellow's name. Pretty fellow. All spit and polish." He wrinkled his nose.

"Well," Susannah continued, "it seems that he was sufficiently enterprising to engineer her escape from Hugo's imprisonment, and they have gone off to be married. She is not too clear on where they intend to settle. She mentions South America, but that's rather vague."

"But that's wonderful!" The prince slapped his hands on the table and beamed at them all. "There is no way Gottfried can expect me to marry his daughter after this. And so I am free to marry Lady Olivia."

The others looked at him with varying degrees of consternation.

While in many ways she thought Prince Conrad would be very fortunate to have Olivia as his wife, Susannah couldn't help feeling that having Olivia's mother as a mother-in-law, even tucked away in Naples, would be something of a drawback for a prince.

Max muttered something about Prince Gottfried and the chance that he might make more difficulties than Conrad realized.

But they were all tired. The problems would have to wait until tomorrow.

Some time later, Susannah lay half beside, half on Max, with his arms holding her in place.

"You aren't going to try to sneak off in the morning, are you?" Her words came out as a drowsy murmur.

A deep chuckle was the first response. "No, no more of that. From now on, we go together." He turned his head to drop a kiss on her hair. "It must be back to Nymburg and the palace tomorrow. But soon we will return to Ostrov. There is so much I want to show you."

"Soon." She sighed contentedly.

Thirty-seven

Somewhere south of Stuttgart

ONCE HE HAD ASSURED HIMSELF THAT THE ONLY actual damage his wife had suffered was to her hat, Lord Penworth turned to the carriage. That had suffered more grievous harm.

It stood tilted at a sharp angle, one wheel in several pieces. The coachman, who had been hired along with the coach, regarded it balefully. "It cannot be repaired, *mein Herr*. It must be replaced."

"That is obvious," snapped Penworth. "It must be replaced, or we must hire another coach. Which is likely to be accomplished more quickly?"

The coachman raised his hands in a helpless gesture. "Who knows?"

Penworth closed his eyes and prayed for patience. He opened his eyes and asked, with a reasonable approximation of calm, "How far is it to the nearest town?"

"Town?" The coachman looked uncertain.

"Or village? Or hamlet? Or any sort of human habitation?" The marquis's calm was rapidly evaporating.

"Phillip." Lady Penworth put a restraining hand on his arm, and he took a deep breath.

The coachman furrowed his brow and thought. "Ah!" His brow cleared and he smiled. "Not far, maybe a mile or so, there is a village. And with an inn. You and your lady can rest there while we fix the carriage."

"A mile or so, you say?" Lady Penworth kept her restraining hand on her husband's arm.

"Yes, gracious lady." The coachman beamed happily. "Down in the valley, and all downhill."

The coachman's good cheer was severely irritating Lord Penworth. He patted his wife's hand. "We could wait here while the coachman goes for help."

"We don't know what sort of help he is likely to find in that village," she said. "Besides, it's quite chilly. No, it's cold. We'll be far better off walking to the village. At the very least, we'll be able to have something to eat and wait out of the wind while the coach is repaired."

She was doubtless correct. It was cold, and it wouldn't be possible to wait in the coach. Not when it was tilted at that angle. But as soon as they had extricated Susannah—and Augusta and Olivia as well, of course—from whatever mess they had gotten into, he was never going to set foot in another German state.

Thirty-eight

BY THE TIME THE VICTORIOUS PRINCE AND HIS colleagues arrived at the palace, none of them were looking their best. The prisoners didn't even make it that far. They were locked away in the barracks of the Royal Guards. In the guest quarters, to be sure, but still under lock and key, with General Bergen remaining there to make certain they were secured. The rest of them rode into the palace courtyard feeling exhausted and longing for hot baths and clean clothes.

Weary though the prince may have been, he strode into his palace with an assured tread and an air of command that had not always been there. Max could not help feeling an almost paternal pride in the way Conrad had grown into his role. Problems lay ahead, certainly, but at the moment, with Susannah beside him, all was good.

Then they were interrupted by one of the palace officials.

He bowed to Max but spoke to Susannah. "Excuse me, Lady Susannah, but there are some visitors who have been waiting for you."

"Waiting for me?" She stopped in surprise. "Who…?"

The visitors were no longer waiting. An older couple stepped into the entrance hall. Their clothes were good, better than good, speaking of both wealth and taste, though a bit travel worn and dusty at the moment. The man—the gentleman—stood tall and straight, with an air of dignity about him. The lady beside him, her dark hair barely flecked with silver, had remarkable blue eyes. Familiar blue eyes. Max looked down at his wife. They were Susannah's blue eyes.

"Mama! Papa!" Susannah went flying across the room to their arms. There were hugs and exclamations and assorted inarticulate expressions of relief and delight before she said, "But what on earth are you doing here?"

"When you told us you will not be able to write to us for a while, what on earth did you think we would do?" Susannah's mother said acerbically. "Just sit there and wait?"

"Your mother was imagining all sorts of dire fates when we received Lady Augusta's letter telling us not to write," said her father, a bit more gently. "We feared you might have been kidnapped or injured or…" He shook his head instead of finishing. "And then when weeks went by without hearing from you…we didn't know what to think."

"I'm sorry." Susannah looked stricken. "We thought at first that it would be just a few days, but things got complicated."

"We have heard a bit about those complications from Augusta and Olivia," said the mother, not sounding placated. Having recovered from her relief, she was sounding increasingly irate. She was also ignoring Max, even though he was standing right behind Susannah, and his size meant that he was rarely overlooked.

Susannah's parents. Guilt struck him as he looked at them. He had not given enough thought to Susannah's family, even though she had spoken of them often enough, he remembered, and with fondness.

In the ordinary way, he would have called on them, asked her father for permission to court her and all that sort of thing. His family would have met with her family. There would have been negotiations, settlements—all the legal and social formalities.

He just hadn't thought about any of that. Marrying Susannah had seemed so definitely the right thing to do. Or, if he were to be honest, the situation had offered a reason for him to do exactly what he wanted to do and to avoid all those formalities.

Susannah—his wife—smiled up at him, and his face relaxed into an answering smile. She took his arm to pull him forward. He clasped a hand over hers. Her parents might see it as a possessive gesture. Well, that is what it was. He was putting them on notice. If only he did not look so disreputable.

"Mama and Papa, may I present Count Maximillian von Staufer. My husband. Max, these are my parents, the Marquess and Marchioness of Penworth." Susannah sounded half defiant, half placating.

There was a moment of utter silence. It seemed no one even breathed. Then…

"Husband?"

Susannah winced. Her mother's shriek had probably

been heard not only throughout the palace but down in the town as well.

"*Marquess*? Your father is a *marquess*?" Max's roar was a good bit lower in pitch, but he did not doubt that it still thundered through the hall.

"How dare you, you blackguard!" Susannah's father advanced and seized him by the collar, ignoring the fact that Max was thirty years younger, several inches taller, and several stone heavier, all of it muscle.

"Villain!" cried the mother as she joined in the attack, swinging her parasol at him. He warded off the blow easily enough, but could barely restrain a laugh. He could not help it. It was so like the way Susannah had tried to drive him off with her parasol the day they met. Her mother was just like her.

"Stop it, all of you." Susannah pushed her way into the middle, and one of her mother's blows landed on her head with a sharp crack. "Ouch!"

That did bring things to a halt.

Max swung her into his arms, warding off the efforts of her parents to reach her, and pushed back her hair to examine her. "There is no cut, but there may be a bruise."

"It's all right." She looked up at him, and her eyes as well as her words assured him that all was well.

He looked up then and announced, "We had best remove ourselves to a less public place." Still with his arm around Susannah, he led the way into a small waiting room. The footman standing in the hall responded to his glare with alacrity and closed the door on them.

At his gesture, Lady Penworth seated herself in the

largest chair in the room. Lord Penworth stood beside her. Even in their dusty traveling clothes, they were far neater, far more polished than he and Susannah. Max suspected that it wouldn't have mattered if he were wearing his dress uniform and all his decorations. Susannah's parents dominated the room. In front of them, Max felt rather like a naughty schoolboy.

He looked down at Susannah, who was looking more nervous than he had ever seen her before. Taking her hand in his, he whispered, "My warrior countess." Her head went up, and she smiled up at him.

They turned to face her parents, but before either of them could speak, her mother did, looking at Max as if he were a pickpocket on trial. "May I ask how it comes about that you claim to be my daughter's husband when you have known her for what? A few weeks? Not even a month?"

He reddened slightly at the imperious tone—there was some justice to her complaint—but answered softly enough. In English. He reached for his English, feeling at a disadvantage in a language he did not speak well. "I realize it may…seem…hasty, but every-thing… It has been not usual."

"Not usual." Lord Penworth snorted, and his whiskers quivered. "That's putting a pretty face on it. My daughter accompanies an elderly relative to a spa and ends up married to some upstart German fortune hunter. We'll see about that!"

"Papa, stop it!"

Despite his anger at the insult, Max could not entirely suppress his smile. Susannah was leaping to his defense. But it was for him to speak now.

Respectfully, he reminded himself. Respectfully. This was his wife's father he was addressing. He clicked his heels and made a stiff bow to the marquess. "My lord," he began. That was, he remembered, the way the English addressed their noblemen. "My lord, I must make assurances to you that my family is of the highest nobility. No one who knows me would speak of me so."

"Bah!" Lord Penworth waved a hand dismissively and turned to his daughter. "You seem to have gotten tangled up in some sort of mess here, but don't worry. We will take you home, and if there has been any sort of marriage, which I seriously doubt, we will have it annulled."

"No!" Susannah's cry was almost drowned out by Max's roar. He put his arm around her shoulders to hold her close by his side and was relieved to feel her arm wrap around his waist. For a moment he had feared…but no. She was his.

"Please, Phillip, this will not help." Lady Penworth reached out a hand to her husband, who went to her at once. She closed her eyes and seemed to be trying to collect herself. Finally, she lifted her head and sighed. "Susannah, we sent you with Augusta and Olivia so you could keep them out of trouble. What on earth has happened?"

"I know I should have stopped them, Mama, but…"

"No, it was entirely my fault," Max interrupted. "I never should have permitted this, this playacting in the first place. And when I saw the danger, I should have insisted that they leave."

"Oh no, that is not fair." Susannah seized his arm

and looked up at him. "You know it is not. You tried to send us away and we refused to leave." She smiled brilliantly at him before she turned back to her parents. "And it really has been wonderfully exciting. I wouldn't have missed it for anything."

That seemed to bring her parents to a halt, and eventually, the whole story was told. It could not be said that the Penworths were pleased, but they were no longer out for Max's blood. At least, not immediately.

Finally, Lady Penworth said, "We are all tired, and I know that I, for one, am sorely in need of a bath." She did not say anything about the others, but the way her eyes flicked over them implied that their need was even greater than hers. "Perhaps we should continue this discussion when we are all more ourselves."

They might continue to discuss it as long as Susannah's parents wished, but it would change nothing. Susannah was his wife, and his wife she would remain. Max did not care if her father was a marquess or a merchant. He did not care how sudden their marriage might appear. All that was unimportant. He and Susannah were bound together in ways far beyond laws and customs. They had faced danger together already. She was his warrior countess. They would defy the whole world if they had to.

Max rang, and a servant appeared instantly, probably having spent the interim with his ear glued to the door. Lord and Lady Penworth were escorted to their quarters. Susannah started toward her old room, adjoining Olivia's, but Max held her back. With an unexpected spurt of pride and possessiveness, he led her to his apartments.

❧

It was an odd feeling. She was no longer Susannah Tremaine. She was now Susannah Staufer, Countess von Staufer, and she no longer had to obey her parents. She would listen to them, of course, and consider what they said, but she was no longer required to do as they said. Not that they had ever tried to make her do something she disliked, except maybe be polite to boring guests, but still…

Now she was Countess von Staufer.

People would have to obey *her*.

That heady feeling floated her through a bath scented with elder flowers. It was a truly appreciated bath after all the riding she had done over the past few days, to say nothing of the other unaccustomed activity. The tub was so deep that when she leaned back, the water came up almost to her chin. She lay back and let her limbs just float in the hot water. Her head rested on the rim of the tub while a maid brushed her hair to get all the dust and dirt and tangles out of it.

The feel of the brush on her scalp was so soothing, and the water was so warm, that she closed her eyes drowsily to enjoy the luxury of it all. The rhythm of the brushing changed slightly, becoming firmer and more regular. Hypnotically regular.

A deep laugh made her eyes pop open. "Do not go to sleep, *liebling*. We must dress and dine with your parents and with the prince."

She sat up with a start, splashing water all over, she was sure, and gasping as she tried to cover herself, which only made Max laugh more. It was just as well that he was not dressed yet either, since the splashes splattered him and the towel that was his only covering. She pointed this out, and he laughed some more.

Then he leaned over and covered her mouth with his, and she stopped worrying about the water. She stopped worrying about anything.

Eventually they were dressed. Her clothes had been brought over from her old room, so to give herself confidence, she wore one of her favorite dresses, a green and blue plaid taffeta dinner gown. Her hair, however, was styled differently. A new maid dressed it in a chignon high on her head, covered with a pearl-studded snood and surrounded by a wreath of ribbons and pearls.

It was all very odd. She was herself and not herself, both at the same time. The new coiffure was more mature than her usual ringlets, and so was suitable for the Countess von Staufer, but the dress belonged to Susannah Tremaine. She had worn it any number of times in London and while visiting her older, married sisters—and even back in Baden. She felt as if she were two people at once.

She was staring at herself in the cheval mirror, still trying to decide who she was, when Max came in behind her. She met his eyes in the mirror, his laughing eyes. Then he reached around and hung a creation of diamonds and pearls around her neck—teardrop pearls hanging from looped chains of diamonds.

She was still staring round-eyed at herself in the mirror when he finished fastening the clasp.

"What on earth...?"

"It is one of the family jewels," he said with a shrug. "Aunt Magda sent it in case you wanted to wear it while we are here."

Susannah began to laugh. "And it will show my father that you are not a fortune hunter?"

His smile was only a trifle shamefaced. "That too," he said. "I must speak with you before we go down." He led her into the sitting room and seated her on the sofa. He sat beside her and took her hand in his, playing with her fingers before he began to speak. "I had not realized that your father is a marquess. I thought..."

"What did you think?" She was quite curious by now, since she had never before seen Max so unsure of himself.

He still did not look her in the face, but his mouth twisted in a wry smile. "I thought it was Lady Augusta who was the important one, and perhaps Lady Olivia. You were so protective of them, so very proper that I thought..." He laughed slightly and finally looked at her. "I thought you were their companion."

"You thought I was a *servant*?"

"No, not a servant." He shook his head to assure her. "Obviously you are a lady, but I thought perhaps...fallen on hard times..." His voice trailed off uncomfortably.

Suddenly things began to make much more sense. She drew in a startled breath and then began to laugh. "You thought I was all alone in the world, or at least from a poor family. You thought you needed to protect me. *That* is why you were so insistent that we marry right away."

He stiffened and turned his head away. "I had feared that you would be offended. I should, I suppose, be glad that you find it amusing."

"My parents will..." She stopped laughing and

paused. "No, perhaps it would be better if we do not tell my parents what you thought."

Scowling down at his feet, he folded his arms. "I do not like that I have put myself in this position with your family. I should have gone to your father, asked permission to approach you... I did not give you the respect that you deserve. It is right that he is angry with me."

She patted his arm. "Well, if it is any consolation to you, I thought you were one of those noblemen who decorate a court, living on sinecures and gifts. I had no idea that you practically ruled a kingdom of your own."

His head snapped up in shock. "You thought me a parasite?"

"No, no. Not that bad." She waved a hand dismissively. "I just didn't know how important you are."

"But anyone could have told you... Our estates cover almost a third of Sigmaringen. Everyone knows of the Staufer family. How could you not know? And if you did not know, you could have asked." He looked outraged.

She responded to his distress with a shrug. "Well, if we were in England, everyone would know of my family. You could have asked as well." Another thought struck her. "You aren't sorry, are you? That we are married, I mean."

"Never that." He reached over, picked her up, and pulled her onto his lap. "Never that. I am sorry that your parents are upset. I did not wish to offend them. But I am glad that I did not ask about your family. If we had to go through all the formality, it would have been weeks—months—before we could be wed."

For the next few minutes, they exchanged unspoken assurances that the existing situation was just what they wanted.

Max sighed and rested his forehead on Susannah's. "Your father, is he only rich or is he also important in England's government?"

"Papa? He doesn't hold any office, but they are always sending him off on diplomatic missions. That sort of thing."

Max nodded. "When you said his title, I thought I recognized the name. I must tell the prince."

Thirty-nine

WHEN MAX AND SUSANNAH REACHED THE DRAWING room, it was clear that Lady Penworth had not mellowed. She was standing by the fire, which did not seem to be warming her in the slightest, and addressed Max in icy tones. "Lord Penworth is with the prince. They wish you to join them."

Max bowed and fled.

Oh, he bowed politely and murmured courteous phrases, but Susannah knew flight when she saw it. She watched him vanish through the door with envy. He was going to have the easier task. Papa was easier to manage than Mama. She put on a serene smile and turned back to face her mother. At least she was trying for a serene smile. She was not sure she was successful.

Lady Penworth shook her head. "Come sit down, my dear. We must talk calmly about this situation."

Susannah knew her mother's "calm" talks. They generally consisted of an explanation of why what you had done or were planning to do was foolish, and why you should do as Mother wished instead.

Mama smiled gently. "Susannah, I know you. You

have always been an eminently sensible girl. I realize that I was being unfair to you, sending you off with Augusta and Olivia and expecting you to keep them in check. But you have always managed to take care of the younger ones and keep them within the bounds of propriety. I hadn't realized how difficult it would be for you to manage Augusta, who is so much older. And I know she can be a bit headstrong. We will forget about that."

She patted Susannah on the hand. "Now please tell me that this, this marriage of yours is only a joke, part of the bizarre masquerade you have all been engaged in."

This was not going to be easy. "No, Mama. It is perfectly real."

"You are married to a man you have known for only a few weeks?" Mama's voice was rising. "I cannot believe you would do something so outlandish, so utterly lacking in common sense. One of your sisters, perhaps, but you?"

A reputation for propriety could be something of a nuisance. "I know it all seems terribly hasty, but Max was just trying to protect me."

"Protect you? Protect you from what, precisely?"

Susannah was not sure just how to explain without raising her mother's ire even further. "He did not know who I was, you see. He did not recognize my name, so he did not realize whose daughter I am."

"Which only goes to show what a benighted backwater this abominable excuse for a principality is. For heaven's sake, child, the Austrian emperor had no trouble recognizing our name when you were in

Vienna, and this piddling little count of yours was unable to do so?"

"That is not fair, Mama, and you know it." Susannah was getting a bit annoyed at being treated like a wayward child. "The emperor might know who the Marquess of Penworth is, but he is not going to assume that any Tremaine who appears is a member of the same family."

Lady Penworth sucked in a long, calming breath before raising her brows. "And was there some reason for you to be keeping your father's position a secret?"

"It just never came up." That sounded sulky and Susannah knew it. More explanation was obviously needed, so she took a calming breath of her own. "I did not realize how important Max is. I thought he was just an ordinary officer, and I didn't want to intimidate him."

"Really, Susannah, this is so preposterous I don't know where to begin." Lady Penworth leaned back and closed her eyes. The silence had grown uncomfortable long before she sat up again and looked at Susannah. "Are you quite certain that this marriage is real?"

"Oh, yes, it is real. We were married in a church with a priest and any number of Max's relatives and the people from the village. Oh, Mama…" She reached out to hold her mother's hand. "I did so wish you were all there. It was all beautiful, but I missed you so."

Her mother did not seem to be appeased. "And such little details as a license? Banns? Your parents' permission? I know you are of age, but still, those are customary even in this benighted place, I assume."

Susannah paused for a moment, uncertain. "I don't think any of that matters. It's Max's village, you see."

"His village? He lives in a *village*?"

"Oh no. He lives in a castle. He owns the village. Quite a number of villages, actually. His estate goes on for miles and miles. I just meant that everyone does what he says."

"That's preposterous." Mama was beginning to sputter. "I don't care who he is. There have to be laws and such. Even Queen Victoria can't simply order a clergyman to perform a marriage out of hand."

"It seems to be different here. It's a bit feudal. On his estates, Max seems to be pretty much the ruler." Much as Mama enjoyed travel and exploration, Susannah suspected that in this case she was having difficulty appreciating what was "different." Explaining all this was difficult, since Susannah didn't really understand it herself.

❧

Max entered the prince's study and almost stumbled. Conrad was seated in the leather chair behind the broad expanse of the desk, looking very much in command and very much like his father. The resemblance had never struck Max so powerfully. It was not just a physical resemblance, he realized. It was the tilt of Conrad's head, the stillness of his hands as they rested on the desk. There was no doubt that the man sitting there was the prince. It was... Max did not know what it was. Disconcerting? Odd? Definitely new.

To the side, staring out the window, was Lord Penworth. He turned at Max's entrance and regarded him with less fury but no more fondness than at their first encounter. "His majesty has assured me that you must not be considered a fortune hunter, and I will accept that you believed this hasty marriage would serve to protect my daughter, but I tell you, sir, I cannot like it. I cannot."

To Max's relief, Lord Penworth spoke in German. Oddly accented, but quite fluent. Max forced himself to meet the older man's eyes. "I can understand your anger, my lord. I…" He was not sure what to say, how much to say. But this was Susannah's father, now his father-in-law. Not someone who would shortly vanish from his life. He deserved the truth.

So he blurted it out. "You are in the right. I should have asked about her family. But I…I wanted so much to have Susannah for my wife that I seized on the excuse. I told myself that she was alone, vulnerable, and that marriage with me would protect her. And that much is true. As my wife she will be safe, always. I myself will protect her, of course, but my people as well. You will never need to have fear for her well-being, I swear it to you."

"You wanted her for your wife?" Lord Penworth took a step toward Max. "That is what matters to you, what *you* want? And what of what my daughter wants? If I see the slightest hint that my daughter is unhappy, or even uncertain, I will have her home in a trice. And I don't care if you are the prince's chief advisor."

The prince's chief advisor? What was… Max gave his head a quick shake to clear it. That was a question for later. "You must, of course, speak with my wife"—he put a light emphasis on the possessive—"but she will not turn from me." At least, he did not think she would.

Lord Penworth bared his teeth, but before he could speak, the prince raised his hand.

"The countess—Lady Susannah—will, of course, decide for herself. I am sure you agree, both of you, that her wishes will prevail. From what I have come to know of her, I doubt any other way will be possible."

Max caught the twitch of a rueful smile on Lord Penworth's face before the cold mask reappeared. Yes, the father knew his daughter. But the husband knew his wife also. At least, he thought he did. He was certain. Almost.

The prince, however, had moved on to another topic. "Lord Penworth, since you appear to be the *paterfamilias* for all these ladies, I approach you. I wish to marry Lady Olivia. Do you give the approval for this?"

"Do I...? But..." The marquess looked utterly taken aback. It appeared to be an unaccustomed state.

Max took some consolation from that. At least someone else was sharing in the confusion. As for himself, his head was in a whirl as he turned to Conrad. "Marry Lady Olivia? But you were so angry..." His voice trailed off.

Conrad spread his hands on the desk and looked down with a secret smile. "It was not her fault."

Penworth harrumphed and seemed to collect himself. "I was under the impression that you were to marry Princess Mila. Was I mistaken?"

"It is obvious that is now impossible, since she has run away. That duty has been removed of her own accord. So, is there any sort of—I am not sure what to call it—any problem, any impediment that would prevent a marriage between me and the Lady Olivia? Please, seat yourself and tell me what you think."

Penworth settled himself and looked almost relieved to be asked to consider a less personal problem—less personal for him, at least. With a slight frown, he said, "I was under the impression that the heart of your difficulty was the need for an alliance with Hechingen. I can see that it is not possible for you to marry Princess Mila, at least at this time, but will it not anger her father still more if you immediately marry someone else?"

"Staufer can tell you that Gottfried will be angry no matter what happens. We will worry about that later. First comes the question of Lady Olivia. What say you?"

The marquess steepled his fingers while he considered how much to say. "It would be an unexpected match, certainly. Has Lady Olivia agreed?"

"She says it is impossible and tells me of her mother." Conrad waved a hand dismissively. "English gossip."

"Yes." Penworth drew out the word. He was relieved that he was not the one who had to tell Conrad about the Dowager Countess of Doncaster. "But that kind of gossip reaches further when the daughter makes a marriage like this one. And Gottfried sounds like the sort of man who would not hesitate to use such gossip."

A stubborn look came over Conrad's face. "With gossip we can deal. Let us put that to the side. Her brother, would he have objections?"

"Not if Olivia herself wished to marry you."

"And there is no legal difficulty? Your queen, Victoria, she would not make problems?"

"Hardly." Penworth permitted himself a smile. "Her own family is so entangled in marriages and relationships with the German states that she will doubtless be pleased by another connection."

"Good. You will tell Olivia so." A smile broke across Conrad's face, a happy, boyish smile of the sort Max had not often seen in recent years.

"Then if you will allow me, Sire, I would like to go and speak with my family."

"Certainly. You may depart. I need to confer with Staufer now."

Max waited until the door had closed behind the marquess before he turned to the prince and burst out, "What is going on?" He took a deep breath to calm himself. "I apologize, Sire, but I am somewhat confused." *To put it mildly.* "Since when am I your chief advisor? What has happened to Count Herzlos? General Bergen?"

"Calm yourself, Max. I seem to have conducted a palace coup of my own." His mouth twisted wryly. "General Bergen is still licking his wounds after the tongue-lashing I gave him when I realized that this stupid comedy you have all been playing was his idea. I believe he is being consoled by Lady Augusta. As for Count Herzlos, he naturally resigned all his offices when I told him of the more tragic games his children have been playing."

Conrad stood and went over to stare out the window. "He truly has served me well, you know.

After my parents were assassinated, he saved us all. Without him, there would no longer be a Principality of Sigmaringen. But now…" Conrad sighed. "Even if this had not happened, it was time for him to go. He will take Hugo and Helga with him to his own estate and keep them there. I owe him that much. And I have given orders for the Black Star Regiment to be disbanded. Those who wish to remain in the army will be distributed among other regiments. But what shall we do with Angriffer?"

Max nodded. "Yes, I see the problem. We cannot put him on trial without bringing the others into it. But we cannot simply turn him loose. He is a viper, and dangerous."

Conrad laughed shortly. "I envy my ancestors. They could have simply wrapped him in chains and dropped him in the Danube."

"A temptation." Max considered possibilities. "It will have to be exile, someplace far enough away that it will not be easy for him to return. South Africa, perhaps. He could make a life there, if he chose."

"Yes. Good. I am tempted to order General Bergen to accompany him, but I fear the trip might be too much for him. Ah, well, it will be arranged, and we will have to trust that Lady Augusta will keep the general in line. They are quite extraordinary, these English ladies, are they not?"

Forty

A WEEK LATER, THE ATMOSPHERE WAS SUBDUED AS they gathered in the throne room to await the arrival of Prince Gottfried. All were seated in couples around the room. General Bergen and Lady Augusta were farthest from the throne, keeping themselves slightly hidden by one of the pillars. Both were still feeling abashed—and perhaps a bit resentful—after the scoldings they had received from members of the younger generation.

Max sat to the right of the throne, with Susannah by his side. He was still self-conscious about his designation as chief counselor and could not help feeling that it was due mainly to the fact that after the banishment of the Herzlos clan and the disgrace of General Bergen, he was the only one left standing. It was not a position he felt ready to fill, and something would have to be done about that. Still, they had eliminated the danger of the Herzlos twins and Angriffer, and Susannah—his wife—was at his side. He felt ready to face anything that came.

Susannah was less optimistic. Max and the prince

had taken care of the physical danger with admirable dispatch, and as Max's wife, she ought to be worried about the remaining threat to Sigmaringen from Prince Gottfried of the irascible temper. However, what really concerned her was Olivia's future. She very much feared that her friend was going to end up with a broken heart. That she was so happy herself made her feel even guiltier about the unlikelihood of a happy ending for Olivia.

Opposite them were her parents. They were somewhat less furious about their daughter's marriage than they had been the day they learned of it. Lord Penworth had even had some interesting discussions about statecraft with Max as well as with the prince, both of whom were quite willing to listen to advice. But the Penworths were still far from happy.

Lady Penworth, in particular, continued to resent a wedding far from home and family. That her daughter would be making her home in a castle was not adequate recompense for the length of time required to reach that castle. Conrad's promise to improve rail service between Sigmaringen and the rest of the world had not reconciled her to the situation. Her concern for Olivia was all that kept her temper down to a simmer at the moment.

Next to Conrad, on a chair that was not quite a throne, sat Olivia. She had spent the past week alternating between euphoria because Conrad truly loved her and despair because marriage to her would bring him disgrace. Judging from her pallor, despair was uppermost at the moment. Could she have fled, she would have done so, but she could not honorably leave the others to face Gottfried's wrath. Not when her appearance was the only thing that had made the masquerade possible.

Conrad was the only one present who seemed to be at peace. Indeed, he seemed to be facing the future with serene confidence, certain that all would fall out as he wished.

The servants had been dismissed in the interests of privacy, though no one present would have cared to wager that the servants were ignorant of the situation. Still, even an illusion of privacy was better than nothing.

Breaking the silence, Lady Penworth asked, "Has there been any news of the princess?"

Max allowed himself a slight smile. "According to the telegram I received, the princess and the lieutenant managed to board a ship in Marseilles two days ago. There was some concern that they would not make it. The men I sent to follow them not only had to offer their carriage when the princess's broke down, but found themselves serving as witnesses at the wedding."

"But they are well and truly gone?" The prince couldn't keep a slight tinge of worry from his voice.

"Unless storms of unparalleled ferocity have raged through the Mediterranean, they should be safely on the Atlantic by now," Max assured him. "And definitely out of reach."

"I suppose it was necessary to keep the news of his daughter's elopement from Prince Gottfried until he got here." Lord Penworth frowned at Max, sounding as if he was still not convinced of the wisdom of this course.

Susannah tensed at his side, as if about to leap to her husband's defense. Max rested his hand on her arm and smiled reassurance when she looked at him. Only then did he turn to Penworth. "I thought it advisable. Gottfried flies into rages and has been known to issue rash orders when in a temper. This way, he will be able to rant and rave in private and will perhaps release some of the anger before he is in a position to order his troops into action."

"It sounds as if the man is a fool." Penworth made a grimace of disgust.

Max was not going to disagree with that assessment, and Conrad managed to restrain the smug smile of one who knows himself to be utterly reasonable.

"Surely he must see that an alliance is necessary for both of you," Penworth continued, addressing the prince. "I will be honest. I do not see much chance of continued independence for any of the small German states. Either Bismarck's Prussia or Franz Josef's Austria will swallow you all up. An alliance, however, may give you the leverage to demand better terms for your countries and your people. If he does not see that, he does not deserve to be a prince."

Now it was Lady Penworth who acted as the peacemaker, putting a restraining hand on her husband's arm. "That may all be very well and good, my dear, but I suspect that this is not the time for a discussion of the duties and responsibilities of a ruler. Like him or not, this Gottfried is the particular ruler that has to be dealt with, and it seems that tact will be needed—great, billowing bushels of tact."

When her husband harrumphed, she continued,

"You know how difficult it can be to deal with even our own queen when she gets some bee in her bonnet. I sometimes think there must be something about a crown that scrambles people's brains." Flashing a brilliant smile at Conrad, she added, "Present company excepted, of course."

The prince smiled back. "I have noted the same in powerful ministers. Herr Bismarck is a prime example."

Olivia had been growing increasingly fidgety during the discussion and now spoke up. "I begin to think I should not be here. Not here, sitting at your side. Surely this will only exacerbate Prince Gottfried's temper."

"No," said Conrad with finality. "You are to be my princess. You must accustom yourself to the irrational people you will have to deal with."

She gasped. "But I have not said yes!"

"You will." Conrad smiled and patted her hand.

Max started to frown his disapproval, but then it struck him that some might say he had been equally high-handed in his treatment of Susannah. He glanced uncomfortably at her and saw from the laughing look she gave him that the same thought had struck her.

Fortunately for his pride, the trumpets sounded and the doors of the throne room were flung open.

"His Royal Highness Gottfried August Leopold, Prince of Hechingen, Prince of Marienberg, and Knight of the Order of Saint Willigis." The herald followed this announcement with another blast of the trumpet.

They all stood to greet Gottfried. He marched in unattended, as was his wont. This was not a matter of humility but of vanity. Gottfried was a short man. He did not want to be towered over by the usual six-foot guards. Nor would he have tolerated a guard of men still shorter than he, which might have looked too much like a parade of children. Or dwarves. So unless he was on horseback, as he usually was out of doors, he walked alone.

Alone, but assured that every eye would be upon him. He wore a pale-blue uniform so bestrewn with orders and decorations that he glittered as he walked. His once-blond hair was now gray but still covered his head, and his mustache blended into side-whiskers so exuberant that his head seemed twice its natural width. It was a style favored by both Prince Wilhelm of Prussia and Emperor Franz Josef of Austria. Max wondered if either of those worthies would be flattered by the imitation.

But it would be foolish to underestimate Gottfried. For all his vanity and short temper, he was no fool, and those hard gray eyes had noted everyone in the room even while his attention seemed focused on Conrad.

"We welcome you to Sigmaringen, Prince Gottfried." Conrad inclined his head just enough.

"And it is a pleasure to be here." Gottfried did the same, and then clasped his hands behind his back to signal an end to the formalities. "Well, Conrad, you said that we needed to speak privately. Why, then, this audience?" He tilted his head to indicate those standing at the side.

"They are all involved in this affair. Please, Gottfried, come and be seated." The prince indicated a chair placed beside the throne. "And I have a letter that was left for you."

A frown began to crease Gottfried's brow, but since the chair was beside, not below, the throne, he seated himself with a flourish and held out a hand for the letter. At a nod from Conrad, Max placed it in the older man's hand.

Gottfried stared at the inscription as if the writing were unfamiliar, but when he turned it over, he seemed to recognize the seal. With a quizzical frown, he looked over at Olivia, who was sitting serenely motionless, looking off into the distance. He seemed about to speak, but changed his mind, broke open the seal, and settled back to read the letter.

A moment later he sprang to his feet, waving the letter in Olivia's direction. "What nonsense is this, Daughter? Have you lost your mind? Lieutenant Bauer, *pfah!*"

Olivia started to shrink back before the attack but quickly recovered herself. She was not going to be bullied by this preposterous little man, no matter what title he bore. "I'm afraid you are making a mistake, Your Highness. I am not Princess Mila."

"Don't talk like a fool. You can't simply decide that you no longer wish to be a princess. Your birth is your birth!" He advanced on Olivia, the letter crushed in his fist. "You are to marry Conrad here and forget this nonsense."

Conrad stood and imposed himself between Gottfried and Olivia. "Calm yourself, Gottfried. You need to hear the whole story. Count von Staufer will explain what has happened."

Max stepped forward and recounted recent events. He introduced all the participants and explained the masquerade as an effort to avoid scandal. His best efforts at a dispassionate recital did not prevent Gottfried's frequent eruptions into profanity.

"Who is this creature who has been masquerading as my daughter? Disgracing my name?" Gottfried sneered at her.

Olivia had been sneered at by ladies in London society. The open hostility of a mere German princeling was not going to intimidate her. She looked at him with icy disdain and said, "I am the Lady Olivia de Vaux, daughter of the late Earl of Doncaster and sister of the present earl."

Taken aback by her failure to cower before him, he turned to another topic. "Their heads! I want the heads of those miserable traitors!" Gottfried shook his fists at the heavens. Or perhaps in some other direction.

Conrad replied calmly, "They have been dealt with appropriately. You need not concern yourself any further."

"And Bauer and my daughter? Where are they now? Have you caught them?"

Max coughed softly. "I fear they eluded us. As best we have discovered, they are now on the high seas, sailing for South America."

"Bauer! I can't believe it. I myself appointed him to head my daughter's guard, and he has served her for three years…" Gottfried's voice trailed off as he thought, doubtless considering that the princess and the lieutenant guarding her had been much in each other's company for those years. And Bauer was a very handsome fellow. A river of curses spilled from Gottfried's lips, though at whom they were directed was not entirely clear.

"I know you!" A new voice broke into the proceedings, reducing Gottfried and everyone else to unexpected silence.

Like an avenging fury, Lady Augusta marched to the center of the room and pointed a finger at Gottfried. "How dare you go shouting at and bullying us? I recognize you now. Willy von Regensburg, that's who you are. Or that's what you called yourself when you were traipsing around London all those years ago."

Gottfried suddenly went bright red again and began to sputter. "Madame, I do not know you." He spun to face Conrad. "Who is this creature?"

Lady Augusta turned to the Penworths. "You must remember, Anne. Or weren't you in London that year? It's more than twenty years ago, but I'll never forget. It was an extraordinary scandal. The fellow had absolutely no sense of discretion. He was carrying on in utterly flagrant fashion with Georgina Doncaster. Everyone commented on it." Her voice trailed off as she realized the implications of what she was saying.

A sudden silence fell on the room.

Pale once more, Gottfried turned slowly to stare at Lady Olivia.

Lady Olivia stared at Prince Gottfried.

The others all looked back and forth from one to the other.

"With my mother?" Olivia's words were the merest whisper.

Lord Penworth was the first to recover. He cleared

his throat and approached Conrad. "Your Highness, this revelation casts a new light on things. Perhaps it would be more comfortable for Prince Gottfried if he were allowed to discuss this situation in private. If you would delegate me to speak for you?"

At Conrad's nod, Lord Penworth led the shaken prince from the room, speaking in a gentle tone suited to soothing a frightened child.

⁓

It took a few days for all the details to be hammered out, but by evening the general outline of the agreement was clear. There would be an alliance between Sigmaringen and Hechingen, creating a small but powerful alliance in Swabia. While there could be no formal treaty with Great Britain, the Queen and her government would be inclined to take a benevolent interest in a principality where the ruler was married to the sister of an admired English earl and a connection of the prominent Marquess of Penworth. The Prince of Hechingen was delighted at a marriage between his ally, the Prince of Sigmaringen, and the daughter of a noble English family with which he had deep ties of friendship.

Of Princess Mila, there was no mention. She had ceased to exist. Privately, however, Conrad intended to send her a handsome wedding present when she and Lieutenant Bauer reached their destination, wherever it turned out to be.

Forty-one

A ROYAL WEDDING WAS NOT SOMETHING THAT COULD be arranged in a matter of days. Or even weeks. The guest list had to include royalty and statesmen from around the globe, all of whom had to be placed in accommodations suitable to their status and not in excessive proximity to ancient enemies.

Banquets had to be planned to welcome the visitors. Butchers and bakers and candlestick makers began to plan ways to expand their businesses.

Activities were needed to entertain the guests during their stay. There would be balls and concerts and plays. That meant that in addition to the wedding guests, Nymburg would be hosting all the musicians and actors and performers. Extensions to hotels were planned, and householders considered how much they could charge for the use of a spare bedroom.

As far as Max was concerned, the greatest difficulty during those weeks was his attempt to convince Conrad that a prince needed a council of advisors, not a single man. Especially not if that man was Max, who felt utterly unqualified for the task of steering the ship of state, and who wanted nothing more than to take his wife home to Ostrov.

Conrad sat behind the desk in his private office and scowled at Max. "I am not asking you to do anything that Count Herzlos did not do. He had no council. He decided everything."

"He had been doing it for decades when he became regent for you." Max strode around the room in exasperation. "He had learned from your grandfather."

"Yes, he learned from my grandfather. And that is why nothing was allowed to change." Conrad's angry scowl remained. "He kept everything in his own hands. And that is why I know nothing."

Max had no answer for that. It was perfectly true.

"That's why I need you. I can trust you, and you will tell me the truth."

"Sire, I will always serve you to the best of my ability. And never again will I conceal the truth from you. But you need advisors who know things—things I know nothing of." Max ran a hand through his hair in a thoroughly undignified gesture. "For example, I know we need more railways, yes. But—"

Conrad interrupted him, nodding impatiently. "We do. We need them badly if we are not to become a neglected backwater. But Count Herzlos disliked them, so they were never even considered. You see the need and tell me about it. That is what I mean."

"But that is not enough! I can see that we need them—I have heard enough complaints from merchants, to say nothing of my wife's parents. But I do not know where it would be best to have them. Should they run to the mines? To the cities? Should they connect us to Berlin? To Vienna? And how should we pay for them? Should the state own them?"

"These are details." Conrad waved his hand dismissively. "Any clerk can find the information for you."

"Yes but…" Max shook his head in exasperation, and an idea came into it. "We could consult Susannah's father."

"The marquess?"

"Yes." Max seized on the idea. "He has been involved in the government of Britain, but he has no interest in Sigmaringen. He can use his experience, but he can also be neutral."

It took a bit of persuading, but eventually Conrad agreed, and Max laid his problem before his father-in-law. Then he had to persuade his father-in-law to help.

That was not as easy as it might sound. Susannah's parents were still distrustful. Max had hoped his request for Lord Penworth's assistance would flatter them, at least a little, and lead them to look more kindly on their daughter's husband. What he got was a pair of icy glares. The sympathy the marquess had shown in his efforts on behalf of Lady Olivia did not seem to extend to Max.

"I realize Sigmaringen is not like other countries, but is it not your duty to serve your ruler in whatever capacity he asks?" There was more disdain than sympathy in Lord Penworth's tone.

Max could swallow the sneer at himself. The sneer at Sigmaringen was almost impossible to swallow. He reminded himself that he needed to conciliate his father-in-law, and beating the older man to a pulp would not accomplish this. Max did not, however, keep the stiffness out of his voice when he replied. "I would think it my duty to give my ruler the best advice I can, and that advice is that my loyalty and friendship are not enough. He needs the counsel of men more knowledgeable and experienced than I am."

Lord Penworth stared at him impassively. Max had never known a man so adept at concealing his emotions. Still, Max saw—or hoped he saw—a slight glint of approval in his father-in-law's eyes.

"Very well. You are meeting with Prince Conrad again tomorrow at two? I will join you then."

Max bowed with meticulous courtesy, turned, and left the room with two pairs of eyes boring holes in his back. He then sought out his wife and spent a few restorative hours in her arms.

In Conrad's private office the next day, Max spoke for what seemed like hours, trying to explain all the areas in which he lacked knowledge or experience.

Conrad kept dismissing Max's concerns, saying, "What I need is someone I can trust, someone who will tell me the truth. You are the only man I know who will do that."

Finally, Lord Penworth spoke up. "If I may make a few comments, Your Highness." He smiled courteously, almost diffidently. Max found it hard to believe that this was the same rigidly correct man he had spoken to the day before.

"I can understand your need for a confidant," Penworth said, "but this does not have to be someone holding an official position. In many ways it might be beneficial to keep Count von Staufer in a private capacity."

"Why?" asked Conrad bluntly.

"I gather that those who saw Count Herzlos before his departure had no difficulty believing that he had resigned for reasons of ill health. However, he was well known, not only in your country but throughout the region, and experienced. If his replacement is an inexperienced young man, your neighbors may view Sigmaringen as vulnerable."

Conrad bristled. "Our army is more than able to defend Sigmaringen."

"But it is always best to avoid the need for its use. And besides…" Penworth hesitated. "I do not know how much you are aware of the ambitions of Prussia."

Conrad snorted. "Max is always warning me that Bismarck and Prussia want to swallow us whole."

"Is he?" Penworth shot a quick glance at his son-in-law. "Well, I think he is right. And if it isn't Prussia, it is likely to be Austria. There is this business with Schleswig and Holstein distracting them at the moment, but sooner or later, they are likely to clash. You, all the small German states, are caught in between them. You must not look weak."

"And you think that having Max as my chief minister would make Sigmaringen look weak?" Conrad looked incredulous.

"Frankly, yes. No one knows him—knows anything about him—outside your borders. You need to surround yourself with men of greater experience."

Conrad snorted. "I know the men who worked with Herzlos. Age did not give them wisdom."

"Perhaps not, but their gray hairs give at least the appearance of wisdom. You can ask them for advice, but you need not follow it. The fact that their names are known to your neighbors will be enough to provide reassurance."

Conrad suddenly laughed. "Playacting! More playacting! Shall we begin another masquerade, Max? Is that what Lord Penworth recommends?"

Lord Penworth looked startled and then turned to Max with a slightly embarrassed smile. "I suppose that is what I am suggesting. So often what matters is the appearance of things."

Max raised a shoulder in rueful acknowledgment. "And now we must learn what lies behind the reputations of others. Who are our friends and who are our enemies?"

"And whom can I trust?" A bitter smile twisted Conrad's lips. "Not any of the men who surrounded my uncle, but who else has any experience?"

"Don't be too hasty," said Max. "Count Herzlos was no fool, and at least some of those who advised him are good men. Valuable men. Baron Helmundt, for example, knows a great deal about trade agreements and finance, and Schussman is a perceptive observer of the diplomatic scene."

"Schussman?" Conrad blinked in surprise. "I thought he was a gambler."

Max grinned. "And you would be wise not to play cards with him. But he can read the people in embassies as easily as he reads those around the card table."

This time Conrad's laugh was more lighthearted as he turned to Penworth. "You see? This is why I want Max beside me. He notices things like this. He always has. People look at him and think that because he is so big, he must be dim-witted, and so they let things slip."

"Yes," said Penworth, regarding his son-in-law carefully. "Yes, I can see where that might happen."

Max retreated to his rooms and his wife feeling somewhat relieved, but still frustrated. There was no way they were going to be able to retreat to Ostrov before the wedding, and no way they were going to be able to avoid the wedding preparations.

Forty-two

A WEEK BEFORE THE WEDDING, THE SUN HAD BARELY set when Susannah and Max tumbled into bed— their newly polished and mattressed and pillowed and bedecked bed in their newly painted and papered and draped chamber in their newly opened and extensively refurbished town house on the finest square in Nymburg. They lay there with their eyes closed, he with his arm around her, she with her head on his shoulder, too exhausted to move.

"Has it been difficult?" she asked as a good wife should.

"Today Conrad had an idea. He thought it would be good to go on procession around the country after the wedding. To introduce Olivia to his people."

Her eyes popped open. "Goodness. How medieval."

"That was his thought—to revive an old custom. I was obliged to remind him that the custom had fallen into disuse because few noblemen or towns could play host to the court without going bankrupt."

She chuckled. "Not the sort of thing the prince would think of."

"Apparently not." Max sighed, but eventually the

corner of his mouth tipped up in a smile. "Speaking of things one would not think of... You know Emil has been pressed into service at the palace?"

Susannah made a noise that could have passed for agreement.

"Well, he came across one of the servants the Russian archduke brought. The fellow was measuring the room that the Austrian archduke had been given to make sure it wasn't bigger than his master's."

Susannah managed a small giggle. "Today I thought two of the bridesmaids—Lady Enid and Lady Bertha—were going resort to hair-pulling over the order of the procession. Each one was waving a genealogy giving her precedence over the other. Order was restored only after Aunt Magda decreed that they would be arranged in size places."

"I wish she could order things at the palace as well. There is a clerk in the College of Heralds who has, I swear, become the most important man in the kingdom. He knows the order of precedence for everyone, down to the babes in arms. And he is the only one in the entire country—possibly the entire universe—who knows."

"I am so glad we were married at Ostrov."

"Even though I cheated you of the chance to have your family around you?" His hand had wandered up and was toying with the ribbon at the neck of her nightgown.

"They will be around me soon enough. They begin to arrive the day after tomorrow. You will not only meet them, but you will have to house them. All of them." She was gently tangling her fingers in the hair on his chest.

"But they'll be diluted by the presence of my cousins." He had turned his head and was nuzzling her temple. "Mmmm. Having you next to me here in this bed is having a remarkably reviving effect on me."

Susannah smiled a smug, cat-like smile. She was feeling revived herself. "Are you sure?"

"Quite sure." His voice was husky. And he proceeded to demonstrate.

⌘

Three days later, Susannah's family had arrived. When the ladies left the dinner table, Max found himself the focus of six pairs of eyes. They were not precisely unfriendly, but neither were they friendly. Distrust seemed to be the predominant emotion here. At least none of them had attempted to assault him so far. He was larger than any one of them, but there were six of them.

Three of them were Susannah's brothers. One of them was her brother-in-law and also Olivia's brother. Another was Olivia's brother-in-law. And the last one, a Frenchman who was also a brother-in-law of Susannah, seemed more amused than hostile.

"I know how you feel," the Frenchman said. "I faced the same scrutiny when I married my Emily."

"At least that was *before* the wedding," growled the oldest of the brothers.

Max did not want to be on bad terms with Susannah's family. Dealing with her parents was tricky enough. In desperation he signaled the footman, who brought out glasses and a bottle of *obstwasser*.

"This is a kind of brandy we make here from apples

and pears," Max said. "I thought you might like to try it."

Not long after the second bottle had been broached, it was agreed that Max was a very good fellow, even if he lived in this odd little country. Susannah could have done worse.

❧

On the night before the wedding, Susannah and Julia, Olivia's sister, stayed with the bride. As foreigners, neither one could be part of the wedding ceremony. That honor was reserved for daughters of the most noble houses of Sigmaringen. But on this night, Olivia wanted to be with her dearest friend and the older sister who had protected her throughout her childhood, and they were all seated by the fireside.

The royal bride was looking panicked.

"You're not worried about the wedding night, are you?" asked Susannah. "Because I can assure you that there is nothing to be frightened about."

"Unless…" Julia hesitated. "I don't know the prince very well. Is there something about him that worries you? Do you think he may be—how shall I put it—less than gentle?"

At that Olivia began to laugh softly. "Oh no. If you did know him, Julia, you would know that he is the sweetest, kindest man imaginable."

"If you say so." Julia continued to look doubtful.

Susannah suddenly realized what the problem was. "It's not Conrad. It's the prince!"

"But Conrad is the prince." Julia looked at Susannah as if she were simpleminded.

"Yes, but…" Olivia looked at her sister as if asking for understanding. "Susannah's right. It's not that I don't want to marry Conrad. He's everything I ever dreamed of. But these last few months, all the preparations, all the people, all the protocol—that's what my life is going to be like. I will forever be on display in front of strangers, and I don't know if I can do it."

"Olivia, think!" Julia said. "How much privacy have you ever had? You have lived all your life in front of servants. And if you do not give a thought to what you say or do in their presence, you should."

"You can make time for yourselves," Susannah said. "Yes, Conrad is a prince and you will be a princess, so much of your life will be lived in public, on display with everyone watching. But it is not so different for the rest of us. Julia's husband is in the foreign service. I'm sure that people are watching every move he makes, analyzing every expression that passes across his face."

Olivia looked at her sister in concern. "Is it very dreadful?"

"Not at all. It's much better than facing the cats in London." Julia grinned gleefully. "Now, you see, when the evening is over and I am at home with David, we send the servants away and I tell him everything I have overheard. It can be very helpful for him because I often hear women talking about what their husbands have told them."

Olivia grinned back at her sister. "Then I will be able to help Conrad in the same way. I'll be useful to him."

The conversation slowly turned to more important

matters, shared memories and dreams, until all three women drifted off into untroubled sleep.

෴

The day of the wedding, the second Saturday in June, dawned bright and clear, as was required for a royal wedding. The cathedral was bedecked in thousands of blossoms, the archbishop and the four attending bishops wore antique copes covered with splendid embroidery in gold and silver thread, and the choir sang the music that had been written for a royal wedding three hundred years before and sung at every royal wedding since then.

The bride wore a gown of cream-colored satin embroidered all over with pearls. The embroidery had been done by a dozen Sigmaringen needlewomen, and the designs were traditional Sigmaringen motifs.

When the prince and princess stepped out of the cathedral, the trumpet blares were drowned out by the cheers of the crowd. Those cheers accompanied them all the way to the palace as they rode slowly in the white landau pulled by six white horses. The joy of the crowd almost equaled the joy on the faces of Prince Conrad and Princess Olivia.

There was a wedding banquet in the palace, of course, attended by visiting royalty, statesmen, and diplomats as well as all the nobility of Sigmaringen, followed by a ball. Down in the town, there were more banquets and dancing for all the citizens of Sigmaringen, from the richest to the poorest.

No one went hungry that day, and there was music everywhere.

Forty-three

THE WEEK AFTER THE WEDDING WAS NOT ENTIRELY free of tension. The departing guests all required careful ceremony to speed them on their way without offending anyone, but it was accomplished. The royal band managed to get through all the national anthems without hitting too many wrong notes and—more importantly—without playing the wrong anthem for any of the visitors.

At last, Max and Susannah were free to return to Ostrov. But not alone. Max had invited her parents to accompany them. He had not originally planned to do so, but during a conversation with Lady Penworth he had somehow issued the invitation. Quite unintentionally, he later told Susannah. She smiled and told him that she understood perfectly. After all, she had a lifetime of experience with her mother.

❧

Lady Penworth was writing a letter when her husband came into their sitting room in Staufer's town house. She gave him an abstracted nod and continued writing. When she finally finished and laid her pen aside, she realized that he had been pacing ever since he entered. This was most unlike him.

After stopping to stare out the window, he turned to speak to his wife. "Staufer tells me you have accepted his invitation to visit his home, Ostrov or whatever it is called."

"That's right." She smiled.

"Anne, did he actually invite us?"

"Why, of course, dear. He may have had a bit of difficulty phrasing the invitation, but I knew what he meant."

"That's what I thought. And I believe he understood as well." He gave a rueful smile. "Perhaps... It is possible... We may have been mistaken... Staufer may not be as stupid as I first thought."

She patted her husband on the arm. "I believe you are right. I confess, my first thought when I saw him was that anyone that big must be somewhat dim-witted. But I admit that was simply prejudice on my part."

Lord Penworth's mouth twitched slightly. "On my part as well."

"After all," she continued, "he never actually did anything stupid."

"He married our daughter without bothering to discover anything about her family." He scowled at the memory of that grievance.

"Foolishly impetuous, perhaps, but he was assuming she was poor and unimportant. A generous and honorable impulse, one might say. Not a fortune hunter, at any rate."

"Anne," Penworth said slowly, standing arms akimbo, "has he won you over?"

She shrugged lightly. "At first I was afraid that Susannah had simply lost her head over his looks. He is an extraordinarily handsome man, you must admit. But when she talks about him, she praises his sense of honor and duty, his loyalty and the loyalty he inspires, not his impressive physique."

Penworth snorted.

"Well, my dear, you can hardly deny that it is impressive," she said. "However, Susannah never was a girl to be misled by a handsome face. It may have been a short acquaintance, but it seems to have been an intense one."

Her husband sat down beside her and leaned back with a sigh of concession. "Our sons seem to approve of him, and I know they were dubious at the outset. Julia's husband says he has a good grasp of the politics of this region, a good understanding of the interests motivating both the powerful figures and the weak ones."

She smiled at her husband fondly. "In short, it appears that he would be an acceptable husband for Susannah if he had only come to you and asked your permission beforehand. And if he did not live so far from England."

Penworth reached over, took her hand in his, and squeezed it. "And if they had not cheated you once again of a chance to arrange a wedding at Penworth Castle."

She shook her head and laughed at herself. "True enough. Why do all my daughters have to marry in foreign lands?"

"Well, I suppose we shall have to forgive Staufer, accept him into the family and all that, but I don't think we should tell him so just yet."

"No, not yet. We must first see this medieval castle of his so we can be certain our daughter will have a proper setting." Lady Penworth's impish grin made her look no older than twelve.

≈

If anyone had asked Susannah to describe her parents' weeklong visit to Ostrov, she would have called it interesting. She retained some sense of propriety, after all.

Aunt Magda had accompanied them as well. She explained that before she retired to her own estate, she wanted to make Susannah familiar with the way things were done at Ostrov. It was a large and complex establishment.

Lady Penworth was certain her daughter was grateful for the assistance, unnecessary though it was. Susannah had, she pointed out, grown up in a castle and was fully conversant with the niceties of managing a noble household.

Aunt Magda was certain that was true and had no doubt that Ostrov would be in good hands. However, every establishment, large or small, had its little idiosyncrasies.

Lady Penworth acknowledged the truth of this, adding that when things had been done a certain way for years and years, a fresh eye was sometimes needed to see how they could be improved.

Susannah kept smiling and thought it very unfair that Max had only her father to deal with, especially since land management was not Lord Penworth's area of expertise. The two gentlemen arrived at dinner every evening more comfortable with each other than the day before, while Lady Penworth and Aunt Magda were increasingly polite to each other.

Mercifully, Aunt Magda left two days before Susannah's parents were scheduled to depart, providing Lady Penworth with two days to fuss over her daughter, admire the castle, and shower her with advice. At least some of this advice, Susannah realized, was actually useful, like using a room closer to the kitchen as the dining room so that food might still be warm when it reached the table.

In a flurry of last-minute hugs and admonitions, the Penworths left in the Staufer carriage. It would take them a comfortable two days to reach Baden, whence they could take trains for the rest of their journey. Improved train service, Max agreed, should be high on the list of improvements for Sigmaringen.

Susannah and Max stood on the castle steps until the carriage disappeared through the gates. Arm in arm, they turned to enter their home.

"Do you know," he said, "this is the first time we have ever been alone?"

Lev, who had been walking beside Susannah, turned his head to look at Max, making them both dissolve in laughter.

When she had recovered, Susannah said, "Alone? You do remember that Ostrov houses some forty servants just indoors? I still don't know all their names."

With the arm he had flung over her shoulders, Max hugged her to his side. "You know perfectly well what I mean." Leading her into the nearest room—a small sitting room that looked out onto a pretty courtyard with a fountain and was furnished with a large, comfortable sofa—he flicked a glance first at Lev, who sat down obediently, and then at a footman who closed the doors firmly behind them.

"Are we truly alone now?" She turned to face him, resting her hands on his chest.

"We are." His own hands slipped around her waist to pull her close to him.

"And no one will disturb us?" She unbuttoned his jacket and began to undo his cravat.

"No one." His voice had grown husky, and his fingers fumbled as he tried to deal with the tiny buttons running up the back of her bodice.

"Good," she whispered as she used his cravat to pull his head down toward hers for a kiss. A long kiss.

Some time later, they lay in drowsy contentment in each other's arms. That the overstuffed sofa was not really deep enough for two did not bother them in the slightest. Nor did it worry them that their clothing was scattered carelessly across the floor.

"There is so much I haven't told you," said Max, nuzzling her hair.

"Anything important?"

"Oh, yes. For example, I haven't ever mentioned that I love the way your hair smells. Like summer."

She smiled into his chest. "And I love that you make such a comfortable pillow."

"I am delighted to offer you comfort, my lady. Because you…" His voice grew serious. "You bring me peace. A kind of peace I never knew existed. You make me complete."

"Yes. That's what it is. With you I am complete. I am what I was meant to be."

"Is it possible that a year ago," said Max, "I did not even know you?"

"No. That isn't possible." Susannah reached up to turn his face to her. "A year ago we had not met, but I feel as if I have always known you. I was just waiting to meet you."

Lady Elinor's WICKED ADVENTURES

London, 1852

Cheerful frivolity reigned in the ballroom of Huntingdon House. The dancers swirled to the strains of a waltz, jewels glittering and silks and satins shimmering under the brilliant light of the new gas chandeliers. Even the chaperones were smiling to each other and swaying unconsciously to the music.

Harcourt de Vaux, Viscount Tunbury, an angry scowl setting him apart from the rest of the company, pushed his way to the side of his old schoolfellow. Grabbing him by the arm, Tunbury spoke in a furious undertone. "Pip, your sister is dancing with Carruthers."

Pip, more formally known as Philip Tremaine, Viscount Rycote, turned and blinked. "Hullo, Harry. I didn't know you were here. I thought this sort of thing was too tame for you these days."

"Forget about me. It's Norrie. She's dancing with that bounder Carruthers."

They both looked at the dance floor where Lady Elinor Tremaine, the picture of innocence, was smiling up at her partner, whose lean face and dark eyes spoke of danger. He was smiling as well, looking down at her with almost wolfish hunger.

"What of it?" asked Pip.

"He's a bloody fortune hunter and a cad to boot. How could you introduce him to your sister?"

Pip frowned slightly. "He introduced himself, actually. Said he was a friend of yours."

Harry spoke through clenched teeth. "You idiot. That should have been enough to disqualify him. Where are your parents?"

"Dancing, I suppose."

Harry caught a glimpse of the Marquess and Marchioness of Penworth on the far side of the room, dancing gracefully and oblivious to everyone else. Turning back to find Carruthers and Lady Elinor again, he muttered an oath. "He's heading for the terrace." When Pip looked blank, Harry shook his head and charged across the dance floor.

⤲

Mr. Carruthers had timed it quite neatly, she thought. As the music ended and he twirled her into the final spin, they came to a halt just before the terrace doors. These were standing open, letting in the scent of roses on the breeze of the soft June evening.

"It is rather warm in here, Lady Elinor, is it not?" he said. "Would you care for a turn on the terrace?"

Before she could answer, a strong hand clasped her arm just above the elbow. "Lady Elinor, your mother wants you." When she turned to object to this high-handed treatment, she found herself staring up at the all-too-familiar scowl of Lord Tunbury. "Harry…" she started to protest.

"If Lady Elinor wishes to return to her parents, I will be delighted to escort her." Carruthers spoke frostily.

"Lady Penworth requested that I find her daughter." Harry's even icier tone indicated that there was nothing more to be said on the subject.

Lady Elinor looked back and forth between them and wanted to laugh. Carruthers was tall, dark, and handsome, or at least decorative, with a pretty bow-shaped mouth. Harry, equally tall, had broad shoulders and a powerful build. His square face was pleasant rather than handsome, his middling brown hair tended to flop over his middling brown eyes, and his wide mouth was more often than not stretched into a broad smile. Not just now, of course.

One would say the two men were not much alike, but at the moment they wore identical scowls. They did not actually bare their teeth and growl, but they were not far off. She could not manage to feel guilty about enjoying the sight. It was too delightful.

Carruthers stopped glaring at Harry long enough to look at her. He may have stopped scowling, but he was not smiling. He was stiff with anger. "Lady Elinor?" He offered his arm.

Harry's grip on her arm tightened and he pulled her back a step. His grip was growing painful, and she would have protested, but she feared it might create a scene not of her own designing, so she smiled. "Thank you, Mr. Carruthers, but if my mother sent Lord Tunbury, perhaps I should accept his escort."

Carruthers bowed stiffly and sent one more glare at

the intruder before he departed. That left her free to turn furiously on Harry. "There is no way on earth my mother sent you to fetch me. What do you think you are doing?"

He caught her hand, trapped it on his arm, and began marching her away from the terrace. "I cannot imagine what possessed your parents to give you permission to dance with a loose fish like Carruthers."

"They didn't, of course. He at least had enough sense to wait until they had left me with Pip." Harry was dragging her along too quickly, and she was going to land on the floor in a minute. "You might slow down a bit," she complained.

"You little idiot!" He turned and glared at her but did ease his pace. "He was about to take you out on the terrace."

"Well, of course!" She gave an exasperated humph.

"What do you mean, 'Of course'?" By now they had reached the end of the ballroom, and he pulled her into the hall and swung her around to the side so he could glare with some privacy.

She shook out her skirt and checked to make sure the pink silk rosettes pinning up the tulle overskirt had not been damaged while Harry was dragging her about. She was very fond of those rosettes. "I mean, of course he was going to take me out on the terrace. That's what he does. He takes a girl out on the terrace, leads her into one of the secluded parts, and kisses her. Marianne and Dora say he kisses very nicely, and I wanted to see if they were right."

Harry made a strangled sound. "Marianne and Dora? Miss Simmons and Miss Cooper…?"

"Among others." Lady Elinor waved a hand airily. "He's kissed so many of this year's debutantes that I was beginning to feel slighted, but I think perhaps he is working according to some sort of pattern. Do you know what it might be?"

He was looking at her with something approaching horror, rather the way her brother looked at her much of the time. "You and your friends discuss... What in God's name are young ladies thinking about these days?"

She shrugged. "Young men, of course. What did you suppose? That we discuss embroidery patterns? Don't you and your friends talk about women?"

He closed his eyes and muttered a prayer for patience. Then he began speaking with exaggerated formality. "Lady Elinor, under no circumstances are you to even dance with a rake like Carruthers, much less go into the garden with him. You have no idea what he would do."

"Fiddlesticks! I know precisely what he was going to do. He apparently has only two speeches that he uses to persuade a girl to let him kiss her, and I want to know which one he is going to use on me. Then I'll know if I am generally considered saucy or sweet."

"Norrie, no one who is at all acquainted with you would ever consider you sweet."

"Well, I should hope not. You know me better than that. But I want to know how I am viewed by the people who don't know me."

He grabbed her by the shoulders and turned her to face him. "Norrie, I want you to listen to me. A bounder like Carruthers will try to do far more than simply steal a kiss."

"I know that. You needn't treat me as if I am simpleminded. But I am hardly going to allow anything more."

"It is not a question of what you will allow. Just precisely how do you think you could stop him from taking advantage of you?"

She gave him a considering look and decided to answer honestly. "Well, there is the sharply raised knee to the groin or the forehead smashed against the nose, but the simplest, I have always found, is the hatpin."

"Hatpin?" Harry looked rather as if he were choking as he seized on the most innocuous part of her statement.

"Yes. It really doesn't matter where you stab. Gentlemen are always so startled that they jump back." She offered him a kindly smile. Sometimes he sounded just like her brother.

He went back to glaring at her. "Norrie, Lady Elinor, I want your word that there will be no strolls in the garden with disreputable rogues."

"Like you?" she interrupted.

"Yes, if you like, like me! Forget about rogues. You may not always recognize one. Just make it all men. You are not to leave the ballroom with any man at any time."

"The way we just left it?"

"Stop that, Norrie. I am serious."

He did indeed look serious. Quite fierce, in fact. So she subsided and resigned herself to listening.

"I want your promise," he said. "If you will not give it, I will have to warn your brother, and you know Pip. He might feel obliged to challenge anyone who tries to lead you into dark corners, and you know he is a hopeless shot. You don't want to get him killed, do you?"

He had calmed down enough to start smiling at her now, one of those patronizing, big-brother, I-know-better-than-you smiles. It was quite maddening, so she put on her shyly innocent look and smiled back. "Oh, Harry, you know I would never do anything that would cause real trouble."

"That's my girl." He took her arm to lead her back to the ballroom. "Hatpins indeed. Just don't let your mother find out you've heard about things like that."

She smiled. He really was quite sweet. And foolish. He had not even noticed that she gave him no promise. And then imagine warning her not to let her mother find out. Who did he suppose had taught her those tricks?

Tunbury hovered at the edge of the ballroom and watched Norrie hungrily. He had not seen her in more than a year, and then two months ago, there she had been. It was her first season, and somehow the tomboy who had been his and Pip's companion in all their games and pranks had turned into a beauty. Her dark hair now hung in shiny ringlets, framing the perfect oval of her face. Her eyes—they had always been that sort of greenish blue, shining with excitement more often than not, but when had they started to tilt at the edge that way? And when had her lashes grown so long and thick? Worst of all, when had she gone and grown a bosom?

But she was such an innocent.

She thought herself so worldly, so knowing, when in fact she knew nothing of the ugliness lurking beneath the surface, even in the ballrooms of the aristocracy. That ugliness should never be allowed to touch her. Her parents would protect her and find her a husband worthy of her, a good, decent man who came from a good, decent family.

Not someone like him. Not someone who came from a family as rotten as his. The Tremaines thought they knew about his parents, the Earl and Countess of Doncaster, but they knew only the common gossip. They did not know what Doncaster had told him, and he hoped they never would.

Yes, Norrie would find a husband worthy of her, but he couldn't stay here and watch. That would be too painful. He had to leave. He would leave in the morning and disappear from her life.

AND DON'T MISS THE SECOND BOOK IN
THE VICTORIAN ADVENTURES SERIES!

Lady Emily's
EXOTIC
JOURNEY

Constantinople, March 1861

CONSTANTINOPLE HAD LOOKED SO PROMISING TO Lady Emily when they arrived this morning, with the city rising up out of the morning mists, white and shining with turrets and domes and balconies everywhere. The long, narrow boats in the harbor all sported bright sails. It had been so new and strange and exotic.

Now here she was, walking with Lady Julia behind her parents on Wilton carpets. Wilton carpets imported from Salisbury! When even she knew that this part of the world was famous for its carpets.

She heaved a sigh. They had traveled thousands of miles to finally reach Constantinople—the Gateway to Asia, the ancient Byzantium, the capital of the fabulous Ottoman Empire, a city of magic and mystery—and for what?

To be tucked up in the British Embassy, a Palladian building that would have looked perfectly at home around the corner from Penworth House in London.

She understood that it was British and represented the Queen and the Empire and all that, but did it have to be so very *English*?

The doors at the end of the hall were flung open and a butler, dressed precisely as he would have been in London, announced, "The Most Honorable the Marquess of Penworth. The Most Honorable the Marchioness of Penworth. The Lady Emily Tremaine. The Lady Julia de Vaux."

They might just as well have never left home.

Emily smiled the insipid smile she reserved for her parents' political friends—the smile intended to assure everyone that she was sweet and docile—and prepared to be bored. She was very good at pretending to be whatever she was expected to be. Next to her, she could feel Julia straighten her already perfect posture. She reached over to squeeze her friend's hand.

"Lord Penworth, Lady Penworth, allow me to welcome you to Constantinople." A ruddy-faced gentleman with thinning gray hair on his head and a thinning gray beard on his chin inclined his head. "And this must be your daughter, Lady Emily?" He looked somewhere between the two young women, as if uncertain which one to address.

Emily took pity on him and curtsied politely.

He looked relieved and turned to Julia. "And Lady Julia?" She performed a similar curtsy.

"My husband and I are delighted to welcome such distinguished visitors to Constantinople," said the small, gray woman who was standing stiffly beside the ambassador, ignoring the fact that he had been ignoring her.

Emily blinked. She knew marital disharmony when she heard it. She also knew how unpleasant it could make an evening.

"We are delighted to be here, Lady Bulwer," said Lord Penworth courteously. "This part of the world is new to us, and we have all been looking forward to our visit." He turned to the ambassador. "I understand that you, Sir Henry, are quite familiar with it."

"Tolerably well, tolerably well. I'm told you're here to study the possibility of a railroad along the Tigris River valley. Can't quite see it myself." Before the ambassador realized it, Lord Penworth had cut him out of the herd of women and was shepherding him off to the side.

In the sudden quiet, Lady Penworth smiled at her hostess and gestured at the room about them. "I am most impressed by the way you have managed to turn this embassy into a bit of England," she said. "If I did not know, I would think myself still in London."

Lady Bulwer looked both pleased and smug. She obviously failed to note any hint of irony in Lady Penworth's words. Emily recognized the signs. Her parents would out-diplomat the diplomats, smoothing over any bumps of disharmony in the Bulwer household, and conversation would flow placidly through conventional channels. Boring, but unexceptionable. And only too familiar.

Then Julia touched her arm.

Still looking straight ahead, and still with a faint, polite smile on her face, Julia indicated that Emily should look at the left-hand corner of the room. Emily had never understood how it was that Julia could send these messages without making a sound or even moving her head, but send them she did.

In this case, it was a message Emily received with interest. Off in the corner were two young men pretending to examine a huge globe while they took sideways glances at the newcomers. This was much more promising than the possibility of trouble between the ambassador and his wife. Refusing to pretend a lack of curiosity—she was growing tired, very tired, of pretending—she looked straight at them.

One was an extraordinarily handsome man, clean-shaven to display a beautifully sculpted mouth and a square jaw. His perfectly tailored black tailcoat outlined a tall, broad-shouldered physique. The blinding whiteness of his shirt and bow tie contrasted with the slight olive cast of his skin. His hair was almost black, and his dark eyes betrayed no awareness of her scrutiny. He stood with all the bored elegance of the quintessential English gentleman. Bored and probably boring.

The other man looked far more interesting. He was not so tall—slim and wiry, rather than powerful looking—and not nearly so handsome. His nose was quite long—assertive might be a polite way to describe it—and his tanned face was long and narrow. Like his companion, he was clean shaven, though his hair, a dark brown, was in need of cutting. While his evening clothes were perfectly proper, they were worn carelessly, and he waved his hands about as he spoke in a way that seemed definitely un-English. He noticed immediately when she held her gaze on him and turned to return her scrutiny. She refused to look away, even when he unashamedly examined her from head to toe. His eyes glinted with amusement, and he gave her an appreciative grin and salute.

The cheek of him! She laughed out loud, making Julia hiss and drawing the attention of her mother and Lady Bulwer. Sir Henry must have noticed something as well, for he waved the young men over to be introduced to Papa.

They both stopped a proper distance away, and the handsome one waited with an almost military stiffness. Sir Henry introduced him first. "This is David Oliphant, Lord Penworth. He's with the Foreign Office and will be your aide and guide on the journey. He knows the territory and can speak the lingo. All the lingoes, in fact—Turkish, Kurdish, Arabic, whatever you run into along the way."

Oliphant bowed. "Honored, my lord."

Lord Penworth smiled. "My pleasure."

"And this young man is Lucien Chambertin. He's on his way back to Mosul where he's been working with Carnac, digging up stone beasts or some such."

"The remains of Nineveh, Sir Henry." Chambertin then turned to Lord Penworth with a brief, graceful bow and a smile. "I am most pleased to make your acquaintance, my lord, for I am hoping you will allow me to impose on you and join your caravan for the journey to Mosul."

He spoke excellent English, with just a hint of a French accent. Just the perfect hint, Emily decided. Sir Henry was not including the ladies in his introductions, to her annoyance, so she had been obliged to position herself close enough to hear what they were saying. This was one of the rare occasions when she was grateful for her crinolines. They made it impossible for the ladies to stand too close to one another, so she placed herself to the rear of her mother. From that position, she could listen to the gentlemen's conversation while appearing to attend to the ladies'. What's more, from her angle she could watch them from the corner of her eye without being obvious.

"I cannot imagine why you should not join us," Lord Penworth told the Frenchman. "I understand that, in Mesopotamia, it is always best to travel in a large group. You are one of these new scholars—what do they call them, archaeologists?"

Chambertin gave one of those Gallic shrugs. "Ah no, nothing so grand. I am just a passing traveler, but I cannot resist the opportunity to see the ruins of Nineveh when the opportunity offers itself. And then when Monsieur Carnac says he has need of assistance, I agree to stay for a while."

"Well, my wife will certainly find the ruins interesting. She has developed quite a fascination with the ancient world."

Oliphant looked startled. "Your wife? But surely Lady Penworth does not intend to accompany us."

"Of course." Lord Penworth in turn looked startled at the question. "I could hardly deny her the opportunity to see the ancient cradle of civilization. Not when I am looking forward to it myself."

"I'm sorry. I was told you were traveling to view the possible site of a railway."

"I am." Penworth smiled. "That is my excuse for this trip. General Chesney has been urging our government to build a railway from Basra to Constantinople. His argument is that it would provide much quicker and safer communication with India. Palmerston wanted me to take a look and see if there would be any other use for it."

The ambassador snorted. "Not much. There's nothing of any use or interest in that part of the world except for those huge carvings that fellows like Carnac haul out of the ground."

The handsome Mr. Oliphant looked worried. Before he could say anything, dinner was announced, the remaining introductions were finally made, and Emily found herself walking in to dinner on the arm of M. Chambertin. He had behaved quite correctly when they were introduced and held out his arm in perfectly proper fashion. He said nothing that would have been out of place in the most rigidly proper setting imaginable. Nonetheless, she suspected that he had been well aware of her eavesdropping. There was a decidedly improper light dancing in his eyes.

She liked it.

About dinner she was less certain. The oxtail soup had been followed by lobster rissoles, and now a footman placed a slice from the roast sirloin of beef on her plate, where it joined the spoonful of mashed turnips and the boiled onion. The onion had been so thoroughly boiled that it was finding it difficult to hold its shape and had begun to tilt dispiritedly to one side.

"This is really quite a remarkable meal," Lady Penworth said to their hostess. "Do you find it difficult to obtain English food here?"

"You've no idea." Lady Bulwer sighed sadly. "It has taken me ages to convince the cook that plain boiled vegetables are what we want. You can't imagine the outlandish spices he wants to use. And the olive oil! It's a constant struggle."

"And in that battle, the food lost," muttered Emily, poking the onion into total collapse.

A snort from M. Chambertin at her side indicated that her words had not gone unheard. After using his napkin, he turned to her. "You do not care for *rosbif*?" he asked with a grin. "I thought all the English eat nothing else."

"We are in *Constantinople*, thousands of miles from home, and we might as well be in Tunbridge Wells."

He made a sympathetic grimace. "Perhaps while your papa goes to look at the railway route, Sir Henry can find you a guide who will show you and your friend a bit of Constantinople. You should really see the Topkapi—the old palace—and the bazaar."

"Oh, but we aren't going to be staying here. Julia and I are going with my parents."

Mr. Oliphant, who had been speaking quietly with Julia, heard that and looked around in shock. "Lady Emily, you and Lady Julia and Lady Penworth are *all* planning to go to Mosul? Surely not. I cannot believe your father will allow this."

Emily sighed. She was accustomed to such reactions. *Lady Emily, you cannot possibly mean... Lady Emily, surely you do not intend...* All too often, she had restrained herself and done what was expected. She intended this trip to be different. Still, she was curious as well as annoyed. Was Mr. Oliphant about to urge propriety, or was there some other reason for his distress? "Why should we not?" she asked.

Mr. Oliphant took a sip of wine, as if to calm himself. Or fortify himself. It was impossible to be certain. He cleared his throat. "I fear Lord Penworth may not be fully aware of the difficulties—dangers, even—of travel in this part of the world. The caravan route through Aleppo and Damascus and then across the desert is hazardous under the best of circumstances, and these days…" He shook his head.

"My friend does not exaggerate," added M. Chambertin, looking serious. "Although the recent massacres in the Lebanon seem to be at an end, brigands have become more bold, and even the largest caravans—they are not safe."

"But we are not planning to take that route." Emily looked at Julia for confirmation and received it. "We are to sail to Samsun on the Black Sea, travel by caravan over the mountains to Diyarbakir, and then down the river to Mosul. And eventually on to Baghdad and Basra. Papa discussed it all with people back in London when he and Lord Palmerston were planning the route. So you need not worry." She smiled to reassure the gentlemen.

M. Chambertin and Mr. Oliphant exchanged glances, trying to decide which should speak. It fell to Mr. Oliphant. "I do not question your father's plan, Lady Emily. These days that is by far the safer route, though no place is entirely safe from attacks by brigands. However, he may have underestimated the physical difficulties of the trip. The mountains—these are not gentle little hills like the ones you find in

England. They are barren and rocky, and we will cross them on roads that are little more than footpaths. It is impossible to take a carriage. If they do not go on foot, travelers must go on horseback or on mules. And this early in the year, it will still be bitterly cold, especially at night."

"You needn't worry," Emily assured him. "We are all excellent riders, and I am told that the cold is preferable to the heat of the summer."

M. Chambertin smiled at her and shook his head. "I do not doubt that you are a horsewoman *par excellence*, and your mother and Lady Julia as well. However, the journey over the mountains will take weeks. We will encounter few villages, and those we find will be most poor. There will be times when we must sleep in tents or take shelter in stables. Nowhere will there be comfortable inns where ladies can refresh themselves."

Emily and Julia looked at each other, sharing their irritation. Male condescension was obviously to be found everywhere.

"I believe you misunderstand the situation, gentlemen." Julia spoke in her iciest, most superior tone. "We are not fragile pieces of porcelain. We are grown women, and English women at that. I do not think you will find us swooning at the sight of a spider. Or, for that matter, at the sight of a lion. Since Lord Penworth has determined that we are capable of undertaking the journey, I see no need for you to question his judgment."

Mr. Oliphant flushed uncomfortably. "I assure you that no insult was intended either to you or to Lord

Penworth. It is simply that ladies do not normally undertake such a journey."

Julia's tone grew even icier. "*Ladies* do not? Are you suggesting that there is something improper about our taking part in this trip?"

His flush deepened. "Not at all. I would not...I assure you...my only concern is your safety."

"You need not worry about that either," said Emily, waving a hand casually in the air. "Harry— that's Lady Julia's brother, Lord Doncaster. He's married to my sister Elinor. He has provided each of us with a revolver."

There was an odd, choking sound from M. Chambertin.

Emily turned to him. "Are you quite well, monsieur?"

"Quite well." His face, when it reappeared from his napkin, was slightly red. "And the Lord Doncaster, he has no doubt taught you how to shoot these revolvers?"

"Of course." Emily smiled rather smugly. "In fact, I am becoming quite a good shot. Would you care for a demonstration? Not here in the dining room," she assured Mr. Oliphant, who was looking more and more distressed.

M. Chambertin, on the other hand, was grinning broadly. "No demonstration will be needed, I assure you. I begin to think that this will be a most interesting voyage. *Bien intéressant.*"

Author's Note

Before German unification in 1871, there were dozens of small independent German states—kingdoms and principalities and duchies. Many of them were located in the north, but in the south, between Baden and Württemberg, were two small states, Hohenzollern-Sigmaringen and Hohenzollern-Hechingen. These two were ruled by branches of the same family that ruled Prussia and were actually absorbed by Prussia in 1850.

For the purpose of my story, I have borrowed their location and half of their names, erasing their actual histories and their connection with the Hohenzollerns. Instead, the ruling families of my fictional principalities are descended from the Hohenstaufens, Holy Roman Emperors in the early Middle Ages and rulers of the medieval Duchy of Swabia. Sigmaringen and Hechingen are therefore still independent in 1863 and, like Baden and Württemberg, worried about the ambitions of both Prussia and Austria. This does not greatly depart from the actual course of history. My story only delays by some twenty years the absorption of Sigmaringen and Hechingen into the German Empire, a fate foreseen by many of the characters in the novel.

Needless to say, the characters and the masquerade are all entirely fictitious, though inspired by one of my favorite books, Anthony Hope's *The Prisoner of Zenda*.

Acknowledgments

With grateful appreciation to all the artists, editors, copy editors, and proofreaders at Sourcebooks for all the work they do to make this book as good as they can, especially Hilary Doda, for her insightful comments and suggestions.

I would also like to thank Professor Robert K. Bloomer, coordinator of German programs at SUNY Stony Brook, for his help with Schwäbisch words and phrases. Any mistakes are my own fault.

About the Author

Lillian Marek was born and raised in New York City. At one time or another she has had most of the interesting but underpaid jobs available to English majors. After a few too many years in journalism, she decided she prefers fiction, where the good guys win and the bad guys get what they deserve. The first book in her Victorian Adventure series, *Lady Elinor's Wicked Adventures*, won first prize in both the Launching a Star and the Windy City Four Seasons contests. She now lives on Long Island, next to a pond inhabited by swans and snapping turtles, with occasional visits from cormorants, egrets, and herons.

Discovery of Desire

London Explorers

by Susanne Lord

The one man who's not looking for a wife

Seth Mayhew is the ideal explorer: fearless, profitable, and unmarried. There is nothing and no one he can't find—until his sister disappears en route to India. His search for her takes him to Bombay, where Seth meets the most unlikely of allies—a vulnerable woman who's about to marry the wrong man.

Discovers a woman who changes his dreams forever

Teeming with the bounty of marriageable men employed by the East India Company, Bombay holds hope for security for Wilhelmina Adams. But when the man she's traveled halfway around the world to marry doesn't suit, Mina finds instead that she's falling in love with a man who offers passion, adventure, intimacy—anything but security…

Praise for *In Search of Scandal*:

"Smart and sexy." —*Booklist*

"Beautifully written, deeply romantic, and utterly magnificent." —*New York Times* bestselling author Courtney Milan

"Delightful… Passionate characters and personal adventures come alive." —*Booklist*

For more Susanne Lord, visit:

www.sourcebooks.com

A Gift for Guile

The Thief-takers

by Alissa Johnson

Never Trust a Thief

Once a famous officer of Scotland Yard and now a renowned private detective, Sir Samuel Brass has better things to do than shadow a reckless hellion in her misguided quest for atonement. But when the daughter of a notorious criminal—and a former thief herself—returns to London to right an old wrong, Samuel is drawn back into the dangerously exciting world of Esther Walker-Bales.

Beautiful and conniving, maddening and brilliant, Esther is everything he shouldn't want. She's a liar. She's a con. She's a thief. And God help him, but he'd do anything to keep her safe.

Esther knows she's put herself in terrible danger, but nothing will stop her from making amends that are long past due—not her family's enemies, not old fears, and certainly not the domineering, interfering, and undeniably handsome Sir Samuel Brass. Yet whenever he's near, Samuel makes her long for a life that can never be hers…and wish she was worthy of being saved.

"Sweet, sexy, and completely irresistible."
—Cecilia Grant, author of *A Lady Awakened*

"Witty, quirky, and altogether fun."
—*Publishers Weekly* Starred Review

For more Alissa Johnson, visit:

www.sourcebooks.com

The Girl from Paris

Paget Family Saga

by Joan Aiken

Ellen Paget's life is irrevocably changed when she accepts a position as governess for the radical Comte and Comtesse de la Ferte, in whose Paris salon Ellen is introduced to the most illustrious artists, writers, and philosophers of the day. The charming Benedict Masham, second son of an earl, and an old family friend, makes it his business to look out for Ellen's welfare. That would be nice, if it wasn't so annoying to Ellen, who wants to flout convention and spread her wings in Society.

Ellen soon sheds the stifling conventions of her proper English upbringing, and contends with the questionable affections of a beguiling writer, whose attentions to Ellen dismay the steadfast Benedict.

When tragedy and scandal force her to beat a hasty retreat back to England, it takes all of Ellen's ingenuity and fortitude to solve the mysteries of the past and present—but can she do so in time to save her father and brother from the machinations of those who mean them harm?

Praise for *Mansfield Park Revisited*:

"Delightful and charming." —*Becky's Book Reviews*

"A lovely read—and you don't have to have read *Mansfield Park* to enjoy it." —*Woman's Own*

For more Joan Aiken, visit:

www.sourcebooks.com